The Changeling's Tale

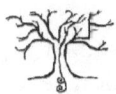

A Paranormal Fantasy

~

{Book One}

The Forest Immortal Saga

Kristina Schram

Mischief*Maker*Media

Published by Mischief Maker Media (USA)

First printing: August, 2014

Cover Design, Interior, and Technical Expertise: GorKee

Cover Photos: 1) Tree with Door & 2) Young Man with Box, from iStockPhoto

ISBN: 978-1-939397-10-2

Visit Kristina Schram on the World Wide Web at:
www.KristinaSchram.com

Acknowledgements

I want to take a moment to thank my readers: Elizabeth Schram, Heather Duane, Gordon Unzen, Keegan Unzen, and Ian More, my newest reader, and an honor to have on board. You put up with my struggles, my errors, my bossiness, and my overachieving ways, and you do it with minimal whining. If I could make you saints, I would.

I should never have an acknowledgement page that doesn't include my husband, Dan. I don't know how he does it, but he does, every second, every minute, and every hour of every day. I'd be lost without you, my oak tree.

Thank you, readers! You rock, you inspire me, you complete me. I love that you read, and I love that you read my books. Because without you I'd be just another starving artist…without the starving part, of course.

And lastly, I thank thee, trees. For without you, we'd all be dead.

To my three sons,
who inspired this series,
and who inspire me always.

If you fear the wolf,
Do not go into the forest.

~ Russian Proverb

Macbeth shall never vanquisht be, until
Great Birnam wood to high Dunsinane hill
Shall come against him.

~William Shakespeare, Macbeth

Within this realm reside mysteries
as tantalizing as the question,
Who brought us here?
Things are not as they should be
in this uncanny wood,
this Forest Immortal.
If enter you must,
I beg you take heed...
and go wisely
into its dark depths.

~Bruce Holt

Chapter One

The Arrival

The voice that taunted Gabriel Hawthorne was low and menacing like the first whisper of a deadly storm.

Gabrielll. Gabrielll...

"Did you hear that?" he demanded of his younger brother.

"Hear what?" Jer asked.

Gabe paused and listened again, then shook his head. He was imagining things. Probably because he was out picking blueberries on a ninety-degree, humid as a Louisiana bayou day, instead of hiding inside like any sane person would be doing. The late afternoon air was so heavy he felt like he was wearing a wool blanket over his head, and a flea-infested one at that.

"Nothing," he muttered. "Go find your own row. You're crowding me."

"You're just mad because you had to leave your girlfriend behind when we moved," Jer stated matter-of-factly. "Don't take your hormonal frustrations out on me."

Gabe hated it when Jer said things like this. Problem was, the little twerp was always saying things like this. He was just too knowledgeable for a twelve-year-old.

"Where's Kris?" he asked, refusing to give Jer the satisfaction of being right. "He's supposed to be helping us pick these stupid blueberries. Look." He thrust out his purple-tipped fingers. "I'm an alien. My fingers will never look normal again."

"He's probably in the barn inventing a blueberry picker," Jer remarked, sitting back on his haunches. His bucket was full, his pale face flushed pink.

Gabe sighed. "He's always getting out of work." He pushed his thick wavy hair back with both hands, leaving behind a faint purple hue amongst the dark blond strands, then wiped the sweat off his forehead with the back of his arm. "I thought Maine was supposed to be colder than California," he complained, the words sounding more sullen than he'd intended.

His family had been living in this bug-infested, blueberry-overrun state for a week now and during that time Gabe had discovered that he hated it here. It was too humid, there were more trees than people and too many chores to do, and he had yet to make any friends. Heck, he hadn't even come close to meeting anyone his age. Since moving to the farm, their mom had kept him and his brothers constantly working, giving them no chance to hang out in town where they might actually meet someone, where they might actually have a life.

"It's probably a lot cooler in those woods," Jer said hopefully, nodding at the dark, forbidding forest that surrounded their new home like a castle wall.

Actually, their home—a rambling white farmhouse built in the late 1600s—was pretty old. The house came complete with a cellar and attic, both of which were likely haunted, and brick fireplaces decorated nearly every room. An unusual stone turret held up the south end of the house, though they had yet to explore it. Mom had refused to let Kris take the locked door off its hinges, as he was prone to do whenever confronted with a locked door. "You can wait until your Grandma May finds the key, which will probably be never," she added in a grumbling tone as she unpacked dishes. Gabe couldn't help wondering, and worrying, about why a stone turret had been tacked on to the house. Turrets belonged on medieval castles, not Maine farmhouses.

Their new home was very different from their modern loft back in San Jose, which had been open and spacious and full of light. Gabe admitted that the farmhouse wasn't half-bad, if you didn't mind the creaks and groans in the middle of the night, the temperamental plumbing, or the old furniture, whose yellowed stuffing popped out in explosive little tufts when no one was looking.

The dark, creepy forest was another story. Jer and Kris wanted to explore it; Gabe did not. The woods made him nervous. Something about all those massive primeval trees lurking at the edge of their yard made him feel uncomfortable, as though strangers hid behind the thick trunks, watching him. Not that he would ever tell his brothers how he felt. They would never stop teasing him about his wild imaginings. Back in San Jose, he'd once seen a strange creature sneaking about in the nearby park. When he'd told his brothers he thought it might possibly be a leprechaun (it was St. Patrick's Day, after all), they started calling him Loony Leprechaun. Not a very clever nickname, but it stung all the same.

"Maybe later," he murmured, sneaking a peek at the looming trees.

"That's what you always say," Jer accused, but he was smiling a knowing smile, fully aware that Gabe didn't like the woods. Gabe decided he'd better distract the little turd before he acted on that knowing look in his eyes.

"I'm going in. These stupid horseflies keep dive-bombing me."

Jer consulted the sky. "It's almost time for supper. Do you think dad'll be joining us tonight?" He asked the question hopefully, though he tried not to show the emotion on his typically expressive face.

Gabe shrugged. "Maybe." Despite all the setbacks his father had suffered, Gabe had his hopes, too. And he, too, kept them to himself.

The two brothers, the younger shorter by a head and slight, the older tall and rangy like a colt, trudged back to the house lugging their red tin buckets filled to the brim with blueberries and bugs. Gabe hoped they'd each get a bowl with milk and sugar to eat after supper, but he wasn't optimistic about their chances. Most likely Mom would say, like she always did, that the berries were meant to be sold at Woodlands General Store in Ranger.

Since moving to Maine, Mom had tried hard not to discuss their dire financial circumstances in front of them, her reticence a sure sign something was wrong. When they had plenty of money, she was always getting on them about watching their expenditures, forcing them to choose between buying a new video game or the much-desired pair of sneakers that everyone was wearing. The cloud of worry that followed her around like a malevolent shadow was another sign that everything was not as it should be.

Gabe adopted her worry, and it ate at him. Their dad couldn't work right now, and hadn't been able to for over a year and a half, so it was up to Mom to make ends meet. Before moving to Maine, they'd lost everything to hospital bills—insurance only went so far—and now they were broke. Dad's disability checks barely paid for the basics— utilities, taxes, food, his medicine, but little else, which was why Gabe and his brothers were out picking berries. No sense wasting free labor, his mom would laughingly remark while handing out the tin buckets, though she wasn't joking. Not in the least.

"Hey, guys, wait up!" It was Kris. At fourteen, he was almost as tall as Gabe, even though Gabe was two years older, and broader through the shoulders. Next to Jer and Mom, Kris looked like a Native American, and not just because of his dark Mohawk. He possessed their father's olive skin and tanned easily, never burning. Complexion-wise, Gabe fell somewhere between his mom and dad. Like his mother, Gabe's brown eyes held a hint of green, though hers carried a more pronounced hue. Some days her eyes seemed to glow like a cat's, especially when she was fuming mad. She often used the effect to her advantage, claiming she was a witch. She wasn't one, or so Gabe hoped, but she could certainly act like one when she wanted to.

Her mother, Grandma May, on the other hand, definitely would have been burned at the stake in the old days. She communed with nature and was constantly concocting unusual herbal remedies for this or that malady. She looked like a witch, too. Her long hair was still black, even in her sixties, and she had sharp, piercing blue eyes. Her skin, pale like her daughter's, was as strangely smooth as a child's, lending more credence to the witch theory.

Even as a little kid, Gabe had always thought Grandma May was weird. Every few years, his family would come visit her and Grandpa May. They once owned the farmhouse where his mom had grown up, but Grandma now lived alone in a tiny cottage nearby. Grandpa May was dead. He'd died last year of a heart attack. Gabe had always liked him. Grandma May, he wasn't so sure about.

Kris ran to catch up to them, tripped, caught himself, and loped onward like a baby giraffe. When he reached them, he gaped down at their buckets. "You're done already?"

"No thanks to you," Gabe snapped. He was not in the mood to support Kris's engineering schemes, which Mom and Dad always encouraged. While Jer and Gabe did the grunt work, Kris had all the fun of drawing and building and inventing. Jer and Gabe wanted to do all that, too, or at least something more exciting than picking berries under the hot sun all day long.

"Sorry!" Kris said cheerfully. "Lost track of time. I was working on an automatic berry picker. It's not easy making something that won't mangle the berries or the bushes. So far, I've come up with the Shaker. Wanna see it?" He looked eagerly at them both, his large, dark brown eyes, just like their dad's, full of excitement.

Gabe shook his head. "Later, Kris. We've got to get these blueberries inside. Since you didn't pick any, you get to clean them. Jer and I will help Mom with dinner."

"We can check it out after supper," Kris persisted.

"We'll see," Gabe unconsciously echoed his mother's standard response to any request made of her. He wanted to go running after they ate, preferably staying as far away from the woods as he could get. He wasn't sure, but he thought the line of trees seemed closer to the house than he remembered from when they flew back for Grandpa's funeral. The forest's sinister presence reminded him of a noose wrapped around his neck, slowly tightening. He wished it didn't exist.

The three boys banged through the screen door into the kitchen and the door slammed shut behind them like a gunshot. Their mom was taking a Shepherd's pie out of a battered, old oven from the seventies. "What was I thinking?" she gasped as the hot air enveloped her. "I shouldn't have cooked." Sweat ran down the side of her heat-flushed face as she set the pie onto a wire cooling rack. She wore her dark brown hair tied up in a bun, though a few rebellious tendrils had escaped the mass and were sticking to her neck like coiled snakes.

They all knew why she had cooked. Their dad needed nourishing meals to get well again. At least, that's what they told themselves. Gabe thought maybe she did it because it was the one sure, tangible thing she could do to help Dad.

"Smells good!" Kris exclaimed, taking the buckets and plunking them on the counter. "I'm starving!" He poured one into a wire-bottomed tray used to sort out the sticks, leaves, and bugs that invariably came with berry picking. Obsessed with all things cooking, Jer scurried over to help their mom. He expertly plucked the crescent rolls from the top rack of the oven while Gabe set the table.

"Why don't you tell Mom how you spent your time while *we* picked berries?" Gabe suggested irritably.

She gave Kris a stern look, but he leaped in to explain, which Gabe knew would get him out of trouble. It always did. Kris had that way about him. Some would call it charm; Gabe would call it the art of bs-ing.

"I was inventing a berry picker, Mom!" he cried. "It's going to save us lots of time."

"It'd save us time if you'd help your brothers pick instead of fooling around in the barn."

His grin was sheepish. "But they're so good at picking berries. Besides, I always spill my bucket," which was true, "and I can never quite get the hang of it," which wasn't.

"You're just lazy," Gabe accused.

"I was working hard!" Kris defended himself, making a sour face at his brother. He tossed a handful of clean blueberries into an antique, blue and white striped ceramic bowl, nearly knocking it to the floor with the back of his hand.

"Working hard at getting out of work," Jer slipped in as he sliced the Shepherd's pie into eight precise pieces.

"Mom!" Kris complained, appealing to her, his brown eyes wide with indignation. "Tell them I'm doing important work."

This time, she surprised them by not taking Kris's side. "I need berries *now*," she told him firmly, "not next week." Jer and Gabe snuck amazed looks at each other, looks that swiftly transformed into gratified smirks. Forehead puckered with worry, Mom wiped her hands on a worn yellow towel that had seen better days. As though realizing her troubled expression, she tried to smile, but the smile melted away, unable to grab hold. "I'm going to check on your father. When I get back, I want dinner ready and the table set. Milk for everyone, Gabe, and set napkins. Okay?"

"Okay, Mom," the three brothers promised.

When she'd gone, Kris asked in a quiet voice, "Is he coming down for supper?"

Gabe shrugged as he lined up a knife and spoon to stand side by side in perfect formation. "We don't know yet."

He didn't come. Mom returned to the kitchen alone, telling them that Dad wasn't hungry; she'd bring him something later. "Perhaps some of your berries!" Her attempt at enthusiasm fell flat. They ate their supper, just the four of them, quietly and morosely, with only the sounds of chewing and silverware clinking against their dinner plates to fill the weighted air.

When they finished with supper, they each inhaled a bowl of blueberries in milk and sugar for dessert, just like Gabe had been hoping they'd get. For some reason, though, the treat didn't taste as good as he'd imagined it would.

It didn't take long before the kitchen was clean and the rest of the berries debugged, detwigged, and measured. They all took turns with their favorite part—pouring exactly sixteen ounces into green containers to haul into Ranger tomorrow. Gabe had gotten his driver's license two months ago, when he'd turned sixteen—the one shining moment in his currently depressing life—so he was going to haul the fruit into the general store, all by himself.

He was both excited and nervous as heck. Having sold their SUV upon arrival to help fund the move to Maine, they were stuck driving Grandpa May's old Ford truck, which actually had wooden boards framing the sides of the pick-up bed. Worse, the manual shift was cranky at best and you had to stomp hard on the brake and pray mightily that your efforts would bring the small tank to a stop. The only good thing about the truck was that once you got it going, it generally didn't want to quit. Though that could be a bad thing, too, Gabe supposed, especially for anyone in its path.

Any spare moment that could be found during the past week, his mom had worked with him on learning how to manipulate the stick shift and clutch. Getting the truck moving forward again without killing it—if he had to stop while facing uphill—remained a challenge. And then there was that whole unreliable brake thing. But he was getting better. Fortunately, the town of Ranger, christened *Home of the Mountains and the Sea*, wasn't as hilly as San Francisco, which they used to visit several times a year before Dad got sick. Unfortunately, the single stoplight in town was situated on one of the hills.

Their work finished in the kitchen, the brothers raced each other out to the old red barn, its peeling paint and cracked windows begging for a spruce-up, to look at Kris's invention. On their first day at the farm, Gabe and his brothers had explored the old building, quickly discovering the immense loft filled with fragrant hay, its rafters dotted with bird nests and splatters of poop. Mice droppings and feathers carpeted the floor, making navigation somewhat challenging. On the bottom level they found several pieces of old, rusty machinery, a stained and bit up workbench covered with antique tools, glass jars full of screws and bolts, nails and mysterious bits, and loads of junk just begging to be rummaged through, cleaned, and put to good use.

Gabe remembered the barn from his past visits, though it had looked more organized and loved then. Cleaning and painting it was on his mother's to-do list, along with a million other tasks she wanted to get done before winter set in. The whole place, house and sheds included, was run-down, beaten by weather, time, and neglect. Grandpa May had been sick for a year before his heart gave out. Once untended, everything had gone downhill fast.

"It's cool, isn't it?" Kris demanded, grabbing a cowboy hat hanging on a railroad spike and plonking it on his head. He liked to wear hats when he worked—said it helped him think.

After examining the strange machine, Gabe had to admit that the Shaker might actually work. He hoped so. He was sick of picking berries and besides, he was worried that the color might never wear off his fingertips. Where he came from, purple fingertips were not cool. In Ranger, the opinion was probably the same.

The Shaker, when Kris attempted to start it, didn't want to cooperate. After fifteen minutes of tinkering and muttering, Gabe left Kris and Jer working on the machine. Kris fancied that Jer was his little Igor, and Jer went along with the game, but only because he liked machines, too.

Gabe did, as well, but today he wasn't in the mood. It was hot and dry in the barn and the hay in the loft was making him sneeze. He hadn't been able to run for a week now and he was itching to get his legs moving. He'd always loved to run from the time he was a little kid. It was the one thing that took his mind off his problems, and he had a lot of them right now.

While picking berries earlier, he'd scouted out a route he could follow, which skirted the edge of the woods. He didn't like how close the path ran to the trees, but it made a nice loop around the yard. One lap should be close to a half mile, he figured, so he'd make the circuit twice. Normally he'd run in the morning, but Mom had kept them busy for the last week, starting early because of the heat. Though it was so hot out right now, he'd probably melt halfway through the first lap.

The sun had begun to ease itself behind the cover of the tall trees and shadows dropped over the yard like swooping bats. Watching the ever-increasing darkness expand its boundaries, Gabe made up his mind. So what if he melted? He really needed to run. He would set himself a good pace and let the moving air cool him.

His tennis shoes were on the porch where he'd left them after hosing down the muddy truck this morning. Dry now, he pulled them on and tied the stiff laces. Without socks he was sure to get blisters, but for once he didn't care. He stood, stretched his arms and legs, then scanned the path, trying to decide where to start. The barn loomed into view and Gabe figured it would make as good a starting place as any.

Muscles loose now, he marched briskly over to the building, watching several bats flit here and there hunting bugs. About fifty feet from the back of the barn, the yard ended and a strange hedge of thick, leafy vines began. The wild and thorny mass, which reached about eight feet tall and was impossible to see through, closed off access to this part of the woods. About fifty or sixty yards back from the hedge, a conglomeration of trees turreted unbelievably high above the ground. He wondered who'd started the thicket in the first place, and why it only grew in certain spots around the yard. Whatever the reason, it offered Gabe the perfect excuse not to have to confront those giant trees. Besides, his roiling stomach warned him not to go in the woods.

With the heel of his shoe, he marked his starting line to run parallel to the back of the barn. Squatting into a runner's stance, he took a deep breath, then, like a whale breaching the surface, he exploded into action. His muscles and lungs protested at the fast pace—it hadn't taken long for him to lose his stamina—but he soon settled into a good rhythm.

The moist air made breathing difficult, but Gabe defiantly picked up speed, helping him outrun the drove of horseflies chasing after him.

They weren't the fastest of flyers—the sloths of the bug world, Jer called them—but when they bit, it stung like a son-of-a-gun, hurting almost as badly as a bee sting, and left behind an itchy bump that could last for days.

Gabe crossed the driveway and rounded the first corner of the yard, his arms pumping like pistons. Here, a faint path disappeared into the woods, leading to a couple neighbors he'd yet to meet, who lived about a quarter mile into the forest. Strangely, the hedge didn't grow along this section of the woods.

Running faster, he swiftly rounded the corner behind the house and the grassy yard straightened out for a longer stretch. According to his mom, this part ran closest to the ocean, where waves crashed against the rocky shore about half a mile away. "On certain days, you can hear them pounding like drums," she told him and his brothers. He inhaled deeply and caught the unmistakable scent of brine, a tantalizing mix of salt and seaweed riding the tail of an oceanic breeze. Gabe felt the breath of cool, moist air on his warming face and welcomed its touch.

The wind picked up, pushing insistently against his back as he passed by the small grove of apple and peach trees, before slipping around him and racing onward to stir up the woods. When the gust hit the trees, their torsos all leaned in one direction, then shifted in unison as the wind changed course. Thunder rumbled, a warning of chaos to come. A storm was on its way and Gabe was glad. A good rain would finally squelch the heat and blow out this wretched humidity.

Rounding the third corner, he heard strange sounds ahead of him. At first he thought it was the breeze rustling the blueberry bushes, but he soon changed his mind. That was a voice he was hearing. The same one he'd heard earlier. He ran faster, caught between the blueberry bushes and the prickly hedge that once again skirted the edge of the woods. Another gust of wind hit him in the back, urging him on as though sensing the challenge of a race.

Gabrielll…

The voice was hollow, haunting…

Gabrielll… There it was again!

Suddenly Gabe figured out what was going on. It was Kris! He was always playing practical jokes. The moment Gabe reached the barn, he was going to hunt down his brother and give him a pounding he wouldn't soon forget.

A couple hundred meters to go. He passed the blueberry rows and was near the neglected vegetable garden now. A warm glow spilled from the barn's open doors. His eyes were locked on them when the light winked out, though the barn's fluorescent outdoor light remained on. Soon after, Jer and Kris left the building, laughing and pushing each other as they ran for the house.

It wasn't Kris playing tricks on him, then. The voice had come from the woods, and neither Kris nor Jer were anywhere near the towering trees. Someone else lurked in the darkness, someone who knew his name.

Gabrielll…

The sweat on his skin turned cold. A tingling, prickling sensation at the base of his neck warned him that he was being watched. In an instant, his sweat and his mouth dried up, and his legs went wobbly.

Gabrielll…

The unwelcome presence was just a heartbeat away. Gabe broke from the trail and dashed toward the house. His left foot hit a tuft of grass and he staggered, nearly falling. He'd just righted himself when strong fingers grasped his shoulder and tried to pull him back with an insistence that spoke of inhuman strength. His heart nearly exploded out of his chest.

He heard shouting and the sensation of touch fled.

Kris and Jer stood on the porch, but they weren't looking or yelling at him. They were peering down at something between them. Feeling safer so close to the house, Gabe stopped abruptly and spun around. He had to know what was behind him, trying to touch him.

Nothing showed itself in the fading light, not even a suspicious shadow, and Gabe's shoulders slumped. He'd been imagining things, just like when he'd come here as a kid to visit, seeing shadows and figures everywhere, hearing voices when no one was there.

Annoyed at his overreaction, he jogged over to see what his brothers were so excited about, though he couldn't help nervously glancing over his shoulder on the way to the porch.

"What is it?" he asked, though the question came out more as a grunt. He was still winded from his run and his fright.

Jer rose and his blond hair and pale face stood out in the darkness of the porch like the moon against the night sky. "We found something, Gabe. Come see for yourself."

Just as he reached the top step, the porch light flashed on and the front door swung open. It was Mom, and astonishingly, right behind her in the doorframe, stood Dad. Despite the heat, his father wore a Hudson Bay wool blanket wrapped tightly around his drooping shoulders. A recent buzz cut of his thinning, light brown hair made his high cheekbones more prominent, emphasizing the telltale hollows of illness beneath them. His eyes, deep-set anyway, were nearly invisible in the shadows thrown by the porch light.

"What is it? What's wrong?" Mom cried. She looked down and gasped. "What...? Who...?"

"We don't know!" Kris exclaimed. "We just found it, sitting here."

Gabe pushed his brother out of the way to get a better look. Sitting on the porch's worn planks was a basket—like the ones you'd find perched atop an old-fashioned baby buggy—only this one was hand-made. Instead of white wicker, supple tree branches formed the rounded basket.

Moving closer, Gabe peered down into the face of a baby—the ugliest baby he'd ever seen.

Chapter Two

You Must Have Been
an Ugly Baby

Mom, thank goodness, took over. "Bring it inside, Gabe," she or-dered as her dark eyes scanned the yard before settling on the woods. Then, her expression grim, she turned and went inside.

He reached down to pick up the basket, trying to avoid looking at the ugly thing. He didn't succeed. That face. He shuddered. A baby shouldn't look so knowing, and it shouldn't have such disproportion-ately large eyes—they were as big as golf balls. The repulsive creature's nose, unlike the little round buttons one is accustomed to seeing on babies, was narrow and hooked. Its fingers, curled around the edges of a woven blanket the color of fresh pine needles, were long and thin, like spider legs. The strange little critter yawned and Gabe couldn't help but stare at its gaping mouth. It was much too wide, the lips too thin and pale. Oh, and did he mention the baby was bald?

As a butt.

With a reluctance verging on revulsion, he picked up the basket and carried it into the house, holding it at arm's length. Once inside, he set the baby on top of the dining room table. Mom, Dad, Jer, and Kris gathered around the basket, squeezing Gabe out of the way. He was only too happy to step back from the gruesome creature.

"Oh, it's darling!" his mom gushed, seeing the baby in the light. "Look at all that hair!"

Hair?

Dad laughed delightedly and Gabe stared at him in surprise. Lately, he'd been so tired and weak that he rarely laughed anymore. And usu-ally it hurt when he did. "She's quite the little cutie pie."

She? Gabe was thinking more along the lines of 'it.'

"She's got my finger, Mom!" Jer cried. "Look, she's trying to put it in her mouth!"

Gabe hurried over to his brother's side, afraid Jer was going to lose that finger. Seeing him, the baby grinned, showing a gummy hole. Its eyes narrowed mischievously, then one of them winked at him. "Did you see that?" He pointed at the babbling baby.

"Ohhh!" his mother crooned. "She's trying to talk."

He stared at her. Hadn't she seen the little monster wink? And why had she said, 'Look at all that hair!' when obviously there was none? Dad had called her a cutie pie, too, an insane term that definitely didn't fit the ugly urchin. Something wasn't right here. Judging by the amused expression on everyone else's face, they weren't seeing what Gabe was seeing.

The baby screamed suddenly and he flinched, slapping his hands over his ears. The sound was horrid, a shrill shriek that would give a tin can in a garbage disposal a run for its money. When the baby finally shut its mouth, he cautiously lowered his hands.

His mother laughed. "She's only hungry, Gabe! We'll have to find something for her to eat. Maybe we'll start with some milk."

"We should find her mother," he replied, thinking a baby like that would probably prefer eating slugs, toads, and snakes, none of which would be found in the cupboards.

"Oh, we will," she replied vaguely.

Gabe frowned. "Uh, when? Do you want me to call the police?"

"I'll do it when I get to it," she said firmly, then hurried to the refrigerator to find some milk.

Gabe shook his head. What was wrong with everybody? Didn't they realize they'd just invited some kind of demon into their home? Mom didn't seem to be in all that big of a hurry to get rid of the thing, either.

Seeing his dad making silly faces, his wan cheeks tinged with a hint of pink, Gabe relented. He didn't know what was going on, but for the moment his dad was happy, so he wouldn't stir up trouble. He would, however, be watching the little monster quite closely, and maybe look into calling an eye doctor, or a shrink, for an appointment.

Mom returned with the milk in a faded red Sippy cup, decorated with smiling pigs, and they took turns feeding the greedy little wretch. When the cup was offered to Gabe, he passed, claiming he was too sweaty from his run. The baby threw him a cunning look. If it could talk, he felt sure it would've crowed triumphantly, "I'll get you, my pretty!"

When the cup was empty, the baby released a ridiculously long burp. Everyone but Gabe clapped in delight as they watched curdled lumps of milk spewing from between the thing's quivering lips. He wondered how they would react if he did the same thing, though he was quite sure they wouldn't clap and cheer. In fact, he'd probably be sent to live in the barn.

Without consulting anyone, Mom voted to keep the little imp overnight and report it missing in the morning. He was pretty sure this violated all kinds of laws. When he mentioned *again* that they should call the police, she argued that no one would know *when* exactly they'd found the baby, and since it looked like she'd been left on purpose, the mother might come back for her at any time. Gabe shut his mouth, quickly deciding that as long as they kept that thing away from him, they could do whatever they wanted with it.

While he watched through the screen door as the storm broke overhead, the others took turns feeding the little gargoyle, burping it, holding it, and entertaining it. They had fallen completely in love. Even Kris and Jer were acting like dopes, arguing about which of them it liked best.

That night, everyone but Gabe went to bed happy and excited to have this new addition. After digging out an old cloth diaper and changing the smelly beast, Mom decided to keep the baby in the small room next to hers and Dad's. She wanted it close by just in case it needed her, but didn't want Dad's sleep to be disturbed by its cries.

Sitting on the floor next to the basket, Jer and Kris took turns singing lullabies to Baby Butt-Ugly. After watching them in disgust for a few moments, Gabe retreated to his room and slammed the door shut.

That night he had trouble sleeping. He kept hearing creaking noises coming from different parts of the house. The storm had cleared out around nine o'clock, so it wasn't the wind making the strange sounds. *It's just an old house*, he told himself. *Old houses make weird noises.*

Like footsteps? his mind insisted on asking.

Finally he drifted off, only to dream of Sadie, his almost girlfriend, and his old life in San Jose, which, though not exactly great, wasn't nearly as bad as this one. When he awoke, he felt tired and cranky and homesick. It didn't help that the baby was throwing a hissy fit, which was what had awakened him.

"Shut it up," he groaned into his pillow. "Make it stop!" Finally, it did, and there was silence for ten blessed minutes.

"Time to get up, lazy bones," his mother called into his room, shattering his peace. He rolled over to beg for more sleep, only to see that she was holding Repulsive, his newly inspired name for the ugly infant. The little monster grinned at him. It was chewing on a bagel, bits of soggy bread all over its thin, sallow face, and it looked like it had thrown up more than it had ingested. Gabe shuddered and gagged.

"I want you to drive into town soon," his mom told him. "You can make inquiries about the baby. But be subtle about it." He stared at her. She had to be kidding! How can you be subtle about something like that? "You're a smart boy," she added, reading his mind. "Figure something out." He wondered if there were any buses leaving town soon. "Now get up and get cracking! I've already let you sleep in, and there's lots to do."

Gabe rolled his eyes—so that his mother couldn't see him, of course—then crawled out of bed. After a quick shower, he dressed in an oversized t-shirt with a picture of the Golden Gate Bridge on it and ragged jeans cut off just above the knee. After running a brush through his wet hair, he joined his brothers and his mom in the kitchen. A cool breeze wafting through the screen door was the first good thing to happen to him that day. The air felt fresh and crisp and he inhaled deeply, hoping to store some of it inside him.

This kind of weather is more like it, he thought.

His mother had taken advantage of the cooler temperature and was baking several batches of May Farm's famous blueberry muffins. A dozen of them cooled on black metal racks on the counter. Near the white ceramic sink his mom wrapped the cooled muffins for him to bring to the store. He stood over the racks and breathed in, his mouth watering. The muffins smelled of brown sugar and cinnamon and tangy fruit. He really wanted one. Somehow Repulsive had scored one, but Kris and Jer were eating plain old cold cereal. Which meant that he wouldn't be getting a muffin, either. They didn't seem to mind, though, engrossed as they were with watching her spew all over herself (emphasis on the gross part).

He sighed and helped himself to a bowl of Crunchies. Pouring milk over the crisp cereal, he felt Repulsive watching his every move. When he could no longer resist, he turned and looked. Noting his attention, the baby lifted the muffin into the air and cackled triumphantly. He curled his upper lip. It cackled again.

He was just about to make a face at the thing when, miracle of miracles, his dad shuffled into the kitchen. The bright sunlight streaming through the windows emphasized his pallor and the new lines around his mouth and eyes, but he looked happy. Especially when he spotted Repulsive. He picked the creature up, then laughed when it spit slimy muffin in his face.

"Feisty!" he said, still chuckling as he wiped away bits of chewed-up muffin.

Gabe's mouth clamped shut. He would not ruin this moment. "How are you feeling this morning, Dad?" he asked tentatively.

"Pretty good for a guy who's just had a kidney transplant." His father smiled, rubbing Kris and Jer's heads affectionately. They beamed at him. This was the father they remembered. Gabe nodded, not trusting himself to speak.

"Sit down, Keith," Mom commanded. "Here, you can give the baby her milk," she amended, pushing him into a chair. The doctor had told them to be sure not to treat Dad like an invalid, even though, for all intents and purposes, he was one. He'd had Type I diabetes since he was five years old, and before they caught the disease and started him on insulin, it had done a number on his kidneys. The damage didn't start to show up until a few years ago, when his ravaged organs began to fail, slowly taking the rest of his body with them.

He'd been sick for a long time before he got his new kidneys, so it was going to take him a long time to recover. In the meantime, they were to feed him good food, make sure to keep his spirits up, and try to make ends meet without letting on that they were having trouble surviving financially.

It wasn't easy.

Mom had wanted to take care of Dad herself so she couldn't work, and they couldn't afford a nurse anyway, even if Mom did get a job. When their money was nearly gone, his parents made the decision to move back to the town where they'd grown up, met, and gotten married. The plan was to take over the family business at the farm. Grandma May had said it was too much for her to handle herself, so here they were.

Despite the obvious downside to living in Maine, it was good to see Dad up and around, happy and smiling. He even asked for a big breakfast and was tucking into it with enthusiasm. If Repulsive could do that for him, maybe she wasn't all bad. He groaned. Now he was calling her *she*! Oh, well. If he couldn't beat 'em, he might as well join 'em. That didn't mean he would feed her or hold her, but he'd try harder not to grimace whenever he looked at the rug rat (emphasis on the rat part).

Finishing his cereal quickly, he stood to go. The car keys were on the table and he reached over to grab them. "Hey, now, just a minute, young man!" his mother called out, startling him. He dropped the keys and they clanged on the wooden table. Repulsive laughed and clapped her skinny hands together.

"What?"

"Do you have your wallet?"

He sighed. No wonder he was so jumpy and anxious about everything. His mother liked to mess with his mind. "It's in my back pocket," he told her. Like he was going to do anything that would mess this up! If he handled things right, he might be able to score some freedom from his family, maybe escape this house once in awhile—without his brothers. His mom had a "no one else but me or your father in the car when you're driving" rule until he proved himself as a reliable driver. Which was fine with Gabe. He was happy to leave his tormentors at home.

She grinned. "You've really got to lighten up, Gabe."

"And you've really got to stop acting like you're going to kick me into next week at any moment." It was his standard reply.

Her eyes twinkled mischievously as she picked up the box filled with muffins, all of which were carefully wrapped in blue plastic and labeled May Farm with a blueberry-shaped sticker. Grandma and Grandpa May had been running the business for a long time before them so everything was already arranged at the store. Gabe was glad of this. Dealing with strangers wasn't exactly his forte.

"Be careful with these," Mom warned him. "If so much as one muffin gets squashed or eaten…"

He held up his hands. "I know, I know. *I* get squashed…or eaten."

She gave him a humorless smirk. "Just as long as we're on the same page." She glanced at her watch, then over at his brothers. "Time's a wastin'. Boys, give Gabe a hand."

Jer and Kris pushed their chairs away from the table, taking the opportunity to tickle Repulsive under the chin. She growled like a mad dog, but it probably sounded like a delighted gurgle to them. It didn't make sense. Gabe had spent a lot of time last night wondering why he seemed to see Repulsive so differently than the rest of his family. Maybe it was simply that they were more accepting of her imperfections. Maybe he was just a big, judgmental snob.

Well, snob or not, he wasn't touching that thing. He didn't really mind that she was ugly—ugly was interesting—but throw vicious into the mix and he wasn't getting involved.

When the Ford was loaded and the hefty tailgate slammed into place, Gabe climbed into the driver's seat. For a moment he thought he was going to make a clean getaway, but seconds later everyone came scurrying out of the house to see him off. This was a momentous event; no way were they going to miss it. He should have remembered that it didn't take much to stir his family up.

His dad approached the truck first, his arms wrapped about himself as though he were cold, even though it was seventy-five degrees outside. The window was down and he placed a trembling hand on Gabe's arm. "Drive safe, son!" he said heartily. After a quick glance over his shoulder, he leaned closer. "And enjoy your freedom." With a wide grin, he pushed away from the car and Gabe felt himself smiling in response. His dad was willing to break a few rules in the house, but he didn't always want their mom to know about it. His body might be weak, but obviously his brain and survival instincts still functioned adequately.

Ignoring the anxious frown on his mother's face, he turned his attention back to the truck. Pushing the clutch and the brake in at the same time, he turned the key with a shaking hand. Oh, why did he have to have an audience? It was hard enough making this ancient machine work without everyone watching him so closely.

The starter whined as Gabe twisted the key hard, then the truck roared to life. Taking his foot off the brake, he slowly began to push down on the gas at the same time he lifted his foot off the clutch. The truck started to hum loudly, then lurched forward, bucked like a wild horse, and died.

"Bravo!" Kris yelled. "Let's see that again!"

"Idiot," Gabe muttered under his breath. Angry now, but determined, he repeated the process, very carefully this time. No way was he going to let Kris see him kill the engine again. His brother had always had a way with mechanical things; he would've started the truck on his first try and be gone by now, laughing triumphantly.

The starter screeched. "Be careful, Gabe!" his mother hollered and his hand jerked off the key. "You're going to break the starter and we can't afford to get it fixed right now. Remember, driving this truck is a privilege, not a right!"

Gabe sighed, refrained from mimicking his mother's reprimand—but only because she was watching—and focused once again on starting the truck. Thankfully, once the engine turned over, he managed to let out the clutch slowly enough this time and the truck began to roll forward.

As the vehicle gained momentum, his confidence grew. Giving a jaunty honk, he steered down the driveway—two dirt tracks with a strip of grass and weeds growing between them. He tried to avoid the potholes, but there were too many of them. Filled with muddy water, it wasn't clear how deep they were so he took it slow, feeling every dip and jerk of the solid truck as he passed beneath the canopy of trees that formed an arch over the drive. The close proximity of their massive trunks and dangling branches made him nervous, reminding him of something he had somehow managed to forget in the uproar of finding Repulsive—the voice coming from the forest…the voice repeating his name.

Well, he hadn't exactly forgotten what had happened; repressed might be a better word. Gabe was a worrier, but when he really didn't want to think about something he simply blanked it out, like it had never really happened. Now the memory came back to him, strong and clear.

Gabrielll...

The eerie voice had called his name like a restless spirit searching for release. Or maybe his imagination had been playing tricks on him—the wind from the approaching storm making it sound like someone calling his name.

He sighed and shifted into second gear. At worse, someone was playing games with him; some local who got a kick out of messing with the new kid's mind. This seemed more rational than believing some kind of phantom had called out to him. At any rate, whatever it had been—his imagination, the wind, someone playing tricks—he decided to run in the morning from now on. No more night runs.

The route into town was relatively simple. There was a turn to make, but he handled it well enough, if a bit jerkily. The shifting part was easy, once he got going, but the dreaded stoplight was only about a quarter mile away and coming up fast. Chugging up the hill, he prayed for a green light; it was bright red at the moment. *Please, please, please, go green!* He stomped on the sticky brake and whipped over into the turn lane, hoping for the best.

Just in time, the light turned green and he was able to make his turn without stopping. The road leveled out a bit where the shops lined up on both sides of the street, before heading downhill toward the ocean. A block after the stoplight, Gabe pulled into a diagonal parking space in front of Woodlands General Store, using all his weight on the brake to stop the truck. The sidewalk helped him a little here, bouncing him back half a foot after he hit it. He quickly cut the engine and shifted into first.

So far, so good!

Feeling inspired by his driving prowess, he cockily opened the door and slid out. His shoelace caught on a piece of metal sticking out of the floorboard, tripping him so that he landed in a heap on the ground. Scrambling to his feet, he glanced around. The sidewalks were empty, and he breathed a sigh of relief. No one had seen him fall. Life wasn't totally working against him today, just enough to keep him on his toes, or his knees, as it were.

Before mounting the wide front porch leading into the store, he took a moment to study Ranger. It was a quaint northern New England seaside town. Old shops crowded together like books on a bookshelf, fronted by faded red brick sidewalks that lined Main Street. The picture window of the gift shop next door, called, fittingly, *Shirt Yourself*, displayed several t-shirts scrawled with Yankee wit: "Moose Crossing," "Got Lobster?" and "Maine: The Way Life Should Be."

Maybe if you're comatose, Gabe thought, making a face at himself in the window.

The town did look nice, though. Each shop was freshly painted, most of them white. A few yellows and pale blues, and one daring red— Woodlands General Store—added a bit of spice to the town, which Gabe found appealing. Lead-glass windows wore boxes of colorful flowers like aprons, and pots hanging from wrought-iron posts or from hooks spilled over with cascades of colorful blooms. The brick sidewalk was garbage-free and only a few bricks stuck up here and there to trip unsuspecting pedestrians.

Main Street led down to the wharf, where sturdy fishing boats and slender sailboats floated peacefully, anchored to buoys painted in a rainbow of colors. The mid-morning sun hit the water at full power, making it sparkle like a billion crystals. Gabe stared at the scene for a moment, mesmerized by the light, before looking around a bit more.

To his left, Shishiqua River flowed around the mountainside and past the looming hulk of an abandoned mill, before slithering down to the ocean like a black snake on the hunt. Thick ivy covered the large mill's red brick walls and its forever-darkened windows stared blankly, though not blindly, at a world that had left it behind. A waterwheel, a few of its planks missing, stood still, seemingly locked in place. The whole structure was dying a slow death. Gabe shivered and looked away, spooked.

From his vantage point on the hill, he was surprised at how much land the forest covered. Running from the top of the mountains down to the ocean's edge, the woods continued as far south as he could see, which was miles on a clear day like today. Strangely enough, relatively few trees grew in town or north of it, where the mill was located, like a line had been drawn, and the trees kept to their side, while the people and their dwellings stayed on theirs.

During the drive to Maine, Dad told them Ranger was one of the rare towns of this size and this close to the coast that didn't have Route One running through it. The highway skirted around the mountains, steering clear of the town. Tourists who visited Ranger must either have heard about it from friends or family, or had stumbled across it on their way to somewhere else. Ranger wasn't easy to get to. Only a small road from the west led into town, and its path followed the northern side of the mountain. No roads cut through the forest, which would have been the easiest and most convenient route. In fact, the road that led to May Farm and Grandma May's cottage dead-ended about a half mile past their drives.

The strangest part was that May Farm sat right in the middle of all those trees. If no one else dared to go through the woods, then why was the farm there? Gabe shook his head. No sense dwelling on it now. He had to get those muffins and blueberries into the store, without damage or spillage, and head back home to do chores. They still had to finish painting and winterizing the house.

It was only July, which seemed like plenty of time to get everything done, but Mom had warned them that winter would be on them soon enough. Maine, she added ominously, was not a state where you messed with winter. Still, he lingered a few more minutes to enjoy the scenery and his brief fling with freedom.

He did wonder what it would be like to experience cold and snow. In San Jose, the most snow at one time that he'd ever seen measured about an inch and a half. All that white stuff coming out of the sky had been such a momentous event that they'd called off school and people even stayed home from work to watch it. The way everyone acted, you'd have thought it was raining fish. When he found out that Maine could get *feet* of snow, he felt a twinge of anticipation, imagining what it would be like to be surrounded by a thick blanket of cold white.

Walking around to the back of the truck, Gabe opened the ornery tailgate, which screeched in rusty protest, and pulled out a box of muffins. Crossing the sidewalk, he made sure not to trip on the bricks that had inched their way up during the winter like gophers poking their noses out of the ground.

Inside, customers stood at the counter with their baskets and he got in line behind them. While he waited, he gazed around the unusual store. There certainly weren't any like this in San Jose. For one thing, this store was a lot smaller than the super-marts where his mom shopped. For another, it looked old, as though he'd stepped back in time. Wide-planked boards, scuffed and nicked, comprised the floor. In the corner, two old men played a game of chess. Or maybe they were sleeping. Neither had moved since Gabe had entered the store.

An assortment of local honey, jams, and homemade breads, along with hard candies and saltwater taffy, packed the wooden shelves. A large pickle barrel huddled close to where the chess players sat and Gabe's mouth watered at the thought of biting into one of the crisp, salty cukes. He should've eaten a bigger breakfast, he realized.

"When will he be back?" he heard the husky woman in front of him ask—or bark, actually. Her deep voice, which filled the store with its force, projected authority, as did her solid figure. She wore a no-nonsense tan blouse tucked into brown slacks, the waistband constricting her middle like a rubber band and creating the illusion that she had a waist. She looked as fastidious as a monk, right down to her square cut nails and highly polished loafers, and her thick, brown hair was chopped short and styled to resemble a head of lettuce. Her look projected the message, *I have no time for such silly things as fashion, fun, or delay.*

"I told you, Mrs. Deacon. He'll be back when he finishes making his delivery to the Thompsons." The other speaker, whom he couldn't see around the formidable Mrs. Deacon, sounded just as no-nonsense, though with the rebellious tone that only a teenager could produce.

"Well, you tell him, *Abazi*," the woman ground out, as though she didn't like the taste of the name in her mouth, "that I'm looking for him."

"Oh, he knows," Abazi replied. "But I think he's avoiding you."

The woman's broad shoulders, which were the same width as her hips, pulled back. "You are impertinent, girl!"

"Oh, that's a great word, Mrs. Deacon," Abazi gushed. "But actually I'm just being honest, not impertinent. Now will that be cash or credit? Other customers are waiting."

Gabe found himself smiling at her daring. He could never talk to an adult like that. Not that he hadn't ever wanted to, but just the idea of it made him sweat. The most he got out was mumbling under his breath at his mom when she made him mad. He wondered if he looked kind of weird, talking to himself all the time, like the bag lady who lived at the park by their old apartment, with her rusty, three-wheeled shopping cart. She fed the squirrels, even though there were fifty signs scattered around the park saying you weren't supposed to, and she talked to herself all the time. He realized he was going to have to find another way of expressing himself if he didn't want to share her fate.

Mrs. Deacon huffed and puffed as she tucked her change back into her wallet, her skin, the texture of wet clay, beaming red. "We need to take some action on that land…"

"…or the town will be losing money," the girl finished for her. "I know. I'll tell him."

"See that you do," Mrs. Deacon warned, shaking a stubby finger at the girl. "Your livelihood depends on it!" With that, she turned and barreled out of the store, nearly knocking Gabe over. She shot a peeved look at him, as though it was his fault for being in the way, before banging out the door clutching two paper bags in her capable arms.

When he'd recovered, Gabe found himself looking at a girl about his age. She wore her straight black hair pulled back into two braids, with tiny wisps sticking out like frayed yarn on a sweater. Her skin was the color of a perfectly roasted marshmallow and her dark eyes boasted long lashes, nearly as long as Gabe's own. His had always embarrassed him. That is until his ex-neighbor, Sara, informed him that girls liked long eyelashes on a guy. She said it made him look like a movie star. After that, for some reason, he didn't despise them so much.

Judging by her high cheekbones, the braids, and the beaded headband she wore around her high brow, he guessed she was Native American. He'd never met a real, live Indian before. He hoped he didn't say something stupid...like that he'd never met a real, live Indian before.

She stared at him. "Yes?"

"Um, yeah, um...here." He banged the slatted wooden box down on the counter. *Smooth, Gabe,* he admonished himself, hoping he wouldn't blush. He blushed.

"Finally!" she cried, startling him. Pulling the box toward her, she pointed a threatening brown finger at him. "You better have the berries, too. That was the deal."

"They're...they're in the truck."

Her smooth brow wrinkled up. "Well?" Gabe watched her uncertainly. "Go fetch them! People keep asking me when we're getting more and I'm sick to death of making up excuses." She shook her head. "The way they act, you'd think blueberries were the answer to old age and infirmity. I mean, they grow everywhere, people. Go pick some yourself."

Without uttering a word in response, he did as he was told, scurrying out of the shop before she could snap at him some more. Grabbing a tray of blueberries from the truck, he carefully carried it into the shop, over to where he saw her standing at the back. This part of the store was more modern and stocked with items you'd find in a regular grocery store, like yogurt and lunchmeat. She pointed imperiously, and he placed all the pints onto a card table she'd cleared. Then he went back outside for the rest.

"So you're the new guy," she remarked when he'd brought in the last box of muffins, her arms folded across her chest as she eyed him up and down. He noticed she was wearing several metal bracelets on her left wrist.

"How did you know?"

"Well, duh!" Her brown eyes slid up toward the ceiling. "How many people do you think live around here?"

"Not very many, I suppose." He was used to the anonymity of big city living. It was weird having people notice him. He wasn't sure he liked it.

She watched him, an amused smile playing at the corner of her lips. "You're from May's Farm, right?" He nodded. "And do you have a name?"

He gulped. "Gabe…Gabe Hawthorne."

"Hi, Gabe Gabe Hawthorne. I'm Abazi Wanibagw." She held out her hand and he shook it. Her skin felt warm and soft. To his dismay, he discovered that he liked the feel of it. "Here's your money," she told him, pulling her hand back and handing him an envelope with the other one. "Now get lost. I've got work to do. I'm *berry* busy." She smirked.

She left him staring at her slim back as she returned to the counter, picked up a book, and began to read. He didn't know what else to do, so he left. She didn't look up. Neither did the two old men. He thought about rearranging a knight and a few rooks while they snored, but resisted the temptation.

As he fished for the car keys in his pocket, he realized something important. Abazi Wanibagw didn't like him. He also realized something else—this bothered him more than he cared to admit.

Chapter Three

Repulsive Has Got to Go

Gabe returned home after a relatively smooth ride—he only stalled out once—to find a note from his mom on the kitchen table. Repulsive was napping, Dad was resting, and she, Kris, and Jer had gone to try out the Shaker. He was to join them as soon as he got back, or else. He grabbed the note and shoved it in his pocket.

Hungry from his trip, he helped himself to a banana and a large glass of lemon-orangeade to keep up his strength before heading out. A long day of work stretched ahead of him. Come to think of it, he'd better make himself a pb & j sandwich, too.

As he ate, he wandered around the house, looking at all the pictures on the walls. Grandma May had left a lot of them behind, claiming she no longer had the space to hang them in her little cottage. In the living room, an old black and white aerial photograph of the farm hung above the battered upright piano. Gabe leaned over and peered at it closely. The farm looked odd sitting in the middle of the woods, like a mushroom growing in a strawberry patch. There were so many trees, growing so close together, that you couldn't see the ground. From this perspective, the forest appeared to be one big lumpy blanket.

But that wasn't entirely true, he soon realized. What were those strange lines and spirals near the mountainside? He was about to pull out the piano stool to get a closer look when he heard a thumping noise upstairs. He stopped what he was doing and cocked his head to listen. Was it Dad? Did he need help?

Swallowing the last bite of his sandwich, Gabe ran for the stairs leading to the second floor where all the bedrooms were located. There were five rooms in all, which meant everyone got their own room. His was the smallest of the five. He didn't like it very much, but it had been the only one left that wasn't right next to Mom and Dad's room. The crappy room was his punishment for being the only responsible kid in the family. When they'd first arrived, he'd grabbed some bags to carry in, like his mother had asked them *all* to do, which had given his brothers first chance at picking out rooms because they hadn't heard her.

Yeah, right.

Once upstairs, he found his dad fast asleep, his chest rising and falling in a steady rhythm. Gabe watched him for a moment, reassuring himself that his father was indeed okay and not dead or in the process of dying. Then he went to check on Repulsive, who was sleeping in the sewing/craft room.

When he entered the small, dusty space, he was surprised to see the basket, which was sitting on the floor next to the sewing table, turned away from the door. Slowly, carefully, he approached the little bassinet. Before he could lose his nerve—he did not have a good feeling about this—he peeked around the side of the basket.

It was empty.

Crud. Mom had distinctly written that she had left Repulsive sleeping, meaning she should've been in her basket. But she wasn't. So where was the little twerp? All his instincts screamed at him to be careful, which scared him to no end. Why would he need to be careful around a baby? Unless Repulsive wasn't really a baby…

Not wanting to make any sudden movements, he slowly straightened up and glanced around the room. There were several cardboard boxes, an old, roll-top desk and its matching chair, and dad's guitar cases stacked in a corner. He tiptoed over to the boxes and breathlessly leaned over to look behind them. No hideous baby back there. Nothing under the desk, either. He began to move toward the door when he heard the thumping sound. It was coming from his room.

As quietly as he could, he crept down the hallway, hoping he could avoid the boards with creaks. He remembered the offenders from his childhood visits, but others could've joined them since then. Still, he managed to make it to his room without a sound. His door, which he'd left open to help cool the room off after all that heat, was shut tight. Someone was in there.

He had a horrible suspicion that it was Repulsive, lying in wait for him, waiting to leap at his throat and suck out all his blood. *Maybe I should just go down and join the others*, he thought to himself. *Pretend I never noticed that Repulsive's basket was empty. If I ran fast, I could get away. She's just a baby. I can outrun a baby.*

But he couldn't make himself move. His dad was up here, alone and weak. Gabe couldn't abandon him. He had to go in that room.

With a shaking hand, he reached for the doorknob. He had almost grabbed hold of the glass knob when he heard it. A giggle. A mischievous cackle that made his hand freeze in mid-air. Someone was in there, all right, and it didn't sound like his brothers or his mom. Come to think of it, it didn't sound all that human.

Summoning his nerve, Gabe forced his rebellious hand to move again. It put up a fight, but he was determined. He had to keep his dad safe. He had to know who was in his room, even if he died of a heart attack finding out.

With a thudding heart and a queasy stomach, he turned the knob. It was slippery in his palm and his hand slid, knocking against the door. He froze. Whoever was in there froze, too—the noises stopped.

Realizing he had muffed it, Gabe grabbed the knob and twisted, shoving against the door at the same time. What he saw as he fell into the room made him stop in his tracks. It was Repulsive, and she was sitting on the floor by his bed chewing on one of his socks. He wrinkled his nose. It was a pair of gym socks he'd worn for a couple days in a row because he couldn't find any clean ones.

"Ga-bri-el?" the baby said, holding out the sock.

He marched over and took it away. "That's not food, Repulsive."

Her odd face contorted into a frown. "Re-pul-sive?"

"Yeah, it means gross."

"Gross?"

Gabe sighed. "Icky. Sorry, kid, but you're not exactly the most attractive thing."

Repulsive's eyes widened with indignation. He stared at her in surprise. Had she actually understood what he'd said? "Not a-ttract-ive? Ick-y?"

He shook his head. He didn't know much about babies, but he didn't think they spoke sentences under the age of one, even two-worded ones. Just to be on the safe side he shrugged in response, then changed the subject, going on the attack.

"How did you get in here? I didn't know you could crawl." He examined her again, hoping to find an answer somewhere in that tiny body as she glared at him defiantly.

"I'm not icky!" she screeched in response, her mouth widening horrifically. "*Ye* are icky! Ye…"

A loud knocking interrupted her. Someone was at the downstairs door. He glanced at the doorway, then at Repulsive. She gave him the evil eye, worse than the usual. He realized she scared him, then felt like an idiot for being scared of a baby. But in his defense, there was something extremely unnatural about her.

Even so, he couldn't leave her here on her own. She could get hurt, maybe fall down the stairs, or into the toilet. He told himself that it wasn't that he was concerned for her welfare—she was obviously stronger than she looked—he was worried about his own safety. If something happened to her and he hadn't done anything to prevent it, his mom would kill him.

Moving quickly, he stepped around Repulsive and picked her up from behind, grasping her tiny waist firmly. Holding her straight out before him, he carried her over to her basket in the other room. Her spindly legs, covered by knit green pants, kicked wildly as she continued to scream.

He had to move fast. Whoever was here was pounding louder and more insistently now, and the sound echoed throughout the house. The visitor, and/or Repulsive, was going to wake up Dad, and he didn't want that. His father needed his rest, and besides, how would Gabe explain Repulsive's words if she decided to speak again? Dad probably wouldn't find his son's nickname for the baby nearly as amusing as Gabe did.

Shoving her thrashing little body into the basket, he hastily tucked her blanket in around her, then grabbed the handle. Pounding down the stairs, he made it to the door in record time and swung it open.

In front of him stood a strange and very tiny woman—the top of her head only came to the bottom of his ribcage. She wore a long, woolen cloak with the hood pulled over her head. The dark purple cape revealed a bit of brown face, the color and texture of a dried apple, and two dark hollows that must be her eyes. Crisp brown coils of hair and yellow fuzzy bits, which resembled the spiky moth caterpillars he would find when they'd once visited the farm in the fall, poked out from beneath the rough material. In one bony, gnarled hand, she gripped the knob of a twisted cane the color of molasses. Her skin, covered with bristly hairs, was rough and cracked like dried mud.

He'd never seen her before, so it was odd that she was looking at him like she knew him. "Yes?" he inquired, trying not to sound rude, but Repulsive was making him nervous with all her caterwauling.

"I come for the baby," the old woman announced in an unfamiliar accent.

Repulsive immediately stopped crying. He spun her basket around to face the stranger. "This one?"

She nodded, though she hadn't even glanced at Repulsive. Perhaps she, too, found the little imp hard to look at. "And I come to warn ye."

His hand flew to his chest. "Me? About what?"

"Stay away from the forest," she replied darkly, her voice echoing, as though coming from deep inside a tunnel. "Ye're not welcome there."

He felt himself getting annoyed, which was stupid since he didn't even want to go into the forest. Still, he didn't like someone telling him what to do. "And if I don't?"

"Then they will get ye, simple as that."

His bravado disappeared. "Wh-who will get me?" he asked, the words slipping out as whispers.

"Just ye stay away," she repeated ominously, stepping forward. He stepped back. "I need the child," she remarked impatiently. "There's not much time."

"Who are you?" Gabe demanded. He wanted to look like he was in charge here, but his hands shook and his voice was uncertain. He sounded more like a child pretending to be an adult. "Why did you leave her here? You don't know anything about us!"

"If ye do not give her to me, I'll be forced to leave her here...with ye."

Gabe didn't hesitate; he handed Repulsive over to the woman. When he saw that the baby was looking up at the old creature with relief, and maybe a little contriteness, he knew they belonged together. He needn't feel guilty about handing her over to a stranger.

As the woman turned to go, he blurted out, "What should I tell my parents, about Repul...about the baby?"

She stopped. "Tell them nothing. They'll not remember. But ye will..." And then she was gone. Leaping off the porch, she scurried, hunched over like a squirrel, across the yard to the side of the barn, and vanished around the corner.

Gabe stood in front of the screen door for a moment, staring at the spot where he'd last seen them, then he ran out onto the porch. His eyes searched the yard, waiting for them to reappear, until he realized something. The stranger didn't leave via the driveway, nor did she head in the direction of their two neighbors to the north. Which left only one place to go.

The woods.

Chapter Four

Meet the Neighbors

"Hey, daydreamer!" he heard someone call out to him. "Where were you?"

He shook his head groggily before turning to see his mom approaching. She gripped a red tin bucket full of berries in each hand. That woman could pick more berries in less time than the three of them put together. She plonked the buckets down on the porch steps, and a couple of the fat berries rolled off the mound and onto the worn wood.

As she leaned over to pick them up, Gabe wondered if his mother had seen the old woman carrying Repulsive away. She wasn't acting as though she had.

"Um, well, I was getting something to eat," he replied carefully.

She shook her head. "You boys are going to eat us out of house and home." She laughed, though she didn't look very amused. "I'm going to go inside and clean up these berries and check on your dad. Go join your brothers. When you're done picking, I'd like you to get started on painting the house now that all the old paint's been scraped off." Gabe and his brothers had finished that dreaded task yesterday. "Grandpa Hawthorne and Grandma May are coming for dinner tonight. I'd at least like to have one side looking presentable." She shielded her eyes from the sun as she gazed up at the cloudless sky. "We're in for a stretch of nice weather so we'd better take advantage of it."

Gabe chose this moment to test out what the old woman had told him. "So, is there anyone else you want to check on?" It sounded stupid, but his mother had heard worse coming out of his mouth.

"Such as…"

He shrugged. "Oh, I don't know. Things that are small and defenseless…"

She narrowed her hazel-brown eyes. "Jer might be smaller than you two boys, but he's certainly not defenseless. Don't forget that black eye he gave you last year."

She didn't remember Repulsive.

He gave her what he hoped was a charming grin. "I was talking about that mice problem. We should really get a cat."

She laughed. "Well, don't I look like the fool? I thought you were making fun of your brother…like you typically do." She ran a tired hand through her bangs. The rest of her brown hair, threaded with gray despite her attempts to color it, was once again twisted back into a bun. "Well, maybe we should. A couple of them so they don't get lonely and tear up the house. Not that they could do much more damage to this old place." She spotted another stray blueberry and picked it up. "Why don't you keep your ears open for anyone with kittens? You could check the bulletin board at Woodlands next time you head into town. It's out on the porch. Or maybe go ask our neighbors later on." She pointed at the stretch of woods on the north side of the yard. "They're through there. There's a path. There was one in my day, anyway."

He knew quite well where the neighbors were, and was very aware it would mean going through the woods to get to them. "Maybe later," he said. Like some time next century.

She gave him a knowing look, but decided not to push it. His mom could be nice that way. "Run along, then. The Shaker actually works pretty well." She gave him a demonstration of how it worked and he laughed at the sight of her whole body convulsing spastically. "Though I'm not sure I can feel my arms anymore."

With that, and a rueful smile, she went inside with her buckets, leaving Gabe alone to wonder whether he'd imagined Repulsive and the old woman, if he should heed her warning, or just forget the whole thing. He hadn't needed her to tell him to stay out of the woods. He had no intention of going in them. But the other part bothered him, the part where she'd said, "They'll get ye." Who was 'they' and why did they want to get him? In fact, how did they even know who he was?

He shook his head. She was probably just some crazy old woman, possibly one of Grandma May's friends, who got a kick out of scaring kids. He should forget about her, pretend she'd never come to fetch her little troll baby, and be grateful he'd forgotten to ask around town about it.

He went to find his brothers in the blueberry patch. When he arrived, Jer was halfway down the third row, using the Shaker, though the machine looked more like it was using him. It was so powerful, it was hard to tell who was in control.

Kris spotted Gabe and waved him over. "It works great!" he yelled over the noise. A streak of dust colored one cheek and a smudge of oil skidded into his left eyebrow. "There's just one problem. It's a bit hard to hang onto!"

"Agh!" Jer yelped. Gabe spun around in time to see the Shaker leap out of his little brother's hands like a fish freed from its hook. Mid-air, the machine began devouring the shrub, before it landed on the ground and started flopping around, resembling a recently beheaded chicken. Jer lunged for it, then hastily retreated as blueberries came flying at him fast as BBs. Attempting to flee, his legs tangled together and he tripped.

Kris dashed over and tried to grab the machine, but it wasn't having any of that, bucking like a wild horse. "Grab it!" Jer yelled, trying to back away, but the thick shrubs gave him nowhere to go. His frightened eyes were wide as the Shaker moved closer and closer.

Gabe pushed Kris out of the way and seized hold of the Shaker just as it was about to maim Jer. Finding the switch, he managed to turn off the machine before it tore his arm out of its socket.

Kris grabbed the Shaker from him and cradled it like a baby. "Are you okay?" he crooned while stroking its skeletal form.

"*Ahem!*" Jer called from his sprawled position on the ground. "It almost *ate* me!"

Kris ignored him. "Looks like there might be a few kinks in the old gal."

"A few kinks!" Gabe yelled. "Someone could've been killed, Kris!"

Kris looked over at his brother, not in the least fazed. "There have been many sacrifices made in the name of science. I'm certain there will be many more."

Jer climbed to his feet, shaking his blond head. "I'm not sure why I always have to be the sacrifice," he muttered.

Kris patted him on the head. "You do it for love."

"Well, you can sacrifice your own life this time, Kris," Gabe told him. "But do it later, please. I've heard that dead people aren't all that great at painting barns and picking berries."

Kris sighed. "Well, at least we did a lot of picking before she had her little temper tantrum." He indicated the six brimming buckets of blueberries.

Gabe blinked at them. *Six* buckets? "Hmmm… I think you might be onto something here. We'll work on the Shaker tonight. Fix her up real good, smooth out all those kinks." The three brothers grinned at each other as they loaded buckets into the red wagon, an old Radio Flyer with four wobbly wheels and a loose handle. Gabe remembered Grandpa May giving him rides in it.

"That'd be cool," Kris replied to Gabe's offer, hefting up the large machine onto his shoulder while Gabe grabbed the handle of the ornery wagon. "We'll be like the three musketeers of engineering. We'll revolutionize the science of berry picking!"

"Now if only you could build a giant painting machine," Gabe remarked, balancing the wagon to keep it from tipping over as they headed in.

"Too bad we don't have a neighborhood," Jer put in, swinging his two buckets back and forth. "We could pull a Tom Sawyer and get the neighbor kids to do it for us." He grinned wickedly at the thought.

Kris snorted. "Kids are too smart nowadays. There's no way we could trick them into doing our work."

Jer sighed. "Whatever happened to the innocence of youth?"

Kris laughed, poking at him. "You *are* the innocence of youth!"

Jer grimaced. "Yeah, well, at least I know something you don't."

Kris and Gabe stopped walking to look at their brother. Blueberries fell from the buckets and scattered about the wagon. "And what would that be?" Gabe asked. Was it something about Repulsive, the old woman? Jer shrugged.

"Spill it," Kris growled, "Or I'll sic the Shaker on you!"

Jer shook his head, his lower lip protruding defiantly. "Not until you promise to show me that time machine protocol of yours."

Kris groaned. He'd been holding that one over Jer's head for a long time. It was always good to have some leverage with him. But Kris couldn't stand not knowing something, so he caved. "Deal. Now what do you know that we don't?"

"It's about the baby, isn't it?" Gabe blurted out.

"What baby?" Kris and Jer both asked, raising their eyebrows at Gabe.

"Just messin' with you," Gabe muttered. "Tell us what you know, Jer."

"We have company," Jer answered, nodding at the woods behind them.

Gabe froze. Had 'they' come—the ones the old lady had warned him about? He slowly turned around. Two figures strolled toward them from the direction of the woods, but at this distance he couldn't see them very well. They didn't look too scary, but he wasn't taking any chances. He prepared himself to run.

Kris had no such anxieties—he seemingly *never* did. He set the Shaker down outside the barn and walked over to greet the strangers, his stride long and relaxed. Gabe parked the wagon in front of the house and reluctantly joined his brothers. Jer was as suspicious about people as they come, had been since he was a baby, and normally wouldn't have gone anywhere near newcomers until he'd scouted them out quite thoroughly, scrutinizing everything about them down to the last eyelash. But whenever he was around Kris, he seemed to take on his brother's confidence. Kris had that effect on people—he made you feel braver than you were. Gabe envied his easy ability to influence others. The worst part was that he didn't even have to try.

As they neared the two strangers, Gabe groaned when he recognized one of them. It was *her*! The Indian—or was it Native American?—girl from Woodlands General Store. What was *she* doing here? When he saw that she was carrying a basket, his stomach started to churn. She couldn't be returning Repulsive! Holy crud, he hoped not. That would mean Repulsive had been real, and the old lady, and her warning, too.

When the two groups came to a stop, standing about three feet from each other, he realized that this basket was very different from the one Repulsive had arrived in—most noticeably, it didn't have a hood and was made from white wicker.

Something alive was in the basket, but it definitely was not an ugly baby. Three little kittens tried to sneak glimpses of the outside world, their little pointy ears and pink noses bobbing up and down. The basket firmly on the ground now, six small paws gripped its edges and three heads popped up. One of the kittens was thin with sleek black fur, like a witch's cat. Another was a black and white ball of long, fluffy fur. The last was a fat tabby that, from the size of it, looked like a Maine coon cat. It kept stepping on the other kittens' heads in its attempt to get out.

"Hey, neighbors," Abazi greeted, scooping up the tabby and putting it back in the basket. "Want some cats? They're Kimber's. Well, not hers, exactly. She didn't give birth to them." Kris and Jer grinned; Gabe refrained. No sense encouraging her. "She rescued a stray cat that was pregnant."

Kimber stepped forward, her progression awkward and jerky. Strawberry blond hair covered her face as she bowed her head low to study her feet. "Just thought you could use a few mousers," she said softly. Gabe's eyes followed hers to the ground and saw the reason for her clumsy movements. She wore heavy metal braces on her legs, each rising to just below the kneecap.

The braces made Gabe nervous and he quickly looked away. He was glad she hadn't seen him looking; she was too busy staring at the lawn.

"So do you want them or not?" Abazi demanded. "They're gonna start eating each other pretty soon."

"We brought some food," Kimber offered, holding up a paper bag.

Jer stepped forward and took the bag from her. She peeked up at him through her blond bangs, then quickly looked back down. "I'm Jer, by the way," he introduced himself. "And these are my brothers, Kris and Gabe."

"I'm Kimber," she said softly. "And this is Abazi." She motioned behind her.

"Nice to meet you. I've always wanted another cat," he said, staring at the top of her head. "We had two cats, a long time ago, but they died of old age." Jer had been very attached to those cats and missed them. After Dad became so sick, Mom never got around to adopting any more.

Gabe missed them, too. He wasn't sure it would be cool to admit it, though. "We do need some mousers," he said instead, "so I guess we'll take them off your hands." He hoped he sounded manly and in charge, despite his sudden nervousness. Making decisions really wasn't his thing. He'd rather have someone else take the consequence if things went wrong. His mom had told him many times that this was one of his 'need to improve on' areas.

Abazi's dark eyes were amused. "Well then, take them!" She shoved the basket into his hands. "My old man gave me the rest of the day off and I've got stuff to do. Come on, Kimber!"

With a quick nod from Kimber, the two girls swung around and hurried off. They were a strangely matched pair, Gabe thought, watching them walk away. Abazi moved like a deer while Kimber labored with each painful step. He wondered if Kimber could feel their eyes on her back and wished they'd stop watching her. He certainly didn't like people watching him walk, and he didn't even wear braces on his legs.

"Come on, guys," he said loudly. "Let's take the kittens to Mom. She'll know what to do with them." Turning toward the house, he felt Kimber relax, or so he wanted to believe.

When they pushed through the screen door and into the kitchen, they found their mom on the phone talking to Grandma May as she rinsed off blueberries in the sink. When they showed her the kittens, she oohed and ahhed over them, telling Grandma that her three cats had dragged in three kittens. After getting their mother's approval, Jer took the little ones away, determined to make them his own.

Kris disappeared, too, probably to the barn to work on the Shaker, which left Gabe to paint the house on his own. Normally, being stuck once again with the job nobody wanted would have peeved him off to no end, but right now he found that he wanted the solitude.

As much as he loathed the idea, he needed to think about the unbelievable events that had happened to him last night and today. To sum up, shortly after hearing a voice calling his name from the forest's depths, a freaky baby had shown up on their doorstep. This morning the strange old woman who'd come to fetch the freaky baby had delivered a warning to Gabe to stay away from the forest. Even more bizarre, after she was gone, no one in his family remembered Repulsive. All this was very mysterious. First of all, why would the lady have left Repulsive on their doorstep? Secondly, who was she? Was she really a friend of Grandma May's playing a trick on him? Finally, why had she warned him against the forest? What lived in there that was so dangerous to him?

Gabe had always felt an unease with the woods, going back long before his family had moved to Maine. When he was a little kid, every two or three years the whole family would fly to Ranger to visit both sets of grandparents. They usually stayed at May Farm because there was more room, then go visit Grandpa Hawthorne in town a morning here, an afternoon there. Grandpa would often take them for rides in his fishing boat, teaching them about the power of the ocean, its mercurial moods, the mystique of its inhabitants.

Gabe had loved those times on the sea with his grandpa. He'd also liked staying at May Farm and enjoyed the house and barn with all their mysteries. The yard was huge and there was always lots to do. Their apartment complex back home didn't have a yard. If they wanted to play outside they had to run across the street to the park. Visiting Maine had always been fun for Gabe.

But those woods… He'd seen the trees for the first time from the car window, through a four-year-old's probing eyes. Even at four, he'd felt there was something wrong with the woods. From his point of view, the towering trees dominated the entire sky like a plague of locusts, and he knew immediately that he never wanted to go near them. Ever.

Yet, because of fate's strange sense of humor, he now lived in the middle of them. He was like an animal trapped in a cage and the tree trunks were the bars. Only this time, he wouldn't be able to escape to California after a few days. He was stuck at May Farm, at least until he turned eighteen, and he wasn't sure he could last that long.

Not without losing his mind.

Chapter Five

The Turret

"Putting you to work, eh?"

The husky voice startled Gabe and he nearly fell off the ladder, which was old and wobbly. He stood two stories up, painting one of the turret window frames with a brush instead of the sprayer so he wouldn't muck up the glass. Holding tight with one hand, he slowly turned around and looked down.

"Oh, hi, Grandma May," he greeted uncertainly, wondering how long she'd been standing there watching him.

She shaded her brilliant blue eyes with a salute as she peered up at him, her black hair looking even more wild than usual. It stuck out from all sides as though she'd touched a static electricity globe. "You'll have to paint the top of the window from inside," she told him. "And you'll have to clean the windows from the inside, too." He already knew this. Cleaning them from the outside hadn't been good enough; he still couldn't see inside the turret.

"That would be ideal, but how can I get into the turret when the door's locked?"

She reached into her pocket and triumphantly produced a skeleton key. "With this!"

His eyes widened and his mouth dropped open. The elusive key! Grandma had been hemming and hawing about that key since they'd arrived, claiming she'd lost it in the move. All that time Gabe couldn't quite shake the feeling that she hadn't wanted to find it. And now, here it was…

His feet thudded down the ladder's rungs until soon he had joined his grandma on the ground. Standing next to her, he couldn't help feeling really tall. The top of her head barely came to his shoulder, and he wasn't even done growing yet. The moment she began to speak, however, that feeling disappeared. She had a way of putting things that made him feel like he was an ignorant child again, and her forceful personality made her seem bigger than she really was. His character paled in comparison to the force of hers. Around Grandma May, he felt like a ghost.

As soon as he reached for the key, she quickly pulled it behind her back and the shrinking began. "Had any visitors?" she asked.

He nodded dumbly. How did she know about that? Abazi and Kimber had been here only this morning. "Um, yeah," he replied. "Our neighbors."

She frowned. "Not those two. Your mom already told me about them. Asked me to bring over some cat food." She pointed to her bike. She didn't own a car now—said it was too expensive. Instead, she rode her adult-sized tricycle everywhere. She'd painted rainbow stripes on the three-wheeled bike, interspersed with shooting stars and half moons with leering faces. Between the two back tires sat a large wire basket, filled at the moment with two hefty bags of dry cat food. "I was talking about another kind of visitor."

Gabe's skin prickled. "What kind of visitor?" he asked hesitantly, keeping his voice low as he glanced around. The yard was empty.

Seeing his expression, she raised a suspicious eyebrow. "Why, that busybody, Deacon. She's been going around talking to people about clearing the forest. Been complaining about it for years, says it's not safe. Now she's adamant about actually doing something. It's that Morrigan woman who's been stirring her up."

Gabe laughed, hoping he didn't sound too relieved. "I saw Mrs. Deacon at the store this morning. As far as I know, she hasn't been out to the farm...yet."

"Well, I better warn your mom. Those women are a menace. Those woods haven't been touched for centuries, and for good reason!"

He swallowed hard. "What reason is that, Grandma?"

She gave him a sly look. "Because most everybody who's tried to mess with them hasn't come back out, that's why!"

"Why not?" he whispered, then cleared his throat. "Did they get lost?"

"Lost! Oh, more than that, Gabe. Those poor people were taken!"

His hands began to sweat, his armpits started to itch. "Taken? By who?"

She shrugged. "Who knows? I've lived here all my life, and my parents before me, and theirs before that. We go way back in this town. There's something about those woods nobody understands and our folk have learned it's just best to leave it be." She said this last part looking directly at him, as though she meant this message to be conveyed to him, too.

He glanced toward the trees, then away with a suppressed shudder.

"Well, I don't plan on having anything to do with those woods. I never did like them."

She smiled approvingly. "Here," she said, thrusting out the key. "It's time you opened up that room. Your brothers aren't going to like it, but I want you to have it. I have this feeling you're going to need it." Again, that assessing look with those eyes. They crawled right into his head and swam around his brain.

"What am I going to need it for?" he croaked, fingering the cold metal with his paint-spattered fingers.

She shrugged and began to stride toward the house. He followed after her like a puppy. "There are things a person knows without knowing why," she said over her shoulder. "That's what I feel about the forest. There's something..." she paused, searching for the right word. "There's something unsettling about it. Never could place my finger on it. I feel as though it allows me to enter certain sections, to search for roots and berries and the like, and the rest is off-limits. I know my boundaries. Do you know yours?" she asked as she climbed the steps.

"Where the trees begin. That's my boundary."

She nodded briskly, satisfied. "Good. Remember that." She opened the door and disappeared inside, leaving him standing on the porch, feeling slightly stranded in his understanding of what had just happened.

Wondering what it was he was getting himself into, he looked down at the key in the palm of his hand. He'd never seen one like it. The bow was a skull that sprouted thorny branches like hair. The shank, the length of his middle finger, had been carved to look like a tree branch. The key ended in two bits, which looked like leg bones.

They sure were morbid back in the old days, Gabe thought to himself.

With a shudder, he pocketed the key and forced himself to clean up the paint supplies before rushing off to explore the turret. Gabe thought about fetching his brothers, but then decided he was supposed to do this on his own. He felt it. Typically he shared most everything with Jer and Kris. In spite of their tendency to bicker, they were close, more like friends than brothers. Since last night, however, he found himself keeping more and more secrets from them. He wasn't thrilled about doing this, and maybe he should tell them Grandma had given him the key, but he had a feeling the turret was meant for him to see first.

Alone.

The late afternoon sun shone brightly as he cleaned up and stored the paint and ladder in the barn—Kris didn't look up from his work on the Shaker once. When Gabe entered the house he found Mom and Grandma May sitting at the kitchen table talking and drinking strong coffee. Grandpa Hawthorne would be arriving soon and Gabe knew that he'd better hurry if he wanted to explore without interruption.

The stairs to the turret sat on the south side of the house. Gabe made his way down a long, dark hallway, lit only by a square window halfway along. He passed the shabby library where Mom had set up Dad's office for when he was ready to work again. She used it now, trying to write what she called The Great American Novel. Mom had always wanted to write a book, but with Dad getting sick she'd put it off. Now, even with all she had to do around here, she'd started writing late at night. He supposed she needed this—something to keep her from thinking about the fact that they were broke and that Dad might relapse at any time. He thought he could use something like his mom's writing, something to make him forget. Something like the turret.

Its door, when he reached it, looked dark and mysterious. Rounded at the top, it was made of thick wood and bolstered by iron bands, and the door handle was a skull's head similar to the one on the key's bow. Gabe stared at the gruesome knob for a few seconds, wondering why someone would put that thing on a door. Every time he wanted to enter the turret he'd be forced to touch death. Gabe didn't want to be reminded of death. The Grim Reaper seemed to lurk around every corner as it was. Maybe later he could replace the handle. Then the turret would truly be his.

Anticipation started his heart beating faster and he grinned. His brothers were going to be so jealous! Of course, the minute they found out, they'd start complaining. He'd simply have to tell them that he was only doing what Grandma had told him to do. They couldn't expect him to argue with an old woman, could they? That would be rude. Besides, they'd gotten first dibs on the upstairs bedrooms.

After fishing the strange key out of his pocket, he inserted it into the lock. Metal clanked against metal and he flinched, glancing back over his shoulder. The hall remained empty. Whipping back around, he quickly turned the key. The door, when opened, creaked like old bones. The sound was exactly like he thought it would be, confirming that the door hadn't been used for years. Who knew what was up there? There could be anything—treasure, junk, skeletons, bats, all of the above. Gabe couldn't wait to find out.

Of course, the way his luck was running, the turret could also be a death trap, full of rats, broken floor boards, and malevolent spirits. He would take it slow.

Peering through the open doorway, he saw a steep set of stairs leading up to another door. His hand groped about for a light switch, and
finding one, flipped it up. Nothing happened. He looked up, but could
see nothing in the dark stairwell. The bulb was probably burned out.
Never having been fond of the dark, he made a note to find a flashlight, or another light bulb, for his next visit.

He almost shut and locked the door behind him—there was a knob
to lock it from this side—but thought twice. He needed the light, dim
though it may be, to find his way up the stairs. Besides, the idea of being caught between two doors in the darkness of an ancient staircase
sounded about as appealing to him as being locked in a dungeon with a
giant spider.

His natural caution kept him from bounding up the stairs, but he did
take two at a time, anxious to see what lay behind the second door.
Similar to the first one, this door was made of thick wood and iron,
though it was smaller—he could barely walk through it without stoop-
ing. A willowy figure had been carved into its center, and her long hair
spread out like a halo around her head. She wore a flowing dress that
fell to her slender ankles and her arms stretched outward as though
summoning to something, or someone, the viewer could not see. The
girl's delicate face caught his attention. Even in the dim light, she
looked alive. He forced himself to look away. There was something
powerful in her eyes, something that could become fascinating if given
enough attention.

To distract himself from her forceful gaze, he studied the skull door
handle, the same as the one downstairs. If he didn't want to be shaking
hands with death every time he went to his room, he was going to have
to find two innocuous door handles, free from symbols of doom.

The second door unlocked easily and Gabe took a tentative step into
the room. He looked around in wonder. The large space, which didn't
look nearly this big from the outside, was filled with old steamer
trunks, a dressmaker's form, jars of colorful marbles, blue glass bottles,
antique toys, old books, broken furniture, and what must have been
nearly thirty wooden boxes, spread all over the floor, packed into corners, and overflowing from built-in nooks and a bookshelf.

Directly before him the half-moon window, whose frame he'd
painted outside, let in a hazy light. It was a magnificent piece of glass,
grand as something you'd find in a Roman cathedral, though certainly
less pristine. The thick, bubbled glass was grimier than a little kid's
hands and was impossible to see through. About seven feet from the
floor, the slightly curved window was too high to look out of properly.

Gabe spotted a small set of stairs that led to a platform level with the bottom of the window. He imagined that he could see forever, sitting on that platform and looking out at the world.

A thick layer of dust covered everything. Gabe sneezed, then again, and again. Nose twitching, he took another step forward, his size thirteen sneakers forming footprints in the dust. It would take an army to clean this place out. There were even cobwebs on the cobwebs. But he liked it. He'd never liked anything so much.

He was about to take another step when he spotted something on the floor, caught in a beam of light coming from a small round window, one of many in the room. Clearly outlined in the dust was a set of footprints. Whoever had made them had been barefoot and had long, unusually thin toes. The tracks looked fresh. Whose were they, he wondered, and how did their owner get in here?

More pertinent, was their owner still in the room?

Gabe glanced around. The intruder could be hiding anywhere. While the turret looked rounded from the outside, it was not necessarily that way on the inside. The dark, wood-paneled walls angled this way and that creating nooks and crannies throughout the room. In some parts, the strange ceiling rose twenty feet into the air, while in others, it dropped so low that even his mom would hit her head. The person who'd designed this room had possessed a strange architectural vision, or been a bit loopy.

"Is anyone there?" he called out, his voice wobbly. He cleared his throat. It wouldn't do any good to sound like that. "I know you're in here." A bit louder now, more sure.

No answer.

He tried again. "Please, just show yourself. I'm not going to hurt you."

"But I might hurt you," a voice growled behind him. Gabe froze. He knew the answer to one of his questions now. Whoever it was, he was most certainly still here...

Chapter Six

Territorial Disputes

Gabe slowly, painfully, turned around, and what he saw made his blood run hot. It was Kris, standing in the doorway to the stairs, grinning like a fool. "Gotcha!"

Jer peered around him. "Thought you could get away with it, huh?"

Gabe stared at his brothers. How had they known? He shook his head. Why bother asking? They always seemed to sense whenever he tried to do something he didn't want them to find out about. Maybe that's why he rarely tried.

"What do you want?"

"How did you get in here?" Kris demanded.

Gabe pulled the skeleton key out of his pocket and held it up. Kris's eyes took on a covetous gleam. He loved keys. "Grandma May gave it to me."

"Why didn't you tell us? We've wanted to see the turret just as bad as you."

"Yeah!" Jer put in.

Gabe shrugged. "Grandma May said she wanted me to have this room. I guess it's because I'm the oldest...and the coolest."

His brothers rolled their eyes simultaneously, pushing past him as they stepped into the room. "That's so unfair," Kris declared, looking around. The acquisitive gleam in his eyes brightened. There were a lot of things in here he would love to get his greasy paws on.

Jer rushed over to a large wicker basket lined with a cushy, yellow pillow. "This would be perfect for a bed! Inky, Gypsy, and Little Joe would love it."

"Inky, Gypsy, and Little Joe?" Gabe repeated.

"The kittens," Kris explained. "Inky's the black one. Gypsy is the black and white, furry one. And Little Joe is the porker of the bunch."

"Oh. Well, take it then. I suppose if I'm going to have this room, you guys can have first dibs on the stuff in here." Gabe tried to sound gracious, then caught himself. "As long as I don't want it."

Kris nodded. "I suppose that might help. But why do you have to have it as your room? We could make it into a clubhouse or something."

"I'm too old for clubhouses." He wasn't, but it sounded good. "I need my own space…away from everyone. Besides, my other room stinks and you guys know it."

"Mom won't let you bring girls up here, you know," Jer informed him with a devilish twinkle in his eyes.

"Girls?" Gabe grunted, the comment touching a sore spot. "What girls?"

"What girls, is right," Kris grinned.

"I saw how you looked at Abazi," Jer went on. "She's very pretty." He and Kris were struggling not to laugh. They didn't want to miss their big brother's sure-to-be-entertaining reaction.

Gabe was stunned. "She's a *snob*! I don't like her one bit. She might be kinda cute, in a weird sort of way, but that doesn't mean I like her. Sadie's more my kind of girl."

"So you like the blond bimbo type?" Kris asked, examining a kerosene lamp.

"Sadie is nothing like that! She's an angel!" She really was. She had long blond hair, with just the right amount of curl, and lightly tanned skin to highlight her amazing blue eyes. She'd been the most popular girl at his school in San Jose—cheerleader, class president, top of her class in grades. She had it all and he'd almost had her.

Truth be told, she wasn't *really* his girlfriend, not officially, anyway. Almost was the operative word here. He'd been working on changing that, right before Mom made the announcement that they were moving to Maine. But Sadie had said hi to him once in the hallway. That had to count for something.

Now it counted for nothing. She lived thousands of miles away, and he was stuck here in this weird place surrounded by unfriendly woods and living next door to an even unfriendlier neighbor who thought she was God's gift to the world.

Kris shrugged. "Whatever you say. Though I never knew angels liked to shoplift."

Gabe nearly choked. "Sadie never shoplifted! She was too good for that. Besides, her mom and dad were lawyers. She didn't need to steal."

"She also smoked, and partied, too," Kris went on, unmoved. "Everyone knew about it. She's been doing it since seventh grade. Sadie had quite a reputation around school, brother of mine, and not a good one."

Gabe couldn't believe what he was hearing. It couldn't be true. Yet even as he thought this, he knew that it very likely was. Kris didn't even try to meet people, but still he'd ended up as one of the most popular boys at school—and he didn't even care. Surrounded by all the right cliques, he had an 'in' that Gabe could only dream of having. He heard things. People went out of their way to tell him things.

"Lies," he replied hoarsely—lamely. "All lies."

"I like Abazi," Jer persisted. "You should like her, too."

Gabe sighed at yet another example of Jer's twisted logic. "You like her because she brought you animals," he grumbled.

"But you like Kimber better, don't you, Jer?" Kris snickered. "She's pretty cute herself. Good thing for you she's too shy for my tastes. It's probably because of her legs, though. What do you think is wrong with them?"

Jer's face turned bright red, his fair skin glowing like a sunset. "I like her because she's nice!" he shot back, glowering at his older brother. "And she probably has cerebral palsy. So what?"

"So, nothing." Kris rummaged about. "I was just curious. Those braces of hers looked pretty clumsy. I thought maybe I could make something better for her."

Jer relaxed. "Well, that would be okay, I guess."

Kris nodded and went back to exploring. As he headed for a pile in one of the corners, Gabe remembered the footprints. "Kris, wait! Don't move." Kris froze, standing still as a statue. "Very funny. You can put your arms down. I thought someone was up here when you guys found me. I saw footprints, but I didn't get a good chance to look at them. I didn't want you to step on them with those clodhoppers of yours."

Kris lowered his arms, but otherwise stood completely still. Gabe scanned the dusty wood floor and saw that only one print remained, right next to a pick-ax with a rotting handle. The long-toed track was slightly smeared. He pointed at it. "There's one right there."

Gathering around the footprint, the three brothers peered down at the strange sight. "It looks like a chicken foot, but bigger and with more toes," Jer commented. He straightened up with a look of confusion. "That's weird."

"Probably just some animal that got caught up here," Kris surmised.

"Yeah, I suppose," Gabe answered, though he didn't really believe it. The track didn't look like an animal print. Whatever their intruder was, he could only hope that it was gone now.

"Boys!" someone called from far away. They rushed to a window and looked down. It was their mother. She was standing on the porch steps, hands cupping her mouth, calling to them.

"Mom's looking for us!" Jer yelped, and Gabe realized that his brothers looked as guilty as he felt. He had the feeling their mom wouldn't like it that they were up here. He wasn't sure why, he just knew.

"Let's get out of here!" Kris hissed. "We'll come back later…after supper."

Gabe nodded. "Sounds good to me."

After locking up, the three boys managed to make it to the kitchen in time to beat their mom coming back inside. She looked at them, startled. "Where have you been?"

"Oh, here and there," Kris replied casually, grabbing an apple.

"You'll spoil your supper," she scolded.

"With an apple?"

She sighed, then laughed. "I suppose not. But still, you better eat a big supper…" She paused. "Oh, Lord! What am I saying? I never thought I'd hear the day when I'd be encouraging you to eat *more*." They all laughed, tinged with relief on the three boys' part. "Your grandparents and your father are in the formal parlor. See if they want anything to drink."

The three brothers ran into the room, anxious to see Grandpa Hawthorne. They remembered him as a gruff old guy with a mischievous side to him. He lived alone in Ranger, down by the docks. Grandma Hawthorne had died before Gabe and his brothers had come along. A few years ago, Grandpa retired from being a lobsterman, but the sea still flowed so deep in his blood that he ran charter cruises for small parties of tourists to soothe his yearning to be out on the water. The extra cash also helped supplement his veteran benefits for service in the navy during the Vietnam War.

They had yet to see him since arriving in Maine. He'd taken a group out to Willow Island for a week, with full services. He hadn't wanted to go—had wanted to be here when they arrived—but he needed the money. He'd given everything he could to help with Dad's medical bills, though the kids weren't supposed to know about that. Back in San Jose, Jer had overheard Mom and Dad talking about it one night while trying to find his pet mouse, King Arthur, who had escaped yet again. Only this time, because Jer spent too long eavesdropping, King Arthur remained undiscovered and free to join the other mousey Knights of the Cheese Wheel Table.

When they entered the formal parlor, which was only formal by name being that there was very little space to actually receive visitors with all the furniture stuffed into the room, Grandpa Hawthorne and

Grandma May were arguing about whose property suffered the most damage from last night's storm. Grandma May was winning. Gabe was beginning to see that she would probably win any argument she was in.

"You boys been up to trouble?" Grandpa Hawthorne greeted them, his slow Maine accent drawing out the vowels. His weathered face looked dour, but the twinkle in his Welsh blue eyes belied his expression. They shook their heads. "Well, why not?" he barked.

Kris laughed, taking another bite of apple. "No time, Grandpa. Mom's been cracking the whip." He performed a spoof of their mother in action, lips pursed, eyes wide, wrist snapping as he made whipping noises.

Grandpa laughed hard, a true guffaw. "Ayuh! I tell you, Keith, that woman of yours is a pistol!" Grandpa Hawthorne always said that about Mom. He also said that if he were twenty years younger, he'd give Dad a little competition. Gabe really liked Grandpa Hawthorne, but he wondered sometimes if all that time on the ocean hadn't maybe affected his brain.

Dad only laughed. "She sure is. Keeps me straight, I'll say."

It was Grandma May's turn to guffaw. "*You*, boy? Ha! You were quite the little pistol yourself as I recall. Always had a smart remark handy, didn't you?"

Dad grinned. "Maybe back then. But it seems I've lost my touch."

"Well, then, you'd better find it again. Your spirit's what keeps you alive, Keith. Don't misplace it." Her look was full of meaning, and Dad frowned and turned away. Gabe had never thought of his dad as a quitter—he wasn't one. But what Grandma had said was true. He needed to get his spirit back. It looked like he didn't want to hear that, though.

"I'll take a whisky, straight up," Grandma May said suddenly. "Nice and neat, mind you. Tell that mother of yours not to water it down. She always waters it down."

"Me, too," said Grandpa Hawthorne, passing a hand through his thick, white hair, which stood up in tufts like March grasses. "But make it a double for me. Those city folks done near drove me crazy this past week. Wanted to go out to an island to get away from it all, then spent most of their time asking for rides back to the mainland to go shopping. So much for roughing it! Damn Flatlanders," he muttered.

Flatlanders was a term Grandpa used for tourists. He also called them the "Summer Complaint," which Gabe thought sounded like diarrhea, and was a far better phrase to sum up what the old man thought of anyone who was 'from away.' Of course, he and his brothers were from away, but luckily Grandpa didn't seem to hold that against them.

"Do you want anything, Dad?" Jer asked. "I could whip you up a Long Island Iced Tea." Knowing Jer, he probably could.

"Hm?" Dad replied, his brow furrowed. He'd obviously been thinking about something else, and whatever it was didn't make him happy. "Oh, just a water. Gotta watch my health." He shifted restlessly in his chair.

"A whisky's not going to kill you, boy!" Grandma cried. "Live a little."

"I thought that's what I was trying to do," Dad said dryly, pulling the red plaid blanket he kept with him at all times more tightly around his shoulders.

"With that attitude," Grandma scolded, "you'll be an old man before your time."

"Fine!" Dad cried. "I'll have a whisky!"

"You will not!" Mom yelled from the doorway. "Mother, what are you doing now? Don't encourage him!"

My father straightened up. "I'm tired of being babied, Ayla. I'm a grown man. If I want a whisky, I'll drink a whisky!"

"Huzzah!" Grandpa shouted. Mom turned a stony look on him and his mouth snapped shut over his dentures.

Lips thinned to whiteness, Mom said slowly, "You may have a small drink, Keith. But I'm warning you, if it makes you sick, I'm not going to be the one holding your head while you puke your guts out!" With that, she stormed out of the room, leaving them all staring after her.

Grandma May broke the silence that had descended over the room. "Score one for your spirit, Keith!" she cheered, giving him a wink. Dad straightened up even more, looking quite pleased with himself. It wasn't easy standing up to Mom. "So how's the turret, Gabe?" she asked, turning to him. He'd just taken a seat on the worn brown couch next to Jer and Kris.

"Turret?" Dad echoed. "But I thought the key was lost."

"It was," she replied shortly. "Well?"

"It's great," he answered, glancing nervously at his dad. "I didn't have much time to explore, but I liked what I saw. It will probably take a lot of cleaning before I can move in."

"No one has been in that turret since I moved here," Grandma May said, staring hard at him. "It's time for it to be used."

"Why Gabe, though?" Kris complained.

"Because he's the one who needs it," she answered. "Besides, you have the barn and Jer's got his critters now."

Jer grinned. "Any chance you can get me a goat?"

She laughed out loud. "A goat! What do you need with a goat?"

"They're interesting."

"Ayuh! They'll eat anything they see, that's for sure," Grandpa Hawthorne put in. "My neighbor owned a billy goat back in the seventies. The darn thing devoured your grandma's flowerbed and she had to drive the beast off with a broom. Then it snuck back and ate her broom! How's that for interesting!"

Everyone laughed, then Dad started to cough. After a couple minutes and some hard wallops on the back by Grandpa, he was finally able to stop. Gabe watched him miserably.

"There was someone in the turret," he blurted out, desperate for a distraction. Everyone's heads swung toward him.

"It was just a raccoon," Kris said quickly, giving Gabe a warning look. "Gabe's always making things out to be more than they are, aren't you, big brother?"

Gabe laughed nervously. "Yeah, I guess it was just an animal. We'll have to really clean the place out good, make sure nothing's hiding in there. I don't want rabies."

"Clean what out good?" Mom asked. She'd just returned with the drinks—lemon-orangeade for the kids, something a bit stronger for the adults.

"The turret," Grandma answered, taking a sip from her glass. She grimaced. "You watered it down."

"The turret?" Mom exclaimed, staring at her mother in dismay. "How'd they get in there? And is it safe? It's probably a death trap by now!"

"It's not a death trap," Gabe hurried to assure her. "It just needs a little cleaning."

She ignored him. "I thought the key was lost!" She hurriedly handed Dad his glass, and a bit of the golden liquid sloshed onto his hand. "I was never allowed in the turret room!"

"You didn't need it," her mother answered. "Gabe needs it."

"For what? Protection against a Viking raid? Have I missed something here?" She shook her head, stunned. "I would've loved to have that room." She plopped down on the ottoman in front of Dad's chair and a cloud of dust flew up. Grandpa grabbed the remaining drink, which had been dangerously close to sliding off the tray, and took a quick gulp of it.

Gabe realized his mother looked hurt. "Well, you can come see it now," he told her. "Now that Grandma's found the key."

"I found it just today, while unpacking a box," Grandma explained. "It really has been lost all these years, Ayla."

"I even tried to remove the hinges once," Mom said softly. "Nothing worked. Those doors are impenetrable."

"They never allowed me to pass, either," Grandma May stated firmly. "You weren't the only one."

"But they allowed Gabe?" Sunlight through the nearby window had changed her brown eyes to green. "How odd." She turned to study him, her ever-changing eyes intense with speculation.

Gabe wasn't sure he liked the direction this conversation was heading. Why was he the only one who could open those doors? What did it mean? "So can I move up there?" he found himself asking, not daring to look his mother in the eye. He picked at a loose thread on the couch, threatening to behead a faceless figure woven into the fabric's tapestry.

She sighed. "I suppose. It's going to take a lot of cleaning and the house still needs to be painted and there are the blueberries and—"

"Oh, give the boy a break," Grandma May interrupted. "He needs this."

Mom gave Grandma May a penetrating look, then turned to Gabe. "Well, your dad might like an office of his own, and I suppose you can clean in the evenings after supper."

Nobody said anything for a moment. In the silence, Gabe sipped at his drink and wondered why his mom was so touchy about the turret room. He also wondered why Grandma May wanted him to have it. Why did she think he *needed* it, like he was in danger or something?

After a bit, everyone started talking again about the storm. Even Dad joined in, announcing that he thought maybe he could start doing some work around the house now that he was feeling better. Mom quickly vetoed that and once more Dad sunk into a funk.

After clearing up from dinner and enjoying a serving of warm blueberry pie with vanilla ice cream, Grandma May and Grandpa Hawthorne left, saying they had to be up with the chickens. Tomorrow was Saturday and Grandpa had to take out a group of tourists for a day-trip and Grandma wanted to be at the Farmer's Market at seven to set up her stand. She sold whatever vegetables were currently ripe, homemade breads and jams, and herbs and herbal remedies. She was a busy woman on summer Saturdays.

When they were gone, Gabe, Kris, and Jer quickly did their chores around the house—a bit of cleaning and straightening, carrying up some canning supplies from the spooky cellar for Mom, and settling Dad into his favorite chair in the library with a book that he probably wouldn't read. Despite his bravado, the visit had worn him out. It saddened Gabe to see him so weak, but only time, and a lot of luck, would help his dad get better.

Without discussing it, the three boys met at the door to the turret at eight on the dot, armed with flashlights, some new light bulbs, and cleaning supplies. Each wore a determined look, as though setting out to do battle. In a strange way, Gabe felt that battle was exactly what they were about to do, and preparing the turret was a part of that.

For the next three hours, they scrubbed and swept and made piles and cleared cobwebs, retiring to bed only when Mom yelled up at them to come down. She didn't come up herself, Gabe noted, which surprised him. After her reaction in the parlor, he'd thought she'd be pounding up those stairs as soon as she could manage. She didn't even ask about the turret when they joined her, watching as Gabe carefully locked the door behind him, but making no comment. Something strange was going on with her.

The following morning, Gabe leaped out of bed at half past five, ready to get started. Once again he met his brothers, already in the kitchen gobbling down breakfast. They were as eager to work as he was. "Time's a wasting," Kris said in response to Gabe's teasing him about what a miracle it was to see him up before eight a.m.

The turret room looked different. The morning sunlight filled the room, flowing dimly through the dingy half-moon window. Gabe hadn't attempted to do anything with it, deciding to wait for daylight to give it a good scrub. Jer and Kris set to work carrying anything they wanted to keep for themselves, after Gabe's okay, down to their rooms, or out to the barn, while Gabe gathered up rags and a bucket of water.

While scrubbing and rinsing and scrubbing some more, he noticed that the glass rose up in several places, like long scars spreading out over the window's surface. He wondered if the window had been broken at one time and then fixed with clear cement. The bumps made cleaning harder, but even with these flaws, the window was awesome. It was *his* window. He couldn't wait until the glass was clean and shining once more.

The dust and grunge was so thick, however, that it took ten minutes to clear even a small patch. When a spot of clear glass finally revealed itself, Gabe couldn't resist peering through it. Down below, he could see their entire yard and beyond it, the woods—lots of woods. He shuddered. The dark world of undulating treetops seemed to go on and on in every direction, traveling up the mountainside and covering the entire peak like a hat, which was unusual—he didn't think vegetation could survive at that altitude, or at least not in such abundance.

With an effort, he forced his eyes to look elsewhere. Because of the curving effect of the turret, he was able to see a great deal. To his left he caught a glimpse of the ocean, a speck of blue and green, and to his right was the town of Ranger and the old, abandoned mill lurking like a spider. In the woods between their yard and the town two houses nestled close together, and one had a paddock behind it. One must be Abazi's house, and the other, Kimber's. He could even see Grandma May's little cottage, along with her massive garden nearly as big as the cottage itself, sitting just off the main road into Ranger.

Unable to help himself, his eyes returned to the woods. He couldn't believe how immense it was. From this vantage point, he noticed how many different kinds of trees there were, with clumps of similar trees grouped together. Not having grown up around many trees, he wasn't sure what the different types were. He knew from his fifth grade science class that there were two main kinds—deciduous (leafy) and coniferous (pointy). From a field trip to Muir Woods he'd learned that Redwoods (pointy) were huge. After that, he was pretty lost.

Not wanting to dwell on the forest any longer—it made him feel weird just looking at it—he returned to his work. A few hours later, finally finished with the window, he realized that he was alone in the turret and had been for some time. Looking down at the barn he saw the doors wide open and Kris, wearing one of Grandpa May's old fedoras, was working inside. Busy with yet another of his inventions, he was using the springs off an old bed he'd found in the turret.

Gabe stretched his stiff muscles and climbed down the small steps. He was glad to see that his brothers had also swept the floor, washed the other windows, and carried away the garbage bags. Kris and Jer could be really cool when they put their minds to it. He would've been at this cleaning for days if they hadn't helped.

Crossing the now nearly empty floor—two stacks of wooden boxes sat in a corner to be gone through later—he set the buckets of filthy water down by the door. Straightening up, he heard someone coming up the stairs. Was it Jer? It couldn't be Kris. Once he got into his inventions, he stayed put for hours. Besides, these footsteps were too light.

He nearly fell backward when his mom poked her head around the door. "Came to see how you're getting on," she said, almost shyly. She stepped into the room and looked around with wonder. "Wow…" she breathed softly. "This place is *amazing*!"

Gabe joined her in looking around. It really *was* cool in here. He knew right away where he wanted to put his bed and dresser, his desk, and his old collection of Star Wars figures and battleships. There was even a good spot for his 50-gallon fish tank, the envy of Jer, but bought with his own money earned from a job at The Hotdog Hut last summer. Later on, he'd figure out where to put his T.V. and Nintendo Wii U.

"Oh, Gabe!" she cried, grabbing his arm. "Look!" She pointed at the half-moon window. When he saw what she was talking about, the air in his lungs left in a rush and refused to return for several seconds.

It was a giant tree, and it was coming right into his room.

Chapter Seven

Hidden Surprises

It was a tree all right, but not a real one. Someone had purposely designed the raised glass to form the shape of a tree. When the light hit the sparkling glass just right, the shadow of a tree was cast across the room, as though it had been brought to life.

"It's beautiful," his mom gushed, and she was not one for gushing. She had good reason to, though. It *was* beautiful. Disturbing, but beautiful.

Hugging herself, she let loose a little sigh. "You're going to love it up here, Gabe. I only wish…" She stopped herself. "Well, I only wish I could've had this place when I was a kid. Heck, I'd take it now, so you better behave yourself." She laughed, but Gabe had the feeling she was serious.

Despite the seemingly live tree reaching into his room, he really liked the turret. He didn't want to lose it. "I'll just get my stuff up here, then go paint the rest of the house," he promised hurriedly.

She laughed, more relaxed this time. "I'll help you. It won't be easy getting that dresser up here. What you're going to do about that fish tank of yours, I don't know."

"We moved it here from California," he reminded her.

"And remember how I vowed that we weren't ever moving it again and you agreed?"

"I'll get Kris and Jer to pick ten buckets of blueberries today."

Her brown eyes narrowed. "It's a deal. But we'll have to move the tank later tonight." She checked her watch. "We'll be spending the next hour hauling your stuff up and I'm bringing Dad in for his blood work after lunch." She glanced around, smiling. "Looks like your brothers didn't leave you much. Just those wooden boxes and that old, mangy trunk that looks like it's sailed the seven seas and then some. Who knows what might be in it?" Her eyes shone with curiosity. "Then there's that bookshelf where the wall sort of sticks out, filled with ratty old books on…" She walked over to it and turned her head sideways to read the titles. "Trees. Go figure."

"Kris owes me a favor," Gabe said. "He can help me with the tank. I'll go dump these buckets, then we can move all the big stuff first. I'll do the rest myself."

Working together, he and his mom managed to shift most of his possessions before lunchtime. The only damage was a scratch on his bed's headboard, which fit right in with the other scratches. When Mom left to fix lunch, Gabe fetched the rest of his boxes, glad he hadn't yet done any major unpacking. His habit of procrastinating had finally paid off.

Cramming clothes into his dresser drawers, Gabe realized that he'd enjoyed himself this morning. It had been a long time since he'd had his mom all to himself. He registered, with a blush, that he missed her.

During lunch he managed to con his brothers into the berry picking. Well, maybe blackmail was the right word. He had only to say 'frogs' and they knew they were screwed. It was a long story, but suffice it to say, it involved a jar, a dead frog, and a pickling recipe. They hastily agreed to pick the blueberries, leaving his mother and father with identical quizzical expressions on their faces.

"I don't want to know," his mother said before leaving them to grab her purse.

After lunch, Mom and Dad left for town, to be gone for the afternoon. After the appointment they planned to pick up vegetables and a few herbal remedies at Grandma May's place. Kris and Jer went to pick the blueberries. The Shaker was back in business and Kris figured it would only take them half an hour to do the job. The house empty now, Gabe began the arduous process of draining his fish tank without getting water everywhere.

An hour later, his brothers returned with a record-breaking *fifteen* buckets of blueberries and purple stained mouths. The load would make their mom very happy, and a happy mom meant a kinder, gentler mom.

"Good job!" Gabe told them and they grinned. "Now let's move that tank so Mom won't have to." With a lot of grunts, bumping into walls and doorframes, and a few bruised knuckles, the three of them hauled the empty fish tank up the turret stairs, setting it carefully onto its sturdy black stand against the wall opposite the half-moon window. He wanted to be able to see the tank from his bed, which he had pushed beneath the window platform so that it formed a little roof over his pillows.

"How are you going to fill it?" Jer asked.

Gabe stared at the tank. He hadn't thought about that part. "I don't know. A lot of trips with a couple buckets, I guess."

"Use the hose. There's that faucet by the porch," Kris reminded him. "Tie a rope to the hose and lower it from this window," he indicated the small, diamond-shaped one to the right of the bookshelf. "Should work."

Gabe grinned at his brother. "I knew there was a reason I let you live."

Kris snorted. "You do it because I'm *so* good looking." Jer and Gabe howled with laughter. Kris feigned hurt. "I *am*!" When his brothers didn't stop laughing, he just rolled his eyes. "I'll go get the hose."

While he was gone, Jer helped Gabe carefully carry the fish up to the turret. Before their trip to Maine, he'd had thirty-one freshwater fish. He now had twenty. Eleven had died on the journey, flushed at whichever rest stop was next in line, along with a small, mumbled-under-his-breath prayer. His favorite, the five silver dollar fish had survived, so he wasn't too bummed out, but still, if the circumstances had allowed for it he would've picked a better burial method for the others that had died. Unfortunately, dead fish, hot car—not a good combination.

The sound of Kris's feet pounding up the stairs startled Gabe and he almost dropped one of the baggies holding the bottom-dwelling loaches that feasted on tank algae.

"Someone's been snooping around in the barn!" he cried, bursting into the room. The green garden hose was looped over his shoulder. The tip of his sandal caught the end that dragged on the floor and he nearly tripped.

"What do you mean?" Jer asked, staring at Kris. Their brother took most things in stride, so when he got excited, it was typically for a good reason. The old lady's warning suddenly came back to Gabe. He'd forgotten all about it after Grandma May had given him the key to the turret. He'd forgotten about Repulsive, too. He thought briefly that it seemed strange, even for him, to be forgetting such unusual events.

"I hate it when people touch my stuff!" Kris roared, sounding like a wounded wookie. He glared at Gabe and Jer accusingly.

"It wasn't me!" Jer cried. "Besides, how do you know someone 'touched' anything?" To call Kris's workspace messy was being polite. Utter chaos was probably a better way to describe it. Yet he knew where everything was and exactly how he'd left it. It was uncanny how he managed it, and very annoying. He'd caught Gabe out several times.

But it hadn't been Gabe this time. "Me, either," he hurried to say.

Kris's eyes narrowed. "Are you sure?"

"Uh, yeah!" Jer exclaimed sarcastically. "Unless I experienced a blackout, I'm pretty sure I had nothing to do with it! Was anything taken?"

"I don't think so," Kris admitted. "I think I interrupted the thief before he found what he was looking for. It's weird, though. I saw something about this height," he indicated a point just below his shoulder, "moving around in the loft, but when I looked, no one was there. I don't know how he got out. I was on the ladder so I was blocking the way down."

"Maybe it was my pet *raccoon*," Gabe suggested, not without his own dose of sarcasm.

Kris grimaced. "Well, see, that's the bugger of it. Those footprints we saw up here? Well, I saw the same ones in the barn."

"It couldn't have been a raccoon," Jer pointed out, telling them what they already knew. From the size of the footprints, that would have been one *big* raccoon.

"So what was it?" Kris demanded. "No one messes with my stuff and gets away with it!"

Gabe wondered if he should tell his brothers about Repulsive and the old lady. To rid himself of the burden would be a huge relief. Maybe they'd even have ideas about who it might have been. Then he hesitated. He had no proof. They'd only think he was crazy, telling them that the entire family had forgotten about a baby that had been in the house and whom they'd held and fed and tickled under the chin. It sounded completely loony, as in Loony Leprechaun loony. He didn't even believe it himself anymore.

"Maybe it was Abazi and Kimber," Jer suggested. "Maybe they were looking for us."

"And the footprints?" Kris argued. "What about those?"

"Some kind of animal we don't know about?" Jer tried. "Something that only lives in Maine?"

Kris frowned. "Well, if I ever meet that animal, I'm going to show him the business end of my fist."

"Well, there's nothing we can do about it now," Gabe said, deciding not to tell them about his visitors. Maybe later, when he had a chance to think about it some more. "Help me with this tank. I've still got a house to paint."

While the tank was filling with water, Kris ran out to the barn to see if anything was missing and Jer went to look in on the kittens. Gabe spent his time exploring the room, finding a few built-in cupboards, their doors practically invisible. He had hiding places! He made a mental note to fill them when there was no chance of being interrupted.

Done exploring, he began straightening up his room. After making his bed, he added water conditioner and good bacteria to the fish tank. He rearranged the landscape several times to evoke an underwater shipwreck scene. When the tank was nearly full, he raced down and turned off the water, then returned to the turret to drop the hose through the window. Before he could forget, he ran back outside to gather up the hose to return it to the barn. If he left it lying around, his mom would freak out, yelling that she was not his servant to be cleaning up after him.

As he was coiling up the hose, he noticed something strange. About ten feet from where he was standing, hidden behind the heavy hydrangea bushes that surrounded the house, was a doorknob. He would never have noticed it if he hadn't leaned over to pick up the hose and seen a movement in the bushes out of the corner of his eye. He stared at the doorknob for a moment, then quickly gathered up the hose to bring to the barn, soaking one of his shoes as the last of the water drained out.

"Kris!" he yelled. "Kris!" Inside the barn, he quickly hung the hose on its rightful hook while struggling to keep it from unraveling. *"Kris!"* he called again as he pushed the same piece of stubborn hose onto the hook over and over. "Oh, forget it. Kris!"

"I'm up here," Kris called back. He peeked over the side of the loft holding a dirty rag in one hand and a screwdriver in the other.

"Why didn't you answer me?"

"I didn't hear you." That was another thing about Kris. When he got involved in something, he was deaf to the world. Jer, on the other hand, heard everything, like he had Superman powers.

"I did find something missing, after all," Kris growled. "Something I grabbed from the turret room."

"You can show me later," Gabe told him. "There's something you've got to see!"

Sensing adventure, Kris scurried down from the loft. "What is it?"

"Come on!"

They met Jer coming out of the house. "What are you guys doing?" he called after them, before running to catch up when they didn't answer.

Gabe pulled back the branches to show them where the door was. It was hard to see from this angle. Behind the hydrangea shrubs, a thicket of briars hid the door from view. Gabe told Kris to run back to the barn to get pruning shears. A few prickly branches weren't going to stop them. They would force the door to reveal itself.

"Don't cut too much," he warned Kris when he returned. "I don't want Mom or Dad to see the door." Or anyone else, for that matter.

After a bit of careful pruning, the boys were able to reach the door without losing an eye. The door looked like the two leading to the turret—rounded at the top, made of wood, and reinforced by metal bands. The only difference was that it measured about half the height of the other two.

Kris was the first to try the knob. "It's locked."

"Let me try," Gabe said. Fingers trembling slightly, he reached over to grab hold of the knob, which, once again, was a death head's skull. He didn't want to touch it, but he had to. He had to know what was on the other side of that door. When he grasped hold of the metal knob, it felt warm to the touch, as though someone had been holding onto it before he and his brothers arrived. The knob turned easily and he glanced at Kris who shrugged.

"I guess I loosened it up for you."

Gabe pushed against the little door and it creaked open, swinging inward. He looked back at his brothers. "Who wants to go first? Jer?"

"Sure," Jer volunteered. The kid might be little, but he didn't back down from a challenge. In asking him to go first, Gabe had wisely (though his mother might have used the word, shamefully) taken advantage of that particular trait in his brother. He figured it was payback for all the times Jer did the same to him, touting Gabe's advanced age to make him go first into potentially dangerous situations. This time Gabe had beat him to it.

"Get in there, then," Kris urged him. "You're the only one tiny enough to fit." It wasn't true, but close enough. The door looked as though it had been made for dwarves.

"Just make sure you come after me if something grabs me in there," Jer said. "Mom will kill you if you let me die." Gabe and Kris nodded their solemn promises while dutifully crossing their hearts with their pointer finger.

Jer ducked low to enter the doorway and Gabe felt the urge to lighten things up a little, but he couldn't seem to find anything to joke about. Who knew what could be hiding in there? What if the creature, who'd made those strange footprints in the turret, lived behind that door? Or something from the woods slept in there? He shuddered convulsively. No. Nothing funny about this at all.

Kris, as usual, had no problems finding the humor. "If something does take you, little brother, make sure before you die to tell them that

I'm all gristle, no flavor at all."

Jer gave an elaborate sigh as he peered into the small opening. "I'm going to need a flashlight. I can't see a thing!"

"Then you won't see what hit you," Kris replied, shoving his brother forward.

Gabe frowned. "You didn't need to push him."

Kris shrugged. "You know how Jer is. Like a wild animal. He would've gone in, I'll give him that, but first he'd have sat sniffing the air like a dog, listening for strange sounds, and pretty much studying everything for the next half hour like he was getting ready for a space launch. I don't have that kind of time. Neither do you. We still need to paint the rest of the house."

He was right. "Do you see anything?" Gabe called into the darkness. He strained to hear a reply, but nothing came.

"Jer?" Kris hollered. "Stop screwing around. What's in there?"

When Jer still didn't answer, Gabe pushed Kris out of the way. "I'm going in. If we don't come out in two minutes, go for help."

"By the time I get back, you'll be dead. I'm coming with you."

Gabe had been hoping Kris would say that. "We're armed, and we're coming in!" he shouted, then ducked his head and scooted his way through the narrow opening. Almost immediately, the space opened up in front of him. It was dark, but enough light shone through the door so that Gabe could tell he'd be able to stand up. "Jer?" he called again as he cautiously pushed himself to his feet.

Kris wriggled in behind him. "What is this place?" Gabe helped him stand up and they both reached blindly about. Gabe's right hand touched a rough surface—stone or brick, he thought—about half the length of his arm away. "It's like a chimney, though somewhat bigger. Probably about four by four."

Gabe reached over to his left, as though he sensed something was there. His hand touched a smooth object…a pole made of wood that seemed to grow out of the floor. It was solidly made, though he could feel vibrations beneath his touch. "Jer?" he called again, louder this time. "Answer me!"

"I'm up here!" Jer's voice called down. They both looked up, but could see nothing. "I climbed the pole!"

"Holy crap! How high are you?" Kris asked.

"About twenty feet. There's another door here. I can feel it. I think it opens into the house somewhere."

"Into the turret," Gabe breathed. "It's an escape route."

"From what?" Kris demanded. "Goblins?"

"Maybe," Gabe answered, not joking in the least. This was getting stranger and stranger. "Can you hold on for another minute?" he called up to Jer.

"No problem."

"I'm going up to my room to see if I can find the opening. I'll start calling to you when I get there. I want you to call back so I can find you."

"Righto!"

"Make sure he doesn't fall," he murmured to Kris as he got back down on his hands and knees. As quickly as he could, he made his way up to the turret. Once inside, he called out, "Marco!"

"Beans!" came a muffled response.

He quickly moved to where the sound was coming from—the bookshelf. He reached out and pushed it. Nothing moved. He wasn't surprised. The shelf stood ten feet tall, five feet wide, and a foot thick, not to mention it was packed with books, at least half of them four hundred page monsters.

"Marco!" he called again.

"Beans!" came Jer's response. Gabe groaned. *Definitely* behind the bookshelf. There had to be another way to find the passage. He searched, but nothing gave itself away...no candle to lift, no sconce to pull. He wasn't going to try pulling out every single book, either. There were hundreds of them!

Frustrated, he kicked at the floor. The tip of his sneaker caught against something and he looked down to see a groove in the shape of an arc about three feet from the bookshelf. He peered up at the monstrosity, then back down at the groove. That was it! The bookshelf must swing open. He moved closer and searched the corner where the bookshelf met the wall. After some poking and prodding, he finally found what he was looking for—a thick latch, carefully hidden from sight. Gabe unhooked the latch and pulled on the bookshelf. With a loud squeal, the heavy shelf swung outward. So this was why the wall protruded behind the bookshelf...to cover up the hidden passage.

As soon as there was a big enough gap, Gabe spotted Jer clinging to the pole. He leaned forward and gave his brother a hand. Jer crawled into the room, a big grin on his face and several cobwebs coating his hair. "That was *so* cool!"

"I can't believe you climbed that thing not knowing where it led or what was at the top. You're usually such a chicken."

"I'm *not* a chicken!" Jer protested, brushing at the cobwebs. "I'm simply picky about what I choose to do."

It was an often-used argument, so Gabe ignored it. Mainly because he had to help Kris, who was right behind his brother. The moment Kris was in the room, he sprang to his feet and began examining the bookshelf.

"This is fierce! Whoever built this really knew their engineering." Like Gabe had done, he poked and pushed and prodded at the mechanism. "It's pretty old," he finally assessed. "Been here a long time. The hinges could use some WD-40."

"Was the pole hard to climb?" Gabe asked.

"Try it yourself," Jer dared. "Then we'll see who's the chicken."

"Maybe I will," Gabe replied. The pole was hard to see in the darkness, but still visible. Made of a dark wood, it was thick as a fireman's pole and smooth as marble. He liked the feel of it in his hands.

He grabbed hold of the pole and wrapped his legs around it. Slowly he let himself descend. As he gained confidence, he picked up speed, rushing downward. Before he knew it, his feet had hit the ground. When he looked up, he saw his brothers peering down at him, grinning. He grinned back. Testing his agility, he climbed back up the pole. The palms of his hands were a bit sore from the friction, but that was it. All the work around the farm this last week was toughening him up.

"We'd better close this," he said. "With my luck, Mom will get home early and find the passage and then she'll never let me stay in the turret."

"We definitely don't want her knowing we have a way to get in and out of the house without her having the faintest clue," Kris said with a wicked smile. He pretended to twirl the tips of a mustache.

"You can't sneak out at night!" Jer cried in dismay. "Not without me!"

"I'm not saying I'm going to be sneaking out at all," Gabe countered. "It's just nice knowing that I could if I wanted to."

"Of course you realize," Kris said, "if you can get in and out without being seen, someone else can, too."

"Like our visitor with the weird feet..." Jer added ominously.

Chapter Eight

Eye of Newt

Gabe had no choice in the matter. He'd never sleep again knowing that someone or something could come and go as they pleased, watching him while he slept, listening to him snore, waiting for the right moment to pounce. Maybe it'd be better to keep the squeak—kind of like having a built-in alarm system. On the other hand, if he had to escape quickly, he didn't want to be struggling to move the heavy shelf or lifting latches.

With a start, he brought his racing thoughts to a screeching halt. *Why* was he thinking this way? Who or what did he have to escape? He was getting a bit paranoid about all this. He needed to just take a deep breath and get a grip before he suffered a nervous breakdown.

In the end, Kris oiled the mechanism so that the shelf moved more easily and smoothly, but despite his attempts to eliminate the squeak, a small squawk remained and Gabe was glad.

Watching Kris work, an excellent idea occurred to him. Wouldn't it be great if the skeleton key worked on the small door down below? He'd feel much better if he could lock it. He told his brothers his plan, then slipped down the pole. When he tried the key, which he now wore on a chain around his neck, he discovered that it could lock the small door from the outside. He also realized that he could open the door from the inside without having to unlock it. These two discoveries made him feel much less exposed to creepy crawlies with funny feet, and if he needed to get out, like in the case of a fire, he easily could.

After locking up the turret, he spent the rest of the day painting the house. Jer and Kris decided to pitch in after he promised to help them with their chores. Typically, Jer was responsible for cleaning the house, though Mom seemed to be doing most of that, and Kris had to clean out the shed and straighten up the barn.

Gabe was both grateful and relieved for the assistance. Grateful for the obvious reasons—painting was hot, tiring work. Relieved because his brothers kept him distracted, talking and screwing around. He really didn't want to dwell on all the strange things that seemed to be happening to him—meeting Repulsive and the old lady, finding an escape hatch to a place no one had entered for years, discovering there might be someone who lived in the woods that was out to get him.

By the time Mom and Dad returned, Gabe and his brothers had managed to paint two-thirds of the house. "Looks good!" Mom yelled from the truck. She sounded tired, but in a good way. Gabe found himself breathing a sigh of relief. He hated it when she was tired and anxious—she got very cranky.

Dad had fallen asleep on the ride home and was still sleeping. Just looking at him slumped against the truck door made Gabe sad. He remembered his dad being so strong and full of energy. He used to play rugby and soccer with them on a regular basis, easily keeping up. But all that seemed a long time ago. It had been a few years since he'd been able to do much of anything with them. Gabe missed the old days. He especially missed running with his dad, racing to see who was fastest. Now he could beat his dad hopping on one foot. That's not how he wanted to win. He wanted to earn his victory fair and square.

While their father slept, the three of them helped carry canvas bags full of vegetables from Grandma May's garden into the house. She also sent some homemade jam along with a few jars of a strange concoction she'd labeled Alder Tea, in her bold handwriting.

"It's probably made from eye of newt," Kris joked when he saw it. "Jer, drink some. See what it does to you."

"Not in this lifetime! You try it."

"No, thanks. I value my life."

"Maybe I should slip a bit into your milk some night. You'll never know what hit you. That is, until you start to grow fangs and a fluffy tail."

"Gabe already has a tail," Kris remarked, pointing at his brother's butt. "Well, he was born with one, anyway."

"Mom!" Gabe complained, having heard this story one too many times. The worst of it was that his parents had started the whole dumb lie. Well, mainly his mom, just because he liked to make fun of the fact that she had been born in a bathroom…while her mom was sitting on the toilet. In revenge, she joked that he'd been born with a tail. He hadn't. He sincerely hoped…

Mom shook her head. She typically stayed out of their sparring and bickering, knowing that nothing she could say would solve anything.

"You got more food for the cats!" Jer exclaimed happily when he saw the huge bag of kitty food on the table.

"Yeah, well, I can't wait until they start earning their keep," Mom muttered. "That stuff's expensive."

"I already started them on some basic skills," Jer replied quickly. "And I'm showing them how to meow to get let out to do their business."

"And who's going to be letting them out in the middle of the night?" she wondered aloud. "This will be worse than having a dog."

"We can keep a litter box for those times," Jer answered, looking worried.

She saw his face. "As long as you clean it," she relented. "I do not clean litter boxes. I can't stand the smell." She jerked her thumb at the truck. "There's kitty litter in the back." He brightened and she ruffled his hair. "You're an odd one."

"Which goes to show that you're definitely my mother," he countered and she cuffed him upside the head, pretending to be mad. Kris and Gabe laughed. It always seemed funnier when Jer sassed Mom. As a little kid he was such a suck-up to her, calling her 'pretty mama' and 'so beautiful.' He even sang songs about her. He still sucked up to her, only now he tried not to do it in front of his brothers.

"What's all the laughing about?" their dad called from the truck as they headed down the steps to grab more bags. He looked groggy and out of sorts. "Laughing at your old man?"

"We're laughing," Gabe explained, "because Jer just told Mom he got his weirdness from her."

Dad smiled. "Well, then, laugh away."

"Keith! I am *not* odd."

"No, just a little unusual."

She gave him a fond look, then set everyone to work, even Dad, to everyone's surprise. Grandma had made them a stew and homemade bread, which Dad sliced with the electric knife, so supper was easy and delicious. Grandma May might be a little strange, but she could cook. They spent the evening frantically finishing painting the rest of the house before it got dark. They'd never had to work like this before. They were covered in white paint, sunburned—except for Kris—and sneezing, but Gabe felt a certain satisfaction when they'd finished. Not that he'd ever admit that to Mom. She'd use it as an excuse to pile on more work.

Too tired to do any more unpacking, he fed his fish and fell into bed. He'd have to do the rest tomorrow. Before long he was fast asleep. Normally, in a new and strange place, he'd lie awake staring at the ceiling, listening to noises. But not here, even knowing about the secret door and the odd footprints. Feeling strangely safe, he drifted off with thoughts of how to arrange his new room floating around in his head.

~~~~~~

The following morning dawned bright and sunny. While eating breakfast, the brothers decided to begin scraping paint off the barn. The forecast called for more rain in a couple days and the fresh paint would need time to dry. Throwing themselves into the job, they managed to clear two sides of the barn before lunch.

Mom was in the cellar sorting out the mess down there, leaving them ample room to fix their lunches. Jer took over the task—the kid actually liked preparing meals, and soon they sat down to eat their grilled ham and cheese sandwiches, which were delicious. Jer had a special talent for turning something as mundane as ham and cheese into a culinary delight. He claimed the secret was the special sauce he'd invented.

"I think I'll go for a walk after lunch," Dad announced while they ate. They all stared at him. "Where?" Jer finally managed to ask.

"Just around the yard. You don't need to look so shocked. My legs still work, you know. Thought I'd check out the woods."

Gabe gulped nervously, then asked a stupid question. "Does Mom know?"

Dad bristled. "She's not *my* mother, and besides I'm only taking a walk. It's not like I'm building an Ark, or something."

"Are you sure you want to go into the woods?" Gabe asked.

"Gabe's afraid of the woods," Kris explained around a mouthful of sandwich. He stuck a few chips in his mouth as he smirked at his older brother.

"Why? Have you seen something?" Their dad was generally pretty easygoing, but he had strong survivalist instincts.

Gabe shook his head, swallowing the lump of sandwich in his mouth. It no longer tasted so good. "It's a big forest and there might be bears. What would you do if a bear came after you?"

Dad grinned. "I'd play dead. I'm close enough to it, anyway."

Kris laughed loudly, earning a pleased smile, but Gabe couldn't bring himself to even pretend to be amused. "Bet you never thought being sick would be a bonus," Kris commented.

"There's a nice path around the yard," Gabe interjected, glaring at Kris. "That's where I run." Yes, he had heard a strange voice while running it, but that had been at night. This was broad daylight. Surely there'd be nothing there now—nothing to harm his father. Besides, he had probably heard the wind, not a person…or a monster.

"You're running again?" His dad's interest was piqued, just as Gabe hoped it would be.

"Just started. I was pretty stiff on my first go, but I think I made good time."

"Well, maybe I'll go check out your track. I could measure it, see how long it is. Where there's a good straightaway, I'll mark the 100 and 200-meter spots. Then maybe tonight or tomorrow I could time you."

"That'd be great, Dad," Gabe replied happily, thrilled with his fast thinking. He'd killed two birds with one stone—kept Dad out of the woods, and got him excited about something. Plus, it would be good to run again, to race the clock.

Mom emerged from the cellar, blinking in the bright light of the kitchen. Cobwebs covered her dark hair like a hairnet and a smudge accented one cheek. "Ah, here's the love of my life now!" Dad held out his arms for a hug. "I need a tape measure, my glorious one."

She stooped low to give him a hug. Unlike Dad, she wasn't naturally demonstrative. Since he'd gotten sick, though, she made an extra effort to be affectionate. "What for?" she asked after giving him a brief kiss on the lips. He pulled her down for another one and Gabe looked away. There was no need to see his parents doing *that*.

When they finally separated, his father told her what for. "I need to set up a track for Gabe. I'll just be walking around it, then measuring off yardage. I'll go slowly and take it easy," he assured her. "That new medicine I'm taking seems to be helping, not to mention your mom's tea." He held up a mug.

"Well, you know where the junk drawer is," she replied flippantly. "And your legs do work, don't they?" Dad grinned. This was Mom's weird way of showing she approved.

"Yes, they do, my dear."

"Put on a hat," she ordered as they began to clear the table. "And take breaks. It can get hot in the sun."

"I'll seek out the shelter of the trees if I feel myself growing light-headed."

"No!" both Gabe and his mother shouted at the same time, earning them strange looks from everyone else at the table.

"Don't you remember what happened?" she continued through gritted teeth.

Dad cleared his throat. "Of course. Right." He turned his attention to his three sons. "I don't want any of you going into the woods. You can cut through the north part to get to the neighbors, but otherwise stick to the yard or to the road. Those woods are just too big. People get lost…"

"Here's the tape measure," Mom broke in, pushing it into his hand. "Now go on, boys, and finish up that barn. It's the last building that needs painting and it'll take a while."

Before any of them could even question their mom and dad's strange reaction about the woods, Mom was ushering them outdoors, handing them their baseball caps as they went.

As they clattered down the porch steps donning their caps, they saw they had visitors. Abazi and Kimber appeared to have wandered idly into their yard. Again. Gabe felt his shoulders slump. This was the last thing he needed right now…more grief.

Dad waved hello as he eagerly made his way over to where the track started by the barn. Gabe was glad to see his dad so excited. The last time he'd looked that way…well, that was when Repulsive had shown up. Now there was another Repulsive to deal with. She just went by a different name…Abazi Wanibagw.

"We came to offer our services," she said as they met up. "My dad told me I had to start doing more charitable work. It's a tribal thing," she grumbled. "Anyway, I thought to myself, who could use some charity around here? And then I thought of you." She stared directly at Gabe, her dark eyes challenging him.

Kris burst out laughing. "He's a charity case, all right."

"Shut up, Kris!" Gabe growled, which, of course, only made his brother laugh harder.

"At least your brother knows what's funny," Abazi remarked. "Look at his hair." She grinned at him, then turned to Gabe, the grin gone. "So what do you want us to do?"

"You're really here to help out?" Jer asked, staring at Kimber.

She glanced up at him through strawberry blond bangs, her hands nervously tugging at the cuffs of her red shorts, and nodded. "I also wanted to see how the kittens were doing."

Jer tugged at his cap. "They're doing great. Kris is going to make them a cat door so they can come and go as they please."

Her smile froze on her face. "Don't let them leave the house," she warned, her soft voice rising.

"She's not kidding," Abazi said. "A lot of cats and dogs have gone missing lately. My dad thinks a pack of hungry coy dogs has come down from the mountains looking for food."

"I'll keep them inside, Kimber," Jer said hurriedly. "We can look at them later, if you want," he offered, stirring the ground with his foot.

Kimber visibly relaxed, her thin shoulders beneath her red and white striped shirt slumping with relief. "That would be nice." She beamed up at Jer.

Her face exposed, Gabe noticed now that she had a pert, uptilted nose with a spattering of freckles splashed across its bridge. Her skin was the color of summer peaches. She was actually quite pretty. His little brother had good taste in the ladies.

"So where do we begin?" Abazi asked, shading her eyes as she looked around the yard. Today she was wearing beaded moccasins and shorts that revealed long, brown legs. Realizing he was staring at them, Gabe quickly looked away.

"We have to paint the barn," he told her. When she frowned, he realized this was a golden opportunity to get back at her for her snarky behavior toward him earlier. "Ready to get started?" When she nodded uncertainly, he said, "Good! You can scrape the paint with Jer and Kimber." Gabe hated scraping paint. It was dirty, gritty work, and seemingly endless. Don't even get him started on the paint chips and where they ended up. The other day he'd found some in his underwear. So, even though he'd look like he'd been in a snowstorm, as he had after painting the house, or in a massacre, as would be the case after he finished painting the barn red, he'd rather run the sprayer.

For the next six hours, with a brief stop for an early supper, they scraped and painted and refilled canisters and sprayed and scraped some more. Finally, miraculously, they were done. The five of them had managed to complete the job, and the barn looked good as new. Later they could wash the windows and replace any broken panes with glass stored in the loft. Grandpa May had kept a bunch on hand for replacements after storms and such.

Gazing at the barn, Gabe felt proud of their work. In fact, the whole farm was looking pretty nice. The house and barn were freshly painted, the grass mown, the garden thoroughly weeded and ready for next spring, and the blueberry shrubs trimmed and stripped of ripe berries...for the moment. Maybe it wouldn't be so bad staying here. Abazi and the weird-footed creature excepted, of course. And the strange voice. And the hallucinations involving creepy babies.

A while back, Dad had gone inside, looking pleased with himself as he whistled a ragtime tune and tossed the tape measure in the air. A healthy sheen of sweat and dirt covered his skin. Gabe's heart had lurched at the sight, mostly with hope. Was Dad actually getting better? He really looked like it. Maybe this new medication would do the trick. Gabe sighed happily. It would be so good to have their dad back.

As the five of them stood and admired their work, he glanced at the

others, his gaze settling on Abazi. Surprisingly, she had worked just as
hard as everyone else, maybe even harder. She and Kris had passed
wisecracks back and forth the whole time, keeping everyone laughing.
Gabe realized that as sore and tired as he was right now, he'd actually
had fun. He smiled as he noticed the paint and dirt covering everyone's
hair and clothes. Kris had spread war paint on each cheekbone and
Abazi wore a red bracelet of paint on her wrist.

She volunteered to help Gabe return the ladders to the barn while
Kris cleaned off the sprayers using Grandma's environmentally
friendly cleaner. Gabe told Jer and Kimber to go inside to see the cats.
Kimber was looking tired and he thought she could use a break,
though she never once uttered a word of complaint or asked to rest.

"Well, I was right," Abazi said as they lifted the ladder up on its
hooks.

"About what?" he asked at the same moment he pinched his finger
between the ladder and the hook. He yanked his finger away and
shook it hard, as though trying to fling out the pain.

"You *did* need my help, charity case." Gabe frowned as she laughed
at him, but kept his lips pressed tightly together to keep from saying
anything back. He was a gentleman, after all, and gentlemen didn't tell
girls to take a flying leap out a three-story window.

They hung the other ladder in silence, then left the barn, with Gabe
keeping his distance. As they walked toward the house, Jer came flying
out the door yelling, "Gypsy is gone!"

Kimber followed more slowly, though she was obviously just as anxious. "She got out," she confirmed, biting her trembling lower lip.
"And now the coy dogs are going to eat her!"

Chapter Nine

Come Out, Come Out,
Wherever You Are

"Are you sure she got out?" Kris asked, coming to join them. A spot of red paint on the tip of his nose made him look like Rudolph, the red-nosed reindeer. "Couldn't she be hiding in the house? It's a big place, lots of corners. Especially in that back parlor where Mom still has all those boxes to unpack."

Jer shook his head. "The kittens never miss a meal. All I have to do is rattle the food dish and they come running, especially Little Joe. He's like a miniature baby elephant. Gypsy must have slipped outside when one of us used the bathroom," he surmised, staring at Kris.

Kris clasped an offended hand to his heart. "Why are you looking at me?"

"Because you never pay attention to what you're doing!" Jer shouted, his eyes brightening with anger. "If Gypsy gets eaten by a coy dog, I'm blaming you!"

"It's not going to do any good blaming others," Gabe interceded. "I'm sure she hasn't gone far." But he wasn't sure. For all he knew, Gypsy might have strayed into the woods. "Kris, you search the barn and shed. Jer and Kimber can look behind the house and in the blueberry patch. Abazi, take that part." He pointed toward the northern section of the woods, where she and Kimber lived. "I'll take the driveway and back behind the barn near the woods." He didn't want to, but neither could he let the others go there. At least he knew enough to be on alert.

The group split up, going their separate directions. Gabe watched as Jer and Kimber's blond heads disappeared behind the house before taking a deep breath and setting off down the driveway.

"Here, kitty, kitty, kitty!" he called as he traversed the length of the dirt drive up to where the trees started, then back again without so much as a meow to guide him. No Gypsy here. He gave vent to a frustrated sigh. There was nothing left to do but search near the creepy hedge. He headed toward the barn.

On the west side, Gabe found where his dad had used the heel of his shoe to make a rut in the dirt and grass. As Gabe was absently adding a little more length to it, he heard a muffled mewing sound coming from the other side of the hedge.

Oh, no. This was not cool. Gypsy had gone to the one place Gabe didn't want to—the forest. He stared at the tangled web of thick, thorny vines that stood between him and the helpless kitten. How had that fur ball gotten herself into this mess?

Gabe took a reluctant step toward the hedge, then another, forcing himself to keep moving forward. When he was about a foot from the wall of brush, something strange happened. The branches began to retreat, like scared snakes, to form an arched doorway in the hedge. He stared at the opening for a moment, completely stunned. He'd just found the answer to his question. There were ways into the forest, as long as you were invited, and he'd just been invited.

Looking back toward the yard, he saw Abazi searching for Gypsy along the edge of the woods. He made to call her, then shut his mouth. No need to involve her in this. Whatever *this* was. Turning about, he squared his shoulders and stepped through the archway. The moment he cleared the wall of tangled plants, he heard a slithering noise—the door was closing behind him. He spun around and lunged at the opening, but it was too late. He was trapped.

As he turned to face the forest, dread spread over his body like a toxic rash. Whatever he feared lay not in the wall he'd just passed through, but in the line of trees in front of him. He felt certain he didn't want his back to those woods, where the trees stood as silently and immovable as the monoliths at Stonehenge.

What amazed him was that many of these trees appeared to be nearly as tall as the Redwoods in northern California, which were thought to be the tallest trees in the world, reaching heights of over three hundred and fifty feet. But Redwoods were so tall because of their rainforest habitat. Ranger, Maine was not rainforest habitat. Something strange was going on in these woods.

His instinct was to race back to the house and hide out in the turret. But Gypsy needed him. He wasn't about to let the kitten get eaten by coy dogs. It was very likely an awful way to go, and Jer would be devastated. Besides, she was kind of Gabe's favorite of the three.

He took a steadying breath and began to walk across the grassy field that separated the hedge and the trees. With one last look back, he entered the dark woods. Silence reigned here, close and suffocating. When his eyes adjusted to the shadows, the first thing he noticed was the absence of undergrowth. No seedlings or small trees waited to take their rightful place in the sky, no little plants, not even ferns grew, only an endless expanse of thick green moss, which spread out before him like a luxurious carpet. With each step it seemed to grow thicker and deeper. His feet sunk and tiny emerald strands tickled his ankles.

Gabe's senses tingled as though electrified. Something was wrong with this unnatural place and he didn't think he wanted to know what it was. He had to find Gypsy and get out of here... *now.*

"Looking for this?" a raspy voice called out.

Gabe swung around, back toward the edge of the woods where the sound had come from. He caught the flicker of a shadow off to his left, then it disappeared behind one of the trees. Was it Abazi? The last he looked, she'd been pretty far away, on the other side of the yard.

He wondered if he should stay where he was, or go on the attack. He recalled what his dad had told him to do if such a situation arose. In high school, Gabe's dad had been able to weight lift over three hundred pounds. Word got out about his feat of strength, which made him a target for Jeff Stevey, the worst of the school bullies. Jeff figured that if he could beat Keith Hawthorne up, it would make him look stronger and, Gabe guessed, more desirable to the girls.

Unable to avoid the confrontation, Dad had made the first move, catching Jeff off guard, and ending the fight without getting touched. Gabe liked that part the best.

"I'm over here," the voice called behind him. He waited a moment, then spun around and dashed after the sound, rounding the massive tree hard and fast.

"Aiyee!" the voice yelped when he grabbed hold of a long, brown arm. "Leave me go!"

He didn't listen, maintaining his grip even though he wasn't exactly sure what it was he had a hold of. The creature before him resembled a human. The torso sprouted arms and legs where it should. There was a head where most humans had a head, with reddish hair growing from it in wild tufts. Yet there was a disturbing wildness about it, about *her* actually. Gabe's captive was a female, he realized with a blush, and she looked familiar to him.

"Repulsive?" he questioned, slowly, carefully. He didn't want the name to sound like an insult, even though it once had been one.

Her little face, long and thin, with a pointy chin, sharp as an elbow, and a narrow nose that curled downward at the tip, crumpled into a ferocious scowl. "I'm Hollie!" she cried, sticking out her thin chest. "And I am *not* repulsive!" He thought he saw her lower lip quiver as she said this last part.

"No," he agreed, studying her uneasily. "You're definitely not Repulsive. Repulsive was a baby. You're not a baby." Despite her thinness, a womanliness flowed beneath the bright green, long-sleeved smock she wore. He noticed that he was still holding her arm. He slowly let it go, hoping she wouldn't run.

A cunning look came into her eyes—odd-looking eyes, moss green, large and knowing, with short, thick brown lashes. "I was one once, though," she answered, her eyes mischievous now. "Thought I'd come and take a look at ye."

"Me?" he said. "Why me?"

"Dame Hazel is so interested in ye, always has been. And now more than ever. I want to know why." She laughed suddenly, a rich, vibrant sound. "We've met before!"

Gabe stared at her in incomprehension. "Before you were the ugly baby?"

She frowned, looking almost frightening. "I was *not* an ugly baby! The others thought I looked quite precious, like a little jewel, I believe yer da said."

"He called you a cutie pie," Gabe answered back. "Not a little jewel. And he's sick so his judgment is screwed up. But I will admit that you look much better to me like this." He indicated her current state. "So did we meet before that or not?"

She cocked her head to one side. "What if I told ye? What if I didn't?"

Her words were purposely provocative. "Does this Dame Hazel know you're talking to me right now?"

The little face suddenly closed up. "I have to go now. Just remember her warning."

"*Her* warning?"

"Stay out of the woods. They'll be comin' after ye."

Gabe looked around, suddenly afraid. "Why aren't they coming after me now?"

"They're preoccupied. But they won't be for long." He gulped. "Here." She reached behind her head and pulled out a black and white bundle of fur. "Keep all yer small creatures in yer house. And stay out of the woods. All of ye."

"You've already said that," Gabe answered impatiently. "But why? Who are *they* and what do *they* want from me?"

"They want yer blood." The wind picked up suddenly, as though on command. "Quick, now. Go! I'll fend them off!"

Gabe grabbed Gypsy from her outstretched hands and spun around
to flee. He knew he had something great to fear here. He'd always
known it since his first visit to May Farm.

Gabrielll.

Gabrielll!

Ye are mine, Gabriel. Come back to me!

The voice was calling to him again. This time, instead of scaring him,
he felt as though he wanted to go to it.

Gabrielll...

He turned back, drawn to the voice.

"Run, Gabriel!" Hollie screamed, her wild, auburn hair flying out all
around her. She seemed to be growing in size as she spun around and
around like a waterspout.

The fear in her voice broke the spell and Gabe took off, dashing for
the wall of prickly vines, the squirming Gypsy tucked firmly under one
arm like a football. When he reached the hedge, he waited for the vines
to open, but nothing happened. No branches unraveled, no door appeared.

The chilling sound of a thousand pursuers' footsteps came at him
from behind. "Open up!" he demanded, his beating heart nearly choking him. "Open up, or I'm going to start cutting!" With his free hand,
he pulled out his Swiss Army pocketknife, the one that had been his
dad's when he was a kid.

He released the blade and the branches parted like a miracle. He
slipped through the narrow space before the door was fully formed,
scratching himself on the thorns. As soon as he was on the other side,
the space closed up again, weaving together as tightly as a knitted blanket.

Behind him, an angry howl soared into the sky. Gabe glanced up, his
mind dizzy with fear, but he couldn't see what had made that horrible
screech. Which was probably just as well. Another wail shrilled close
by and the wind blew harder. The trees along the edge of the woods
began to thrash about as though commiserating with the howler.

Gabrielll...

The air went still and the whole forest quivered to a stop.

"Don't ever do that again!" Gabe shouted at the wall, shaking from
head to foot as he took several steps backward. Was it his imagination
or did the greenery cower before him? He shook his head and slowly
backed toward the barn, facing the woods the whole time. He wasn't
sure what had happened, but he wasn't about to be taken unawares
again.

"So you found her?" a voice rang out, startling him. He wheeled around. Abazi, hands on her hips, looked annoyed. He never thought he'd be glad to see her, but he was. "Good," she went on, giving him a strange look. "I've got to get home or my dad will worry."

"But not your mom?" he asked, saying the first words that came to mind.

"My mom's dead." She grabbed a writhing Gypsy and headed back toward the house. Gabe could only stare after her as she walked away, an arrogant jut of her hip marking each step. When she was out of sight, he sank to his knees, suddenly overwhelmed.

He didn't move when Kimber and Abazi left, nor when Kris and Jer went inside with Gypsy. He was stunned by what had happened in the forest. Had he really been chased, or had it only been the wind mimicking howling moans and the sound of footsteps?

And who was this Hollie, a.k.a. Repulsive? How had she transformed from a baby to a young woman, and so quickly? It was impossible. She must have used a sibling for the baby. That seemed more likely than her morphing from baby to young adult in one day. But then why claim that she wasn't an *ugly* baby; that the others had found her appealing? How could she know they'd thought that unless she'd been inside the house, as the baby? A real baby couldn't have communicated all that information. But, Gabe recalled, Repulsive hadn't been a normal baby.

So what the heck was Hollie? Some kind of mutant? The possibility was certainly something to consider. On the drive out to Maine, Gabe had read a book Grandma May had bought him and his brothers about the strange people and places of New England. The authors had devoted several pages to reports of reclusive families hiding themselves from the rest of the world. One family had blue skin, another sprouted noses like pig snouts. The writers concluded that these traits were most likely the result of genetic mutations passed down from generation to generation.

Hollie might be one of those strange creatures. Her unusual appearance would explain why the townspeople were scared of the woods, and maybe even why there'd been disappearances in the past. Outcasts wouldn't want strangers snooping around. But would they go so far as to kill to keep themselves safe from prying eyes? What about the missing dogs and cats? Were the forest folk responsible for those disappearances, too?

Dame Hazel, the person Hollie had said was interested in Gabe, was yet another enigma. Was she the old woman who had fetched Repulsive, the one who'd warned him to stay out of the woods? And why was someone he'd never met before yesterday so interested in him?

And last, what had happened to Abazi's mother?

These uncomfortable, and seemingly unanswerable, questions plagued him like a swarm of black flies as he sat on the soft grass, plucking at the green strands, one by one. A cool breeze picked up, lifting the hair off his forehead and soothing his hot skin.

He'd just started to relax, to let down his guard, when he heard the voice.

Gabrielll... Come to me, Gabrielll...

He didn't hesitate this time. Jumping to his feet, he ran as fast as he could to the house. Whatever it was, it couldn't get him there.

Could it?

Chapter Ten

The Visitor

"Cat got your tongue?" Kris asked. The three brothers were eating an extra slice of blueberry pie a la mode as a treat for getting the barn painted. Since Gabe had returned to the house, Gypsy had attached herself to her savior and was curled up at his feet purring like mad and batting lazily at Gabe's shoelaces.

He looked up from his plate. For the last several minutes, he'd been pushing bits of crust around and around, unable to forget his experience in the woods. "Huh?"

"You haven't said a word since you came in. That's totally unlike you, spaz. Usually we can't shut you up."

Gabe shrugged. Each new event that happened made it more difficult to come clean with the whole strange story. *Do you know that baby you guys don't remember? Well, I met her in the woods today. She's no longer a baby, if she ever really was one, and she talked to me. She doesn't really look quite human and she told me that something is after me. Then I was chased by that something. Well, I think I was, because I never actually saw anything. But it talked to me, and actually called me by name.*

Uh, no. Best to keep his mouth shut.

Kris gave him a speculative look. "So I figured out what's missing from the barn." He kept his voice low so that Mom, who was washing dishes, wouldn't hear. "It was a chest," he went on. "An old wooden one with designs carved into the wood. It was pretty fancy looking."

"What was in it?" Jer asked, leaning closer.

"I don't know. It was locked. That's why I borrowed it from the turret. Figured I could try and open it somehow. But now it's gone. I wonder who took it."

"Well, it couldn't have been Kimber," Jer said. "She was never out of my sight."

"I'll bet she wasn't," Kris snickered, and Jer scowled at him.

"I wouldn't put it past Abazi," Gabe muttered.

"What's your problem with her, anyway?" Kris asked. "I think she's cool."

"She's all right, I guess," Gabe backed off. This was not a topic he was going to get into, not with his brothers. Give them an inch and they'd rip off his arm. "I didn't see her leaving with anything, though, so I guess we can rule her out."

"Then it must be our visitor with the weird feet," Kris deduced.

Gabe nodded absently, a new thought occurring to him. Could Hollie have gotten into the house and left the footprints in the turret? If so, how had she done it? Both of the doors had been locked…except the back one, Gabe suddenly remembered. The baby could've been a distraction, allowing Hollie to sneak into the turret, unnoticed.

It was a good theory, but it still didn't answer his questions. What did she want from him? Why had she come to check him out? 'Dame Hazel is so interested in ye, always has been,' she had said. 'I want to know why.' The strangest part was when she remarked, 'We've met before!' But he was pretty sure they hadn't—a face like that a person would remember. Still, she seemed quite positive. So why had she been evasive afterwards, when he'd started asking questions? Why bring something up and then not tell him anything more? Maybe she'd meant to elaborate, but couldn't because his unseeable pursuer had interrupted.

The more he thought about it, the more he figured he and Hollie had probably met during one of his visits to the farm when he'd been younger. Maybe she lived in a house in the woods and had come to visit and he hadn't been very nice to her. He could see that happening. She had a way of pushing his buttons.

"Maybe our visitor is a mutant raccoon," he finally ventured. He needed his brothers to stop thinking of their intruder as human, at least until he was ready to tell them everything. "I've heard of stranger things."

Jer shook his head ferociously. "No way! The prints we saw were too big for even a mutant raccoon, more the size of a bear, I think. Bears are known to have human-like footprints."

"How did a bear get into the house, dipwad?" Kris challenged. "And without us noticing?"

"When you're into your stupid experiments you wouldn't notice a spaceship landing on your head and little spacemen climbing up your nose," Jer accused.

Kris considered this. "You could be right. But Mom would've noticed. You can't get anything past her."

"Noticed what?" she asked, coming up behind Kris. She smelled lemony and was drying her hands on a dishtowel.

He played it cool. "If we had a bear in the house."

"Very funny. What are you guys really talking about?"

Gabe looked away. He was a terrible liar. Always had been. He couldn't stand breaking the rules, and if he did break one, he always ended up confessing. Or worse, his mom simply knew when he was lying. She said he tended to look everywhere but at her when he was making the attempt.

Kris, on the other hand, could lie like a rug if he wanted to. He rarely did, though. He thought lies were for sissies. The truth was often more unbelievable, anyway, and therefore more of a challenge. Jer's approach to getting away with murder was to baffle the person with his own twisted form of logic. He was very good at it.

"Gabe?" Mom questioned. She knew, of course, that her oldest son was the easiest target.

"We found a strange footprint in the barn. We were just wondering what kind of animal it could be. Maybe we could check out the woods, see if we can track it?" It wasn't a lie, but he was definitely dodging the truth by throwing this red herring out there.

Mom took the bait. "You are *not* to go in those woods!" She glanced out the screen door at the dark line of trees. "The forest is too big; the trees go on for hundreds of acres. It's just too easy to get lost." He noticed she was breathing funny.

"Okay, Mom," the three boys replied. Nobody actually said the words, "I won't ever go into the woods, Mom." All they'd actually said was, 'Okay.' Jer had taught them that trick. Never commit yourself to an action you can't promise not to undertake.

"Now finish up here and wash your plates like good little boys. Dad's in bed and I'm going to do some more cleaning in the cellar." Dad had gone to bed early, leaving Mom fidgety and anxious. The new medication he was taking had upset his stomach. *And he'd been doing so well,* Gabe thought mournfully.

They did as they were told, waiting for her to gather up her cleaning bucket and head downstairs before renewing their conversation.

"I think we should set a trap!" Kris suggested, his brown eyes wide with excitement.

Gabe shook his head. He was afraid of what they might catch. "We might hurt one of the kittens."

Kris scowled, his hand on the door, ready to go outside. "It doesn't have to be a painful one...just a tricky one. Like flour on the floor, or something."

"That's a great idea!" Jer exclaimed. He was all for anything that involved espionage.

Gabe decided he'd better compromise before they got too suspicious. "Fine. You guys work on your trap. I'm going to fix those barn windows."

"The flour won't take long to do," Jer said, rooting around in the cupboard. "When we're done, we'll help you with the windows."

Gabe realized he was actually starting to like the sound of the flour idea. He definitely wanted to know if the creature was continuing to visit the house unnoticed, especially while he was sleeping.

"Dangit!" Jer grumbled, sitting back on his haunches. "There's hardly any left." He shoved the depleted sack back into the cupboard and went over to the fridge to add flour to the grocery list. Mom tended to freak out if she found out that they knew a household item was low or out and didn't put it on the list. She was a demanding woman, their mother.

"It's already on the list," Jer reported. "I wrote donuts instead. Maybe she'll buy them thinking Dad wants them."

"Genius!" Kris cheered, then snapped his fingers. "Speaking of genius...we can use dirt instead of flour! That way the trap won't look so obvious. There's that pile by the garden."

"You guys fetch the wheelbarrow, and I'll get shovels," Gabe said quickly.

Full of enthusiasm for their mission, they headed out the door and were soon spreading dirt in front of the barn doors, by the front steps of the house, near several of the cellar casement windows, and finally, by the small door leading into the turret.

"I still wish we could set a few snares," Kris grumbled when they were done. "Could've caught me some rabbits!"

"The last time you set a snare," Jer reminded him, "you caught a little kid. I can't believe you managed to lure Booger Johnson in by promising him a cookie."

Kris grinned. "Oh, yeah. That was pretty funny. I can still picture it in my head... Poor little Booger swinging back and forth, hanging in the air by one foot, finger up his nose and screaming like a stuck pig. Even though it cost me a whole bag of Oreos to shut him up, I deemed it a successful experiment." He shook his head and sighed wistfully. "Those were the days, my friends."

"I thought they'd never end!" Jer sang. "When we turned Booger into a piñata! He struggled and he screamed, he wet his pants, he did..."

"Those were the days!" Gabe finished in a falsetto. "Oh, yes, those were the days!"

All three burst out laughing, pushing and shoving each other as they staggered about, clutching their stomachs. When they finally settled down to a few shuddering sighs, they put away the wheelbarrow and went to work washing and fixing the broken barn windows, using a lightbulb in a cage for light. The sun had already set when their mom called them in. She fixed them a snack, ruffling their hair and joking with them. Gabe could tell she was very pleased that they'd finished the barn.

When they were heading off to bed, his mom called him back. "Say, Gabe?" He turned around. "Could you make another run into town tomorrow? Woodlands has already sold out of the blueberries you brought in."

"*Already?*"

"It's those tourists," she explained. "They can't seem to get enough of 'em." She smiled wearily. "I'll get up early tomorrow to package up what your brothers picked the other day and make some more blueberry jam. We're almost out of flour, though, so I won't be able to bake any more muffins."

"Yeah, I know," he said without thinking. She frowned. "Um, Jer was looking for something in the cupboards."

She nodded absently, abnormally satisfied with his explanation. Gabe often thought his mom should have worked as a spy. She typically never missed a beat.

"Well, could you pick up some more? Maybe get the rest of the stuff on the list, too. We can't keep doing all this running back and forth with gas prices so high. I would've gotten more things yesterday, but with your dad..." She trailed off, looking up at the ceiling as though searching him out in his bed to check on him.

"Is he going to be all right?" he asked, hesitantly.

She nodded briskly. "Oh, yes. Just a minor setback. I think once he adjusts to the new medication he'll be better than before." Her face was bright, but her eyes were not. She looked tired. "Anyway, why don't you get yourself to bed?"

He nodded. "Goodnight, Mom."

She pulled him to her and gave him a hug, then stood on her tippy toes, made him bend over, and kissed him on the forehead like she'd done since he was a little boy. "Goodnight, Gabie Baby." He blushed and hoped fervently she'd never call him his special nickname in front of Abazi. It was bad enough she did it in front of his brothers. Luckily, they had their own corny nicknames—Jer Bear and Kris Bliss. "Now scootch!" She waved him off.

As he was heading down the hallway, he glanced back over his shoulder to see his mom still standing at the kitchen table staring off into space. He looked away. He hated seeing her like this. He wished, somehow, that he could help her out more, but he didn't know what to do.

He was unlocking the second of the two doors to the turret when he heard a shuffling noise by his feet. Images of nasty, bloodthirsty rats leaped into his mind and his hands started to shake.

"Meeewww!" came a little voice from down below and Gabe's shoulders dropped with relief. It was only Gypsy. "What are you doing here?" He bent over to pick her up. "You're supposed to be with your siblings." Gypsy started to purr, clinging stubbornly to Gabe's shirt. "Fine. You can sleep with me tonight. To be honest, I wouldn't mind the company."

Once upstairs, Gabe stripped down and donned his favorite San Francisco t-shirt and a pair of old gym shorts. Despite being so high up, the turret was surprisingly cool, which was great because Gabe easily overheated. His mom often joked that his blood must be magma. Snuggling under the covers, Gypsy joined Gabe, settling in right by his ear. The warm body and the sound of purring lulled Gabe to sleep within seconds.

Hours later, he sat up, wide awake. He'd heard something. Thousands of tiny bumps erupted on the surface of his chilled skin as he scanned the room. He wasn't one to wake easily. The noise must either have been very loud, or very insistent, especially for him to notice it over the hum of the fish tank.

"Meeewww! Meeewww!"

Gypsy. But she wasn't in bed; she was over on the far side of the room, close to the bookshelf. Gabe gulped when he realized he was going to have to leave his safe, warm bed and go after the kitten. Gypsy sounded quite piteous, giving Gabe little choice.

He placed his reluctant feet on the wood floor and crept over to the bookshelf. The closer he got, the louder the noise became, but it wasn't Gypsy making it. The sound was muffled, far away, yet quite obviously something more than just the wind or the creaking of an old house. Someone was trying to open the little door. Was it Hollie? Dame Hazel? Or that other one…the one who had called his name? Maybe it was *them*, the ones who were after him. He snatched up Gypsy and backed away from the bookshelf. Soon he was under his covers, clutching the warm kitten tightly to his chest, senses ticking like a time bomb.

Even though he was pretty sure the sounds stopped not long after he returned to bed, there was no way he was going down that pole, alone and at three a.m., to make sure. He spent the rest of the night staring at the bookshelf, waiting for it to open. Gypsy, of course, went directly back to sleep.

The moment the first ray of light shone into one of the east-facing windows, Gabe was out of bed, and together he and Gypsy hightailed it downstairs. Gabe fed the cats and then fixed some breakfast for himself. When he had somewhat satisfied his hunger, he set to work measuring out the blueberries into the green cardboard pint containers. He needed something to do while he waited for his brothers to wake up, plus he was helping his mom at the same time. This alone, he figured with a grin, should push him into the favorite son position.

Two hours after Gabe came down, his dad shuffled into the room. He wore his favorite pine green terry cloth robe and a pair of ratty old slippers they'd given him for Christmas several years ago. He looked at Gabe in surprise. "What are you doing up?"

Gabe had already cleaned up and put the packaged blueberries into cardboard boxes. Wiping his hands on a towel, he answered casually, "Oh, I couldn't sleep. Thought maybe I'd go for a run."

Dad beamed. "I could time you."

Gabe gave a cautious nod, not wanting to get his hopes up. "How are you feeling?"

"I don't know what happened, but I feel great! Grandma's tea really cleaned me out last night. I felt like I was getting roto rootered." He laughed. "The funny thing is, I feel full of energy today. And I'm starving!"

Gabe grinned. His dad did look good. "I'll whip you up some pancakes. There are a few extra blueberries. I'll make some for everybody." The smell should get his brothers out of bed quickly. Energized, he got to cooking while his dad measured out his insulin for the meal, then scanned the town paper Grandpa Hawthorne had brought over when he visited.

"Says here there's a job opening at Woodlands." He tapped the paper. "Flexible hours. Good pay. You should give it a try."

Gabe felt his good mood deflate. "I don't know, Dad. There's an awful lot to be done around here."

"Your mom said you guys have finished a lot of your work these last few days. She's real proud of you, Gabe." Gabe blushed, remembering all the complaining he'd done while working. "You don't have to work too many hours, it says, and you'd be able to earn some pocket change.

Maybe start saving for college again."

"I'll look into it," Gabe replied, busying himself with making orange juice while the bacon, eggs, and pancakes cooked. He thought about the job as he flipped the bacon. Working with Bossy Abazi was the last thing he wanted to do, but the idea of having his own money was appealing. He wouldn't rule it out.

Dad inhaled deeply. "Smells like you're about done. I'll go fetch the lazybones."

"Don't bother," Gabe replied. "I think I hear them now."

Kris and Jer came pounding down the stairs and into the room, followed by their yawning mom. "What's going on?" she asked, taking in the scene.

"Gabe made breakfast," his dad announced proudly.

"You packaged the blueberries, too," she said quietly, gazing steadily at Gabe. He looked away. "What's wrong?" His mother tended to be suspicious when anyone did anything nice without being asked. Typically she had good reason to be.

"I couldn't sleep," he said quickly. "Gypsy kept waking me up." That was the truth, but again, only part of it.

"Don't look a gift horse in the mouth, Mom," Kris told her. "Or it might end up biting you in the butt."

She gave him an amused look. "More likely it would be my nose."

"Probably. But I like saying butt." She shook her head as she pulled out a chair.

Jer poured the orange juice into juice glasses, shaking his head in awe. "He made bacon and he didn't burn it this time! He even used my trick of adding pepper to one side to bring out the flavor. Wow!"

Gabe had burned the bacon one time, and had never heard the end of it after that. It wasn't his fault he'd gotten caught up in his favorite TV show and had forgotten to flip the strips.

Before long, everyone was tucking in. These days they rarely enjoyed a hot breakfast, typically only cereal or toast. Mom wasn't much of a morning person. If they got one, it came from Dad, and he'd been too sick to make anything for a long time. Gabe missed those morning times. He missed what they meant and the security the warm food in the morning made him feel.

But now, seeing the color in his dad's cheeks and the way he was putting away the pancakes, Gabe started to feel a little hope. Dad looked really good. Maybe things were finally starting to return to normal.

"So how about that run?" Dad asked. He wiped his mouth with a cloth napkin and pushed back his chair. "I'll go fetch the stopwatch."

The boys watched him go, each with a pleased expression on his face. "He looks good, doesn't he, Mom?" Kris asked. "Maybe this new medicine will work better for him. Not make him so sleepy all the time."

"That's the idea," she replied, sipping her juice. "All we can do is hope and pray for the best." She picked up her plate. "Well, I'm off to shower. I'll clean up this mess later."

When she was gone, Gabe jumped to his feet. "Come on!" he yelled to his brothers. "Quick, before Dad comes back."

Jer frowned and Kris shoveled a few more bites into his mouth. "What's going on?" he asked around a mouthful.

"I heard something last night. Outside. Gypsy kept meowing at it."

"Ahh…" Jer nodded knowingly. "So that's why you're up so early. I figured there had to be something."

"Just come on!"

After one last forkful, Kris left his plate and followed after Gabe and Jer. They hurried over to the small door. Eager to see what story the dirt had to tell, they pushed their way through the shrubs, earning several scratches for their troubles. The dirt, spread out in a thin layer, covered several square feet of space. Right in the middle were two prints, exactly like the ones they'd seen in the barn and in the turret room.

"Looks like our bear is back," joked Kris. "Let's check out the other traps."

At each spot, they found more prints in the dirt. Strangely—disturbingly—several came in different sizes and looked more like boot prints than bare feet.

Gabe felt his blood go cold when he realized what this meant. There was more than one of them. And he highly doubted they were looking for Gypsy.

Chapter Eleven

These Woods Have
Got to Go

The brothers were quiet heading back to the house. Dad met them on the way out, spinning the stopwatch around his finger. "Why the long faces, guys? Does Kris have bad gas again?"

Jer laughed loudly, slapping his knee. He loved this story. When they were little kids they had camped out in tents Mom had set up in Kris and Jer's bedroom. Because they had only the two tents, Kris and Jer ended up sharing one of them. In the middle of the night, Kris started farting so badly that the stench woke his three-year-old brother, who proceeded to try and escape. When Dad came to check on them before bed, he heard Jer call out, "Help me!" his voice tiny and weak. Apparently, the zipper was stuck and he couldn't get out. Dad rescued Jer, who decided to bed down *outside* the tent for the rest of the night. Kris slept through it all.

The fart story had grown to be a legend in their family.

"I'm ready to go, Dad," Gabe said with a smile—he'd been sleeping in the other tent at the time. "I just need to stretch a bit."

Dad readjusted his Red Sox baseball cap. "Maybe I'll stretch with you. Can't have all those pancakes going straight to my gut." He patted his flat stomach. Despite the medications he was taking and the lack of exercise, he'd somehow managed to maintain his physique. Though probably only because he'd lost a lot of weight before the operation, and now, didn't eat much.

"Can I run, too?" Jer asked, batting his dark lashes charmingly.

"Sure, kiddo," Dad grinned and Gabe had to stifle a frustrated groan that struggled to be heard. He never got to spend alone time with Dad. His little brothers were always tagging along. But he didn't want to ruin things so he bit his lip instead.

"Me, too!" Kris put in.

The half hour Gabe had figured they'd spend together turned into an hour and a half. Dad was enjoying himself so much that Gabe didn't have the heart to end the fun, nor did he really want to. When he thought he might puke his guts out, his dad called it a day, which was probably a good thing since they still had the shed to clean out. Having finished their last race, Jer and Kris ran ahead to the house to change out of their sweaty clothes while Gabe stayed behind with Dad.

"You're running really fast, Gabe," Dad said. "You haven't lost a second of speed. You've maybe even gained a millisecond."

Panting and gripping his knees, Gabe managed a grin. "It won't be long before you'll be out here running with me."

His dad nodded thoughtfully. "You know, I think you're right."

Inside, Gabe headed upstairs to shower while his dad joined Mom, who was making blueberry jam. Dad considered himself to be the official jar tightener and allowed no one else to move in on his job, which, of course, no one else wanted.

"What took you so long?" Kris demanded when he showed up at the shed.

"I actually took a shower, dorkwad. You guys only faked washing up."

Kris grinned. "True."

So…" Gabe said slowly, grabbing a stack of newspapers from the 1990s and dumping them into a cardboard box to be recycled. "What do you think is going on with all those footprints?"

"We've been talking about that," Jer spoke up. "We think it could be neighbor kids."

"Neighbor kids?" Gabe echoed in disbelief. "The only neighbors we have are Kimber and Abazi. From what I can see out the turret, there aren't any other houses for miles, other than Grandma May's. That's an awful long way for kids to come just to spy on us." Which reminded him…where did Hollie actually live? Up in the mountains?

"This is Maine," Kris reminded him. "What else is there to do?"

True. "Listen," Gabe said, making a decision. "There's something I've got to tell you guys. But you have to promise not to laugh. Okay?"

Jer and Kris nodded solemnly. Gabe shook his head. "Say it."

Jer grinned while he and Kris intoned, "I promise not to laugh at my wacko brother."

Gabe moved to sit down on an old tractor tire. "Well…" Two loud honks interrupted him.

"What the heck?" Jer ran to the shed door. "We have company. Whoa! You won't believe this!"

The other two boys quickly joined him. "Holy canoli, would you look at that!" Kris whistled. "It's a Hummer, H2 SUT! But it's *pink*," he muttered, his eyebrows drawn together in dismay, the experience completely ruined for him.

They were checking out the vehicle when a blond woman slid out of the driver's side. She was very attractive, Gabe thought, instinctively looking her up and down. His brothers must have thought so, too—they both stared at her like she was a bowl of strawberry ice cream on a hot summer day.

Crisp and efficient in pink Capri pants and a white blouse, she marched up the porch steps and knocked briskly on the screen door. A moment later, Mom appeared, opening the door without a word. The woman disappeared inside.

"Come on!" Kris hissed and slipped out of the shed. As quietly as they could, they tiptoed up the steps and scooched in close to the screen door. Gabe leaned forward as far as he could. He could see his mother and the stranger facing each other.

"Of course I remember you, Candi," he heard Mom saying. She didn't sound happy about the memory, and Gabe wondered why. Candi looked like a nice enough person to him. "You were a year ahead of me in school, I believe."

"I suppose I'm hard to forget." Candi smirked. "I was captain of the boy's basketball cheerleading squad, Class President, voted prettiest hair, and I was the lead in the senior play. I always kept my finger in many pies!"

"I definitely remember *that* about you." The tone of Mom's voice veered on sarcastic. "So, to what do I owe this, um, pleasure?" She was really struggling.

"Why, I'm here to welcome you back, Ayla." Candi waved a well-manicured hand at Mom.

"Oh?" she replied, not impressed.

"And, well, to ask you a favor."

"Ahhh…" Their mother was being very conservative with her words, which usually meant trouble.

"Well, you've heard the plans about the forest, right? Cornelia Deacon has been getting the word out." No reply. "So you haven't heard anything?"

"I've been rather busy, Candi. Keith has been ill."

"Oh, yes. I heard about Keith. Poor guy." She didn't sound as though she meant it. "I remember when he danced with me at prom. Of course, everyone wanted to dance with me. I wore a pink dress and was voted prom queen. That was the best night of my whole life." She sighed wistfully. "So what's wrong with him?"

Mom bit her bottom lip. "He had transplant surgery."

"It's not from something catching, is it? I mean, I have the constitution of a horse, but there are the kids. Jake Jr. and little Jen-Jen are in so many sports. Their teams can't afford to lose them for any length of time."

"He has diabetes."

"He got *fat?*"

Mom stifled a curse and Gabe could tell she was working very hard not to slap some sense into the woman. "You went to school with him, Candi! He has Type I diabetes, remember? Mr. Moroney dedicated an entire class period to it!" Candi looked blank. Mom sighed. "It means his pancreas doesn't work, and it's not catching."

"Oh, well, that's a relief." She paused. "A *whole* class period? I don't remember that at all. I must have been absent that day." She laughed. "Anyhoo, as I was saying…there are plans in the making to clear the forest. I'm the top realtor in town so the townspeople decided to put me in charge of everything. I guess they knew I'd get the job done."

"What do you mean? You can't clear the forest, Candi!"

"Ayla, Ayla!" Candi gave her most winning smile, all bleached white teeth and pink lipstick. "We can, and we will. The place is a hazard. Nobody seems to own the land. I mean, there was some kind of trust fund set up years ago, which has been paying the property taxes on it, but I'm sure we can do something about that. A good lawyer, which my husband, Dick, happens to be, can make all that go away. Ranger is expanding, Ayla. We could become rich off that land! Hotels, restaurants, a nice theater, a little wine shop, a better road! All right on the ocean. Ranger would be spectacular."

"You can't do that," Mom echoed weakly. "You just can't."

Candi didn't seem to hear her. "So we need your help. You grew up here. You know the woods. I want you to guide some assessors around the place, help them get a feel for the size and scope of the land. We'll pay you for your time, of course."

"How can you ask me that after what happened?"

"Oh, that! That was years ago! I'm sure he's recovered by now…"

Gabe tensed. What were they talking about? More importantly, who?

"I won't do it, Candi."

"But it's for the town! You'd be helping out a lot of people."

"Like you," Mom accused.

Candi's voice hardened. "I'm trying to make Ranger a better place to live, Ayla. That's not a crime. Think of your father-in-law, your own mother. The increased business would set them up for life."

"They don't want that kind of life."

Candi sighed, rolling her close-set eyes. "I'd forgotten what an innocent you always were. So naïve." She gave Mom another fake smile
with her perfect white teeth. "Well, it looks like I'll have to dig up *something* to change your mind."

The kitchen grew awfully quiet and Gabe leaned in closer. Footsteps
sounded and Dad entered the kitchen from the cellar. "I found the
pectin for the jam," he announced, holding out several little boxes.

"Why, Keith!" Candi exclaimed, her face a contrast of studied con-
cern and difficult to conceal curiosity. "I heard you were sick!" Dad
turned to face her. He looked confused. "You poor, poor thing. You
certainly don't look sick," she purred, reaching out and placing her
hand on Dad's arm. Gabe's eyes widened. Was she actually putting the
moves on Dad, right in front of Mom?

Oh, she was so dead.

"Who are you?" Dad asked, his tone sharp.

Candi gave a nervous, fluttery laugh. "Why, it's me! Candi! We
danced at prom together!" Her heavily made-up eyes narrowed to slits
as she brushed back her highlighted blond hair. "I guess that surgery
you had affected your mind."

Dad nodded. "Ahh… I remember you now. Candi Mara."

She brightened. "Well, it's Morrigan now." She flashed a large diamond ring at him.

"You were always trying to get me to date you…" Dad went on,
oblivious.

Candi's blue eyes widened. "I was not! I… Oh, you're just kidding!
You always were a teaser, you silly thing." Gabe thought Dad didn't
look the least like he was joking.

"Well, I have a house to show so I shall leave you to your *domestic* du-
ties." She waved a dismissive hand at the canning jars. "Call me if you
change your mind. Ciao!" She fluttered her long pink nails and the
boys scurried down the steps, gaining only just enough time to lean
against the railing and try to look nonchalant before she came out.

"Hello, boys," Candi trilled as she clattered down the steps in her
pink heels. She didn't seem surprised to see them. "Who'd like to earn
some money?"

"I would." Kris stepped forward.

"Well, aren't you a strapping young man." She peered at him over her
white, oversized sunglasses.

"He doesn't know the woods, Candi," Mom called through the
screen. "None of them do."

Candi pouted. "In that case, I'm outta here. Bye, boys." She flounced down the last of the steps, leaving them to watch her climb into her pink Hummer. Without bothering with a seatbelt, she took off in a roar.

"You can put your eyes back in your head," Mom said dryly. The three of them turned around to look at her.

"But it's a Hummer, Mom!" Kris protested. "Even if it is *pink*."

She smiled, reaching down to ruffle his Mohawk. Once again, Kris had said the right thing. "All right, gang. Let's get back to work. Kris and Jer, I want you to finish cleaning that shed. After that, more blueberries please." There was some good-natured grumbling, but she ignored it, as usual. "Gabe, could you head to the store now? I want to make more muffins while it's still relatively cool." She looked at the woods, her expression far away, then she and Dad went back inside, talking in low tones. She made no comment about her typically nosy sons, who hadn't asked a thing about the hot Mrs. Morrigan.

When they were gone, Kris turned to Gabe. "So what were you going to tell us before Blondie showed up?"

Gabe shook his head. "There's not enough time. I'll tell you when I get back."

"You'd better," threatened Kris, pointing a finger at Gabe. "Because I won't be able to think about anything else until then."

Gabe promised and headed into the house to fetch the boxes of blueberries and still-warm jam, quickly loading up the back of the truck. Before he left, his mother told him to pass along that the jam still needed to cool and set, but should be ready to sell tomorrow.

"Oh, and tell Mozi—he's the one who owns Woodlands, by the way—we need to set up a delivery system for the muffins. I don't want to be driving into town every day."

Gabe nodded. "Got it."

"And say hello for me. We went to high school together. I always liked Mozi. He's Abazi's father, by the way."

Gabe had already figured that out. "Done and done, Herr Kommandant," he replied, giving his mom a mock salute.

She cuffed him upside the head. "Go on now, and watch that stoplight on the hill. And don't forget the grocery list." She snatched it off the fridge and handed it to him along with two twenties she'd left on the counter.

Grabbing the keys off the hook by the door, he strolled toward the truck feeling surprisingly light-hearted. He was going to be getting away from the woods for a while. It was a good feeling. He slid into the warm cab and quickly lifted his legs to avoid burning them on the seat. That's when something in the passenger seat sprung up beside him.

"Greetings, Gabriel!"

He suffered a mini heart attack. "What the heck are you doing in here, Hollie? Get down!" His heart, once it had kicked back in, was now beating wildly. She made a face at him, but did as she was told, crouching on the floor of the truck. Luckily, Jer and Kris were already working in the shed and hadn't seen a thing.

With a shaking hand, Gabe managed to start up the truck and head down the driveway without mishap. When they reached the part of the drive that passed under the trees, he slowed down and glared at his passenger. She had popped back up and was now sitting on the seat looking quite pleased with herself.

"So...?" he prompted. She was busy examining the insides of the old truck, fumbling with knobs and digging her bare toes into the small hole in the floorboard at her feet. He gasped. He recognized those long, narrow toes. "It was you! In the turret and in the barn. And you were snooping around the house last night. I thought so!" He said this last part half to himself, feeling quite triumphant that he'd figured it out.

"Not just me," she replied nonchalantly, though she watched him carefully as she said it.

He stared at her, feeling a chill. "Then who else? Why do you keep coming back here? What do you want?"

She gave the smallest of shrugs, her green shift lifting slightly. "I told ye, Gabriel. Dame Hazel is interested in ye and I want to know why."

"Well, me, too. I also want to know where we met before."

"Ah, that!" Her green eyes lit up. "Now that's an interesting story!"

He waited for her to begin, but she seemed to have no inclination to do anything of the sort; her eyes were focused on the road ahead and she was humming a strange tune, her feet dangling happily. She seemed to be enjoying the ride.

"Okay, then, who are the others you were talking about?"

"Some are of me own sort," she casually explained. "Some are of the other..."

Gabe gulped, his foot lifting off the gas. The truck drifted to a stop and he quickly stomped on the clutch and brake, letting the engine idle. "Of the other? What do you mean? Who? Those things that were chasing me yesterday? When I saw you in the woods?"

Hollie shrugged. "Ye're wanted by all sorts, Gabriel. It's a mystery to me as to why. I'm just as bamboozled by it all as ye are."

"I really don't think that's possible," he replied dryly. "I mean, I don't even know if you're one of the good guys or the bad guys."

Hollie wasn't listening. She was looking out his window, her strange eyes squinting as they darted about searching for something he couldn't see. Finally her gaze settled on one spot and Gabe followed the line of her sight to see what had caught her attention. They had visitors. Several dark figures emerged stealthily from the woods on his side of the road. They moved like wild predators, fast and with a violent determination to catch their prey. No one in the group was very tall, yet their black cloaks and hidden faces screamed of malice and intimidation.

"Um, Hollie..." She looked his way. "Are these your sort, or...?"

Her thin little face sharpened as she shook her head in denial. "Go, Gabriel!" she cried. "Make this metal contraption move now!"

In his panic, he let out the clutch too soon and the truck bucked and died. The figures were close to them now, gliding across the ground like puppets on a string. Within seconds, they had surrounded the truck. A thin, almost skeletal hand reached into the open window and Gabe knocked the pale, grasping thing away.

Gabe's hand took on a life of its own, jerking and spasming as he tried to turn the key. "Come on!" he begged the truck. "Start!"

Gabriel! Come, Gabriel!

The voice sounded malevolent, threatening, not like the other one at all. He immediately knew this voice wasn't the same one he'd heard on his run or by the hedge, and he felt no urge to go to it. In fact, the hideous voice made him want to run home and stick his head under his pillow.

"Get back, ye dregs!" Hollie shouted, striking at the cloaked figures with the solid knob at the end of a short stick. Polished and decorated with leaves and berries, the club looked like a work of art. Despite its fancy appearance, however, the cudgel was an effective weapon. "His blood is not for the likes of ye!" Screeches, like that of an angry eagle, rattled Gabe's ears as the wood made contact with briefly exposed patches of rough, pale skin.

Gabe looked around. More of the ghastly creatures poured like beetles from the boundaries of the woods. Too many to fight. Soon there would be no way out. He turned his attention back to the key, struggling to make it turn.

"Stay back!" Hollie warned the attackers. "Don't make me come out there after ye! Ye'll be feelin' the sting of me bata until it rains on ye in hell!"

Finally the key rotated into place and the truck roared to life. Gabe's leg quivered like a plucked rubber band as he let up on the clutch and punched down the gas. The vehicle sprang forward and the creatures leaped out of the way, howling and hissing at him. The truck tore down the drive.

The dark figures fled, but then the trees themselves appeared to close in on the truck, threatening to cut off the way entirely.

"Faster, Gabriel!" Hollie shouted, shaking her cudgel, or bata, as she'd called it.

The wind blew back tangles of her reddish hair, revealing a narrow forehead crumpled in anger and fear. The force of the air pouring in through the window pulled back the pointed tips of her delicate, thin-skinned ears. Branches scraped the truck like desperate claws. Sunlight faded and soon they were trapped in a tunnel of darkness. Gabe was driving blind now; his vision blocked by trunks and branches. They weren't going to make it through the thicket of wood; they were going to be crushed. Gabe clenched the steering wheel tightly and prepared himself for impact.

It didn't come. The light returned, flooding the cab, as the truck broke free of the wooded realm like a charging bull. Gabe saw the main road up ahead and punched the gas again. A quick glance in the rearview mirror shocked him. The way behind them was clear; the drive was empty. No trees, no little goblins—or whatever those things had been. Nothing.

"Ye can let me out here," Hollie told him, tapping her bata on the truck's dashboard like a conductor bringing the orchestra to attention.

He stopped the truck, but kept his feet on the petals, ready to take off if need be. "What just happened back there?"

"We had visitors." She put her hand on the door handle. "I best be goin' now."

"Do you live close by? I didn't see any houses from my window." Gabe was fishing for information, but Hollie wasn't falling for that.

"I live close enough," she replied as she scanned the line of trees. On the other side of the main road, the tree-covered mountain began, erupting from the earth like a pirate's craggy tooth.

"But what about those...*things*? Won't they come after you?"

She gave him a luminous smile, revealing surprisingly strong, even teeth. For some reason he'd expected rotting stumps to match his mutant theory. "Why, Gabriel. Ye care about me! I was hopin' ye had goodness in ye."

He frowned. He wasn't sure about goodness. He just knew that he'd feel terrible if something happened to her and he hadn't done anything to prevent it. "I could give you a ride home, you know. I don't mind."

She laughed. "I don't think ye can get there-ah from here-ah." She spoke the words with a broad Maine accent, sounding eerily like Grandpa Hawthorne. "But thanks all the same, Gabriel."

A scary thought occurred to Gabe. "Um, not to sound totally self-centered," he started, "but how am *I* going to get back home? Won't they try to get me again?"

"We're on the lookout for ye this time, Gabriel. Don't ye worry about that."

"Why were they after us in the first place?"

Hollie's moss-colored eyes sparkled. "They weren't after me. They were after ye, ye knob. Maybe they thought ye'd make better eatin' than cats and dogs."

Gabe blanched. "You're kidding, right?"

"Just keep those kittens inside, hm?" She looked around her again, her eyes alert. She didn't seem comfortable being out in the open. "Now go on. Deliver yer goods."

"You're sure you'll be okay?"

She nodded, solemn now. "Just stay out of the woods, Gabriel."

Nodding in return, he pushed down the gas and drove away, his entire frame, from his head to his toes, trembling. Hollie didn't move from where she stood, and he soon lost sight of her as he rounded a bend in the road.

'Better eatin' than cats and dogs…' she'd said.

Holy crap.

Chapter Twelve

Working For a Living

Gabe pulled into an open parking space in front of Woodlands Store, glad to have finally arrived. During the short drive, he'd gone over what had happened to him and Hollie. A lot of different ideas had popped into his head about what was going on, and not one of them related to anything paranormal or mythical. The more he thought about it, the more he realized that this whole thing had to be an elaborate hoax. Most likely Abazi had set up the chase scene. She lived here, she more than likely knew enough kids, and she didn't particularly like him.

Of course, when he'd first heard the voice calling him, he hadn't yet met Abazi. Though maybe that wouldn't have mattered to her. Maybe she picked on anyone new to town. With a sigh, he opened up the back of the truck and grabbed a box of jam. Knowing the jars were still warm, he wrapped his hand around one. The heat and the feel of glass on his skin were soothing, a balm to his shaky nerves.

Finally, realizing someone might be watching—like Abazi—he let go of the jar. This little bit of goodness and normality made him feel better and he entered the store briskly and competently, the little bell announcing his arrival.

Except for a brown-skinned man behind the counter, the store appeared to be empty, the chess players gone. The thickset man was squinting at a receipt held an arm's length away. "Kokwiz!" he muttered. "They print these words smaller every day." He glanced up at Gabe and smiled. "Excuse my French, but I'm getting old."

Gabe flushed, feeling awkward. This had to be Abazi's dad. Like his daughter, he wore his hair in a thick, black braid that lay heavily on his back. His long-sleeved shirt bore a colorful Native print and a watch with a silver band inlaid with turquoise hung loosely about his wrist.

"Um, hi. I brought the jam." He held out the box like an offering.

"Ah, yes! You must be Gabe, Ayla's son." He stepped around the corner. "I'm Maskwamozi, but my paleface friends call me Mozi. Probably because they can't pronounce my real name." He chuckled, his stocky frame shaking with mirth. "Here let me take that." He grabbed hold of the box and studied the jars with a small smile teasing the corners of his mouth. The jars did look nice, Gabe had to admit, with their sky blue lids and a yellow ribbon tied around the rim. Mozi inhaled deeply. "I swear I can smell the jam right through the jars. I hope you've got more of these?"

"Two more boxes, though Mom says the jars have to cool and set before you can sell them. There's also a bunch of fresh blueberries."

"Ah, good man." Mozi smiled, the movement emphasizing a deep scar, shaped like a half-moon, pitting his left cheek. "I'm starting to think your grandfather has been sending the tourists my way. They get bored roughing it and want to spend their hard-earned money, and he gets bored listening to them complain, so he sends them here. I'm sure he tells them they can't truly say they've been to Maine unless they've bought some blueberries."

Gabe grinned. "That sounds like Grandpa, all right."

Mozi set the box on the floor at the back of the store. "Shall we fetch the rest?"

Gabe nodded and together they hauled in the remaining boxes, storing the jam jars on a bare shelf until they could be unpacked in the morning. The blueberry containers went on a table, in the middle of which sat a sign proclaiming, "Eat Like a Mainer…Get the Real Thing!"

It sounded kind of hokey, but tourists liked hokey. Gabe did, too, actually, but he'd never let on to Grandpa. He'd be labeled a Flatlander before he knew it.

"You didn't need to help," Mozi said when they were finished, "but I appreciate it. I'm a little short-handed right now. My last employee left for the big city in search of better things." He chuckled. "I suppose Portland doesn't seem like much of a city to you, coming from San Jose."

Gabe shrugged. "I like Portland. We passed through it on our way to Ranger." The small city had a nice feeling to it, Gabe recalled. He'd especially liked the old, red brick buildings and cobblestone streets. "We stopped for chowder in a tiny café along the waterfront. They served it in huge bread bowls. It was really good."

Mozi laughed loudly. "Leave it to a teenaged boy to focus on the food! Your poor mother."

Gabe ducked his head, not sure how to respond. He'd always thought Indians were calm and quiet, wise and thoughtful. Mozi seemed to be more of the exuberant kind. "Um," he ventured when

Mozi finished laughing, "my dad said you were looking for someone to fill in part-time."

"I sure am. I want Abazi to get more involved in our tribal activities. There's a lodge up north. Her mom died when she was young and I've been so busy with raising her and working the store that I'm afraid I've neglected a few things." He frowned for a moment, his black eyebrows nearly joining together, then they parted and he smiled. "Are you looking for a job?"

"You want me to fill in for Abazi?" Mozi nodded. "Then, sure. I'd be happy to. I had a job back in San Jose. I'm a good worker."

Mozi beamed and slapped Gabe on the back. "I didn't have a doubt about that! Your mom was no slacker, as I recall. Back in our day, she was quite the star here in Ranger."

Gabe had heard the stories many times. Dad wasn't shy talking about what Mom had done. He loved bragging about her. Of course, Dad had been quite the star himself in track, and Mom returned the favor, telling them about Dad's comeback from a broken leg his senior year after the doctors said he would never run again. Gabe loved that story, asking to hear it whenever Dad's health took a turn for the worst. It proved that his dad wasn't a quitter, and reminded Gabe that Dad was going to beat this latest setback, if only through sheer determination.

"So what would you want me to do?" he asked.

"Well, you'd start out stocking shelves and keeping the place tidy. That should be easy enough. When it's slow, I'll show you how to run the register. That isn't too hard, either, although the credit card machine acts up sometimes."

"And Abazi will be at the, um, lodge?"

"As much as I can make her go. She's kinda shy around them, so some bribery might be in order." Gabe didn't think shyness was Abazi's problem. "I'm sure she'll come around. A lot of her mother's family lives up that way."

Gabe smiled to himself. That was exactly what he wanted to hear. "Well, I'm interested, if you want to take me on."

"Why don't we start this coming Sunday? There's a tribal event then. Abazi's aunt is going to pick her up."

"Okay. Oh, my mom was wondering how you want to do deliveries. She doesn't want to be coming into town every day, with the price of gas, I mean." Gabe flushed. Their lack of money was something he was not used to, even after these last couple of years of having to cut back. It was kind of embarrassing to have to be so cheap.

"No problem. I'm not awfully fond of spending all my money on gas, either. Abazi can pick them up in the evening, or one of you can drop them off at our house." Gabe nodded, making a mental note not to be around in the evening, or to find a way to blackmail one of his brothers into making the delivery. Better yet, since Kimber's house was close to Abazi's, he might point this out to Jer and let his brother figure out the rest.

Gabe remembered the shopping list in his pocket. "Do you know where I can find flour?" Mozi directed him toward an aisle and returned to the counter and his pile of receipts. Gabe quickly gathered up the necessary items, deliberating over the donuts Jer had requested before deciding against them. Maybe he could get Jer to make homemade ones.

"Well, I've gotta get back," he said awkwardly after paying for the groceries. He never knew how to end a meeting with someone. He had long since learned that while staring at them might prove effective, it wasn't exactly socially acceptable. "There's a lot to do around the house, you see, and I should try to get most of it done before I start work here."

"I like your attitude," Mozi remarked. "Adio. Wli nanawalmezi. Take care of yourself."

"You, too, Mozi. It was nice meeting you." It was. Mr. Wanibagw was a good guy—very different from his daughter. Gabe wondered how that had happened.

"Likewise, Gabe."

This time Gabe made sure to check out the inside of the truck *before* he entered it. He didn't want any more surprises, like strange creatures trying to hitch a ride home with him. Reassured that nothing was lurking, he climbed into the cab. He was nervous about the trip home...more specifically, about the ride down the driveway. Maybe if he just gunned it and drove really fast, he'd be okay. Hollie had assured him that she and her 'kind' would be looking out for him, but he wasn't sure what they could do to fight off the weird creatures that had chased them. Then again, if this was all a prank, he shouldn't have anything to worry about. Still, it was best not to count on his prank theory. His motto, "Better safe than sorry," had saved him a lot of grief over the years.

When Gabe reached the turn-off, neither Hollie nor her friends were visible. He wasn't sure if this was a good thing or not. He could only hope that her gang was hiding behind trees, laying low. Not wanting to depend on his hopes, Gabe took a deep breath and floored it as he made the turn onto their driveway, spraying loose gravel into the ditch.

The truck roared through the tunnel like a tank. When Gabe burst out on the other side, alive and well, he took his foot off the gas and released the air he'd unconsciously been holding prisoner in his lungs.

He'd made it.

After dropping off the groceries and parking the truck on the side of the barn, went to find his brothers. They had finished cleaning the shed, he was glad to see, and had moved on to blueberry picking.

Kris operated the Shaker while Jer maneuvered the buckets around. Today Kris wore protective goggles—a new addition—and had laid out a gray tarp to catch the stray fruit falling from the shaking plant. The tarp would be Jer's suggestion. Kris had a lot of good ideas, but sometimes he missed the most practical solutions. Since Jer hated inefficiency, they made a good team.

"We're almost done!" Kris shouted over the ratcheting noise of the machine. Jer grinned up at Gabe, pointing to the overflowing buckets. Giving a thumb's up, Gabe grabbed a couple of the burdened pails and loaded up the red wagon. When it was full, he pulled it to the house and set the buckets on the kitchen counter, quickly returning to the blueberry shrubs. When the last of the buckets were filled, the boys headed back to the house to clean the berries.

Once in the kitchen, Kris couldn't stand it any longer. "So what's going on, Gabe? I'm gonna lose it if I don't find out soon!"

"Jer," Gabe motioned with his head, "go see where Mom and Dad are."

Jer gave a mock salute and took off. He didn't mind taking orders when intrigue was involved and he got to be a part of it. While he was gone, Kris prodded at his brother with questions, but Gabe waited for Jer to return. He didn't want to have to tell the story twice.

"They're in the attic," Jer reported. "Mom must have finished cleaning the cellar."

"Did they see you?" Gabe asked.

Jer shook his head. "I'm too good for that. Besides, they were looking at an old yearbook."

"Reminiscing about the good ol' days, back when dinosaurs roamed the earth," Kris joked.

"They were talking about our visitor, I think," Jer corrected. "They were also laughing at her 'Farah Fawcett' hair, whatever that means."

"Mom really didn't like her, did she?" Kris said. "Wonder why?"

"You know how Mom is," Gabe replied absently. "So do you guys want to hear this, or not?" At the moment, he wasn't entirely sure he wanted to share. If his brothers didn't believe what he had to tell them, he'd never hear the end of it. Though it would be worse, he decided, if he didn't say anything and something bad happened to one of them.

"We're all ears," Kris announced as he dumped a handful of twigs and leaves into the compost bucket. Jer made a place for himself at the table next to his brothers and started to work on his own bucket.

Gabe took a deep breath. "Well, it all started a few days ago. When I was running… I, well, I heard someone calling my name, but no one was there."

Kris laughed. "We already know you're crazy, dude."

"You said you wouldn't laugh," Gabe accused.

Kris immediately sobered. "So I did. Sorry. Won't happen again. Go on."

Gabe did. He told them everything that had happened, from hearing the voice and finding Repulsive, all the way to the recent goblin attack on the way to the store. When he was done, he waited for the inevitable jeers. Said aloud, his story sounded bonkers. He wouldn't blame his brothers for thinking he'd lost his mind.

"Well, that explains the footprints," Jer remarked after a few moments of silence. Gabe stared at him. Jer never believed anything until he'd thoroughly analyzed and dissected it. Probably because when he was younger, his two older brothers always tried to fool him. Well, they still did try, though now they rarely succeeded.

"You believe me?"

Jer shrugged. "I might have seen something, too."

"What did *you* see?"

"Well, it was on our first night here. By the woods. I tried to convince myself that it was just some wild animals, but they looked an awful lot like people. They stood on two legs, anyway."

Kris pursed his lips in thought, his left eyebrow arched. "So what do they want with *you*, Gabe? I'm so much more interesting."

"Not everything's about Kris Hawthorne, you know."

"Well, it should be," Kris proclaimed, then grinned. "It seems like Maine isn't going to be so boring after all, eh, mates?" He liked speaking in different accents, feigning a cockney one this time. He was almost as good at it as their mom.

"I don't think me losing my life is all that exciting."

"Now that's where you're wrong," Kris insisted. "I mean," he went on to explain, "you're *not* going to lose your life. We're going to be prepared for next time."

"How?" Gabe wanted to know. "When? I'm starting my new job Sunday and we still have work to do around the house. There won't be time for extras."

"Tsk, tsk," Kris tutted. "When something's important," he mimicked their mom's voice, "you make time for it. And Jer and I think you're important, if only to keep Mom off our backs once in awhile because she's yelling at you instead of us."

"Ha, ha. You're just lucky I don't beat the crap out of you and deflate that big head of yours."

"Guys, guys," Jer intervened. "We need to talk about what this means." He looked at the two of them. "We've got some big questions here." He held up his hand and ticked them off. "First of all, who are these people? Hollie and Dame Hazel and the goblins. Second, what do they want with Gabe? Third, does it have something to do with what that lady, Mrs. Morrigan, mentioned about what happened years ago and Mom being scared of the forest? Finally, what's in that missing trunk?"

Kris snapped his fingers. "I'll bet Gabe stole something from someone when he was a kid, and he put it in that box. Or maybe he stole the whole box. Now they want it back."

"I didn't steal anything!"

Jer frowned. "Whether you did or not, how did the box get into the turret? Mom and Grandma May told us no one's been in there during their lifetime."

Kris's shoulders lifted. "I don't know. It was just an idea."

"We need to find that box," Jer decided.

Gabe dumped the last of his blueberries onto the cleaning tray. "I'm not going in those woods."

"They say the best defense is a good offense," Kris replied, raising an eyebrow hopefully.

"You didn't see those little monsters, or whatever they were. When they came at me, I felt like I was the main course at a cannibal convention. If they're real, then I'm in big trouble."

"That's why we need weapons!" Kris insisted. "We've got our slingshots." Kris claimed he could knock a fly out of the air at fifty feet. He couldn't.

"Why don't we search the house first," Jer suggested. "Gather clues."

Kris's lip lifted in a sneer. "Count me out. I'm going to be doing a weapons check."

"A what?" Mom asked, coming into the kitchen. All three boys jumped guiltily. "What's this? Why, I believe you three are up to something. I guess that means I should give you more work. You know what they say about idle hands…"

"They're well-rested and look very nice?" Gabe ventured.

"Nice try. So what's left on the list?" She laid a finger against the side of her cheek and looked at the ceiling as though searching for inspiration from the god of chores. "Ah, yes. I remember. We need firewood. Lots of it. I want to use the woodstove and fireplaces as much as possible this winter to save on fuel."

"I thought you didn't want us going into the woods," Gabe protested, suddenly chilled, as though he'd seen hundreds of eyes peering in at him through the screen door.

"Yes, I did say that," she admitted. "But this part isn't really the woods, *per se*. It's the section behind the house between our yard and the ocean. Close to the apple and peach trees. There's a lot of deadwood and brush back there that need to be cleared out."

"So it's safe?"

"I wouldn't let you go in there if I didn't think it was safe."

"I'll run the chainsaw!" Kris volunteered.

"Not in this lifetime, buster," she told him. "I'll be doing that part... You can wipe those stunned expressions off your faces! I *am* a native Mainer, you know. We're very self-sufficient. Anyway, Gabe can split the wood, Kris can haul it to the woodshed at the back of the house, and Jer can stack it."

Kris continued to argue that the world would be a much better place if she let him wield either the saw or the ax while Gabe thought about going into the woods. Maybe it wouldn't be so bad if their mother were there with them. Surely those weirdos in the dark robes—the dark ones—wouldn't attack in broad daylight when an adult was around. Right? Then again, mad, hungry goblin creatures most likely attacked any old time they pleased.

"What about me?" Dad asked as he entered the kitchen. They all turned toward him, flabbergasted. The man had a hard time making it through the day without taking a nap. "What?" he demanded, looking hurt. "I'm not totally helpless! I want to *do* something around here!" Fists clenched, he looked like a defiant child. At the sight of him, Gabe felt his heart contract.

"Okay, okay! You can gather brush and small sticks," Mom decided, her brow furrowed. "We'll need kindling." He nodded, looking pleased, and his fists uncurled. "All right, then!" She clapped her hands together. "Leave the blueberries for now, and let's gather everything up. Then we'll have lunch and get started."

A half hour later, gloves, goggles, an ax, and an ancient chainsaw had been collected from the shed and barn and stowed in a wheelbarrow to be used for hauling the split wood. Everyone ate their lunch quickly, strangely excited about getting to work as a family. As he bit into an apple, Gabe found himself growing more and more curious about this part of the woods. Why did his mother deem it safe when the rest of the forest was off limits?

After lunch, Dad went to sharpen the ax and oil and gas up the chainsaw. While he was doing this, Mom decided to take the boys on ahead to check out the woods where they'd be working. With Mom in the lead, the little group trudged across the yard, toward the woods behind the house. The smell of brine was sharp today and Gabe inhaled deeply, enjoying its salty scent. It was nice back here—the land dipped downward a bit and the ground was still soft from the rain, the grass lush.

Just past the apple and peach tree grove, a path led into the woods that he hadn't noticed during his run a couple nights ago. Similar to the northern section, no prickly hedge blocked the way here. Gabe glanced over his shoulder and noted that the wall of vines disappeared into the shadow of the trees about a hundred yards away.

When they reached the woods, Mom plunged into a grove of tall trees, their gray bark thick and fissured like elephant skin. Dark green, round glossy leaves covered the branches. What looked like tiny green pinecones, roughly the size of jellybeans, peeked out from beneath the leaf clusters.

"Black Alders," Mom noted as they passed by the silent beings growing out of the soft, moist ground. It was strange, but Gabe didn't feel afraid amongst these trees. He thought that if they could, they would protect him.

The grove of alders quickly thinned out and the four of them headed into another grouping of trees. The ground beneath their sneakers felt like a sponge, soft and wet and springy. The trees here were quite different from the alders. Their long, supple branches, covered with narrow green leaves, fell from the trees' tops like Arabian horsetails. Some of the branches lay on the ground, tempting him to pick one up and crack it like a whip.

"Weeping Willows," Mom said. A fitting name, Gabe thought. The drooping trees sighed and bent in the soft breeze, exuding an aura of suffering. "Your great-great-great-great Grandmother May planted them. According to legend, the willow is an enchanted tree. If you're out walking on a night when the moon is full and you pass near a willow tree, you might end up somewhere you weren't expecting. The willow supposedly serves as a gateway to the Fairy world." Gabe waited

for her to laugh, but she didn't. Instead she quoted a poem in a strange
Celtic accent,

Ellum do grieve,
Oak he do hate
Willow do walk
If Yew travels late.

Gabe shivered. She sounded as though she believed all that stuff was
real. He hoped it wasn't. If fairies and gateways and enchanted trees
truly existed, then those things in the woods might not be just kids
dressed up as goblins. They might be *real* goblins.

No. Gabe shook his head. *Not possible.*

About fifty feet ahead a stream dissected the woods. The fast flowing
water measured about twenty feet across at its widest, with narrower
sections here and there, where small waterfalls formed. Moss-covered
stones stuck their noses out of the water, making the brook bubble and
froth as it flowed downhill toward the ocean.

"I wanted to show you this spot before we started work." Mom
watched Gabe as she spoke. "I'm surprised the stream is still in the
same place," she added, almost to herself, as she turned her gaze back
to the water. Gabe thought it was an odd thing to say. The stream
looked like it had been there for centuries, following the same course
year after year, despite sudden rainstorms and heavy spring run-off.

"So we can come here?" Kris asked, climbing onto a boulder. He
stood up and surveyed the land as though he were king.

Mom didn't answer right away. "I suppose so," she said finally. "I
feel safe here. But if you sense anything weird, or hear something that
doesn't sound right, head straight for home. Fast." She sounded deadly
serious and the three boys gave her identical questioning looks. "Promise me," she ordered.

"Are you worried about bears?" Jer asked, again neglecting to promise anything.

Mom bit her lip in thought and her eyebrows drew together as
though struggling with a secret. "Maybe," she finally conceded.

"Wildcats?" Jer sounded too interested, Gabe thought. He was going
to give them away.

"I'm worried about *something* wild coming after you," she answered.
"So be careful out here. The creatures in these woods aren't like your
pets. To them, you're a threat or just dinner." She scanned the woods
one last time, then turned to head back. "Come on. I just wanted you

to see this place. It's so beautiful that I couldn't resist sharing it."

Maybe you couldn't resist, Gabe thought, *because some things are simply more powerful than fear.* The concept seemed strange to him; fear was the most powerful emotion he knew.

They headed back toward the house, Jer and Kris sword fighting with sticks the whole way. Unlike the other part of the woods, the moss here was of reasonable height and there was dead brush on the ground. But again, no seedlings or small plants. It had likely been a hard winter and the deer had cleaned out the woods.

Completely? Even being a city kid, that seemed a bit extreme to him.

As they grew close to the yard, a stand of pine trees greeted them, their bark thick and red and their needles pungent and fresh. Evergreens were one of the few trees Gabe could recognize, mainly because he liked the smell of them, but also because that's what Redwoods were.

"I don't take down live trees, only ones that are already dead," Mom told them. "Soft woods, like this pine," she indicated, "dry the fastest, so we'll start with them. Eventually I want to harvest the hardwoods because they burn longer and cleaner. We'll do that this fall. It takes time to season wood to make a good fire, so I want to get going on building up our stores. Really, we should've started this months ago."

They found Dad waiting for them at the edge of the woods with the wheelbarrow and essential tools. For the next couple hours, the family sawed and chopped and hauled wood and brush. They were sweaty and itchy and sticky. Overall, though, Gabe found he didn't mind the work, and the smell of pinesap was rather intoxicating.

After half an hour of gathering up brush, Dad was happy to quit, heading back to the house to 'oversee' operations there. Kris and Jer took turns fetching the cut wood and stacking it in the wood crib.

Rubbing her right arm, Mom finally called it a day. "Maybe we'll do some more tomorrow," she said. "Wouldn't want to cut off a foot." Gabe heartily agreed.

Jer was hauling a load back to the house, leaving Mom and Gabe alone. Shoulders aching from the unfamiliar job of splitting wood, Gabe was only too happy to head back himself. As they made their way through the trees, he decided now might be the time to ask the question that had been bothering him.

"Why don't you want us to go in the woods, Mom?"

"I just don't think it's safe," she answered tersely.

"I heard what that lady said," he persisted. "About something that happened a while back. What was it?"

His mom stopped and swung around to face him. "You want to know, Gabe?" she demanded, looking anxious and upset. "Do you really want to know?"

He flinched. "Probably not. But don't you think I should?"

She blinked a few times, then sighed. "You were four years old. Something took you, Gabe. Something came right out of the woods and took you."

"Oh." She was right. He didn't want to know.

Chapter Thirteen

A History Lesson,
and More

Gabe was too stunned by his mom's revelation to ask any more questions. Before he knew it, they were back in the yard and Mom was admiring the stack of wood that now filled the wood crib near the house. Close to the crib, Grandpa May had installed a small door to get firewood inside. You pushed the wood through the opening and it slid down a chute to land in a box in the cellar.

"This is so cool!" Kris marveled as he pushed another log down the chute.

"Now you know where you get your engineering genes," Dad commented.

"I wonder if we could mechanize it?" Kris muttered to himself, not hearing Dad. He was in his own little world.

The conversation sounded quite normal, at least for their family. "What do you mean something came and took me?" Gabe finally managed to get out. "What was it?"

Mom set the chainsaw and her leather work gloves in the wheelbarrow. "We'll leave this here tonight," she said to no one in particular.

"Um, *Mom*? What was it?" This was one subject she wasn't going to avoid.

"What was what?" Jer asked.

"Mom is afraid to let us go into the woods because when I was four something came and took me."

"I thought we weren't going to tell him that, Ayla," Dad said. "Now Gabe is going to be paranoid about every little sound he hears."

"And we all know Gabe doesn't need to be *more* paranoid than he already is," Kris added, sliding another log down the chute. "I mean, he used to worry that we were going to be swallowed up by a black hole." Apparently he had tuned into the conversation at the same time Dad had. Gabe gave his brother a dirty look.

Mom sighed. "He asked and I didn't want to lie about it. Besides, I think it's a good idea that they know what could be out there. They'll be more likely to do as we ask."

"What *could* be out there?" Jer clapped his hands. "It *is* a bear, isn't it? A mutant one!" His blue eyes were bright.

Mom shrugged. "All I saw was something dark. It happened while we were home for a visit. We were outside in the yard, and Gabe was playing along the edge of the woods, chasing butterflies, I think. I went into the house to fetch a basket of laundry to hang on the line. When I came back out a few minutes later, I spotted a small figure darting into the woods. That's when I realized Gabe was gone."

"Gone?" Jer breathed. "Just like that?"

"Just like that." She shook her head. "Two days later, he returned. A group of us were about to go search the woods again when he walked into the yard, smiling. I was so relieved to see him I almost passed out. I was pregnant with Jer at the time and Kris was only two and kept wanting to come with us. And it had been *two days*! We were exhausted from forty-eight hours of searching and worrying." She wrapped her arms around herself as though suddenly chilled.

"To make things even more difficult, once in the woods, we kept getting lost. It seemed almost as though the landmarks were shifting around, confusing us. The search was slowed even more because we couldn't split up for fear someone would get separated from the group and end up lost for good. Not to mention the fact that we always felt like we were being watched, and at times, hunted. Wild animals, I imagine, but still…not a nice feeling."

She took the ax dangling from Gabe's limp hand and set it in the wheelbarrow. "There are stories of people going into those woods and not coming out, and they're not just rumors. Twenty years ago it happened to Bruce Holt, a man who lived in town. He was a bit of a recluse, but a nice guy. I think he was a poet, actually. Anyway, the story goes that he went into the woods and never came back out."

"There's nothing weird about that," Jer argued. "Thousands of people get lost in the woods every year and some are never found."

"Yes, but he's not the only one who's disappeared. He's just an example." She looked at all of them, her eyes intense. "The town records show over a hundred disappearances, dating back to over three hundred years ago when immigrants first settled Ranger. Only just last year a surveyor from Newcastle got lost. No one ever saw him again."

Gabe gulped, then looked back over his shoulder at the woods. He felt as though they were watching him, biding their time. "So what did I say when I got back?"

"That's the strangest part. You didn't say anything. You acted like someone who'd only just stepped into the woods and then right back out again. You didn't remember being gone, you weren't hungry or tired or cold. It was like whoever, or whatever, had kidnapped you had taken good care of you."

"Maybe it was that one guy," Kris ventured. "The recluse."

"Bruce Holt would've been dead by then," Dad stated firmly. "There's no way he would've survived the winter, let alone several of them on his own, in Maine."

"You don't know that," Kris protested. "How do you think they did it in the old days?"

"Bruce had a heart condition," Mom explained. "A very serious one. I think that's why he was a recluse. Interacting with people was just too hard on him."

"So now what do we do?" Gabe gulped. His whole world seemed to be closing in on him.

"We stay away from the woods," Mom said simply. "That should be easy. After you returned, a giant hedge grew up in front of certain parts of the forest, seemingly overnight, thick as a wall. The funny thing is, I couldn't remember it being like that when we went to search for you." She frowned before continuing. "Anyway, for some reason, the part of the woods by the stream seems to be okay, so you can go there. If you do happen to get lost, head east toward the ocean. At midday, if you're facing the stream, the sun should be above you. I think. Maybe I should get us all compasses," she added in a mumble to herself.

"I don't know about you guys," Gabe said, "but I'm staying away from those woods." He didn't like that part about them feeling hunted.

"It's probably just as well," Mom agreed, smiling at him. She looked relieved.

Dad stretched and patted his stomach. "I'm starved. Let's go eat."

Mom and Dad headed around the house, talking in low voices, with the boys following more slowly after them. "I guess that explains why you don't like the woods," said Jer. "It's weird that you don't remember what happened. You don't, do you?"

"Not a thing. Though when I get too close to the trees I get nervous. It's not that I feel *truly* afraid of the woods; it's just that there's something peculiar about them. Something I can't explain. I don't like that feeling."

"I feel the same way about mysteries," Kris remarked. "I like them, but I don't. I can't stand not knowing the answer." He grinned suddenly. "You know what we're going to have to do, right?"

Gabe groaned. "We're not going into the woods. The hedge won't let us."

"It let you in," Jer reminded him. "When you were looking for Gypsy."

Gabe frowned. He'd hoped they'd forgotten about that part, as he had. Unfortunately, Jer never forgot about anything, absorbing whatever was put in front of him, like an amoeba, only with arms and legs.

"Hollie probably did something to the vines to make them open up like that." Gabe didn't really believe this, but nothing else made sense, either.

"But what was she doing?" Kris asked. "How did she make the branches part like that? Did she use strings? Her bird friends? I've been thinking a lot about it and I can't figure it out. You said you didn't see anyone nearby when the vines parted and that it happened very fast. Whoever did it must have used some kind of machine."

"Or magic," Jer suggested. They looked at him and he shrugged, a little defiantly. "Stranger things have happened in this world."

"I'm still not going back there," Gabe insisted, yanking open the screen door and tromping inside. He felt hot and itchy and his arms ached. He just wanted to take a shower and forget.

~~~~~~

After supper, Grandma May and Grandpa Hawthorne came to visit for a couple hours. They ended up playing Monopoly while Grandma told them a bit of history about the house. Hoping to be distracted, Gabe listened intently.

"Your ancestors," she began, "were among the first white folk to settle this area, coming over from Great Britain in the late 1600s to start a better life. There was some mystery about why they left. Rumor has it that they'd been forced to leave their home country, though no one today knows why.

"After claiming this patch of land, the first thing the Mays did was build the turret. The stone walls are two feet thick. They built it to be impenetrable." She looked at Gabe as she said this, her blue eyes hinting at something. "Of course, there were a lot of Indian raids, and whatnot, back then. But our folk always got along with the Abenakis— the Indians who lived here before us—so it was thought that building the turret was just a strange whim." She snorted, showing what she thought of that theory. Gabe wondered what the real reason was. What did his ancestors feel they needed protection against? "The rest of the house was added on afterwards, and a half-century after that, the barn was raised.

"The family has always been blueberry harvesters, picking them wild for the first couple hundred years. Now pay attention. History lesson coming your way. In the early 1900s, Elizabeth White, along with Dr. Frederick Coville, domesticated the wild blueberry bush. This led to the high bush plants we grow out in the backyard. Our ancestors, being pragmatists of the highest order, were quick to jump on the high bush wagon. It was much easier to move up and down nice, neat rows than to risk the bugs, bears, and moose in the woods where the fruit thrived. Blueberries are very healthy for you, full of antioxidants," she ended her story. "Eat a few handfuls every day, especially you, Keith."

"I will," Dad agreed heartily. "That alder tea you sent over seems to be doing the trick. I had so much energy today. I felt like I could run a marathon." His whole family groaned and he laughed. "Well, maybe just trot down the driveway and back, but that's a start." He leaned over to grab a cracker off the snack tray Mom had put together, wincing as he did.

"You okay, Son?" Grandpa Hawthorne asked, his expression worried. Grandpa might look tough, with his tanned, leathery face and ever-present white stubble, but Gabe had learned at a young age that the old man was a softie at heart. He'd do anything for his family.

"I don't know," Dad answered, sounding a bit out of breath. "I was pulling out some brush in the woods when something scratched me." He held out his right arm. A long, purplish cut streaked down it. It looked awful.

"Did you see what scratched you?" Grandma asked quietly, and Mom glanced sharply at her.

"I think it was some sort of shrub. Thick, hard to see into. Funny thing is, I don't remember noticing any shrubs when I started working in that spot. Did you see any, Gabe? I was close to you when it happened." Gabe shook his head. He hadn't noticed any shrubs back where they were cutting wood.

Mom went pale as she examined the vicious gash. "It looks pretty bad, Keith. I should put something on it."

"Try lavender and tea tree oil," Grandma suggested. "Both fight infection. I can make something up for you to drink, too, Keith."

Mom nodded. "I think we'll put some oil on it right now. Boys," she said, standing up, "why don't you start cleaning up. We've got another long day ahead of us tomorrow."

Grandpa Hawthorne and Grandma May both took the hint, grabbing their empty glasses and heading for the kitchen.

"I don't want to spoil the fun," Dad protested, looking distressed.

Mom yawned. "Get over yourself, Keith. We're all tired and you're giving us a good excuse to get some sleep."

Dad's face relaxed. Gabe had the feeling that he worried he was always ruining things for them. "I'm so tired, I could sleep through a tornado," Gabe added, wanting to make sure his dad wouldn't feel guilty.

"Me, too!" Jer and Kris chimed in.

"Goodnight, everybody," Grandma May called out.

"Need a ride, Eleanor?" Grandpa Hawthorne asked, setting his glass in the sink.

"I wouldn't say no to one. I'd hate to cheat you out of spending more time with me." They left together, laughing. Well, Grandma was laughing, anyway.

Dad said goodnight, then Mom hurried him upstairs to treat his cut. When they were gone, Kris started in again about going into the woods. "We won't go far, and we'll leave a trail," he promised.

"No."

"You're such a wuss, Gabe."

"If it were you who'd been kidnapped and dragged into the woods by some strange creature, you wouldn't be so quick to return."

"At least I would've remembered what happened," Kris grumbled.

"It's called a repressed memory, you dolt," Jer intervened. "It's when you experience something so horrific that if you didn't 'forget' all memory of it, you'd go insane. The worst part is that the memory's still there, just waiting to pop out and get you when you least expect it."

Gabe stared at his little brother. "So *horrific*? What do you think happened to me in there?"

"Who knows? But I'm sure it was awful. Otherwise, why wouldn't you remember it? I mean, I can understand forgetting after some time had passed—after all, you were only four, but you remembered nothing immediately afterward."

"Mom said I was smiling when I came out; that I looked well cared for."

"Here's my take on it," Kris offered. "I think you remembered everything and it drove you mad. *Then* you repressed the memories, but you stayed loony."

"Very funny, Dr. Freud," Gabe growled.

Kris puffed on an imaginary cigar. "My theory does explain a lot of things," he claimed, speaking in a German accent. "Like your love for the Sadistic Sadie, ja?"

Gabe's fists curl up. Kris had a real talent for pushing his buttons. There were times when he wanted to punch his brother and knock the arrogance right out of him. His mom was always saying, "Don't let him get to you, Gabe. The less reaction he gets, the faster he'll give up and walk away." Gabe knew this was true, but sometimes it was too hard to follow good advice even when it was the right thing to do.

"Go in the woods if you want," he said, winning the battle with his temper—this time, anyway. "I'm going to bed."

Kris grinned. "Don't you want to know why she was called Sadistic Sadie?"

Gabe turned and walked away, determined not to respond. Gypsy scampered out from under the table and followed after him. "Because she liked to pick on little kids!" Kris shouted after him.

Gabe only shook his head as he headed toward the turret. The sound of Kris's laughter and Gypsy's padding paws accompanied him down the dark hall. He ran up the turret stairs, two at a time, glad the thick door blocked out any outside noise. Kris had a very loud laugh.

After taking a few deep, calming breaths, he spent some time cleaning up his room and organizing. He unpacked his last box of books, then fed his fish. As he worked, he realized that he really liked the feel of the turret. Despite all the windows, especially the big half-moon one with the tree, he felt safe here. Protected.

Still, he made sure to check that the hook connecting the bookshelf to the wall was securely latched and no strange noises could be detected. When his inspection was complete, he remembered that he hadn't brushed his teeth and zipped downstairs to use the small bathroom off the kitchen.

He was heading back through the kitchen when he heard a heavy clicking sound on the porch, like dog claws on wood, and froze. Wanting to do anything but approach the door, he had to fight some very strong instincts to make himself move forward. He couldn't just walk away, he argued to himself as he tiptoed along. What if those weird goblins had come? Most likely it wasn't them, only a raccoon searching for scraps, or one of the kittens had gotten out and was trying to get back in. Either way, Gabe had to be sure nothing dangerous was out there. His family wasn't protected like he was in the turret, with locked doors and thick, stone walls. Mom and Dad wouldn't expect a thing. They were completely defenseless.

After creeping forward a few more steps, he decided that using loud noise might be a more effective weapon. He began to stomp across the pine planks of the kitchen floor singing, "Fee, Fie, Foe, Fum! I smell the blood of an Englishmun. Be he alive, or be he dead, I'll grind his bones to make my bread!"

He placed his hand on the doorknob and there came a shuffling noise, like several feet, and what sounded like whispers, too. Definitely not a raccoon or a sweet little kitten out there; it was something human.

Gabe didn't hesitate. With one swift twist, he turned the lock and ran out of the kitchen, up the stairs to the second floor where the bedrooms were located. He needed to know if everyone was safe in the house and also confirm that it wasn't one of his brothers playing a trick on him.

They weren't. Both Kris and Jer lay fast asleep in their beds while Mom had dozed off in a chair next to her and Dad's bed. She'd been trying to keep watch and Gabe could understand why. He didn't look good. The wound on his arm was red and inflamed and his sleep was restless as though monsters pursued him in his dreams.

"Mom?" He shook her shoulder lightly. "Wake up."

"Huh? What?" She started up, looking wildly about her.

"You fell asleep in the chair."

She glanced over at Dad, blinking groggily. "I wanted to keep an eye on him," she sighed. "But all that woodcutting tired me out. We might have to bring him to the doctor's office tomorrow. I don't like the look of that cut."

Gabe didn't either, but he didn't want to add to her worries by saying so. "Then you better get some sleep, hm?" he said instead. "At your age, you need all the beauty rest you can get."

She smacked him on the arm. "If I get any more beautiful, I'd be impossible to look at. Like the sun…" She stretched her neck, getting a crick out. "Or an angel."

"Just as long as you remain humble about it," Gabe answered with a laugh.

"Could you lock up for me?" she asked. "Just the front door. Oh, and you'd better check the cellar. Make sure the wood chute door is shut tight. I don't think Kris closed up after he was done trying out Grandpa's contraption. We wouldn't want any coons getting in." She yawned.

"Sure, Mom." He leaned down and kissed her on the cheek. She rubbed his head drowsily. "See you in the morning."

He left her and hurried back downstairs, feeling sick to his stomach. Neither his brothers nor the kittens had made the noise outside. Gypsy was in the turret and Inky and Little Joe were sleeping with Jer, cocooning his blond head between their little bodies. Still, he would bet his right pinkie finger that he'd heard human voices.

In the kitchen he grabbed the flashlight, shook it several times to charge it, then headed toward the cellar door. As an afterthought, he backtracked and took a butcher knife out of the drawer. He wasn't taking any chances. Besides, he hated the cellar. The dirt floor was always damp, there were lots of spiders, and the darkness…shudder. An odd smell lingered there, too. No, the cellar was definitely not his hangout of choice.

He switched on the light in the stairwell, though it didn't do much good. The single, 40-watt bulb gave off very little light, leaving lots of dark corners for monsters to lurk in. The only way to turn on the other lights was to pull a string. That meant crossing the dark space, giving whatever might be down there plenty of time to grab him. He promptly turned on the flashlight.

As he crept down the wooden steps, he whipped the bright beam back and forth in an attempt to catch off guard anything that shouldn't be there. When he reached the bottom step, he swept the light around the room in broad arcs. His mom had done a great job cleaning. When they'd first arrived, the cellar had been a cobwebby, dusty mess full of overstuffed boxes and broken furniture. Now there was nothing to hide behind.

To the left of the steps a decrepit washer and dryer leaned against one another. Judging by the look of them, they were quite possibly the first electric washer and dryer ever invented. An old cement sink hunkered down next to them. Underneath, Mom had stored stacks of flowerpots and a few bags of potting soil. Several cheap metal shelves lined one of the uneven, cement-patched stone walls. Not much sat on them right now. Mom had thrown out a lot of Grandma May's stash, including several Mason jars containing pickled eggs, and a couple jars nobody could figure out what was in them, not even Grandma.

A worktable covered with boxes labeled Nails and Screws and Mysterious Bits took up more wall space. Then there was the usual stuff you find in a basement—water pump, furnace, hot water heater, and a couple chest freezers. Some of the wires and tubes on these appliances had been heavily duct-taped. He hoped the pitiful looking machines would hold up through the winter. Everything down here looked pretty old and they had no money to replace anything if it broke.

The beam from his flashlight finally found the wood chute. Beneath it was a sturdy wooden box about four feet wide and four feet tall, to catch the incoming wood. Next to it, an old, potbellied woodstove squatted like a black toad.

Gabe cautiously approached the chute. Readying his knife, he peered over the side of the box, flashing the light around inside like a deadly laser. Several pieces of fresh-cut wood sat at the bottom. Nothing else. Not even a bug.

Then he heard it.

Thump, thump, thump.

Gabe aimed the light up the chute, only to find two coal black eyes staring back at him. He broke out in a cold sweat and the hand holding the flashlight started to shake. The chute was open and something big and creepy was trying to get into the house.

Seeing Gabe, it screeched loudly, but didn't pull back out. Instead, it writhed and squirmed like a worm on a hook and Gabe realized that the intruder was forcing its way in. Gritting his teeth, he thrust the knife into the opening, hoping to at least scare it off.

It didn't scare.

Not wanting to kill whatever it was, Gabe started looking for something long, spotting a broom his mom had used to clean the cellar. Dropping the knife, he grabbed the broom and shoved the handle into the chute. The wood made contact with a sickening thud.

"Eeehhh!"

Gabe cringed. If the creature was an innocent animal, he didn't want to hurt it. He began to poke at it lightly, yelling, "Shoo! Get out of here!" as loudly as he could. Hampered by the tall sides of the wood box, he pulled out the broom and climbed awkwardly into the box so that he would have a longer reach.

Once inside, he peered up the dark chute. It was quiet in there—no sounds of squirming or wiggling. He lifted his flashlight for a better look and spotted a skull-like face in the beam before the head ducked low. Gripping the broom tightly, Gabe thrust it into the chute, much harder this time. That was no innocent animal.

The intruder bellowed in pain, sounding very human this time.

His theory proven, Gabe shoved harder, banging his elbow. Wincing, he noticed he'd banged it on a small, thick door with a large, rusty bolt on it. Without stopping to think why Grandpa, or Grandma May, would've needed such a big bolt on such a small door, he pulled out the broom, slammed the door shut, and tried to secure it.

As he struggled to slide the bolt home, his feet slipping on the wobbly logs at the bottom of the bin, something hit the door hard, jarring it. Gabe tried to make his treacherous hands move faster, but the bolt was stuck. Another bang rattled the door and it popped open. A skeletal hand reached out and clawed at Gabe. He whacked at it with the flashlight and the hand withdrew. Before it could return Gabe slammed the door shut and rammed the bolt hard with his palm, leaving a purple dent in his skin. After protesting, the metal bolt finally slid home. The little door was locked.

"Get lost, or I'll skin you alive!" he shouted, thinking that last part sounded pretty intimidating.

Scratching, snuffling noises whispered inside the chute like deranged rats, but the sounds grew dimmer with each passing second. Whatever was in the shaft was backing out of it. It had given up trying to get in—for the moment, anyway. Gabe fell back against the side of the box, breathing hard.

This is not cool. Not cool at all. What if there were other doors, other ways into the house? Gabe decided that he'd better go check everything out, and fast.

He spent half an hour searching the house, from the attic on down. Every window and every door was now shut tight and locked behind him. It might get a bit warm in the house tonight, but they'd be safe. Tomorrow he would do the securing before he went to bed.

Finally finished, he raced back to the turret, grateful he'd had the foresight to lock the two doors before going to brush his teeth. Sometimes his paranoia really paid off.

Once in bed, he pulled the covers up to his chin and a sleepy Gypsy close. It took a long time to fall asleep.

Chapter Fourteen

The Woods Come to Gabe

By the time Gabe woke up it was already nine o'clock. He lay in bed for a moment, blinking his bleary eyes. When he attempted to sit up, he wondered if he'd suffered a stroke during the night. He could barely lift his arms and his neck felt like someone had taken a giant wrench and tightened it one revolution.

Groaning like an old man, he managed to pull himself out of bed. As always, the half-moon window drew his eyes and he looked up, only to discover that a gray mist had taken over the world. The heavy fog pressed against the glass as though trying to steal into the room, and was so thick Gabe couldn't see the sky, or anything else for that matter.

Throwing on some dark blue shorts that hung down to his knees, a stained and rumpled t-shirt, and his running shoes, Gabe hurried downstairs with Gypsy galloping after him. The round, fluffy little kitten was determined, but not very fast, and Gabe had to wait every few seconds for her to catch up. When he arrived at the kitchen, Jer and Kris were already there, eating breakfast and staring gloomily out the window at the foggy day. Unlike Gabe, they could feel the cold and had dressed in jeans and long-sleeved shirts. Kris's pants sported a hole in the right knee, as did all his pants.

"Where're Mom and Dad?" Gabe asked, immediately sensing something was wrong.

"Dad's sick," Jer replied morosely. Kris didn't move or answer, just continued to stare out the window, a stubborn expression on his face.

"But I thought he was getting better!" Gabe cried.

"His wound got infected," Jer explained, and Gabe belatedly remembered what Mom had told him last night. "Grandma May and Mom drove him into Ranger to see the doctor. They left about an hour ago."

Unsure of what to do, Gabe poured himself a bowl of milk and cereal. Sitting at the table, he looked at his despondent brothers, each handling their fear in different ways. Jer scrunched down and got real quiet, like a mouse. Kris got mad.

"We had visitors last night," Gabe found himself saying. He hadn't particularly wanted to relive the experience, but figured it would serve as a distraction.

"Visitors?" Kris swung around. "Who?"

"Or what?" Jer put in.

"I don't know." Gabe went on to tell them what had happened, leaving nothing out. When he was done, Kris looked almost happy again. The idea of a good fight thrilled him, and this one, against goblins and ghoulies attempting to breach their fortress, was as good as it got.

"We should go after them, Gabe! The best defense is a good offense, remember?. Besides, I'll bet what's going on isn't even anything weird, just some town kids giving the newbies a scare. See what we're made of. Well I say, let's show them!"

"Mom said we're to stay close to the house today," Jer reminded him. "She doesn't want to be worrying about us *and* Dad." Kris's shoulders drooped. "And she wants us to clean the attic."

Kris groaned. "That'll take all day!"

Jer looked bleak. "We're supposed to put away the wood-cutting stuff that's in the wheelbarrow, too."

"I'll do that!" Kris immediately volunteered. Both Gabe and Jer frowned at him. "What?" he said, trying to look innocent, though the devious gleam in his eyes completely ruined the effect.

"If we let you go out there, unattended, we won't see you again for hours."

Kris smiled sweetly. "Would you rather have me outside working, or in here complaining the entire time?"

The two brothers looked at each other, then said at the same time, "Outside."

Kris grinned. "Thought so."

At that moment, the phone rang and Gabe, who was closest to it, snatched it up. "Hello?" The connection was staticky. "Is that you, Mom?"

"Gabe? We're heading to Augusta. Grandma, too. Dad's pretty sick and Dr. Statin wants to hospitalize him overnight."

Gabe's hand started shaking and it was hard to hang onto the phone. "Is he going to be okay?"

There was a pause. "I think so. We caught the infection early. We'll know for sure after the first twenty-four hours. Dr. Statin said they'd give him an IV of antibiotics at the hospital. That should fight the infection pretty fast and keep it from spreading."

"Sounds positive…"

"It's very positive. Just...pray for him." Static crackled. "Look, I'm breaking up. We're heading around the mountain. Watch out for your brothers. I'll call at supper to check on you."

"Okay, Mom. Tell Dad..." He swallowed hard. "Well, just tell him we love him."

"I will. Bye..." The phone cut out.

Gabe hung up and turned to his brothers. They looked painfully hopeful. "He's going to be all right, they think. Mom and Grandma May are bringing him to the hospital for an IV to fight the infection."

Kris let out a pent-up breath. "Dad's a fighter. He'll be fine. It's just a cut, anyway. Right?"

Both Jer and Gabe nodded. Kris was the toughest of them in some ways, yet sometimes also the hardest hit. Gabe knew that Jer wasn't as taken in by his optimistic report, but he kept his mouth shut. He knew how Kris could be.

"I'll clean up the kitchen and get some bread going for supper," Jer volunteered. "Just in case they're able to make it back tonight." He was doing his darndest to look cheery.

Gabe nodded. "Thanks, Jer. Why don't you go ahead and fetch the wheelbarrow and put it in the barn, Kris. I don't want you inventing anything while you're there, though. I want you to do some straightening up. Okay?"

Kris nodded solemnly. "I promise I'll do my best to try."

Jer groaned and threw the dishcloth at his brother. "You're so full of it!"

"Full of charm and good looks, I'm sure you mean," Kris retorted. Laughing, he left them to go about his business of avoiding doing any real work. Gabe had to admit that his brother wasn't lazy, just easily distracted. Still, it made more work for the rest of them and that got old quick. Though, truth be told, he hadn't exactly been super-volunteer-guy when he was fourteen. He sighed. It was hard being grown-up. He wasn't sure he liked it.

Even though they were cleaning, he and Jer had a good time up in the attic. They found a lot of ancient clothes stuffed into musty old trunks or hanging on wooden hangers in a couple of tall wardrobes that smelled of lavender and dust. They tried on sparkly bellbottom pants and funky-colored polyester shirts with insanely long collars, and a variety of worn fedoras that must have been Grandpa May's. Gabe made a note to show them to Kris. There were even a few fancy ball gowns, but they decided they'd better not try those on. As funny as that would be, it would also be the same time Kris showed up with a camera.

At noon, they headed downstairs, each carrying three garbage bags full of junk or recycling. Jer checked on the rising bread, which filled the room with the scent of yeast, then started lunch while Gabe went to fetch Kris. The fog was so thick now that even though he had turned on the porch light, he had to find his way to the barn relying more on a sense of direction than sight. Although San Jose had fogs on occasion, none were ever as bad as this. He was practically blind in this soup.

With each shuffling step forward, the mist seemed to change, almost into a living thing. Gabe shivered and wrapped his arms about himself. A part of him liked the fog—how it turned the world he knew into something foreign, almost fantastical—but it also scared him. Fog, with its evanescent embrace, was too adept at hiding things.

When he finally reached the barn, he found a dusty Kris up in the loft. He was singing opera, or his version of it. "Do you have to sing that crap?"

"You're just jealous because I'm a multifaceted kind of guy. The ultimate Renaissance man."

"Yeah, jealous," Gabe snorted. "That's the word for what I'm feeling when you make that noise. More like an overwhelming desire to pop my own eardrums with an ice pick."

"Jealous, you are jealous, soooo jealous of my manly voice!" Kris sang in a falsetto.

"Were you actually cleaning up there?" Gabe asked, wanting to stop the singing, as he wiped little droplets of water off his face. Even his hair was wet, making the waves turn to curl. It wouldn't be long and he'd look like a cherub. For the hundredth time, he wished he had straight hair like his brothers.

"Yes, I was cleaning!" Kris's eyes widened in wounded dismay. He was very good at looking offended. "I had to! I couldn't find something. Whoever was looking for whatever it was they were looking for made a mess of my stuff. They screwed up my whole organizational system." Which also happened to be a system nobody else could understand since it didn't look any different from a chaotic heap.

"Well, it's lunchtime. Did you get the wheelbarrow?"

Kris made a face. "Oops! Forgot about that. I'll go fetch it now."

"Kris! You had one thing to do and you didn't do it!"

"Well, I'm doing it now, so stop acting like an old lady."

Gabe bit his tongue, but only because he kind of was acting like an old lady. "Fine." He turned to go, then stopped at the gray wall of fog.

"Maybe we should go together. This stuff is pretty thick. I wouldn't want you getting lost."

"I have the navigational system of a submarine," Kris boasted. "I never get lost."

"Yes, you do. All the time!"

"Oh, well, that's because I'm busy thinking and not watching where I'm going. If I'm paying attention, I'm better at tracking than a hound dog." His eyebrow popped up as he waited for Gabe to challenge him.

"Maybe one who's been hit on the head several times. Come on. The fog's getting worse by the minute and I'm hungry."

Kris scurried down from the loft and joined Gabe at the barn door. "Boy, it *is* thick," he remarked, peering out. "Maybe we should just leave the wheelbarrow until this clears."

"Which might not be for a couple days. I remember Mom saying something about the fogs along the Maine coast and how unpredictable they can be. They can last an hour, or go on for days. If that's the case, all our stuff will rust."

"Crap. Mom will kill us."

"Correction. Mom will kill *you*. I turned on the porch light before I left the house. All we have to do is head toward it."

"Can you see it?" Kris squinted through the thick fog.

"Not so much as a twinkle. Actually," Gabe looked down. "I can barely see my feet."

"Let's hope for the best, then. Grab my arm. I'll lead the way."

Gabe felt a qualm of doubt, but grabbed onto Kris's arm anyway with the wild hope that his brother would actually follow through on the task at hand, without getting distracted.

With Kris leading the way, they plunged into the murky mix and charged straight ahead. With each step, Kris's confidence faltered and he slowed until they were putting one foot in front of the other as cautiously as a baby learning to walk. The way the fog swirled and leaned on them, as though nudging them along, seemed almost unnatural.

Gabe stopped walking and the mist bathed him in its cool breath. "We should be at the house by now."

"Hmmm… I think you're right."

"We're lost, Kris. Because of you!" Gabe could literally feel his blood pressure rising.

"We can't be lost, Dumkopf! We're still in the yard."

He was right; the grass under their feet was short from being mowed. But this didn't make Gabe feel any better. Stuck in the middle of the yard, they were unprotected and clueless about where to go next, blatant targets for anybody to start taking potshots at them.

"Let's just stand here a minute," he suggested, "and try to get our bearings."

"Oh, fine," Kris reluctantly agreed. He was all for blundering onward, never mind where they might end up.

Standing still felt strange to Gabe, like he was trapped inside a dark, soundproof room. Nothing around them offered a clue as to where they were. Not a light, not a building, not a living soul. Or so Gabe hoped. The dark ones could be out there…waiting for something like this to happen. Waiting to steal his blood. He drew in a deep, shuddering breath.

Gabrielll… His heart seized up. *Gabrielll…*

They'd found him!

"*Kriiisss!*" Now they were calling Kris's name! They knew about him, too! "*Gaaabe!*"

"Jer!" Kris exclaimed. "He's calling for us. Smart kid. I knew we kept him around for a reason. Let's follow his voice. Keep yelling, Jer!"

Gabe's shoulders drooped with relief. No darth goblins, then, just his little brother. "Marco!" he cried out.

"Beans!" Jer called back. He never tired of that game.

The brothers called back and forth until finally Gabe saw the porch light, a tiny glow that grew steadily brighter. He breathed a sigh of relief. The fog had distorted Jer's calls, fooling them several times into thinking his voice had come from somewhere else. For a few heart-stopping minutes he thought they would never reach the house.

"Isn't this fog awesome!" Jer said excitedly as they approached the porch.

"Totally," Kris heartily agreed. "It's so thick, we got lost going from the barn to the house."

This is one big adventure to him, Gabe realized. He hadn't been scared at all. "We still haven't fetched the wheelbarrow."

"Mom parked it by the woodshed. We can just follow along the house."

"I don't know…"

"You're scared!" Kris turned on his brother. "It's just fog, Gabe."

"Fog that can hide stuff," he mumbled.

"You know Mom'll have our hides if we don't put that stuff away. She'll go after you first because you're the oldest. By the time she's moved onto me, I'll be hiding out in the barn."

"Fine!" Gabe snapped, knowing Kris was right. "Let's get moving."

"Hurry back, you dorks," Jer ordered. "I've got soup on and I'm making grilled cheese sandwiches."

"Don't worry, we will," Gabe said sincerely. He had no intention of moving slowly.

He and Kris shuffled quickly along the front of the house, around the turret, to the back side without incident. The wheelbarrow was where Mom had left it, though water droplets coated everything in it. Gabe was glad they'd gone to fetch it. Much longer and the salt air and moisture would have rusted everything. He was grabbing the handles of the wheelbarrow when he remembered something important…he needed to close the outside door to the chute.

"Where's the lock?" he asked Kris.

"I don't know. Somewhere around here." Eventually Gabe found it on the ground nearby using his hands to feel around. When the padlock was snapped shut, they pushed the wheelbarrow back to the house and carried it inside to dry off. Once the door was shut behind them and they were safe in the warm, bright kitchen, breathing in the tangy, rich scents of tomato soup, frying butter, and melting cheese, Gabe finally relaxed. It was good to be out of that fog and away from what it did to his imagination.

After devouring their lunch, they cleaned and dried off all the wood-cutting tools while Jer did the dishes. Gabe set Mom's gloves out to dry on the radiator next to their box of sports equipment that Dad, even though he couldn't play much of anything these days, had set up by the door. As he laid a glove out, spreading each finger for quicker drying, he said, "You know, Jer, you sounded just like Mom when you called me Gabriel instead of Gabe." He gave a casual laugh, as though Jer's answer meant nothing to him. "But since you saved our lives, I won't tease you about it. If you hadn't called for us, we'd still be wandering around out there."

Jer's blue eyes were confused. "I didn't call you Gabriel. I called you Gabe…and I called Kris, Kris. I know you guys think I'm a mama's boy, but I'm not that much of one. I don't do *everything* like her. I'm my own man, you know." His lower lip jutted out petulantly.

"Well, then who called me Gabriel?"

"I didn't hear anyone calling *Gabriel*," Kris put in. "Just Kris, then Gabe. Like Jer said."

Gabe looked back and forth between them. "You mean…"

The phone rang, startling them. Gabe picked it up and said a cautious, "Hello?" half expecting to hear a voice calling, *Gabrielll…*

"Gabe?"

It was only Grandpa. He clapped his hand over the phone and let loose a sigh of relief, before answering, "Hey, Grandpa."

"Just called to check in on you boys. Your mom told me about your dad. Looks like this fog's going to stick around for the day so I wanted to be sure you didn't need anything."

Other than an army, which he was pretty sure Grandpa couldn't provide, they were good. "We're fine, Grandpa. Jer just made lunch."

"Well, be sure you stay inside until this cussed mess lifts. Grown men have disappeared in fogs like this, never to be heard from again."

Gabe shivered. That had almost happened to him and Kris. "Sure, Grandpa. Will do. Have you seen lots of fogs like this?"

"A few times. This one's a doozy. Dungeon thick, right enough. It's so thick you could pound a nail into the dad-blamed stuff and hang your hat on it." He chuckled. "I remember the last time we had a fog like this, one of my neighbors decided that since he wasn't going to be able to do any fishing, he might as well shingle the roof. Took him all day to do it. When he was done, he went into supper and said to his wife, Berda, 'This sure is an awful long house.' Well, old Berda knew something wasn't right. Their house was tiny; she should know, she'd had to raise ten kids in it. So she went out to take a look-see and what did she find? Well, I'll be an oystershucker, her husband had shingled past the edge of the roof and out onto the fog!"

Gabe laughed. "That's a good one, Grandpa."

"Ayuh, that it is. So you're all set? Maybe I should swing by, just in case."

"We're fine, Grandpa! I don't want you driving over here in this fog. If Mom found out, she'd whack you a good one, then me for not stopping you. We'll let you know if anything comes up."

Grandpa chuckled. "Good enough. Bye, now."

"Bye, Grandpa." Gabe hung up the phone and relayed the fog story to his brothers. They both got a good laugh out of it.

"So I take it you're hearing voices again," Kris said when he'd stopped laughing.

"You didn't hear it? Nothing?"

"Looks like he, or she, is only talking to you," Jer determined.

"Well, isn't that great?" Gabe groaned. "And by that I mean, *not*! I'm either going crazy or something's after me. Lots of somethings, judging by all those different footprints we saw."

Kris carefully set the chainsaw back in the wheelbarrow. "I vote that you're crazy."

"You believed me before!" Gabe stared at his brother in disbelief.

"I'm trying to stay open-minded," he announced smugly. "But since I know you have a history of paranoia, I'm starting to have my doubts about your ability to distinguish reality from delusion."

"Fine," Gabe huffed, feeling hurt and betrayed. "I'm going to go clean the attic."

"Well, I'm going out to the barn," Kris answered back, unperturbed by his brother's hissy fit.

Gabe swung around. "You can't go to the barn! Remember we almost got lost?"

"I'll tie a rope to the porch. I remember seeing some clothesline down in the cellar."

"Fine. It's your funeral." On that note, Gabe stomped upstairs to the attic, fuming over his brother's words. Jer stayed behind to help Kris with the rope and to make sure he made it to the barn. When Kris was safe, Jer joined Gabe in the attic where they spent the rest of the afternoon cleaning. About a half hour before dinnertime, Jer left Gabe to bake the bread.

Gabe worked another half hour before quitting himself. He gathered together several more garbage bags and hauled them downstairs, lured by the enticing smell of fresh-baked bread. He entered the kitchen at the same time the porch door swung open.

"I can't believe someone cut the rope!" Kris shouted. "If you guys hadn't come along…"

"We were bored," a familiar voice replied from the porch. It was Abazi. Behind her was Kimber. "My dad's stuck at the store and Kimber's mom is stuck in town, too, at her own shop. So we were all by our lonesomes, with nothing to do."

The three of them spilled through the doorway and Gabe stopped in his tracks, thrown for a loop. He'd never been very good at handling the unexpected. Seeing Abazi and Kimber in his house was certainly not something he'd expected.

Abazi had foregone the braid today, wearing her hair down instead. The black mane reached halfway down her back, falling thick and straight as a velvet cape. Thousands of water droplets coated her hair, making it sparkle in the bright kitchen light.

"What?" she demanded, catching him staring. "Never seen a girl before?"

Kris roared. "Oh, he's seen them! He just doesn't know what to do with them."

"Shut up," Gabe growled. It was the best he could come up with in his stunned state. "I was just wondering how you made it here in this fog."

"I'm an Indian, in case you didn't notice." Abazi smirked at him.

"Well, *I'm* glad you came," Kris remarked. "Gabe, you didn't cut the rope, did you? I mean, I can't see you doing something like that, but I was being a bit of a butthead to you earlier."

"A bit of one?" Gabe challenged, then relented. "No, I didn't do it. Ask Jer. I was with him the whole time."

"He was," Jer spoke up, waving a dripping spoon. "You guys want to stay for supper? Our parents are in Augusta. We've got the house to ourselves!" He grinned mischievously. "What say you, ladies?"

"I'm not sure Mom would want us to have visitors," Gabe heard himself say, then wished he could pull back the words. Could he sound like a bigger idiot? "She wouldn't like it," he added, immediately realizing that yes, he could sound like a bigger idiot.

"Mom doesn't need to know," Kris said. "Besides, she's not going to care that these two came over. She's been worried about us making friends. Well, now her worries are over."

"I'll bet she can't sleep worrying about Gabe," Abazi quipped. "Can't imagine he's a friend magnet with that pouty look he always wears." Gabe refrained from scowling, and thus, proving her point.

"Would you grab me that tomato, Kimber?" Jer asked, heading back toward the stove. "I want to start a salad."

"Sure," she said softly, making her way over to him.

When she reached the counter, Jer started singing into his spoon. "I can bring home the bacon! Fry it up in a pan. And never let you forget I'm a man. Cause you're a wooooman!"

The other three laughed and Gabe sighed. It was out of his hands now. Jer was determined to have his way, and when Jer decided he wanted something, he got it. And he wanted Kimber to stay. Fighting him wasn't worth the cost, because in the end Gabe knew he would lose. Anyway, even if he won, he'd lose by proving himself to be a total drag.

"So what's this about a cut rope?" he asked.

"I was about to head back to the house," Kris explained. "Getting hungry, you know, and I went to grab the rope, then realized it had been cut. I just about sh—, um, had an aneurysm," he deftly avoided swearing in front of the 'ladies.' "I started calling you guys, but Abazi answered instead. She came right to me. A regular laser beam, that girl."

She grinned at him, but when she looked at Gabe, the smile dropped off her face. "Is something going on here I should know about? I mean, a cut rope in this fog...that's serious stuff."

Abazi was the last person Gabe wanted to know about what was happening. "It's nothing." He nodded at the counter. "Who's going to cut the bread?"

Soon everybody was pitching in to help Jer get supper ready, laughing and talking about the strange fog as they worked. Kris repeated Grandpa's fog story for the girls, with a few variations—casting himself as the main character and putting Jer in the role of the wife, which Jer didn't appreciate. In no time, the spaghetti, covered with Jer's special marinara sauce, was ready to serve, along with his homemade garlic bread and a fresh garden salad. At the dinner table Kris dominated the conversation, telling Kimber and Abazi about his blueberry picking wonder, the Shaker.

"I wondered how you guys picked them so fast." Abazi looked at Kris with what might have been admiration. "How'd you make it?"

Kris told her all about every agonizing detail and she listened without interrupting—something Gabe was sure she'd never do if it were him speaking. On the other side of the table, Kimber and Jer were immersed in their own little world, discussing food and animals. Apparently Kimber had horses and had invited Jer to come see them.

Gabe found his attention wandering. He wondered how long these strange events were going to go on. Something had to give, and soon. Either this whole experience was going to turn out to be real and the dark ones would capture him and eat him, or he was truly having hallucinations and would soon be receiving a one-way ticket to Funny Farm, USA. Neither outcome was appealing.

When dinner was over, they cleaned up the kitchen. As Jer was putting the last of the dishes away in the cupboard, the phone rang. Gabe motioned everyone to be quiet, then picked up the receiver.

"Hello?"

"Gabe?"

"Mom! How's Dad?"

"Well, he's holding his own." Her voice was choked up, as though she'd just tried to swallow a mouthful of food. This was how she sounded when she was trying not to cry.

Gabe bit his lip. "Well, that's good."

"You guys are all right?" Kris started making faces and the girls giggled. Gabe glared at them, which only made them laugh more.

"We're fine, Mom. Jer made supper and we just finished. The attic is all clean," he added, wanting to distract her with good news.

"Oh! Good! I wasn't looking forward to cleaning out all that stuff. My father saved everything, even cereal boxes."

"Yeah, I found those. I'll haul the recycling and trash to the Redemption Center tomorrow. We should make some money off the glass bottles, right?"

"Um, yeah. Tomorrow." She didn't sound too certain. "We'll have to see about that."

"Oh, okay. Well, we've got some chores we want to finish before bed. Tell Dad we love him."

"I will."

They said their goodbyes and Gabe hung up. "Dad's holding his own," he responded to their questioning looks. "He has an infection," he explained to Abazi and Kimber. "You've probably heard he has diabetes and that he had to get transplant surgery." They both nodded solemnly, and he thought Abazi actually gave him a sympathetic look. Though that was probably just wishful thinking.

"So what should we do now?" Kris started to ask, when a knock on the front door interrupted him. Everyone jumped, feeling a wee bit guilty about having boys and girls in a house together while the parents were elsewhere. They weren't doing anything wrong, but that didn't matter. Not to the parents, anyway. They always thought kids were up to something.

"Must be Grandpa," Gabe muttered. "I told him not to bother coming over. He could've ended up in the ditch." He turned the knob and swung open the door. There, on the porch, stood five figures shrouded in dark cloaks.

"That be the one!" a gruff voice called out.

Before Gabe knew what was happening, the screen door flew open and the cloaked figures swarmed him, grabbing his arms and legs and upending him quicker than two blinks. "Hey!" He struggled to fight them off, twisting his body this way and that. But they were too strong, already carrying him down the steps and away from the house, into the deep, dark fog.

Chapter Fifteen

The Ko-goks

After seeing his brother disappear out the door, Kris grabbed a baseball bat from the sports box and charged, bellowing like a berserker. Before he could do anything, the door swung shut, though he did manage to give the arm closing it a good whack and whoever owned it shrieked in pain. Jer grabbed the doorknob and tried to turn it, but it wouldn't move. After struggling for what seemed like a very long time, but which was probably only a few seconds, the knob gave way. Jer yanked open the door and he and Kris peered out. The shrieker was gone, and so was Gabe.

"Gabe!" they shouted, their voices loud in their ears. Only the fog greeted them back, swirling and dancing before them in macabre fashion. Gabe had disappeared.

"What the heck just happened?" Kris roared. "Where is he? *Gabe!*" He swung back around to confront Abazi. She, Kimber, and Jer were huddled in the doorway staring out at the thick fog. "Did some of your friends set this up?"

"Don't be stupid!" Abazi snapped. "I don't have friends. Other than Kimber, that is."

"All right, then tell me what happened out there. There were five of them, kind of short, and dressed in black. Do you know who that could've been?"

"The boys around here can be real cretins," she replied thoughtfully. "This could be their idea of a practical joke. It's a stretch, though, even for them. People in Ranger generally stay away from this part of town and they definitely stay home when it's foggy like this."

Kris stared at the gray wall of mist, thinking that she and Kimber hadn't stayed home. "We have to go after him." He stroked the wooden bat. "Now."

"Where do you think they went?" she asked.

"The woods," he answered grimly.

Abazi looked suddenly less poised. "Are you sure about that?"

"Of course I'm sure. Why?"

"Well, it's just that my people call these woods the place where the chi bai, or wandering spirits, reside. They don't go in there lightly, if at all, and neither do I."

"Sounds like my kind of adventure." Kris gripped his bat. "Arm yourself, Jer. We're going in."

"Well, if you're going, then I'm coming, too," Abazi declared as she pulled a red rubber band off her wrist and swiftly tied her hair into a ponytail. When it was secure, she headed for a beat-up tomahawk hanging on the wall. It was their mom's, one she'd had since she was a girl and had used to win hawk-throwing competitions. She'd promised to show them how to throw it once they found a good block of wood to use for a target. "I'll take this."

"You know how to throw that?" Jer was in awe.

"Duh. I'm an Indian, remember?"

"Not all Indians practice Indian things, Abazi," Kimber spoke up. "You of all people should know that."

Abazi grinned. "I do. I just like giving these guys a hard time."

"You like giving everybody a hard time." Abazi grinned again as she got a feel for the hawk's weight and length, gripping the handle and extending her arm outward.

Jer grabbed another baseball bat from the sports box for himself. He swung the wood slugger back and forth a few times. Kimber watched him, a worried frown lining her forehead. "You know, Kimber," he said to her, trying to put it gently, "I think you should stay here."

She shook her head, the frown growing stubborn. "I have to come with you."

"But your legs are going to slow you down." Kris didn't need to finish the rest of that sentence, *and slow us down, too.* Kimber knew. He grabbed the flashlight and shoved it into the waistband of his pants.

Kimber gave him a sweet smile. "Did you happen to notice where I was when you were being led back to the house?"

"Of course. I was last, then Abazi...I remember keeping my eyes on her hair. And you were in front of us." He snapped his fingers, pointing at her. "*You* were the one who led us through the fog! Why didn't you say something?"

She tilted her blond head to one side. "I like to let Abazi have her fun."

Abazi laughed. "Busted! I really do know how to throw hawk, though, so I'm taking it. My dad made me learn. Kimber, you take this." She grabbed an old wooden mallet from the counter and handed it to her friend.

Eyeing the mallet doubtfully, Kimber took hold of it with her small, pale hand, nearly losing her grip on it. "We should go now," she said, sounding surprisingly in charge. "I don't want to lose the trail." She smiled mischievously at Jer.

"Let's do this, people!" Kris shouted as he headed out the door, and his thunderous voice bounced back at him from several directions at once, like light off a mirror.

The four of them hustled down the porch steps, stopping at the bottom to let Kimber take the lead. Her red, hooded sweat jacket helped them see her in the white fog that billowed around them. As they shuffled along, Jer made sure to stay close to her. She was so small and delicate; she could easily slip into the fog bank and not be able to slide back out.

"Remember when we told you not to let the kittens out?" Abazi asked, barely visible even though she was only a few steps ahead of Kris. He grunted in response, his eyes on the awesome howling wolf dominating the back of her sweatshirt. He hadn't seen it the first time, when her hair covered its magnificence. "Well, a lot of people's pets have been disappearing lately. Some wacko could be offing them, or a wild animal is going after easy prey, or…"

"Or…" Kris prompted when she paused.

"Or, that Malsumis and his Ko-goks are real."

"Malsumis and his Ko-goks?" Kris repeated. "What the heck are those?"

"They're like the bogeyman, I guess. Malsumis is supposedly the evil twin to Gluskab, who's sort of an Abenaki hero. Gluskab started the Golden Age, teaching us how to fend for ourselves—you know, hunting, fishing, building shelter. He taught us about science, too. My tribe believes that the white man angered Gluskab so he left us. But he will return again someday. Malsumis, on the other hand, has never gone away and continues to seek out evil to this day. He especially likes to go after white people."

"Now you're messing with us," Kris scoffed.

"I am not!" she protested, then she laughed. "Well, maybe the part about going after white people. I might have made that up. Anyway, it's just a stupid legend. I don't believe any of it."

"So what exactly are Malsumis and those Ko-gok thingies?" Jer asked.

"I'm not sure," she grumbled. "I can never pin the tribe elders, or my father, down on the subject. Believe me, I've tried. When I was a little kid, the boys used to tease me and warn me that Malsumis's Ko-goks were going to get me if I didn't do what they said. I never gave in, of course, but that didn't stop them from trying to manipulate me."

Her brow furrowed as she relived the memory. "Anyway," she shook herself, "according to those jerks, Ko-goks are some kind of monster more terrible than your worst nightmare. Their descriptions always started with the words dark and evil, continued with the Ko-goks' long, bony hands, and ended with their deep and overwhelming thirst for human blood. Ko-goks' faces are like death's heads and they possess the ability to change form; into what, I'm not sure." She tried to sound bored by the whole thing, but a tiny tremor in her voice belied the truth. She was scared of the Ko-goks, despite her defiance against the bullies, and despite claiming she didn't believe the stories.

With this disturbing image set firmly in their minds, the group quietly passed the looming barn, which appeared before them like a ghost ship. After several long minutes, they blundered into the massive hedge. The living tapestry looked more than impenetrable; there was an air of threat about it—a feeling that if it could communicate it would scream at you to go away.

"Stand back!" Kris ordered the others, readying his bat. "I'm going in."

He was about to start swinging when a slithering noise, like snakes rushing at him, stayed his hand. Numerous vines in the hedge retreated, revealing a door. Arched and low, the opening looked quite small and not very welcoming. Jer took a step toward it. A thorny branch brushed against his arm and a delicate tendril wrapped around his finger. Another threaded itself through his hair. He backed away from the wall, thoroughly spooked.

"I guess that solves the mystery of how Gabe got through the hedge," Kris remarked.

Jer peered suspiciously at the opening, his hand rubbing the spot where the vine had scratched him. "I hope this isn't a trap. It looks like a trap, you know." He glanced about. "I've got a funny feeling about this."

The others gathered around the uninviting door. Unintimidated, Kris ducked low. "Well, here goes nothing." He stepped through to the other side. Seeing that he was all right, the others quickly followed, not wanting to be left alone. In their feverish minds unseen enemies lurked everywhere, just out of sight, though perhaps not out of reach.

Once they all stood on the other side of the hedge, the door disappeared completely, as though it had never been there. Now, any escape route was closed off. Unnerved, they hurried away from the strange hedge, across a grassy clearing, until they reached the edge of the forest. Here, they paused for a moment to stare up at the massive trees facing them like soldiers on guard.

After a moment's hesitation, they slowly stepped into the forest's realm, the light dimming within like clouds passing over the sun. The trees grew thick here, clustered together as a herd of cows would gather in a storm. Their grayish-brown trunks were the legs of giants standing with their heads touching the sky, unseen through the fog. These trees were at least a couple hundred feet tall and centuries old.

Kris turned around, his cheeks glowing with excitement. "Do you think they came this way?" he asked Kimber.

She nodded. "I can sense your brother. I can smell his fear." No one asked how she could do this. In fact, they could smell something, too. The odor permeated the air around them like rancid perfume.

Jer swallowed hard. "Is he going to be okay?"

Kimber looked up at him, her blue eyes luminous in the white fog. "I don't know. We'll have to move fast."

"Show us the way, oh, Great Guide," Kris invited as he ushered her ahead of him.

Kimber took the lead. With each hesitant step into the dark woods, Jer noticed something strange. Not a bird-like chirp or a rustling of leaves were to be heard, no scampering squirrels or fleeing deer to be found. The fog could be swallowing all evidence of their existence, but for reasons he couldn't fathom, he didn't think that the heavy mist was the answer. All the animals had simply gone away. *Or been eaten*, he thought, remembering what Abazi had told them about the disappearing pets.

Thankfully the thick, emerald green moss, a plush carpet beneath their feet, muffled their footsteps, giving them some protection. After a few minutes, however, the moss became a hindrance. It grew deeper with each step, making progress increasingly difficult. Poor Kimber struggled along, bits of moss catching in her leg braces.

This is not a typical forest, Kris thought as he looked around. The animals had yet to show themselves. No shrubs or saplings decorated the forest floor, not even the hardy wintergreen or the typically abundant fern. There were no dead leaves to crunch on, nor broken branches, rotting logs, or half-fallen trees to trip over. Not even any pinecones or acorns. Just the tall trees, many with roots growing above ground, resembling the legs of an octopus, and moss-covered boulders dotting the forest floor like green warts. It was eerie here in this wild, forbidding place, and Kris shivered suddenly in the cool air.

They were not welcome here.

Kimber put up her hand. "Do you hear that?" Everyone stopped to listen, and then Kris heard it, too. They all heard it. A soft shushing sound, as though something were being dragged along the forest floor, its body scraping against the ground.

Suddenly the sound was all around them. They could see nothing in the fog, but they felt in their bones that something was there. Whatever it was refused to be ignored.

"Who's there?" Kris demanded, brandishing his bat. "Show yourself or get a taste of this puppy!"

The shushing grew louder. They were completely surrounded by it now, as though caught in a tornado. They huddled against each other as they felt the unseen threat grow closer. They pressed backward until finally there was no more room to press. They were trapped, and by something they couldn't see.

"It's the Ko-goks..." Abazi whispered, her usually cocky voice shaking. "They've come for us."

~~~~~~

The dark ones have me, Gabe realized as he fought to free himself. His captors were the same creatures he'd seen from the truck, the same ones that wanted his blood. At around five and a half feet tall, his kidnappers were short, but surprisingly strong, and wore cloaks with hoods so he couldn't see their faces. *There are four of them*, he determined, rapidly counting the hands grasping and pinching him. *I might be able to take four...if I could just get free.*

As they hurried along, the cool fog caressed his fevered skin. Once in a while they would pass through a warm patch, which might sound nice, but was not. To Gabe, the heated air felt like something was breathing on him. At times, the fog would lift and he could make out the grand trees rising upward, or a stand of boulders grouped together like sleeping elephants. Quiet ruled here, as though the whole world was asleep. Yet the noise that he could hear—the dark ones' breathing—echoed in his ears, taunting him.

"This be dumber than dumb," one of the kidnappers hissed in frustration. "Me feet hurt from touchin' deadwood and he's too heavy and wiggly, anyway. I'm gonna drop him if'n he keeps this up. We should just eat him now!"

"And get banished to the *Other Side*?" another one bellowed, his voice echoing off the fog. "Un, uh. We're supposed to deliver him and that's what we're gonna do. Now quit yer whinin' and do yer job."

There was a loud, fretful sigh. "I don't know what Straif is wantin' with him, anyway. He can't be too bright, openin' the door like that. Didn't even look, did he, Dorn? Ye could just say we didn't find him, then I'll eat him all up! Num, num, num!"

"Barb!" the other voice scolded when Gabe had tried to take advantage of their distraction by twisting his body hard toward the complainer. "Stop arguin', ye drisk-headed podunk, and hold up yer end!"

Gabe felt the thin, dry hands on his left leg grip tighter. They weren't going to let him go that easily. What in Hades was he going to do now? He didn't know which fate would be worse, meeting Straif or getting eaten by these creeps. Gabe was pretty sure Straif wasn't the kind of guy to serve him tea and crumpets, but he also didn't like his chances with these jokers, either.

"Let me go!" he cried, kicking and twisting about as hard as he could.

"Ye stop that cruckel right now, *Gabriel*," the name came out in a sneer, "or we're gonna do as Barb here suggests. Eat ye right up."

Vicious laughter rang out as the dark ones enjoyed the joke, or threat, as Gabe saw it. "You'd better let me go!" he yelled, searching for a threat of his own. "Or my brother, who likes nothing better than to humiliate and defeat others in battle, will hunt you down and make you wish you'd never been born."

There was silence for a moment. "We aren't fearin' yer brother, *Gabriel*," retorted the one who seemed to be in charge.

"I be fearin' him, Dorn," he heard another whisper. He thought it might be Barb.

"You *should* fear him," Gabe warned. "He's fierce. He's not scared of anything. I'll bet he's in these woods right now, tracking you."

Another burst of laughter mocked him. "Then he's as good as dead," Dorn snarled.

"Why?" Gabe cried out, fearing for Kris, and Jer, too. Their little brother would not allow Kris to leave him behind.

"Ye're thinkin' we're the only ones in these woods? Oh, no. We're everywhere. We rule the Forest Immortal!"

"Don't you mean Straif does?" Gabe muttered.

Another silence fell over the dark ones, then, "Oh, just shut yer yapper! We still got a ways to go, and Dorn is growin' hungry."

Gabe decided to obey. He didn't want to set Dorn off—he seemed to be the one most likely to eat him, and toe by toe just to prolong the agony. Gabe decided to shut his mouth and start working out a plan in his head. If they still had a ways to travel, he figured the dark creeps would grow tired of carrying him soon enough. He weighed a hundred and sixty pounds, mostly muscle, he figured, not an easy load to haul.

They'd already been complaining about dropping him—Barb had, anyway. All Gabe had to do was bide his time, lull them into complacency, and then *bam!* start thrashing about like a fish on deck. They wouldn't even know what hit them, and he'd be free. But what was he going to do once he got away? Finding his way out of this maze of trees, through thick fog, wouldn't be easy. Just the thought of it made him want to hyperventilate.

"Where are we now?" Barb whined after fifteen minutes had passed. "I hate how everythin' keeps changin' round here. Me arms hurt from carryin' this lug, me feet burn from that dratted wood, and me skin is all itchy."

"Not far," Dorn growled. "So keep yer knickers on."

Gabe decided that he'd better move now. He'd learned in Driver's Ed that most car accidents happened close to home. Within a few miles of their destiny, drivers relaxed, thinking they were as good as home, safe and sound. He only hoped these idiots would do the same. Over the last few minutes their breathing had regressed to heavy panting and the occasional grunt, and he thought that their grip had loosened.

Steeling himself mentally, he relaxed his entire body, letting it droop. Not expecting this, the pea brains lost their grip and their long fingers scrabbled to grab hold. With a violent twist, he tore free, landing on the soft ground with barely a thump. Before he knew it, he was on his feet and running, tramping through the thick moss as fast as his feet could carry him. Angry voices rang out behind him and he hoped it was only the fog that made them sound so close.

Quick as a frightened deer, Gabe leaped over rocks and dodged around tree trunks. If only the trees didn't grow so close together, he might be able to gain ground on his shorter captors. But the little guys stuck to him like a burr. Gabe was a sprinter, not an endurance runner, and he was starting to get winded. He might be able to outrun them at first, but over distance, they'd catch him in the end.

From out of nowhere, hundreds of sharp, grasping thorns raked at Gabe's clothes and skin. The pain brought him up short, ending his mad dash. He'd blundered into a patch of black, spiky trees, standing not much taller than he did. He turned to go another way and found more of them. He ran in a different direction, and there they were again. This stupid fog was so disorienting! He heard voices and froze where he was, hoping against hope that his pursuers hadn't heard him crashing about and were now passing him by.

"We got ye now, *Gabriel*," Dorn's voice drilled into Gabe's ear like a cloud of locusts. He sounded very close. Gabe spun around, hoping to find where he'd first entered the swarm of thorny trees, but the opening remained elusive. He couldn't see anything in the fog beyond the thousands of black branches surrounding him, trapping him in a prison of spikes and thorns.

His gaze fastened on a dark figure pushing his way through the thorny trees without so much as wincing. The thick cloak took the brunt of the spikes, protecting its wearer. Perhaps if Gabe had been wearing more than a t-shirt and shorts he would have been able to do the same.

"Ye can come peacefully, or we can leave ye here to starve. What say ye?" Dorn was so close now that Gabe could actually see a bit of his face—a white oval marred by two dark hollows for eyes. There was something disturbing about his countenance and one fleeting glimpse was enough for Gabe. He didn't want to see any more.

"I know you won't just leave me here. Straif wouldn't be too happy if you failed to bring me to him." A guess, but it was all Gabe had. He needed to stall as he crept backward, giving him time to find a way out of this trap.

"We'll tell him where ye be. If'n ye made him come for ye, he'll be awful scorched. Who knows what he might do to ye then." Evil laughter chilled Gabe's heart.

"Straif is not as nice as us," Barb felt compelled to add.

Gabe gulped, feeling dizzy with fear. He didn't know what to do. Take his chances here, hoping to find a way out before Straif came after him, or leave with Dorn. Neither sounded like the way to go.

He'd decided to take his chances in the thorn patch when long fingers suddenly seized his arm. "Got ye!" Dorn howled triumphantly. Instantly, the others jumped Gabe and grabbed hold of him, lifting him off the ground like a pig to slaughter. He hadn't even had a chance to run. How had they got so close without him noticing a thing?

"All that we see or seem is but a dream within a dream," he mumbled dazedly to himself, thinking Poe's quote could've been written about what he was going through right now. Nothing was real here; it couldn't be. Strange, dark creatures. A haunted forest. Voices that knew his name. This all had to be a dream. But despite all the pinching the dark ones inflicted on him, he didn't wake up. Could this all really be happening to him?

Lord, he hoped not.

Chapter Sixteen

In Enemy Territory

"Wwhat are ye doin' here?" a voice whispered from behind them. "Where's Gabriel?"

"We're looking for him," Kris answered carefully. He had no idea who or what was talking to him, because whoever it was was staying out of sight.

"What do ye mean? Why did ye come *here* to look for him?"

"Because someone came to the house and took him," Abazi snapped. "What's it to *you*, whoever you are?"

A girl dressed in vivid green leaped down to land in front of them. She must have been hiding up in a tree, Kris figured, which was really cool. "*Ye* are rude," she accused, pointing at Abazi, and her narrow, freckled nose quivered indignantly.

She's quite pretty, in a woodsy sort of way, he thought. *I like woodsy.* He also liked how her flushed cheeks and bright lips highlighted her dusky skin.

"I am," agreed Abazi. "Sometimes I can't help myself."

The girl looked taken aback. "Oh, well! Hmm… How odd just admittin' it like that," she muttered to herself. "Well, back to what I asked ye… Why here? Why did ye come to the Forest Immortal? It's the worst thing ye could've done."

"We think Gabe's kidnappers brought him here," Jer explained. "There were five of them, all dressed in black. Kris nailed one on the arm with his bat before they fled with our brother."

The girl's face drained of its lovely color. "They have him? They have Gabriel?" She wrung her long-fingered hands together. "Oh, this is not good. I knew I shouldn't have lured him in here that day. I wanted to get back at him for callin' me Repulsive! Oh, we must tell Dame Hazel right away!"

"What we must do *right away*," Kris corrected her, "is find Gabe."

"Dame Hazel is wise. She'll know what's goin' on. I only know that if the Ko-goks have him, then he's in trouble."

Abazi drew in her breath. "Did you say Ko-goks?"

The girl nodded. "That's what we call them now. They're evil creatures, and they want Gabriel. But I don't know why."

"Where are they taking him?" Kris growled, tightening his grip on his bat.

"To Straif, to be sure. He's their leader. He's worse than all of them put together. I met him once. I'll never forget it. I wish I could…" Her words trailed off as she looked around, her eyes full of dread.

"Not Malsumis?" Abazi questioned.

"That's another name for him."

"Do you know where Straif is now?" Kris asked.

"Sort of. He's always changin' the way to his place—what we call the Dark Domain. But Dame Hazel will know how to get there. She knows everything. She's very old and very wise. We must go to her."

"So what are *you*, then?" Abazi demanded. "There's something different about you."

"My name's Hollie," she answered, deliberately choosing to misunderstand Abazi's question. "I live in the forest. And ye are Abazi. The tall one goes by the name Kristofer." She pointed to Jer. "Ye're Jerome and the small one is Kimber." Hollie smiled at her. "Ye're the tracker, and a very good one, at that."

Abazi pointed the tomahawk at the strange girl. "How do you know our names?"

Hollie shrugged. "It's easy to be informed when one observes."

Something clicked in Kris's mind. "You're the baby! Gabe told us about you. He said we all adored you. I can see why." He grinned at her. "That must be how you found out our names." His brow wrinkled. "We never call each other by our full names, though. That was a good guess on your part." He shook his head. "So why don't we remember you?"

Her answering smile was mysterious. "I shall take ye to Dame Hazel now. If we hurry, Gabriel will still have a chance."

"A chance to what?" Kris asked.

"A chance to live."

"Ah. Then show us the way." She gave him a penetrating look, which he felt all the way to his toes. He rather liked the sensation.

With a little nod, she turned about and plunged into the forest. The group hurried after her, not wanting to be left behind in the deep and twisted woods.

"We must move fast and keep our voices low. There are enemies all round us, watchin' us, trackin' our every step." Nobody answered her. There was nothing to say to that.

Abazi fell back to walk alongside Kris. "Do you trust her?" she whispered. "She's a bit odd, isn't she? I mean, she doesn't look entirely human, nor does she act it."

"She seems all right to me. Gabe said she helped him get away the first time the dark ones attacked him."

"This has happened before?" She sounded incredulous.

Kris told her about what Gabe had gone through over the last couple days. "I kinda didn't believe him," he admitted. "I thought maybe somebody was pulling a practical joke on him. Or he was just being paranoid. Gabe's always coming up with a million scenarios for what something might be, but typically never is."

"How do we know we can trust Hollie? Maybe she's leading us into a trap."

"Maybe. I don't know. We'll just have to stay on alert and see where we end up."

"I'm not sure I like the sound of that. There's something wrong with this place. I can feel it." Abazi shivered. "No birds, no squirrels. And this moss! It's practically tickling my nose, it's so high!"

"I bet this is how the woods looked before humans came along and started cutting down all the trees," Kris said, his eyes far away. "This forest must be really old." Lids half-closed, he conjured in his mind a world of ancient times, populated by dinosaurs and sea monsters. His fingers itched for a drawing pad to capture it all.

"Did you hear what Hollie said about the Ko-goks?" Abazi interrupted his imaginings. "She seems to think they're real. Maybe my clan knows something after all." She frowned as though this was a fact she'd rather not accept. "I always thought those old farts were full of it whenever they talked about spirits and stuff like that. But now—"

"Since we don't know anything for sure," Kris interrupted, "let's not make any assumptions. I'm still not entirely sure this isn't some kind of stupid joke. But I like to keep an open mind. However it turns out, I'm up for it." He flicked his wrist, spinning the bat resting on his shoulder.

"I hope we find this Dame Hazel soon. I'm sick of walking through this fog. It's like trying to find your way through a cloud." Abazi wrapped her arms around her. "I'm getting creeped out and I just want to get out of these woods."

Kris nodded, even though he didn't feel the same way. He was worried about Gabe, but he liked the challenge these crazy woods gave him. He'd waited his whole life to be tested. Now that the time had come, he was determined to enjoy every second, even if it included walking blindly through thick moss and fog.

Up ahead, Kris heard Jer ask Kimber, "What kind of horses do you have?"

"An Appaloosa named Spunky and a Shetland pony named Patches," she replied. "My mom bought them cheap from Mr. Johnson—he's the local horse trainer and vet—to help me build up my muscles. You know, for my…"

"Your cerebral palsy," he finished for her. "I did some research on CP the other night. You must have a mild case. I can barely even tell you have it."

She gave him a little smile. "Other than these?" She glanced down at her braces, "and the dorky walk and fumble fingers?" She laughed at the pained expression on his face. "I'm actually very lucky, Jer." His eyebrows shot up in surprise. "You should come over some time. I'll introduce you to Spunky and Patches."

"I'd like that."

Hollie swung round. "Ye've got to be quiet! Ye talk so much. On and on. Have ye not heard of a little thing called silence?" She turned back around, her narrow shoulders hunched in annoyance. "Sheesh!" The four friends gave each other guilty smiles.

They were only able to take a few more steps when Hollie stopped again, holding up her hand and tilting her head to one side as though listening. "Oh, now ye've done it! They've heard us!"

"Who's heard us?" Kris demanded.

"The Ko-goks! Yer dark ones. I can't let them see me. It's too late now for ye to escape, but I'll be close by." With a dash and a leap into the air, she was gone, swallowed up by the fog.

"She set us up!" Abazi cried. "I knew it!"

"Hollie!" Kris called. "Come back!"

His mouth clamped shut when he saw a mass of dark figures in black cloaks emerge from the fog like shadows at dusk. Before he could blink, he and the others were surrounded. One of the cloaked figures, taller than the rest and wielding the deadly clout of arrogance and leadership, stepped forward. Instinctively, Kris and Jer pushed Kimber and Abazi behind them. Both girls resisted the chivalrous act, but not for long. They sensed the evil oozing like poisonous gas from the crowd of veiled strangers.

"Ye are not welcome here."

"No," Kris agreed. "But we came all the same."

"That's the last mistake ye'll be makin' in this world, then," the creature growled. His hood was draped in such a way that they couldn't see his face.

Kris hefted his bat. "Don't be too sure about that."

Jer readied his, too. "Yeah. We came here for a reason. Why don't you and your friends just walk away and we'll pretend this meeting never happened."

The cloaked figure chuckled—a dry, stepping on dead leaves sound. "Ye are fools. Four against forty. Do ye think ye can win?"

"Hmmm…" Kris pretended to ponder. "Well, I plan to take down as many of you as I can before I'm taken myself. I figure that should be about thirty-five of you."

"Brave words," the hooded figure sneered. "But are ye willin' to risk yer friends' lives?"

He pointed and Kris and Jer spun around. Somehow, under the cover of the fog, the creatures had snuck up and grabbed Abazi and Kimber, then slipped back again, hands smothering the girls' mouths, all done without a sound.

"The game changes," the leader remarked.

Kris gave him a brief nod. "So it has."

"Put yer weapons on the ground and step away from them."

Kris and Jer reluctantly did as they were told, both feeling completely vulnerable without their bats. Abazi and Kimber dropped their weapons, too. Strangely enough, the Ko-goks, or whatever they were, didn't take the weapons for themselves. In fact, they avoided them completely.

"Ye're comin' with us and don't be thinkin' of tryin' to get away."

The hooded figures herded their captives forward into the waiting fog. Abazi and Kimber were released, but there would be no escape for any of them. They had no weapons and they were completely surrounded by dark cloaks.

Despite their threatening presence, the Ko-goks were awfully quiet. Kris thought that if these jerks were a bunch of kids dressed up, they played the game awfully well. Everything about them gave off an aura of danger. He sensed they would be tough opponents and he had the experience to know. Back in San Jose, he'd been in a fair number of fights. There was always some kid thinking he was tougher than Kris Hawthorne, until Kris proved them wrong, of course. This situation was different. He and Jer and the girls were hugely outnumbered, plus they didn't know who or what they were up against.

"Where are you taking us?" Abazi shouted, unable to bear the quiet any longer. "I want to know!" she bellowed when no one answered her. "Is Hollie working for you?"

"Ye seen Hollie, did ye? I need to pay her a visit, thank her personal-like for what she's done."

"You can't do this to us!"

"Father'll be quite pleased with Feltry this day," the leader murmured, as though speaking to himself. "I'll bring ye to him to do with ye what he will. Most likely, he'll want to eat ye."

"What in Hades are you talking about?" she demanded. "And what kind of stupid name is Feltry?" She shook her head in disgust. "This has got to be some kind of sick joke. Nobody practices cannibalism anymore. It's against the law, you know." There was a burst of snickering.

"Father won't be breakin' no laws eatin' *ye*," Feltry answered her in an ominous tone.

Abazi glanced over at Kris. He only raised an eyebrow at her as if to say, "No clue."

"You're saying he's not human?" Kris pushed.

"I'm not sayin' nothing," Feltry muttered.

Kris had a feeling that Feltry hadn't liked Abazi poking fun at his name. He thought he'd better keep his mouth shut for the moment and definitely not comment on Feltry's use of a double negative. Instead, he trudged through the clinging moss and thought about his dad, wondering how he was doing, if they'd been able to treat his infection. Kris was starting to have his suspicions about how Dad had come by his wound. He'd told them he hadn't noticed the thorny shrub until he'd scratched himself on it. Maybe, Kris postulated, someone had been hiding in the shrub, waiting to make a sneak attack. He'd seen something like that in an old war movie once. A spy disguised himself as a bush, then slowly crept closer to the guard keeping watch. When the secret agent made his move, the soldier didn't even see the knife coming. The moving bush was a classic stealth maneuver, though he wasn't sure how realistic it was. At any rate, however Dad's injury had come about, Kris felt certain it had something to do with these dark strangers, and with Gabe's kidnapping.

When they stepped from the woods into a clearing, he felt as though he could finally breathe normally again. He inhaled deeply and the smell of death and decay filled his nose, effectively squashing his triumph at being free of the forest.

About ten minutes into their trek across the field, they met up with another stand of trees, none of which stood over thirteen feet at its highest point. Deadly thorns pierced the black bark of the trees' wild, malformed branches as profusely as goose bumps. The shiny, black thorns grew long and thick, with strong, sharp tips that could pierce a person's chest with one good thrust. Could these thorns have been the cause of Dad's wound? If so, he was lucky not to have been sliced up like a stick of butter.

They entered a short tunnel, about ten feet long, its walls and ceiling made of intertwining tree branches. A thorn whipped out at Jer as he passed by and he batted it away with a karate chop. The tallest of the bunch, Kris stooped over to avoid getting his hair combed by the tunnel's ceiling, which weighed heavily with thorns. Kimber stumbled and Jer caught her arm. Kris could tell she was getting tired. Feltry had kept them moving at a rapid and unrelenting pace and even he was feeling the burn.

After a short stretch in the tunnel, they entered a smaller field, completely surrounded by the dark, thorny trees. The fog was thinner here, as though even the mist didn't want to linger. In the middle of the field, a boulder protruded from the ground like the nose of a shark. On it sat a creature, regally, as though the rough boulder were a throne. Like Feltry and the others, he wore a dark cloak, his face hidden from view.

About twenty yards in front of them, four hooded creatures marched toward the boulder and its forbidding occupant. Between them, they carried something heavy and they were in a hurry.

A growl erupted from Feltry. "What are ye doin' here, Dorn?" he shouted. "I got something to show Father. Get yerself out of the way, Brother." Feltry swiftly herded the group toward the boulder, racing to reach it before Dorn.

Dorn glanced behind him as he struggled along with their heavy burden. "Dorn caught him, Father!" he bellowed triumphantly. "Dorn caught *Gabriel!*"

Kris's stomach flipped.

That thing they carried like a beast to slaughter was his brother!

Chapter Seventeen

The Powers That Be

Gabe heard the shouting behind him. He wrenched his neck around to see what was going on and spotted Kris, Jer, Kimber, and Abazi. He'd never been so thrilled to see anyone in his life. Heck, he'd even plant a big one on Abazi's contemptuous mouth to show how happy he was. She'd probably smack him across the face, but he wouldn't mind.

His joy was short-lived, however, when he realized that they were prisoners, too. A taller dark one, who looked ten times nastier than Dorn, herded them forward. A menacing figure, sitting perched like a vulture on a large boulder, stood up, and Gabe's kidnappers froze in their tracks. Gabe peered up at the strange creature, who was surprisingly short, yet somehow managed to convey the illusion that he was the tallest one there. A bony finger extended from his cape's billowing sleeve and he beckoned them without a word.

Dorn was obviously frightened; his body was tense and his chest rose and fell in rapid, jerky bursts, but he didn't loosen his grip on Gabe, nor did the others. No way were they going to blow their mission now.

No command was issued, out loud anyway, yet all Gabe's captors set him down on the damp, prickly ground, at the same time. He scrambled to his feet, searching out his brothers and his friends. The fog was lighter now and he could see them huddled together about ten feet away. Before he could call out to them, Dorn pushed him forward, toward what had to be Straif. Dorn had called him Father, which Gabe hoped was just a term of respect the gang used for their leader. If Straif was an adult, Gabe and the others were in big trouble. An adult involved in something like this either had to be crazy or evil, or both.

Gabe stood only a few feet from the makeshift throne now, but Straif did not look at him, nor did he make a sound. A seething shadow, he stared up at the sky and his silence made a more disturbing impression than if he'd howled and thundered.

After some time had passed, Gabe couldn't take it any longer. "Listen, if we're trespassing, we'll leave right now. I'm not sure what kind of game this is, but we don't want any part of it. We want to go home." No response. "So if you don't mind, we'll just be going." He made to turn around.

"Ye'll not speak until spoken to, *Gabriel*," the voice boomed and Gabe froze.

"Leave him alone!" Kris shouted. "You're nothing but a bully and a tiny one at that. I could take you with one hand tied behind my back." Gabe and Jer unwittingly echoed each other as they groaned in dismay. One of these days Kris was going to get them killed. Maybe this was the day. "Let's see what you've got, Darth Ugly!"

With chilling deliberation, Straif's skeletal hand reached up and slowly pulled back his hood. Gabe's stomach heaved a little when he saw Straif's face, which was hideous—skin white as death; his eyes, set deeply into hollows, like black, gaping wounds. The skin rimming each lashless orb was red and covered with sties. An array of shiny black spikes, about two inches long, crossed his scalp in an arc, from one ear over to the other, except Straif had no ears, just holes drilled into moldering flesh.

There is no way that thing is human, Gabe thought in a panic.

"I've been waitin' a long time for ye to come back," Straif finally spoke again. His voice was old and dry, though surprisingly strong coming from one looking so close to death. "So that I can finish ye once and for all." The dark followers howled in triumph, and the sound chilled Gabe's blood.

"But why?" Gabe forced out. "Why me?"

"When ye're dead, them'll be givin' up. Easy as that."

Gabe swallowed the acidic bile flooding his gullet. "Who are *they?*"

"The Rogues." Straif glanced back over his shoulder, into the mountains behind him. The movement showed more spikes protruding from his pale head, which looked, from the back, like a puffer fish. "They live up there." He pointed at the mountain with a long finger. "I chased them into the hills to hide like rats. But they don't always stay up there."

"What would they be giving up?" Gabe asked, stalling for time. In all this, time was the only weapon he had. The malevolent fog had returned again, growing thick and dark around them. He could barely see Straif now, which perhaps wasn't such a bad thing. Even if the guy was only wearing some kind of elaborate mask, he scared Gabe.

"The fight," Straif replied simply. His weird spider leg fingers pulled his hood back over his spiky head. "Now I'm growin' hungry. For meat and for power." He chuckled, like snakes hissing. "Ye've been a thorn in me side for too long, *Gabriel*. Prepare yerself to die."

"Wait!" Gabe cried out. "You can have me, but you have to let my friends go."

"Yer friends'll be just as tasty as ye."

"We'll fight," Gabe warned, though his beating heart made it difficult to get the words out as forcefully as he would've liked. "We'll take out as many of you as we can before we die." It was something Kris would say. Gabe was finally getting why his brother could be so intimidating.

"They have to be *live*, Father," Dorn spoke up. "Or they're no good!"

"Quiet!" Straif snapped. "They're no match for us."

"How about us, then?" A single, lilting, yet powerful, voice came from all around them, echoing and mocking. A chaotic chorus of whoops and cries rang forth as a mob flew from out of nowhere to surround Straif and the dark ones. Gabe couldn't see them clearly in the billowing fog, but he knew there were a lot of them.

One of the newcomers stepped forward out of the mist. He was tall, about Gabe's age, with curly, reddish-brown hair the color of sunlight through autumn leaves. Dressed in dark greens and browns, he gripped a long staff of pale wood spotted with numerous dark diamond shapes. "Let them go, Straif, and we'll let ye live."

"Fools!" Straif shouted. "Ye're surrounded." He swept his arm around to indicate the unseen circle of black, thorny trees. "Ye can't be gettin' out unless I say so."

"We have our ways, Straif. Remember?"

Straif hesitated. "This is a trick. If'n ye had the advantage, ye'd have killed us by now."

The boy smiled. "We're not like ye, Straif. We don't kill unless absolutely necessary. And then, we try to make it as painless as possible. We know what ye do here. We've heard the screams. Ye follow a different path from us now."

"Get him!" Straif bellowed, and the dark ones charged the stranger. "Destroy him! Make him wish he'd never been born!" With a triumphant smile, the stranger leaped back into the heavy fog. The dark ones chased after him, pulling long, lethal looking thorns from beneath their cloaks. Gabe knew those thorns. He'd encountered them in the woods, then in the tunnel to get here. He hoped the stranger would be all right.

Realizing he'd been left alone, Gabe glanced up at the boulder. Straif was peering angrily into the fog where the boy had disappeared. Now was the time to make his escape. Unable to see his brothers and friends now, he crept slowly backwards until Straif disappeared in the mist.

Out of his sight, Gabe swung around and headed toward where he'd last seen the others.

Strange noises and grunts of frustration echoed all around him as he made his way through the fog, seeing nothing. He was starting to despair of finding the others when he spotted them a few feet away, clustered together for protection.

"Hey, guys!" he hissed. "It's me!"

They all turned to face him and Kris and Jer grinned. "We thought we'd let you come to us," Kris said, slapping him heartily on the back. "More efficient that way."

"Yeah, thanks," Gabe replied dryly, though he was smiling. "Now let's get out of here."

Nobody spoke as they hurried in what they hoped was the direction of the tunnel. Muffled by the fog, the sounds of the battle behind them faded to whispers. The group soon reached the thorny trees, but there was no tunnel to be found. The way out was completely blocked.

"There's no way we'll be able to get through that!" Jer pointed at the massive wall of spiky branches. "Those thorns will rip us to shreds." Gabe stared hopelessly at the mass.

"We should keep looking for the tunnel," Abazi ordered. "While they're still distracted."

A nearby shout told them they'd already run out of time. "They're gone! After them!"

Gabe took a step toward the wall. "Get behind me, and be ready to move. Jer, take Kimber's hand and bring her through with you. We're going to have to go fast and she's going to need your help."

"Done and done!" Jer replied, happily seizing hold of Kimber's hand. The rest lined up behind him, with Kris going last.

"Ready?"

"Ready," came a chorus of replies.

Facing the short, spiky trees, he growled in what he hoped was a threatening voice, "Open up, you stupid trees, or I'm going to rip you apart with my teeth!" There was a flutter and a twitch of branches, barely noticeable in the fog and shadows. "You've got five seconds," Gabe tried again, using the same threat his mother used when they were kids and weren't obeying. (Okay, maybe she'd used it last week because they were spending too much time playing video games and not enough on packing. Still, it had worked.) "If you're not open when I get to zero, I'm going through and you're not going to like it."

To everyone's amazement, the branches began to hastily unweave, writhing like exposed worms as they slid backwards in a mad scramble to part ways. Soon a small opening appeared in the thick hedge. Though not very wide or high, there was enough space for them to crawl through. Gabe got down on his hands and knees and scrambled through ten feet of hedge, scratching his cheek along the way. Jer followed, pulling Kimber after him. Next came Abazi. She was halfway along, with Kris right behind her, when the gap in the branches began to close.

"Stay open!" Gabe commanded. The branches stopped moving.

Abazi started crawling forward again, then jerked backward. Her sleeve had caught on a thorn, or perhaps it had caught on her—on purpose. Either way, she was stuck. Kris tried to help her, but he was too big and awkward in the tiny space. He couldn't free her.

"Come through, Kris!" Gabe ordered. "I'll get her." Kris slipped around Abazi and crawled to the end. Gabe hurriedly pushed past him. The tunnel had already grown smaller, the branches rapidly reuniting. Abazi was breathing hard as she wrestled with her shirt.

"Stay still!" he yelled. She frowned, but obeyed. He reached out and grabbed, not her shirt as she was expecting, but the base of the thorn. "You shouldn't be messing with me," he snarled as he gripped the thick stem. With a hard wrench, he snapped the thorn right off.

His action was like throwing a switch. The branches began to move faster, reaching out for each other, threatening to trap them in a deathly embrace. Grabbing Abazi's hand, Gabe yanked her along as he hobbled along on his knees. The way ahead was dim, the branches racing at lightning speed. Furious, Gabe used his free arm to smash at the frantically writhing limbs. They fought back, swinging at him like fists, slapping his face, pounding his head.

With one last burst, he dragged himself and Abazi through the opening. With an angry hiss, the gap closed, leaving them panting on the ground, bleeding from several scratches.

"Wow!" Kris nodded in approval. "I'm impressed, Gabe. And here I always thought you were such a wuss."

Gabe gave his brother a tired, slightly puzzled smile. He hadn't ever expected to see such behavior from himself, either. "I got mad, I guess."

"You saved my life," Abazi wheezed, reaching up to touch a bleeding scratch on her chin. She peered at him through narrowed eyes, which didn't look very grateful.

"Not completely." Gabe stood up. "Soon enough, those dark dorks are going to figure out that we managed to get outside their tree fortress. We better keep moving." He reached out and took Abazi's hand.

When their skin made contact, a sucker punch of electricity hit him right in the gut. He looked down to see her gazing up at him, a different expression on her face now—one he wasn't sure how to read. He quickly let go of her hand.

"Kimber knows the way," Jer said. "She's a good tracker."

"Fine by me," Gabe agreed. He'd had his turn as leader. He was ready to follow for a while. He wasn't sure how he'd pulled off being so macho, getting those branches to part, pulling Abazi to safety. He was shocked by his own actions, by his take-charge attitude, and thought maybe he needed to cool it before his luck changed.

Kimber took the lead and the five weary teens soon crossed the field and entered the forest. The way darkened instantly, as though someone had pulled a mourning shroud over the treetops. But they forged ahead, knowing their pursuers could be on them at any moment.

They'd been walking for several minutes when Kimber stopped, spun around, started in another direction, then stopped again. "Things are changing," she said, her soft voice confused, a little frightened. "Just as I get a bearing on where I am, everything shifts about. I have this feeling that things are constantly moving. The trees, the stones..." She trailed off.

"It's this fog," Jer spoke up. "And it's getting dark. Do you still have the flashlight, Kris?"

"Holy crap, I forgot all about it!" Kris pulled it from his waistband and turned it on. The beam hit the wall of fog and bounced back at them, unable to penetrate the cotton ball of mist. He swore and pointed it at the ground instead. The small glow helped show the way a little. "Hey, what's this?" He shined the light at something metallic lying on the ground.

"Mom's tomahawk...and all our weapons!" Jer hurried forward to grab his bat. "I can't believe we found them. We thought we might need some protection going after you," he explained to Gabe. "We didn't want to waste time so we grabbed whatever was close and headed out. When Feltry and his gang took us, they made us drop them."

"Why didn't they take the weapons for themselves? You'd think they'd at least hide them."

Kris shrugged. "Couldn't tell you. All I know is that they had those wicked thorns to do their talking for them. Maybe they're weapon enough." He shouldered his bat and handed Abazi the tomahawk.

Jer offered the mallet to Kimber, but she shook her head. "Give it to Gabe. He'll be able to do more with it than I could. I can't always make my arms do what I want them to. I might end up beaming one of you guys on the head!"

Jer laughed and handed the heavy wooden weapon to Gabe. He hefted it in his hand, feeling a little like Thor, god of Thunder.

"What are we going to do now?" Kris asked. He'd found that if he kept the flashlight beam on the ground, aimed slightly ahead of them, they could see enough to keep from running into things.

"We keep moving," Gabe replied.

Abazi snorted, now back to her normal self after nearly being swallowed by trees. "For all we know, we could be going in circles and heading right back to those Ko-goks."

Gabe laughed. "Ko-goks! Where you'd hear that? Sounds Russian."

"It's Abenaki, bonehead. You know, Native American? My tribe's language?"

"Sorrr-y. I certainly didn't mean to insult your people." Gabe made sure each word dripped with sarcasm. After he'd saved her life, he would've thought she'd be nicer to him. Apparently not.

"Apology accepted," she smirked, once again baffling him.

"We can't stop here," Kimber interrupted. "We're not going in circles, but we're also not heading for home. Every time I try to go in the right direction, which is due east, something nudges me along in a different direction. A direction that they want me to go."

"They?" Jer echoed. "You mean, some other creatures?"

"Maybe it's Hollie!" Kris exclaimed.

"Hollie?" Gabe echoed. "You know Hollie? Did you see her?"

"She found us. She was taking us to see Dame Hazel when the Dark Dork Brigade caught us. I guess we were talking too much."

"Like now," Gabe remarked dryly. "Hollie mentioned Dame Hazel to me, too. If she's directing us somehow, maybe we should go along with it."

Kimber nodded her approval. "I agree with Gabe."

"Me, too," piped up Jer.

"Fine by me," Kris shrugged.

"I think Hollie led us into a trap once already and now she's doing it again," Abazi argued. "But if you guys don't mind heading toward your deaths, why should I?"

They continued to follow after Kimber, who'd taken over the flashlight, making their way around boulders and trudging through thick moss. The woods were completely dark now.

"Maybe we should hold hands," Kimber suggested. "So no one gets lost."

Everyone agreed, though after that, the going was even slower than before. Still, Kimber never wavered, simply kept bumping steadily along in her awkward gait.

After half an hour, their guide finally faltered, then came to a reluctant halt. "I need to rest," she panted. "These stupid braces are a real pain in the butt."

"Don't you mean pain in the leg?" Kris joked.

Jer winced at his brother's insensitivity, but Kimber only laughed. "I stand corrected. Well, maybe I should sit corrected. Though after all this walking, my butt hurts, too!"

The small group started giggling, covering their mouths to stifle snorts of laughter. "Mine, too!" Jer gasped.

"And mine!" Kris choked out.

Both Abazi and Gabe refrained from admitting that their butts hurt, but they snickered all the same.

"Shhh!" a voice behind them scolded. "Do ye always have to be so loud?" Hollie held out before her an old kerosene lantern that gave off a warm glow. "I see ye found yer weapons all right. I was doin' me best to lead ye to them. This fog is thicker than Dorn's brain. Now I need ye to follow me, and be quick about it. Ye were lucky to escape, but we must be gettin' to our safe place before they find ye. They're still huntin' ye, ye know!"

"Hey, Hollie!" Kris greeted.

"Hey, yerself," she replied saucily, giving him an impish grin. Then she turned to Gabe. "I can't believe ye let them take ye like that, Gabriel."

He gaped at her. "I didn't *let* them! I thought it was my grandpa coming to check on us and—"

But she had already turned and plunged into the woods.

"I guess she told you," Abazi sniped. Gabe glared at her back as she marched on ahead of him. Realizing he already couldn't see the others, he hurried to catch up. He was mad, but he wasn't about to cut off his nose to spite his face. The woods were full of deranged creatures who would happily do that for him...

Chapter Eighteen

King of the Forest Immortal

After the third time Kimber stumbled and fell, Hollie gave vent to her frustration. "We must keep movin'. We can't keep stoppin' like this!" She sounded afraid, and Gabe had a feeling that Hollie did not scare easily. Especially after seeing how she'd handled the dark ones—the Ko-goks—when they'd come after the truck. "Listen!" she hissed as Jer bent down to help Kimber to her feet. The poor girl looked beat, and now guilty on top of that. Hollie's thin little face tilted and her bright eyes narrowed with concentration.

Gabe heard it, too—a whispering, wanting sound.

Gabrielll...

Gabrielll...

Gabrielll!

He glanced over at Hollie, who was staring at him in surprise. Judging by everyone else's lack of reaction, he thought maybe she was the only other person who could hear the voice. "We must hurry." She glanced over at Kimber. "But first we must do something about this one. She's slowin' us down."

Jer's blue eyes widened in alarm. "Over my dead body!"

"That as well may be," Hollie replied, a gleam in her forest eyes, "but I'm thinkin' along the lines of someone carryin' her."

Jer's indignant chest deflated. "Oh, well, then I'll carry her."

Kris stepped forward. "I'll do it, half-pint."

Jer's fists clenched and his cheeks flushed. He looked like he wanted to kick his brother in the shin, which is what he used to do when he was a little kid. The blow never stopped Kris, but it certainly made Jer feel better. "I can handle it, Kris."

"When you're my age, Jer, you can carry all the ladies you want. But this is life and death, so I'm carrying her. You take my bat and protect us if anything attacks."

Jer was still frowning and Gabe mentally groaned. When his little brother decided to dig his heels in about something, a long battle would ensue and eventually he would win, even though he might be wrong. Mom said Jer's determination was the only way he was going to get ahead in life, having to live with two bigger, older brothers. Though she was also sympathetic to Kris and Gabe. She, too, had to deal with Jer's 'determination.'

"I'm not some kid, Kris, I'm twelve. And anyway, Kimber's light. I can carry her just as well as you can."

Kris laughed. "I'd like to see you try."

"Knock it off, you guys," Gabe intervened. "You're acting like idiots." As usual, he'd said the wrong thing. Jer's expression went from stubborn to uncompromising as a raging bull.

"I'm not the idiot who got us into this mess," he growled.

"I didn't plan to be kidnapped, you little snot. And I didn't need your help." The first sentence was truer than a blue sky, the last pure lie. Gabe didn't care. He was tired and he wanted to go home, not argue with his brother about carrying Kimber, something he would regret the moment he made the attempt.

"Good, because I won't be giving you any more of my help."

"All of you shut up," Abazi snapped. "Listen, Jer. Today is not the day to prove a point. I'll bet you're quite strong for a twelve-year-old, but you're not yet strong enough to carry someone on your back through these stupid woods. Sometimes being strong means admitting that you can't do something."

Gabe was surprised at her diplomacy, then wondered why she never applied any of that patience and understanding to him.

Jer worked at his lower lip as though trying to chew through it, then slowly began to nod. "All right. I guess I'll be the lookout." Gabe and Kris stared at their little brother in shock, then over at Abazi. Though Gabe had been sure he'd catch her gloating, she was looking up at the dark sky and not at him.

Kimber smiled at Jer, handing the flashlight to him. "Good thinking, Jer." He grinned, already adopting the idea as his own. He was appeased for now—later this might come back to haunt them.

"Up you go," Kris said to Kimber before hauling her onto his back. Jer looked jealous, but when he saw that Kimber didn't look too thrilled with her new ride, either, he kept his mouth shut. She obviously didn't enjoy being treated like a baby any more than anyone else did. "Just think of me as one of your horses," Kris told her and she smiled a little.

"Well, then, giddyap!"

The group hurried forward into the woods. Hollie's lantern and Jer's flashlight did little to help guide them; the fog was simply too thick.

With each step, Gabe felt more stifled, as though the swirling mist had come alive, growing desperate hands that reached out and grasped his throat like the Grim Reaper. The trees huddled closer than ever to one another and then, suddenly, the woods filled with threatening sounds—eerie groans, hundreds of footsteps all around them, beguiling voices.

Gabrielll! Come to me, Gabrielll!

A strong desire to turn around and follow the voice pumped through Gabe's veins, plaguing his mind with wishes that weren't his own. He shook his head, trying to clear it, and focused on the howling wolf on Abazi's sweatshirt. But his mind refused to cooperate and his limbs felt full of warm liquid. He found himself stopping; his eyelids fluttered, threatening to close. Would it be so bad to simply fall asleep and let whoever it was come?

His heartbeat slowed, his breathing calmed. The voice was nearer now, sweet and tempting. *I'm here, Gabriel. Come to me...* He turned around.

"Where?" he called out. "Where are you?"

Come toward me voice, Gabriel. Come this way...

Something hard slapped his cheek. His hand flew to the stinging spot as his eyes sprang open to find Abazi facing him, her expression fierce. "What are you doing?"

He shrugged, feeling stupid. "I don't know..."

Her lips twitched. "Well, you look like an idiot." She grabbed his arm and yanked him about. "Come on. They're getting ahead of us."

"Thanks," he said, the word coming out before he'd fully considered whether or not he wanted to use it.

"Now we're even."

"Looks like it." He spotted the lantern not far ahead of them. "There they are." They caught up to the rest of the group, though only Hollie glanced back at them. From the closed look on her face, Gabe had the feeling she knew about the voice. Yet she hadn't done anything to stop him from following it. Maybe Abazi was right about her.

"We're here," Hollie announced, after forging through a thick grove of sharp-needled spruce trees. Gabe peered around, amazed. The fog had completely disappeared and a nearly full moon shone down into the woods, lighting the way. Ahead of them stretched a wide path, bordered on both sides by tall, stately trees. The mighty trees looked solid and strong, protected by thick, fissured gray armor and topped by a heavy helmet of dark green leaves.

"The Oaks will protect us," Hollie said as she led them onto the path.

At the end of it, numerous pale trees formed a large circle. Gabe recognized this tree, with its peeling white bark and slender trunk. It was a birch tree. In the moonlight the band of trees looked like skeletal soldiers standing in formation, tattered yet proud.

The group entered the circle, only to discover that it curved around and around like a metal spring. At one point, Gabe heard a strange noise and glanced behind him only to discover that the trees now blocked the way they'd come. He blinked rapidly. Most likely he simply couldn't see the path in the shadows; it was dark enough to mask the way. Even so, a chill ran down his spine. He hoped this wasn't some kind of trap—a maze leading them into a maelstrom.

The line of oaks and the spiral of birches...this is what he'd seen in the aerial photograph above the piano. He glanced up at the sky and saw stars shining brightly overhead, as though no fog had ever existed this day; had, in fact, been conjured up by evil. Seeing the stars twinkling up there, seemingly as immovable and unchangeable as anything could be in this world, Gabe felt some hope that they were going to get out of this. Then he remembered Straif's desire to destroy him and that tiny spark of hope was snuffed out.

The spiral ended abruptly and the group entered a small clearing illuminated by the moon. A massive tree dominated the space, its bulky roots rising up out of the earth and forming tiny caves and tunnels between root and ground. As Gabe grew closer, he could see that the tree's bark was pale and smooth in some places, mottled in others, a camouflage pattern of browns and greens, like algae speckling a whale's hide. The tree's plentiful branches were far reaching, nearly touching the sky. Viewed from above, the mighty limbs might appear as a river with countless tributaries, or as veins in an ancient and gnarled hand. It was a beautiful and immense tree and Gabe could only stand in awe of it.

As though sensing their approach, a figure appeared from out of the moon shadows to greet them and Gabe recognized Dame Hazel immediately. Same height, same mouse-like walk, same majestically purple cape. Hollie left them and approached her nervously. "He's here."

Dame Hazel looked over at Gabe. He couldn't read her face in the dark, though he could tell that she had pulled back her hood. "It has begun, then," she said.

"I'm sorry for me curiosity." Hollie's voice was wretched. "I shouldn't have lured him in."

Dame Hazel chuckled. "Tuck yer worries away, little one. I'm curious, too, as are the others. But they don't know what I know. They don't understand. They only know they're drawn to him. As we all are."

Gabe had the uncomfortable feeling they were talking about him. If that was the case, he figured he should at least be involved in the conversation. He stepped forward, but Dame Hazel held up her hand. "Ye're safe here tonight. In the morning, in the light, we'll take ye home. The danger is too high now. This is *their* time."

"But—" Gabe started to protest.

"Dame Hazel is wise. We should listen to her," Hollie counseled. Gabe wondered if she was only saying that because she'd gone against the Dame's wishes. He'd done the same thing a few times himself, sucked up to people he didn't like, though he wasn't proud of it. Sometimes survival came at a price.

"Our parents are going to be worried," Abazi spoke up, coming to join him. "They'll come looking for us. They'll come into the woods."

"Yer parents are otherwise occupied," the little woman said ominously. "They know not that ye've gone, nor will they be aware ye've not yet returned."

"If we even *can* return," Kris muttered, looking around him. He and the other two had come to join Gabe and Abazi. "We don't know our way back and the fog screws everything up anyway. Kimber says the trees and rocks keep moving around so she loses her bearings. Are you doing that?"

"Ye'll have an escort on yer return," Dame Hazel dodged his question. "We'll see ye safely home."

Gabe didn't know what to do. He was exhausted and couldn't think straight. "All right," he gave in. "We'll stay here. But we need to leave first thing in the morning."

"Show them where to bed down," Dame Hazel ordered Hollie, suddenly business-like. "Then come with me. We must wait for the others to return." Before she took her leave, Dame Hazel raised her hand in the air and brought it downward in front of them. Then she turned and drifted away into the darkness.

Hollie escorted them to a pile of thick moss on the north side of the giant tree. A light breeze shivered amongst its leaves, making hushing sounds as a mother would a restless child.

"Drink this," she said, handing Gabe a jeweled goblet, old and dented. "The nectar will quench yer thirst." She watched him carefully as he took the cup. He sniffed at it, feeling suddenly parched as though he'd been in a desert for years. Unable to resist, he raised the cup to his lips and took a sip, then another and another.

Taking turns, each drank from the seemingly bottomless cup. The cool liquid tasted of apples and spices and the waters of spring; it made their tongues tingle and their throats sing. After drinking deeply, the entire group felt leaden with tiredness. All they wanted to do was sleep.

"Rest ye well," Hollie bade them. They barely heard her as they sunk into the thick moss, unconscious even before their bodies had settled. The night closed in around them.

~~~~~~

"Gabriel!" The voice woke him from a deep and dreamless sleep. He sat up, ready to run. "Gabriel!" He blinked, rubbed his eyes a few times, then opened them to see Hollie. The sky had turned a purple-golden blue that heralded the rising of the sun, but for the moment shadows still ruled the world. "Dame Hazel wants to speak to ye. Alone," she added.

"Why?" he croaked. His throat was dry, his scratches burned, and his arms still ached from chopping wood and being carried like a trussed-up calf. The last thing he wanted to do was move.

"She has something she needs to tell ye."

"Hmmm…" He really didn't want to get up. He was still feeling groggy and the moss was soft and surprisingly warm, like sleeping in fuzzy, half-baked bread dough.

She grabbed his arm. "So that means ye have to come with me."

"Can't she come here?" he mumbled, feeling his body leaning backward, away from Hollie, away from wakefulness.

"I don't think she can tell ye in front of the others. It's, um, rather personal."

Gabe straightened again. If she had meant to catch his attention, she'd succeeded. Now he was curious. "All right. I'm coming." He stood and stretched, amazed, and a bit envious, that everyone else still slept. Fully awake now, he could feel the morning chill along with every bruise and scratch he'd acquired the night before. Even his eyelids hurt.

He followed after Hollie and she led him around to the other side of the tree, which was even bigger than he'd first thought. His fingers trailed along its trunk before reluctantly leaving it behind. Side by side, they headed toward another birch tree spiral at the base of the mountain. In the open space, lingering clouds of haze hovered like ghosts, waiting for someone to come and tell them where to go. Gabe passed through one and shuddered. The moist air felt cool on his skin and left behind a residue that seemed to be more than just water. The miasma crawled over his tongue and down his throat, tasting of despair.

Shaking his head roughly, he tried to rid himself of the gloomy sensation. He was always making things out to be more dramatic than they were. His mom had spent countless hours talking to him about this. She did it herself, she told him, and one just had to knock it off or end up going nuts. Of course, the last time they'd had this discussion, he told her she needed to remember that she often only accused him of overreacting when he was arguing against an unfair punishment she'd imposed on him. He'd earned a "very funny, smart guy," for that one.

Still, he would try to do as she suggested. He would focus on what he could see in the here and now, not dwell on or go beyond what he could process with his five senses. Soaring above him, the mountainside looked spectacular and imposing. The steep wall of stone rose to a golden summit spotlighted by the rising sun. Trees covered the mountain's rocky side, clinging to its rough surface like lichen. He thought they looked scared, almost desperate, as they huddled together, then decided he was being dramatic again.

When he looked at the birch spiral he noticed that a group of strangers had congregated there. All of them were young, tall, and as sturdy as the oak trees they'd passed earlier. Each wore a dark green cloak and a bow with a quiver of arrows, and gripped a staff, some using it to hold their weight. These must be the ones who'd saved them from Straif.

Two figures, facing each other, appeared to be arguing. "It's mine, Dame Hazel. I'll not give it back!" Dame Hazel responded, but Gabe couldn't make out her words. He wondered what they were talking about. "The law is that ye keep what ye reap," the low, husky voice persisted.

"That's stealin'!" Hollie called out. The one who'd been shouting swung around to face her. "It's not ours in the first place, Oswald!"

Oswald, Gabe realized upon seeing him more closely, was the one who'd confronted Straif. His fists were clenched—one of them around his staff—and his dark brown eyes blazed fiercely. "Stay out of it, Hollie. This is none of yer business!"

"I'm the one who fetched the box, Oswald, so it's mine," she declared. "And I choose to give it back to its rightful owner. I tried once already, but the door were locked." She frowned at Gabe, as though he'd locked it on purpose to thwart her.

A shock of auburn hair fell over Oswald's eyes and he swept it back impatiently. "As ruler here, I'm the one who should make that decision."

"Ye're always actin' like ye're King of the Forest Immortal, Oswald,"

Hollie scoffed.

"That's because I *am* the King of the Forest Immortal, Hollie! That's what me name means! And because of it, the Rogues made me their leader. Not once did I ever take the position lightly. I've worked hard as ruler, though leadin' hasn't always been easy, as ye well know."

Hollie chewed on a ruby lip for a moment. "Fair enough. But we still are in disagreement. I think Dame Hazel should decide what's the best thing to do. She's the one who knows what all this is about."

As though hearing her cue, Dame Hazel left Oswald to greet Gabe. "Hello, Gabriel." In the dim light, he could see that she was indeed the odd woman who had come to fetch Hollie, seemingly ages ago. With her hood pulled back, he saw her face clearly now. Her skin was nut brown and covered by craggy, acorn-sized moles; her eyes were dark and deep. She had surprisingly large ears, slightly pointed at the top, and her hair was a mix of thick yellow and brown curls. Like Hollie, she was different than anyone he had ever seen.

He stifled a strange impulse to bow. "Hello, Dame Hazel."

"Ye've walked into a right mess, Gabriel. I'm sorry about that. Even though I am the one who knows what all this is about, I now doubt what I did." Her calm, rather magisterial, expression belied her words. She didn't look particularly sorry, or doubtful, for that matter.

"What are ye talkin' about?" Oswald demanded. "What does this Knobby have to do with us, and how do *ye* know him, Dame Hazel? Hollie has told us nothing." He scowled at her. She returned the favor.

"Yeah, what do you want with Gabe?" It was Kris, and behind him stumbled Abazi, Jer, and Kimber. Gabe felt awfully glad to see them. He needed someone on his side in this strange standoff.

"We want to keep him safe," Dame Hazel answered.

"Safe from what?" Jer stepped forward. As small as he was, it was strange how he sometimes reminded Gabe of a bull. "We want some answers."

"Yeah," Gabe put in. "What did those jerks want with me? Why do they keep calling my name?"

"The Ko-goks sense there's something special about ye, Gabriel. They're right, but it isn't them who's callin' ye—not all the time. The one callin' is..." Her eyes narrowed for a moment. "Well, it's yer mother."

"My mother?" he replied dumbly. "But she's in Augusta."

Dame Hazel peered down at her gnarled hands, then back up at Gabe. "As hard as I tried to sway her thinkin', she was never quite convinced ye weren't hers. She has always sought ye out. She took ye,

ye know. When ye were a little one." She used her hand to show how
tall he'd been...about the same size as a four-year-old.

Gabe's insides quivered at the implication. "You mean some crazy
lady took me because she thought I was her son?"

"She's *not* crazy!" Oswald protested, his eyes wild.

Gabe held up his hands. "Sorry. But, crazy or not, it *is* a weird thing
to do."

"Yer lineage is a big reason why Straif seeks ye, Gabriel," Dame Hazel interrupted.

"But Straif said he didn't know why he had to kill me, other than that
it would stop the others from fighting him."

"Straif's a liar. He knows who ye are. He just doesn't want anyone
else to know."

"Then who am I?" Gabe asked.

"Ye're the true King of the Forest Immortal."

"What?" Gabe and Oswald both cried, gaping at her.

"That can't be!" Oswald glared at Gabe. "*I* am the King, Dame Hazel! Ye told me so. And I'm the one who's spent his life fightin' Straif
and his like. I'm the one keepin' us safe, organizin' our bands and
makin' sure we have weapons. If I am certain of anything, it's that *I'm*
King of the Forest Immortal!" He wasn't bragging, Gabe noted. He
looked too astounded for that.

"There must be some mistake," Gabe spoke up. "I'm Gabe
Hawthorne, which, as far as I know, doesn't mean king, and I grew up
in California."

"Hollie." Dame Hazel nodded at the girl. "Show Gabe what we are."

Hollie glanced at Dame Hazel, then at Kris, and lastly, at Gabe. She
seemed torn, as though she wasn't quite certain she wanted to do what
she was being asked. Dame Hazel gave her a stern look and Hollie finally acquiesced. With a skip, she took off, ran several steps, then
leaped high into the air where she began to spin around like a whirling
dervish. When her feet came close to touching the ground, her lithe
body blossomed into a blur of color and light, and her feet disappeared.

When the movement came to a standstill, Hollie was gone. In her
place stood a tree—a small tree with bright green, shiny leaves and
bold red berries. Gabe blinked, then peered around the other side of
the tree, thinking Hollie must be hiding behind it. Then something
even stranger happened. The tree began to move. Delicate roots jerked
free of the soft grassy ground and pulled the tree forward, step after
step. The closer it came, the more he could make out a slender body

forming the outlines of the tree, branches for arms, rounded hips, trunk legs, and a face, the eyes and mouth dark impressions, the nose a protruding bump.

"Holy crap!" Kris shouted. "That is so fierce!"

After giving a violent shiver that shook its leaves, the Hollie tree leaped up into the air, spun about once more, and landed several feet away as Hollie, the human. She looked hard at Kris, challenging him to say something. He returned the stare, obviously impressed. She smiled impishly.

"You're *trees*?" This had to be a dream. The cup they'd all drunk from last night must have contained drugs, and the drugs were causing this strange, unbelievable dream.

"Not quite," Dame Hazel said calmly. "We're Dryads, or tree spirits. We're mostly human, with the exception that we can change ourselves into trees. Though not all Dryads can change. There are those who can absorb the tree and show as their human form, then change back again whenever they wish, and then there are those who have lost the vision to transform. They stay always as trees, unable to remember or imagine bein' anything else. But do not underestimate them. They're awful powerful as trees. They can move and they can fight. They'll grab and hold ye tight as a creeper vine, strangle the life right out of ye, pierce yer heart with thorns."

Gabe remembered the thorny trees that had closed in on them, the ones that had nearly killed him and Abazi. Why could he accept that the vines and branches had parted way for him, moved on his command, yet not believe they were thinking creatures? He couldn't have it both ways.

"Ye're our leader, Gabriel."

He shook his head, wanting to deny everything he'd just heard...*seen*.

"Should we show him the box?" Hollie asked, sensing his disbelief.

Oswald groaned and turned away. "Ah, now ye've done it!"

"Yes, show him. It might help him to understand."

Hollie dashed back to the giant tree, returning quickly with an old wooden box. She handed it to Gabe. He hesitantly took it, his fingers trembling despite his willing them not to. The small chest was made from dark wood, with amber and agate swirls. Carved into its lid was a tree, raised in relief like the one on the half-moon window. Its broad trunk started at the bottom of the box and rose up the front, transforming into wild branches that spread out over the top like a brush fire. Gabe set the chest down on the ground.

"That's the box!" Kris cried. "The one that went missing from the barn. It's locked, though. You guys must have the key." He looked at Dame Hazel for confirmation.

"A key is not necessary. Open it, Gabe," she directed.

He reached out and pressed a small metal button on a clasp, which held the box shut. There was a click and the metal piece popped up. He glanced at Kris who shrugged. "I tried everything to open that box. Well, not everything." He grinned. "Sadly, I'm in short supply of dynamite at the moment."

Gabe felt himself smile; Kris never changed. But when he looked back at the box his smile faded. He was meant to open it, but he wasn't sure he wanted to. Who knew what might be in there? A skull? A dagger? A cute, little jack-in-the-box armed with a pistol?

Still, he was curious. His fingers reached out and lifted the lid, slowly and carefully. As it rose, the contents of the box were revealed. Gabe frowned. Clothes? He reached in and pulled out a finely woven, dark green cape. The heavy cloak looked the same as what Oswald and the others wore, except for the embroidered image of a white flower the size of his hand, five petals encircling a delicate stamen with a bright pink tip, sewn onto its back. Without thinking, he lifted the fabric to his nose and breathed in the scent of apple wood, warm sunshine, pine and honey, fresh air and magic. Then something strange began to happen. He felt funny, as though his body wanted to grow and stretch and... He flung the cloak to the ground, popped to his feet, and backed away.

"What's wrong, Gabe?" Abazi asked sharply. "What happened?"

"I...I don't know."

"Ye felt the callin' of the Forest Immortal," Dame Hazel told him.

"Why do you call this place the Forest Immortal?" Jer asked. He was looking at Gabe as he spoke, a thoughtful expression on his face.

"We are the Forest Immortal because those who live here never die. When it's time for our shell to decay, we create a seedling and grow another tree, another home for our spirits." Her face darkened. "But no longer can we make any young. If anyone is lucky enough to attain success, the Ko-goks devour the weeuns before they have a chance to thrive."

That explained the lack of seedlings in this part of the forest, Gabe thought. Something unnatural was keeping the trees from reproducing offspring, or if they managed to make any, the dark ones ate them. His stomach soured at the images of greed and raw desperation this knowledge conjured up.

"The old ones are in danger of havin' no home to go to," Dame Hazel continued. "We can't survive without our homes, ye see." She glanced up at the sky. Rays of sun spread long fingers over the canopy of trees. "Dawn breaks. It's time to get ye and the others home."

Just like that? She springs this totally insane story about him being some kind of king and them being trees, then sends him off? No way. "But what happens after that?"

She shook her head. "We wait and see."

"Sorry, Lady," Kris interrupted, sounding like John Wayne. "But that's not my style."

Dame Hazel looked grim. "Don't be blind to the point where ye put yerselves in danger."

Kris grinned. "Danger's my middle name. I'm always ready for it."

The old woman smiled for the first time since they'd met. "I can see that. Ye're a good guardian."

"I'm a good brother," he corrected.

She nodded. "Of course. Oswald and Hollie, escort them to their homes. Watch for the changes. They come quick and fast. Straif has confused the other trees with his magic, makin' them move about, givin' them doubts. We can't trust them; they're not themselves." She frowned, her hooked nose quivering. "Be very careful, young ones. There's evil afoot."

"I'll take them safely home, Dame Hazel," Oswald replied. "And when I return, we will talk."

She gazed steadily at him. "Yes, we will talk."

"Come on, then," Oswald said to the group, his expression thunderous. "We'll see ye home."

Chapter Nineteen

Three Thousand Years

The tired group trailed after Oswald, glad to finally be escaping the woods. They passed the giant tree, which, according to Hollie, was a sycamore named Isis. They hurried through the birch tree spiral, open once more (though Gabe wondered if it had ever actually closed), and down the long oak tree corridor.

At the end, Oswald stopped and turned to face the group. "Our next steps are unprotected ones. Stay close to each other and stay on alert. I know this forest like I know me own heart, and even I am wary." His dark eyes regarded each of them in turn, his penetrating gaze settling on Gabe last, challenging him. "Are ye ready? Do ye think ye can handle this?" The questions seemed so clear in Gabe's mind that he wanted to answer them, but he kept his mouth shut. No need to antagonize the one person who knew how to get them out of the forest. Despite Oswald's animosity toward Gabe, he seemed like the kind of guy who would not shirk his duty. Or so Gabe hoped.

At first the going was relatively easy. The moss didn't grow nearly as thick here and the trees were spaced a good five feet apart. But it wasn't long before the way grew harder, the trees closer together, the moss deeper. Gabe couldn't remember at what point he started seeing things. He thought maybe the trees were moving around, shifting a bit here; over there, something darting, always just out of the corner of his eye. The shadows made him question his own senses. Despite the rising sun, an aura of darkness dominated, and the otherworldliness of this secretive place made it hard to know what was real and what was not.

His mind drifted back to what Dame Hazel had told him—that he was a king. It didn't seem real. Perhaps Dame Hazel really had spiked the drink they'd shared. He remembered waking up feeling dazed, as though drugged. But why? What would she get out of convincing him he was a king? It made no sense.

With a start, Gabe realized that his pace had slowed considerably and he'd fallen behind. He began to run to catch up when something grabbed his ankle. He flew forward and his chest hit the ground—oddly devoid of moss—and the air in his lungs whooshed out. The others were either too far ahead or too preoccupied to notice what had happened. Gabe couldn't cry out to get their attention; he could only lie there heaving and grunting, waiting in agony for his breath to return. He rolled over onto his back and drew his knees up to his chest, trying to urge the air back in.

He was still struggling to breathe when a snake-like object slid over his right ankle. Just as quickly, it crossed over to the other, immobilizing both legs. Within seconds, more tendrils joined in, trapping him like a moth in a spider web. He struggled to sit up, but was slammed back to the ground. "Guys, help!" he tried to yell, but could only give an oxygen-deprived squeak. And then the worst happened...the tendrils covered his mouth.

He squirmed and wiggled, trying to escape, but the shackles around his wrists tightened, forcing him to release his mallet. He was defenseless now; completely helpless to fight against an attacker he had yet to see. His head pounded from lack of air and stars appeared in his vision like a front-row view of a distant galaxy.

"Hiii-yah!" a voice cried out and a heavy thud sounded by his feet. Kris with his bat! His brother lifted the weapon to strike again, but a green-feathered branch whipped out and snatched it from him. "Hey!" he shouted, but before he could do anything more, another branch grabbed him around the waist and lifted him off the ground.

"Kristofer!" Hollie yelled. "Gabriel!" She leaped into the air, spun around, and landed in the form of a tree. Her slender branches slashed furiously at the rough-barked tree that appeared to be Gabe's attacker. "Back off, Yew! They aren't yers!"

A howl arose from within the tree, like lost voices echoing out of the earth. "Miiine! Miiiine!" Like a malevolent troll, the tree loomed over Gabe, and he felt as though he was in his grave, the tree serving as his tombstone.

"There is death after life, and life after death," Oswald spoke as he strode forward, calm and assured. "Yew, this is yer choice!" His voice rose with each word, echoing around the forest so loudly that many listeners heard it, and not all of them friendly.

"Miiine!" the tree cried out, less strongly now. "Liiife!"

"Straif isn't the answer!" Oswald persisted. "Straif is for Death. We, the Rogues, are for Life! Choose yer side!"

"Liiife..." the yew moaned, then dropped Kris onto his back at the same time releasing its hold on Gabe. Hollie, seeing that the battle was over, jumped up, spun about, then landed as a human. She brushed back her wild tresses and straightened her dress. Gabe could only stare at her dumbly.

Kris scrambled to his feet and grabbed Gabe's arm, pulling him away from the writhing tree. "She's dyin'," Oswald explained, watching her with a distant pity. "She doesn't want to, of course. Her line goes back three thousand years. This'll be the end of it."

Gabe was still fighting for air. "But...why...did she attack me? How...could...I help her?"

"Do ye not see? When our seedlings failed to thrive, or were devoured, Straif turned to other measures to keep himself alive."

"The missing cats and dogs," Jer guessed, taking Gabe's arm and pulling him to his feet with Kris's help. "They're using animal blood to survive. The yew thought she'd do the same with you, Gabe."

"Straif and his followers think that yer blood is the best blood, and will save them." Oswald shook his head. "They're mistaken, but who am I to correct their foolishness?"

Gabe rubbed at his scratched arms. "They should want your blood. *You're* the King of the forest."

"Not in their mind," Oswald answered shortly. "Not anymore." He bowed to the tree. "I'll return, Yew. I'll help ye, best I can." From deep within the shuddering tree came the cry of a grief-stricken child. His expression stony now, Oswald turned to go. "Come, let us leave this place." He looked at Gabe. "Don't linger again. I may not hear ye fall next time."

Gabe stared after him. So it hadn't been Kris who'd known something was wrong, it had been Oswald. Yet he was the last to arrive. Had he hoped he'd be too late? What an easy way to get rid of the interloper—let the crazy tree do your dirty work for you.

Gabe picked out some pine needles stuck in his shorts. He wasn't so sure now about letting Oswald lead them to safety. The boy obviously had problems with Gabe, but what choice did they have? No one here could lead them out of the woods, not even Kimber with her tracking abilities. The forest was too wily.

The group started off again, more wary this time. Every tree became a potential enemy, every branch a weapon. Abazi dropped back to walk beside Gabe. "You dropped this," she said after a few minutes. She handed him the mallet.

"Thanks," he replied as he took it. He felt better simply having it in his hands.

"Do you think this is real?" she asked, looking straight ahead.

"I don't know. I'm starting to think we were drugged."

"That makes more sense than you being King of the tree spirits." Her voice was scornful, yet he noticed she didn't look at him.

He pulled a bit of bark out of his hair. "Something weird is going on, but I'm pretty sure it's not *that* weird."

"My ancestors believed in tree spirits," she said after a few moments of silence. "Many in the tribe still do."

"But do you believe in them?"

She shrugged. "I didn't use to. But now—" She cut herself off. "Do you hear that?"

"Hear what?" He could only hear their footsteps and the soft voices of the others up ahead.

"I thought I heard something in the woods. A sort of cry."

"It was probably just *yew*."

"Or you," she quipped.

"Or ewe."

She snorted. "That was really baaaa...d."

"Look who's talking...or should I say, baaaing?"

Abazi started to say something else, likely more clever than what he'd said, then snapped her mouth shut. Her head swiveled back and forth as she studied the forest around them, her shoulders tense and dark eyes watchful. "I wasn't kidding about hearing a noise. Something's out there."

He paused and listened. "I don't hear anything unusual. Maybe you're hallucinating. We all could be. We did see Hollie turn into a tree, and I thought a tree attacked me."

"You really think Dame Hazel drugged us?" Gabe nodded. "Maybe she did. But she didn't exactly look like the dealer type to me, and I'm pretty sure I'm not having hallucinations right now. I know your white ears can't hear it, but I can. My people can hear the earth speak. Something's back there...and it's getting closer."

"Why do I have the feeling it's not a deer?" Gabe said dryly. "Come on. Let's get moving." They quickly caught up with the others. "I think we've got company," he told the group, making sure his voice carried to Oswald.

Unfazed, Oswald said over his shoulder, "They're me band. They're keepin' an eye on me."

"You don't trust us?" Jer exclaimed disbelievingly. He never considered that other people might be as suspicious about him as he was about them.

"Why should I? Ye're strangers to me. Who knows who ye really are?"

"He's got a point there," Kris said.

He certainly did. And what he said went both ways. Gabe knew his brothers, but he didn't know Oswald or his band. For that matter, neither he nor his brothers knew Abazi or Kimber all that well, about as much as they knew Hollie, in fact. Perhaps they should all be on better guard, a thought that made Gabe feel uncomfortable. Unlike Jer, he preferred to give everyone the benefit of the doubt, whether they deserved it or not. His optimism in, or naïveté about, the human race had gotten him hurt more than a few times.

"Are you sure they're your people?" Abazi spoke up.

Oswald stopped and swung around to face her, then smiled charmingly, as though he were seeing her for the first time. "Positive. And ye are...?"

Abazi flushed. Gabe couldn't believe it. She never blushed like that when he talked to her. "Abazi Wanibagw."

Oswald nodded respectfully. "Ye're one of the dark-skins. We have much respect for yer kind."

Her eyes widened. "You do?"

"Ye're a wise and gentle folk, though brave warriors when need be. And ye believe in us...unlike some of ye." He gave Gabe a measured look. Gabe wished he'd stop looking at him every time he delivered one of his loaded comments.

"We do?" she managed. "I mean, um, yes, my people do believe in tree spirits. I remember something about the legends...that tree spirits are mostly good, but there are some bad ones, like the Ko-goks."

"The Ko-goks can be fierce and frightening. When preparin' for battle, they bring their branches together, as though clappin' up a thunderstorm. The louder the clack, the stronger the tree, for the number of their limbs is greater and more powerful."

"How can banging branches together be scary?" Gabe asked. "Sounds kind of dumb to me." He didn't like being left out of the conversation, though he wished he could have come up with a more insightful conclusion than 'sounds kind of dumb to me.'

"Ye'd not think that if ye were the one they were clackin' at."

"I'd like to see them try that on me," Kris said, spinning his bat in his hands.

Oswald shook his head. "It'd be the death of ye."

"Ah, but what a death!" Kris sighed. "A warrior's death!"

"Don't be talkin' that way!" Hollie admonished. "Ye're askin' for trouble."

"I like trouble."

Her thin nose wrinkled in annoyance. "Ye never had to face real trouble, Kristofer. Real trouble is watchin' yer elders get killed off, one by one. Real trouble is havin' yer whole family uprooted from their homes. Real trouble—"

"How much farther?" Gabe interrupted her tirade. He was growing anxious. "Mom might be trying to reach us, and then there'll be real trouble if we don't answer the phone."

"She'll think we're sleeping," Kris told him.

"We need to stop," Jer said behind them. He and Kimber had fallen back. "I need to rest."

The two brothers spun around. Jer never admitted to weakness. He'd learned the hard way to be tough around others—namely his brothers—who mercilessly took advantage of any show of weakness. When they saw Kimber leaning on him hard, her face pale and drawn, they realized what was going on. *She* was the one who needed rest. Jer's expression warned them they'd better keep their mouths shut about it.

"You know," Gabe said, "after that stuff we drank I haven't felt like myself, either. I could do with a break, too."

Oswald shook his head. "We can't stop here." He peered anxiously around the restless woods and Gabe's heart skipped a beat. Oswald was about as cool as they come, so if he had reason to be worried... "We can't stop at all."

A rush of wind battered them from behind, followed by a strange keening noise. Kris shoved his bat into Jer's hand. "Cover me!" he cried and pulled Kimber up onto his back. "We ride again, fair lady!" Kimber clung to him desperately as they began to run for their lives.

"Move!" Oswald shouted, pushing the others ahead of him. "Something has gone wrong!"

Unthinkingly, Gabe grabbed Abazi's hand and pulled her along with him. They ran after the others, picking up speed as the sounds of a forest coming alive echoed around them. Branches thrashed, roots groaned, and sap bled as trees reached out to grab them.

The Ko-goks were coming. Gabe knew this for certain. Coming to kill them...*him*. He didn't know how he knew this, but he did, and he was afraid. Perhaps that would explain why he did something so stupid.

He turned around.

Splotches of black surrounded Oswald like spilled ink, threatening to overwhelm him. He swung his staff at them with a strength and skill that told of many such battles. Gabe pushed Abazi on ahead of him.

"Get out of here!" he yelled, then turned and raced back toward Oswald. He should be making sure his brothers and the girls got out of the woods, but Kris would have to do it. The dark ones weren't interested in the others anyway. Right or wrong, they were interested in Gabe. Solely in Gabe.

Fortunately for Oswald, none of the creatures wanted to get too close to the stick he swung in a wide arc. But there were so many of them and only one of him, eventually they'd wear him down.

Oswald's band was nowhere to be seen, which meant Gabe was Oswald's only hope. His one advantage was that the dark ones hadn't spotted him yet. He glanced at the mallet in his hand, which suddenly seemed startlingly inadequate. He looked around for a better weapon, but the forest floor was bare of even a twig.

He was about to give up and charge in when a loud crack above his head startled him. A moment later, a thick branch crashed to the ground at his feet. He grabbed the heavy club, then glanced up, wondering who to thank. Nothing but branches and sky waited above him. He said a quiet, "Thanks," anyway, saluted for good measure, then prepared for the fight of his life. His hands trembled and his heart thudded and he wanted to run, but the gang of dark ones was closing in on a weakening Oswald like a voracious pack of hyenas. Oswald didn't stand a chance.

"Hey!" Gabe called out, swinging the club over his head. "Anyone want some of this?"

Oswald jerked around to gape at him, as did the others. He recognized Dorn and Barb, along with the one who'd captured his brothers and his friends—Feltry. Seeing him, Feltry cackled wickedly, the sound grim as a ghost train.

Still laughing, he leaped into the air, spinning around to land only a few feet away. Gabe swallowed hard, his throat tight and dry, and hoped what he was seeing was drug-induced. Feltry had transformed himself into a tree, but not just any tree. Unlike Hollie's petite and brightly colorful tree form, Feltry's boasted hundreds of black, twisted branches, barren of leaves, but not of thorns. His tree eyes and mouth were gaping black holes, craggy and mad.

Straightening to his full height, which was twice as tall as Gabe, he raised several branches into the air and began to smash them together. *Clack! Clack! Clack!* The eerie echoes were like bone striking bone, teeth gnashing teeth. It was a horrible sound, just as Oswald had said, and not dumb at all.

"Flee!" Oswald shouted at Gabe. "They routed me band! We're on our own. Ye have to get the others out of the forest!"

"I can't leave you here alone!" Gabe shouted back.

"Ye can! Ye must!"

"I can't," Gabe argued stubbornly. "I *won't*"

It was somewhat of a bluff. Seeing Feltry towering over him, his club-like arms raised high, Gabe seriously wanted to throw up, and then run, or vice versa. But both options were pretty much out of the question. He possessed enough insight into his own psyche to realize that he wouldn't be able to live with himself knowing he'd saved his own butt at the expense of someone else's.

One of Feltry's branches slashed out, swift as a cobra, and a thorn tore into Gabe's shoulder. He stifled the cry of pain panicking to get out and raised his makeshift club high into the air, beating back Feltry's branches, flying at him like whips. Blood roared through his brain as he swung and smashed with the long, heavy stick and much smaller mallet.

Feltry screeched and struck out again, a huge branch swinging straight toward Gabe's head. At the last second, he leaped out of the way, landing next to Oswald. The boy hoisted him to his feet. "We be dyin' together, then," he stated calmly, and lifted his staff to attack.

"I guess so," Gabe answered back, wondering if those inane words would be his last. It seemed shock had dulled his senses and made him stupid.

The Ko-goks gathered behind Feltry and moved in for the kill, long, sharp thorns in hand. With a violent howl, they attacked. Oswald knocked back three with one swing while Gabe brought two more to their knees after hitting them on the head with his mallet.

But there were more, hundreds more, and they kept coming. Feltry in his tree form was the worst of all. His long branches, with their fang-like thorns, flailed at them quick as a windmill in a hurricane. They wouldn't be able to hold him off much longer. He was growing sneak-ier and quicker with his strikes, while they were tiring.

"Attaaack!" cried a familiar voice, and a series of howls rang out as Kris drove a wedge through the mass of dark-robed bodies, knocking them aside with his slugger. He looked like Paul Bunyan, swinging the bat back and forth with ease. He'd pushed his shirtsleeves up and his forearms rippled with each swing. Close behind him strode Hollie, a princess warrior. With ruthless effectiveness, she smacked her bata on bony heads, matching Kris knockdown for knockdown.

Jer and the others were nowhere to be seen. They must have gone on ahead, back to the house. Gabe shuddered. Without Kris, his brother and their friends were sitting ducks now. Straif may want Gabe in particular, but he'd also said his men needed meat, and humans were meat.

But it was too late to change course. Feltry, spotting Kris, reared angrily up into the sky like a cobra. "Get the warrior!"

The Ko-goks screeched and howled as they advanced toward Kris. The noise rattled in Gabe's chest as he continued to swing his club at whatever came his way. He didn't even need to hit the dark ones very hard to make them hiss in pain and hastily retreat. Sometimes all he had to do was poke them.

Gabe was jabbing at several dark ones surrounding him when Kris shot off the ground like a rocket ship. One of Feltry's thorny branches gripped him tightly around the waist. Kris's sneakered feet kicked hard as he struggled to free himself, and his bat swung in wide arcs, each one a resounding whiff. He couldn't reach Feltry; the tree spirit was too fast.

With Kris firmly in hand, the Ko-gok raised another spike-tipped branch into the air. Gabe's stomach dropped. Feltry was going to drive a thorn right through Kris's head! He lunged forward to stop him, but couldn't seem to make any progress through the mass of dark cloaks attacking him. He shouted desperately at Feltry, trying to distract him, but Feltry ignored him.

Something whistled through the air over his head, slamming into the tree spirit's trunk with a sickening thud. Feltry roared and Gabe took the opportunity to escape his attackers. He raced toward the tree, desperate to reach his brother. Thrashing about in pain, Feltry's hold on Kris loosened. Gabe jumped up and grabbed hold of his brother's leg, and his added weight quickly freed Kris from Feltry's clutches. The two brothers dropped to the ground and rolled away from the spasming tree.

Landing in the thick of the battle, they jumped to their feet and resumed fighting the increasingly frenzied dark ones. Catching a glimmer of metal lodged in Feltry's trunk, Gabe realized that the irritant was a tomahawk. Abazi! Swinging his stick with more intensity, he frantically searched amongst the mass of dark capes for signs of her, and at last he saw her. Ducked down low, she was watching Feltry, her brow furrowed.

No... Gabe thought. *She wouldn't.*

She would.

With a cry of horror, he crashed through a wall of dark ones, knocking them aside like a bowling ball. He had to stop Abazi from going after the tomahawk. She was going to be killed! How could she be so stupid? It was merely a weapon, not worth her life!

Suddenly she dashed toward Feltry. "No, Abazi!" he cried, but she couldn't hear him, *wouldn't* hear him over her own insistent resolve. He raced after her.

She was quick, weaving around dark ones and ducking beneath flailing branches like a running back. In only seconds, she was at the tree and standing on tiptoe, reaching for the tomahawk. Feltry's constant movement made her task difficult; the weapon kept bobbing out of her reach.

With grim determination, she waited for the right moment, then lunged and at last grabbed hold of the handle. With a wrench, she clutched the tomahawk in her hand. She grinned triumphantly and turned to leave, but she'd celebrated too soon. Once the weapon was removed, Feltry stopped moving. Abazi froze, sensing her mistake.

Gabe, only a few feet from her now, realized too late the danger they were both in. Feltry lifted two of his branches and grabbed both Gabe and Abazi in one fell swoop, snatching them off the ground as swiftly as a hawk. Hard to call it good luck, but the branches Feltry used to grab hold of them bore only half-inch thorns, otherwise they'd be dead by now.

"What are you doing here?" Abazi grimaced in pain as she struggled to get free.

"I was trying to save you!" he yelled back.

Her expression was less than grateful. "Thanks for nothing." She glanced around, searching for a way to escape. Remembering the tomahawk, she flashed Gabe a triumphant grin. Knowing she only had one chance, she chopped swiftly and surely at the branch holding her until it cracked like ice. With a yip, she fell to the ground ten feet below. Right before she hit the ground, one of Feltry's branches whipped out, striking the side of her head. Her dark eyes rolled back and she crumpled onto the forest floor like flattened grass.

Gabe stared down at her, stunned. "Abazi!" he yelled, the word warped and dull, coming in slow motion. "Get up!" She lay still as death, the tomahawk still clutched in her hand.

Feltry roared victoriously and turned his back on the fighting. Using his roots, he loped awkwardly away from the battling group. The other trees of the forest cleared a path for him, their movements accompanied by bows. Gabe fought to get free, using his mallet to beat on Feltry's branch, but the tree spirit either ignored the pain, or didn't feel it.

"I'm the favorite now," he mumbled to himself. "Father'll make me his heir. Dorn's a Knobby. He knows nothing about nothing. I'm the smart one, the strong one. I'm the next King." He chuckled ruthlessly. "Father'll have to share Gabriel's blood with me, that is the way of it now. He needs me strong to wipe out the Rogues. He can't do it alone."

They clomped further and further away from the battle scene. For the first time since this whole nightmare began, Gabe felt a sense of hopelessness settle over him. Abazi was seriously hurt, possibly dead, and he could do nothing about it. He wasn't going to be able to stop Feltry, or escape. The mad tree spirit was intent on proving himself to his father, intent on becoming the heir...

Chapter Twenty

Blood is Tastier Than Water

Gabe didn't want to die. The whole idea of death scared him—it always had, ever since he was a little kid. Death meant being alone and lonely. Death was cold and dark; it was a gluttonous monster that hunted down life and snuffed it out like a tiny flame. Death was breathing hard down Gabe's neck right now. Its wicked hand reached out to snatch his soul away and all he wanted to do was scream and scream and—

A low hanging branch smacked his face, bringing him around. What was he doing? He wasn't dead yet. He couldn't give in; he *wouldn't* give in. He had to think, and he had to plan. Feltry was taking him back to Straif, something Gabe couldn't let happen.

"Let me go," he shouted as loudly as he could, "or I'll…" He paused, unable to think of what to say next.

"Or ye'll…*what?*" Feltry's raspy voice demanded.

"Or I'll go medieval on your trunk!" The moment the words left his mouth, Gabe regretted them. Was that really the best he could come up with? If Kris had been in this situation, he'd have said something like, "Let me go, or your name's gonna be Stump!"

Feltry began to shake, his branches clacking against one another. It took a moment for Gabe to realize that the tree was laughing at him. This was a new, all-time low.

"Hey!" a familiar voice shouted and Gabe turned to see Dorn running after them. "Where are ye goin', Feltry? *Gabriel* is mine, ye know!" Feltry kept walking and laughing. "Put him down!"

Feltry swung around. "*Gabriel* is mine now! I'm the one who caught him this time, not ye. Father'll be glad to have him back. Too bad we need to keep him alive." He pulled Gabe close to his trunk and sniffed, and Gabe's skin tingled as though a raptor had caught his scent. "I can smell his blood. It's full of life. Aagghh!" he suddenly gasped in pain. "Stop it, Dorn, or I'll turn ye into kindlin'!"

'Turn ye into kindling.' *Now that was a good one*, Gabe thought bemusedly as Feltry swung a branch at Dorn, who'd just stomped on one of his roots.

"Ye can't change back and still keep hold of the human, Feltry!" Dorn shouted, ducking low. "Dorn can take ye down easily when ye're like this."

"I'd like to see ye try."

Feltry swung his branches wildly about and one of the larger ones knocked Dorn to the ground. Instead of jumping to his feet, he stayed low, shoulders hunched like a hyena, and crawled, not away from Feltry, but toward him. Feltry tried to hit him, but his brother was too hard to reach so near Feltry's trunk. Once Dorn was close enough, he lifted his arm and drove it downward, the thorn in his hand sinking deep into the wood.

Feltry's entire tree body convulsed, then, like a melting snowman, he began to shrink, returning to his human form in seconds. When Gabe felt his captor's grip loosen, he wrenched free, landing with a thud on the ground several feet away. He kept rolling with the momentum, losing his staff along the way, before ending up behind a large tree. For once, luck was on his side. The brothers, blinded by rage, had forgotten about him. They faced each other now, solely occupied with the desire to kill the other.

A force of dark ones appeared out of the woods. Having realized that their leaders had abandoned the hunt, they felt obligated to do so, too. Hooting gleefully, they gathered around the brothers, eager to watch them fight.

Keeping low to the ground, Gabe crawled backward until he felt safe to stand. Then he tucked his mallet into his waistband and began to run. Behind him, the brothers' grunts and curses rang out, followed by cheers urging one or the other on. Gabe forced himself to run faster. There wouldn't be much time to get away. Sooner or later someone was going to notice he was gone and the hunt would begin again.

Hoping he was heading in the right direction, he let his legs take over. Before he knew it, he was back where the first battle had taken place. The moss was torn up and flung about, and splashes of blood spotted the green. The Ko-goks weren't the only ones to abandon the area; his brothers and friends had disappeared, as well. He hoped they were all right, especially Abazi. He was sorry he'd ever doubted that she and Kimber were anything but their friends.

Did Kris carry her out? The thought of his brother being Abazi's new hero was strangely aggravating, but Gabe managed to push his feelings to the back of his mind. Knowing what could be lurking in the forest, he had to keep his thoughts trained on moving forward, and his ears on listening to what followed behind him.

His vigilance saved his life. While leaping over a mossy stone, a black branch shot out, nearly beheading him with its razor sharp thorns, which had been flattened to make a battalion of blades. He managed to duck in time and ended up sprawled on the ground on the other side of a boulder, instead of flattened against it.

When he saw who had tried to guillotine him, he wondered if he would have been better off with Feltry and Dorn. Straif had removed his hood and was staring at Gabe with sunken, dead eyes. He looked as though he hadn't eaten for centuries.

"We meet again, *Gabriel.*"

Gabe nodded warily, keeping his eyes on Straif the whole time, hard as that was. Looking at him was like looking at someone's open, infected wound. "Your sons are looking for you."

Straif's eyes darkened. "As usual, they've disappointed me. I asked them to fetch ye and they end up fightin' each other. Stupid saps. Their brains have gone to rot, I tell ye."

"Dame Hazel says you lied to me." Gabe didn't know why he was saying this now. Perhaps he wasn't sure he could trust Dame Hazel, either, and needed to put her to the test. Straif cackled, but didn't answer. "Okaaay..." Gabe began again, unsure where to take this. "So what's the truth? Why do you want to catch me?"

Straif clacked broken, yellowed teeth together. "That's an easy one. Ye see, *Gabriel,* if I take yer blood, I'll live forever."

Gabe swallowed hard. "I doubt that, but I'll go with it. So why *my* blood?"

"Because ye're the only one who can undo what has been done to us."

"What was done to you?" Gabe asked breathlessly. Barely able to move a muscle, he felt ensnared in Straif's intense presence, like a fly caught in a web.

"A crime was done to us. I'm tired of payin' for something we didn't do."

"But I still don't see how *my* blood can help you."

"Yer blood'll set things right. It'll make us whole again."

"Shedding blood can't do that!" Gabe protested. "You can't right a wrong with a wrong." He'd learned that in kindergarten. Straif had apparently skipped kindergarten. "I think you're lying to me...again."

Straif's lips, if the bloodless lines could be called that, twitched with amusement as he glanced upward at the sky. There wasn't much to see through the thick canopy of leaves. "Well, ye won't ever know, will ye?" The question was barely a whisper. Straif swung his arm around hard and Gabe jumped back. He'd been expecting the move—it was Jer's favorite, after all—lure the enemy into complacency, then clobber them a good one.

Before Straif could attack again, Gabe was off, racing through the woods. This time he didn't make the mistake of looking back. He was pretty sure he wouldn't like what he'd see.

The wind picked up, turning the still woods into a violent storm, and tree trunks and branches clashed against one another with hurricane fury. When the trees in front of him moved to cut him off, Gabe knew he was in big trouble. He barely made it between two of them before their trunks smashed against each other. They had almost squashed him like an ant. His adrenaline surged, making his legs wobbly, but he didn't stop running. He couldn't.

"Stop him!" Straif shouted from somewhere behind Gabe. Like machine-gun fire, thorns ripped into the trees he dashed past. He began to bob and weave, to make it harder for Straif to hit him. One thorn skimmed his bare leg, but he didn't slow. A mistake now would mean his life.

His jerky movements confused the trees, forcing them to collide against one another too soon, again and again. They seemed unable to adjust or try anything different. Perhaps Dame Hazel was right, that Straif had cast a spell on them, taking away their free will and pressuring them to do things they wouldn't ordinarily do.

A cavalry of noise behind Gabe made his heart beat harder. Others had joined Straif in the hunt. Dorn and Feltry must have realized that their prey had given them the slip.

"Cut him off!" Straif ordered. "Get round front of him. Stop him!"

Fists clenched to fight, Gabe ran like a wildcat, quick and wily. They outnumbered him by far, but they'd have to use their brains if they wanted to catch him. Luckily for him, one of them wasn't very smart and was inadvertently helping his cause.

"Get yer big trunk out of the way, Barb!" someone shouted.

"Me feet hurt!" Barb bellowed. "Slows me down!"

"Then stop runnin'! Ye keep cuttin' Dorn off, ye big waste of space!"

Gabe smiled to himself. *Thank you, Barb.*

The edge of the forest was close now—he could tell by the way the light brightened, as though a field awaited him. The trees grew farther apart with each step he took, but what he saw next knocked the hope of reaching freedom right out of him. A swarm of malevolent shadows raced to cut him off. They flanked him on either side, their black cloaks flapping in the wind like crazed bats. As soon as they could, the two lines would merge, creating a wedge that he wouldn't be able to avoid, trapping him like a wild animal.

Chapter Twenty-One

He's in the Trees!

"Gabriel!" a voice called to him, and he skidded to a stop. The sound had come from above him. He glanced up, but couldn't see anything amongst the heavy canopy of leaves and branches. He was about to start running again when a thick vine dropped in front of him. Without stopping to consider whether or not this might be a trick, Gabe grabbed hold of the vine and felt himself rising like an elevator.

About twenty feet from the top of the tree, and a hundred feet too high off the ground, a hand reached out and clasped his own. He raised his head and found himself looking into unexpected eyes. Oswald. The boy lifted a finger to his lips. As quietly as he could, Gabe crawled onto a thick branch next to him and crouched low. Together they watched as the dark ones filled the space below them like a murder of crows.

"Where is he?" Straif bawled, directly beneath them.

A sudden gust of wind knocked against the tree and an old lullaby chose that inopportune moment to fill Gabe's head.

Rock a bye baby, on the treetop.
When the wind blows, the cradle will rock.
When the bough breaks, the cradle will fall
And down will come Gaby, Oswald and all.

He cringed and tried to think happier thoughts. The wind blew harder.

"He's got to be close!" Feltry called out. "Our net's tighter than a spider's web."

"It isn't tight enough," Straif sneered. "He must have doubled back somehow."

"Then the fault's on Feltry's side," Dorn insisted. "Dorn and his mates are the best at this game."

"Game?" Straif snapped, and Dorn cringed, realizing his mistake.

"This is no game, spawn." Straif pointed a long, bony finger at the group gathered around him. "If we can't catch that boy, we'll be dead. Simple as that. Now go! Feltry, that way. Dorn, this way." The two groups ran off, but Straif stayed behind. He threw back his hood, letting his dark, soulless eyes scan the woods, and his head bobbed up and down as he sniffed the air like a starving wolf.

"Blighters!" Oswald cursed under his breath. "Don't move!" He wrapped his arms around Gabe and his whole body began to shake. Gabe watched with horror and fascination as Oswald's skin turned rough and brown. His arms stretched and grew until his limbs transformed into branches that hid both of them amidst rapidly sprouting leaves, exactly like those of the tree in which they sat, and those that lined the corridor leading to the birch spiral. Oswald was one of the magnificent oaks.

Straif finished his sniffing and looked straight up. Gabe could hardly see him through the leaves, but he felt as though the dark creature's coal black eyes could see him. He tried not to move. He tried not to breathe.

He was doing quite well until the tip of his nose started to itch. To make matters worse, a spider landed on his arm and crawled up his sleeve. Biting his lip, Gabe struggled to fight off the screaming impulse roaring through his brain to scratch his nose and fling that spider to kingdom come. Every muscle and nerve in his body protested, urging him with all their strength to tremble, stretch, anything! But he did not flicker so much as an eyelid.

With a disgusted shake of his head, Straif finally stalked off, heading back into the woods. Oswald had saved Gabe's life. No wonder he thought of himself as King of the forest.

"He's gone," Oswald declared after another minute of waiting to be sure Straif wasn't faking his departure. His branches transformed back into flesh and blood and he quickly separated from Gabe. "That was too close."

"Where are my brothers and my friends?" Gabe asked, scratching his nose, the sensation a delight. The spider, thank goodness, had strolled back down his arm again. He gently flicked it onto a leaf.

"They're safe. Me band met up with us after Feltry took ye. They're watchin' out for yer kin."

"They haven't made it out of the forest yet?"

"I cannot say. We went separate ways."

"Why?"

"I promised Dame Hazel I'd bring all of ye safely home, and one of ye happened to be missin'." He glanced over at Gabe. "Yer brothers didn't want to leave ye behind, but I told them I'd take care of ye."

"And Abazi? Is she all right?"

"When I left her, she was awake, but looked a bit wilted."

"Wilted?"

"Weak. Wobbly. Ye know." Gabe finally made the connection. "I'll take ye across the Briar Borders, then I'll go and fetch the others." It wasn't a suggestion; it was an order.

"I can't do that."

"Ye'd only be an encumbrance."

"I'm not leaving my brothers and my friends behind in this forest!"

Oswald's chin lifted slightly. "Do ye see this scar?" He pointed to a thick, white mark running along his jaw. "I got it takin' down a rogue Rowan tree. He had canker rot and it were drivin' him mad." He pointed to a thin slash over his left eye. "This one came during the Sycamore Rebellion. The whole lot of them got it into their fool heads that they could make it on their own without the rest of the Forest Immortal. We would've let them go, if only to teach them a lesson, but they wanted all rights to Shambolic Stream. After a bit of a struggle with me and me band, they decided they were happy as they were. I'm pretty sure it was Straif who incited them. It wouldn't be the first time." He reached up and gripped the branch above his head. "I know what I'm doin'..." he paused. "And I know how to handle those who give me a hard time."

"That was a nice speech," Gabe replied steadily, though inside he was nervous as heck. He might know what he had to do—not back down—but that didn't make the task any easier. He didn't like confrontations. They often ended up backfiring on him. "But I'm still coming with you."

Oswald pulled himself to his feet. "Ye aren't the only one who stands to lose in this."

"I know. My brothers and my friends could lose their lives because of this forest of yours. I won't let that happen."

The boy narrowed his eyes. "Yer kind is a pain in me neck. Ye know that?"

"You wouldn't abandon your band, would you? So how can you expect me to?"

"Ye aren't scared for yerself? The Ko-goks are after ye, don't ye see that?"

"I never said I wasn't scared," Gabe admitted. "Every little bit of sense in my brain is screaming at me to get out of these woods and as far away from Straif as I can. But I can't listen to those bits."

"Even when those bits are right?"

"I can't leave them here."

Oswald looked around the forest, squinting a moment before point-ing off to the west, back into the depths of the forest. "They headed that way. We must travel by tree." Oswald began to climb higher and Gabe reluctantly followed after him. Soon they were nearly to the top, clinging to thin branches that bent beneath their weight. Gabe won-dered if maybe Oswald was right. Maybe he shouldn't go with him. He could run on ahead, distract the dark ones from his brothers and friends. He didn't especially like this kind of height—the killing kind. He stood more of a chance against the Ko-goks.

"Whatever ye do, don't look down and don't let go of me." Oswald held out his scarred hand. Gabe hesitantly reached out and grabbed hold; it was callused and rough—a hand that had seen years of hard work and been through many battles. "Ready?"

"I suppose so, but...aagghh!"

Oswald leaped from the tree branch and Gabe was yanked forward. His stomach stayed behind as they flew through the air toward the next tree, which seemed a mile away, but was probably only ten feet. When they landed lightly on a small platform of interwoven branches, his gut caught up to him, making him feel slightly queasy. Several of the tree's slender branches wove together right in front of them, creat-ing multiple platforms along the way, like stepping-stones across a stream. Oswald ran along the makeshift path and made another jump, pulling Gabe after him.

Once Gabe got his rhythm down, Oswald ran faster and leaped far-ther. Soon they were racing along the treetops, though Gabe wasn't sure how he was managing to make his size thirteen feet land on the right spots. After a few more leaps he decided that the trees were help-ing him out. He was not normally this sure-footed, always running into walls and furniture at home. Without their assistance, he would have misstepped by now. He could do this!

A loud crack sounded below them and he looked down. That was his first mistake. His second was to let go of Oswald's hand.

"Blighters!" Oswald shouted as Gabe began to fall.

And down will come Gaby, his mind sang as he plummeted toward the earth. The branches slapped against his face and body like whips. He was falling face first in a swan dive, arms stretched out in front of him. The ground rose up to meet him with a swiftness that belied its impas-sivity. From far away, the thought came to Gabe that he was going to die.

He didn't want to die.

"Catch me!" he cried out, to whom he didn't know. To Oswald? To God?

No one answered.

The feeling was irrational, but Gabe didn't want to meet the ground face first. He didn't want to see death coming. He pulled his legs in and twisted his body to land on his back. It wouldn't do him any good, but he did it anyway.

A second later he hit at full force. But it wasn't the ground—whatever had caught him was soft, like a trampoline. His hands groped about and found branches. The trees had caught him!

But he wasn't out of trouble yet. The net of branches stretched lower and lower, racing toward the ground at an incredible speed. Gabe wrapped both hands around a couple limbs and hoped for the best, all the while thinking that they couldn't possibly hold his weight.

But they could.

He sprung up, bounced several times, then settled to a stop. It seemed that he'd found the mother in the lullaby, the one not mentioned, but who would certainly be there to catch her baby, cradle and all. This time, the mother was the tree itself.

"I've got ye," he thought he heard someone say in a voice lovely and ethereal, but there was no one around.

Shaken, but alive, he rolled off the web of branches and dropped ten feet to the ground. Once he'd steadied himself, he looked up at the trees that had saved him. Strong, straight trunks topped by an umbrella of glowing, green leaves surrounded him. The trees' bark was smooth and gray, blotted with occasional patches of pale green moss.

Not just one mother, but many. He bowed to them all. "Thank you for saving my life," he said. It seemed right, if a little bizarre, to express his gratitude, as he had for the club, and he thought that maybe the trees returned the gesture, their limbs sweeping low.

Oswald landed beside him, his expression a contrast of awe and annoyance. "The Beeches saved ye?" He gestured wildly at the gray trees. "Are ye a son of a Beech?"

Gabe's lips twitched and a small snort escaped. "Kris and Jer call me that sometimes, but I don't think my mom would like the term."

"But she's…" He looked up. "Well, this one in particular is a right difficult one to please." One of the beech tree's branches swung down and smacked Oswald on the back of the head. "Hey! What was that for?"

But he wasn't to find out, nor would Gabe.

"Gabe!" He spun around to see Kris, Hollie, and Jer racing toward him. "You're okay!" Behind them the woods came alive with an influx of forty or so young warriors, male and female, and all dressed like Oswald. Two of the males carried Kimber and Abazi, who, while looking pale, was conscious. The Rogues had arrived.

"How'd you get away from the Bozo Brothers?" Kris demanded. "We were going to bring the girls back to the other side and then come for you. Abazi's half out of it and Kimber's got some bad blisters. Stupid braces." He reached over and patted Kimber solicitously on the back.

"I got lucky," Gabe told him. "Dorn and his brother started fighting. While they were duking it out, I snuck away."

The three brothers grinned at each other. "Good thing *we* never fight," Jer remarked. They all laughed.

"We need to get ye out of the forest now," Oswald interrupted.

"Lead the way, my good...um...forest man," Kris told him, slapping his palm with his bat.

Gabe moved up to Abazi's side. A tall youth carried her on his back with an ease Gabe wasn't sure he, himself, would be able to pull off. "You okay?" She smiled blearily up at him, brandishing the tomahawk. "I saved your mom's hawk."

"She wouldn't have cared if you'd lost it." Well, she might have been a little mad at first, but she always got over things after blowing and blathering about it first.

"But I would've cared."

"Next time you're just going to have to sacrifice your pride."

Her expression turned funny, as though she were in pain. "Sometimes pride is all a person has."

"Well, thanks for getting it back," he said awkwardly.

"I didn't do it for you, dipwad." With that, she laid her head against her ride's back and closed her eyes. Gabe watched her face as the boy went on ahead, wondering if she was going to be all right. She looked awfully pale.

"Ye didn't answer me question," Oswald said in a low voice, interrupting Gabe's thoughts. He realized with a start that Oswald was walking next to him. He wondered if he had heard Abazi calling Gabe a dipwad. Man, he hoped not.

"What question?"

"How do ye know the Beeches? Why did she, um, they save ye?"

Gabe shrugged. "Before you pointed out what they were, I didn't even know what a beech tree was. They're beautiful."

"They're known as the Queens of the Forest. They keep to themselves, ye see. They're quite exclusive."

"You mean they're snobs?"

"Snobs?"

"They think they're better than other people...or rather, trees."

"Yes. Well, no. It isn't that they think they're better, they just *are* better."

"By whose standard?" Gabe wanted to know what made someone or something better than another. What was that elusive element? The one that always confounded him, kept him up nights searching for the secret code everyone else always seemed to know but him.

Oswald had no answer for him. "I's just that way. I still don't understand why she, I mean, *they* chose to help *ye*." He shook his head, confused, and perhaps a bit annoyed.

Gabe was curious, too. "Maybe they didn't want my blood and guts splattered all over their bark."

Oswald nodded thoughtfully. "Ye may be right. They are fastidious, the Beech."

Gabe smiled inwardly. He hadn't really been serious. "We should probably get moving, don't you think? The dark ones are bound to figure out that we tricked them."

"That's exactly what I said earlier. Glad ye're finally catchin' up to me." He left Gabe to consult with his band. Soon after, the band members pulled into a tight formation around the smaller group. "Our only hope now is to outrun Straif and his Ko-goks," he said to them.

"Let's do it, then," Kris growled impatiently. Hollie, sticking close to his side, nodded in agreement.

The pack began to run. Gabe tried to stay alert, but it wasn't easy. Strange noises chattered all around them. Out of the corner of his eye, he caught a shadow flitting here, a blurred figure dashing there. Were these members of the band, or something more dangerous?

When a branch snapped somewhere farther back, Gabe knew that the sound didn't come from anything good. Something was hunting them, waiting to make its move. He had the uncomfortable feeling that they were being herded into a trap. He moved up to join Kris, Jer, and Hollie. Oswald had taken the lead and was several paces ahead.

"We've got company," he whispered.

Kris's fingers kneaded his wooden bat. "I thought so. I can feel them out there."

"What do you think we should do?"

"Act like we don't even know they're there," Kris murmured. "But let everyone know and tell them to be ready. Maybe pick up the pace a little. Grandma can run faster than this." To be fair, Grandma May was a pretty fast runner, but still, Kris was right. They had to get out of this forest, *soon*.

Gabe approached Oswald. "I know," he snapped, before Gabe even said a word. "We all know, and we know who it is. They want to trap us where the Wych Elms live."

"Witch Elms? What are they?" He thought an elm was a kind of tree, but anything of the witch variety couldn't be good.

"W-y-c-h..." Oswald spelled it out for him. "The word means flexible. Nothing to do with yer human witches. But..." he paused. "Well, they're a bit tetchy at times. They have a dark side to them. Ye never know with Wych Elms what they're about to do. Flexible can mean lithe, but it can also mean to go either way, good or bad. Ye see what I'm sayin'?"

Gabe thought he was starting to. "So it wouldn't take much to bring out the worst in them?"

"That's it in a nutshell. Ye're quicker than rocks, Gabriel."

"Can we go faster?" he asked, ignoring the jab. He'd heard worse.

"We don't want to provoke an attack sooner than necessary. We can't let them know we know they're near..."

Gabe nodded and dropped back to Kris. He was whispering with Hollie, and Jer had moved up to be by Kimber. "He says that if we start running faster, we'll give away that we know the Ko-goks are following us."

"And in the meantime let ourselves be herded into a trap!" Kris hissed. "I say we split off and go on ahead on our own."

Hollie scowled. "Oswald is a right bossy sort, but he's smart. He knows what he's talkin' about. We should listen to him, Kristofer."

Kris shook his head in disgust. "Now's the time for action!"

"What about Kimber and Abazi?" Gabe asked. "How do you propose we carry them and fight at the same time?"

Kris's mouth scrunched up in thought. "That would be a challenge."

"I say we stick with Oswald. I'd rather have him and his band helping us than to try and fight Straif and the Ko-goks on our own."

Kris didn't look convinced. "It's never good policy to let yourselves be drawn into a trap."

"We don't have a choice," Gabe insisted. "So wipe that look off your face!"

"What look?" Kris asked innocently.

"Just don't," Gabe warned.

"We should at least be ready. Do you still have your mallet?"

Gabe pulled it from his waistband and held it up, wishing he still had his big stick. As he showed his weapon to Kris, he tripped over something and crashed to his knees. Scrambling to his feet, he saw the source of his fall. His stick? It was! He recognized the bark and the gouges made from their earlier fight. Strange that it had ended up here. He picked it up and quickly rejoined Kris and Hollie, who were waiting for him.

"This, too," he brandished the stick.

"Good. Jer and I are armed and so is Oswald's little army. I guess we're gonna have to fight our way out. Or..." he grinned mischievously. "We take them now!" With a roar, he broke away, dashing back toward the ring of band members, which parted before Kris, the raging bull.

"Kris!" Gabe screamed. "Get back here, you idiot!"

But Kris didn't listen. He never did.

Chapter Twenty-Two

Let My People Go

One moment there was nothing to see but trees and rocks. The next, dark ones were everywhere—like a swarm of ants, with Gabe and the others, the sugar. *Oh, Kris!* Gabe bemoaned. *What have you done?*

There was nothing left to do but fight. He sprinted up to the band members carrying Abazi and Kimber. "Get the girls to the border. Do whatever it takes. Hollie, you lead them. Jer, you go, too. Your job is to make sure they get there safely. Now go!" He pushed them forward.

"I want to fight!" Jer cried.

"I need you to watch over the girls. They're injured. You have to guard them!" It was the best he could come up with to convince Jer to go.

Jer glanced at a tense Kimber, then nodded. "Come on, guys."

Gabe watched anxiously as the small group rushed past Oswald, soon disappearing amongst the trees. Gabe thought that the edge of the woods was close—it had to be. He didn't think they'd last much longer. He also couldn't rely on Jer doing what he was supposed to. He hated being left out and was most likely still sulking from their earlier argument when he wanted to carry Kimber.

Kris's roar caught Gabe's attention and he spun around. A tide of cloaked maniacs slashed at his brother with long, deadly thorns, pushing him backward. He leaped away, all the while striking out with his bat like a warrior Babe Ruth. He was holding them at bay, but for how long?

Oswald pointed his staff at the mass. "Attack!" His band dashed forward, staffs and batas in hand, and the two groups clashed, dark green against deepest black. "Get out of here!" Oswald shouted at Gabe as he fought two Ko-goks at once. "We'll hold them off!"

Gabe worked his way over to Kris, his mallet and staff cracking against the hard, wood-like bodies of the dark ones. "Come on! Jer and the girls have gone on ahead. We have to catch up!"

"I'm busy!" Kris grunted, swinging his bat.

"But what if Jer decides he should be here with us instead of with them?"

Kris instantly changed gears. "I'm on it." He let the Rogues take his place and turned to flee with Gabe. As they ran, Gabe glanced back. It wasn't a fair fight. Far more black capes filled the woods than green ones, but he didn't know what else to do. He had to get everyone safely out of this cursed forest.

Before long they caught up to the others, who were slowed by their burdens. Hollie was leading the pack and looked glad to see them. Jer eyed them angrily, but didn't say a word.

The way lightened up ahead and Gabe's heart leaped. They were close! The sun shone brightly, just beyond the reach of the trees, its light a treasure they all desperately wanted to capture. All they had to do was make it to the other side of the hedge—what Oswald called the Briar Borders—and they'd be safe.

"Fall back!" Oswald called in the distance. The band was retreating, heading their way like a stampede.

They raced toward the light. Gabe's breath came in gasps and his lungs burned like fire. They were only about ten seconds from the edge of the woods when the disaster happened. A line of grayish-brown, crack-barked trees moved in unison, forming a wall that blocked the way as effectively as a tank. They screeched to a halt.

"What the heck?" Kris cried. "What's going on?"

"They're the Wych Elms!" Hollie cried. "Straif has muddled them!"

Gabe's head pounded. "Let us through. They're coming!"

The sound of whispering filled his ears. "It's Yggdrasil! He's our beginning. The other one is our end." The voice echoed forth from the tree directly in front of Gabe. Its branches slashed through the air with each word, as though emphasizing an important point.

"I like t'other better," the one to the right remarked. Most of its leaves were missing. "He's very grand, very scary. I like scary."

"Ye liked the Gorse, too, and look what they did to ye! Stripped ye bare of all yer lovely leaves!"

Gabe looked over his shoulder. The Rogues were only a few hundred yards away and behind them came the dark ones, a tidal wave of evil and despair.

He squared his shoulders. "I am Gabriel! Let us through and I'll see that you live long!" He had no idea where such dramatic words had come from, but they sounded good.

"Ye will?"

"Of course! That's why I'm here."

"He's trickin' ye, Ailem."

"Ye knothead, Weachu! The other is trickin' *ye!*"

"But what if...?"

"But what if...*nothing!*" Ailem growled. "I'm lettin' him through. If'n he's trickin' us, he'll be finished. We're Wych Elms. We can cross both ways. He knows this, sure enough. He's not like those dratted, spike throwin' fiends..."

Gabe wasn't entirely sure he knew what Ailem meant, but he didn't care. He just wanted to get through to the other side, to the sun. A creak and a groan sounded and the two trees parted. The others stayed where they were, maintaining the wall. Gabe urged everyone through, shoving Kris, who looked like he might try for one last battle.

The last to come was a vexed Oswald, followed quickly by Gabe himself. Once through, he glanced back and found himself staring at a wall of dark ones surging toward him. "Run!" he hollered to the others. Feltry was only two steps away from the opening now. He lifted his arm and aimed his thorn at Gabe's chest.

Then he disappeared as the trees closed ranks once more. Feltry grunted in pain as he slammed into the unmoving wood and the dark ones bellowed and shrieked angrily at being cut off. Gabe glanced up at the line of trees. "Thank you, Ailem. I won't forget this."

"See that ye don't. I'm tired of growin' old. Me branches ache something fierce."

Gabe smiled and hurried after the others. About ten more feet of thinning trees, and he was out in the sun. He was safe, and he finally felt warm again. Despite all the running he'd done, through all that deep moss, he hadn't been able to shake the chill of the woods.

The rest of the group, including the Rogues, was nearly to the hedge. Gabe ran to catch up to them. "I did what I promised," Oswald said when Gabe came alongside him, panting hard. "Now it's up to ye to stay safe. Do ye know the secret of the Briars?" He stepped up to face the hedge.

"I do!" Kris cried. "There's a door somewhere around here." He looked about. "Here, I think." He began pulling on the thick, woody vines. "Come on, show me the door!"

Oswald chuckled. "That's not the secret." He glanced over at Gabe. "Do ye know it?" His expression told Gabe he assumed the answer would be no.

"I think so." Gabe stepped forward. "Open!" he cried, lifting his arms. "Open *now!*" Slowly, reluctantly, the prickly vines began to part. "That's it, right?"

Oswald looked sick. "Something like that."

"Way to go!" Kris slapped Gabe on the back. "All right, people, let's move out!"

Jer helped Kimber through the small opening, followed by Kris and Hollie supporting a wobbly Abazi. Kris, Jer, and Hollie soon reappeared.

"Come on, Gabe," Jer urged, looking back at the woods. "Let's go. Who knows how long the trees can hold off those creeps."

"Will they cross the Briar Borders?" Gabe asked Oswald. They'd already done so once to kidnap him.

"They can, but they'll not. Not at the moment, anyway." He glanced up at the sky. "They don't like the sun, or rather, the sun doesn't like them."

Jer frowned. "That doesn't make sense. Sunlight is how you guys survive, right? Well, at least the tree part of you."

"Not for them. Not anymore," Oswald said ominously. "Not since they partook of blood. They have tainted themselves. Ye mix sap with blood and it'll burn more quickly than either on its own. It's a deadly, unnatural mixture and nature seeks to destroy it."

"So what do we do when it's nighttime?" Gabe asked, his eyes frozen on the woods. For the moment, the elms were holding their line, but a lot of noise rang out from the other side of the wall of trees. Angry noise.

"Ye're safe in the house. Or in any wooden place with the doors shut tight. They don't like the touch of dead wood. They can stand it for only a wee bit, then they must leave its touch, for it burns them something fierce. Ye cannot eat yer folk and escape the consequences of it."

"That explains why they didn't touch our weapons," Jer remarked, half to himself. "All of them are wood."

"And why I didn't have to hit them very hard with my staff to hurt them," Gabe realized. And also why Barb had complained that his feet hurt 'from that dratted wood' after Dorn's gang had stood on the porch to kidnap Gabe.

"Ye see the way of it now," Oswald said. "Time we be goin'. Me band grows restless to return home." Oswald turned to the group, who'd retreated back toward the edge of the woods. "We'll stay on this side until we reach Shambolic Stream and then..."

A shriek pierced the air, cutting him off. One of the elms had given way, several black thorns impaling its rough bark. Branches swiped at the painful spikes, desperately working to remove them. Undeterred by the whipping branches, an army of dark ones poured through the opening. Gabe could feel their pounding footsteps in his chest.

"Get out of here! *Now!*" Oswald ordered, then raced toward the woods, bata raised and staff swinging. Halfway across the field, a giant brute launched himself at Oswald, catching him off guard and knocking him to the ground. He didn't get back up and the dark one leaped on him.

"Stay there, Kimber!" Gabe cried. Before she could protest, the three brothers sprinted back toward the battle. They would rescue Oswald, then get out of there. Kris knocked several dark ones backward with a couple swings of his bat and Gabe struck out at a short one trying to grab Jer. The three made their way toward Oswald, but couldn't reach him. Surrounded by capes, he and his opponent wrestled fiercely, rolling and flipping each other.

"Get the boy!" a chilling voice rang out. Straif waited at the edge of the woods, not daring to risk himself in the sun. The heavy cloaks the Ko-goks wore, along with their pulled-up hoods, made sense now. Their hands, however, could not escape exposure. Little puffs of smoke drifted up from the bone-white skin, and the smell of burning wood, laced with the sickly sweet stench of spoiling blood, filled the air. Straif's minions screeched in pain, but seemed more afraid of their leader's wrath than the effects of the sun's rays. They continued their attack.

The heavy odor pulled itself into Gabe's lungs, writhing and jerking like a living creature. A cough wracked his body. "Kris!" he shouted between hacks. "Watch out for Jer!" He was attempting to fight off three warriors at once, trying to prove himself as strong as any of them. The attackers lunged at him with their thorns, again and again, until one finally made contact, scratching Jer's cheek. The strike distracted him long enough for the other two Ko-goks to grab his arms.

"Let me go!" he howled, kicking and screaming like a two-year-old. His ferocity surprised the dark ones; they had not expected such strength in one so young. One lost his grip and Jer jerked his arm away from the other one. Gabe rushed the group, swinging his mallet. There was a crunch as it connected with one of the dark one's shoulders. The monster screamed in pain.

It didn't take long for Gabe to realize his mistake as Dorn and four of his lackeys appeared from out of nowhere. He had used Jer to get to Gabe, and Gabe had played right into the scumbag's hands. The five Ko-goks rushed at him, their bony hands reaching out to grab him. One knocked away his staff with his cloaked elbow. Another whacked Gabe's head with his balled-up fist.

"Good one, mates!" Dorn cried. "We got him!" The dark ones closed the circle, with five of them against two. "Father'll like Dorn best after this!" His fist rose high into the air before quickly dropping as his skin started to sizzle.

"I had it taken care of, Gabe!" Jer shouted. They were standing back to back now. He could feel Jer shaking, but the tremor came not from fear, but fury. "I didn't need your help, you superhero wannabe!"

Gabe couldn't believe what he was hearing. "So you're saying I should've let them kill you?"

"At least it would've been a glorious death."

"No death is glorious!"

"It is when you die for a good reason," Jer argued.

"There's no good reason to get yourself killed!" Gabe bit his lip hard to stop the threatening tears. Dad had been fighting death for years now. Nothing about it was sublime. "Especially when you're meant for better things, Jer." *Like Dad is,* he whispered to himself.

"Shut it, ye two!" A cloud passed over the sun and Dorn spun around to face the woods. "Father!" he hollered over the noise of the battle. "Dorn got him! Dorn caught *Gabriel!*"

A dark figure pushed his way through the fighting crowd. Dorn grinned and Barb, his sidekick, snorted wickedly. Soon Straif was inside the circle of dark ones. The battle was still being fought around them, but inside the ring, it seemed as though nothing else was going on in the world. Gabe tried to push Jer away from Straif, but his brother was reluctant to go.

"I'm going to need some room," he whispered. Jer's blue eyes regarded him defiantly, then slowly he backed away.

"Come with me, and I'll let yer brothers live," Straif growled. Even though he was getting what he wanted, he did not look happy. "Dorn, take him."

"Leave now," Gabe replied with deliberation, knowing he had to get this right, "and I'll let *you* live." At these words, Dorn stopped his approach. Slowly, he began to back up, pulling his hood up as he retreated. The sun had returned.

Straif laughed his dry, raspy laugh. "Ye're amusing, Gabriel. Stupid as grass, but good for a laugh."

"You misunderstand me, Straif. I'm not joking."

Straif looked around at his followers. "This seedling thinks he can take me on and live to tell about it!" The watchers laughed uproariously, enjoying the spectacle.

Gabe stood his ground. He had this strange feeling that it wasn't really Gabriel Hawthorne who was talking. It was some other kid; one who had courage and who didn't worry about death or dying or getting good grades so he could go to a good college, whose guilt ate at him daily like a parasitic worm. This other Gabriel lived a different kind of life. He was brave and he was a fighter, a man who lived in the moment. He was the person Gabe had always wanted to be, but was simply too scared.

A dark one approached Straif, bowing and shuffling as he came forward. "We have them all," he said, keeping his head low. Gabe glanced around, feeling his heart sink. The Rogues had been captured, including Oswald. Feltry had Kris and Hollie.

Gabe peeked back at the Briar Border, but the door was no longer there. He hoped the girls were still safe on the other side. He was about to turn back when a movement caught his eye. He peered closely, but nothing more happened. He returned his gaze to Straif.

"I guess ye're ready to bargain now, eh, *Gabriel?*" the dark leader sneered, his hood sliding back just enough to show his rotting features.

"He doesn't bargain!" Kris shouted from the crowd. "Don't give in, Gabe!"

Gabe gave a tight smile. That was Kris, through and through. Fight every battle like you were fighting for your life, for your family's life, for everything. Maybe that's why Kris often won.

"I don't plan to." He pulled back his shoulders and stuck out his chest, hoping the gesture would give him strength and courage. "So, Straif, do you want to be the first to die?"

Straif's expression shifted for a moment. "Are ye tryin' to tell me ye want to fight me?" He looked intrigued.

"I'm not sure I can make it any more clear. When I win, you let us all go."

Straif grinned a horrible grin. "And when *I* win?"

"Then I'll come with you willingly. Just me, though. You have to let the others go."

Straif nodded. "So be it."

"I have your word?"

"Oh, yes. Ye have me word. But ye won't be needin' it."

Gabe raised his fists. "Let's do this."

"Gabe, no!" He glanced back. Abazi had somehow managed to climb up on top of the Briar Border. "Don't do this!" Her dark eyes suddenly widened. "Gabe, look out!"

He swung back around in time to avoid Straif's first strike, his arm swinging over Gabe's head. The dark one backed off, grinning. "Ye want to give in now?"

"No, but I'll make you the same offer."

Straif threw back his head and roared. "If only me sons had yer grit." Both sons sneered at Gabe. If Dorr and Feltry hadn't hated him before, they certainly did now.

"Let's get this over with," he growled.

At that moment, a thick band of clouds blotted out the sun. Straif smiled and the triumphant expression further marred his maggoty face. "I'll be takin' a different form then," he announced as he pulled off his cape. Thick black spikes rose from his palms and spread upward along his elongating arms. Thorns sprouted from his chest, piercing his rough, white shirt like needles. Straif was half tree now, yet maintained most of his human attributes. In this mutated form, he was stronger and bigger, yet still agile.

Staring at the new and improved Straif, Gabe knew he was in big trouble. This no longer looked like such a fair fight. He had thought he could take Straif as he was—short and slow. But not like this. Fighting him now would be like fighting a giant, rabies-crazed porcupine.

"Are ye ready to die?" Straif inquired, almost politely. "Because I'm ready to take yer life!"

The dark ones hooted wildly, a strange cacophony that evolved into a deep-throated chant. "Blackthorn! Blackthorn! Spill the blood, return to life! Blackthorn, Blackthorn! Take the power, end the strife!"

Feeling sick, Gabe glanced around one more time. Kris stood next to Jer at the edge of the ring surrounding Straif and Gabe. Ko-goks restrained both brothers' arms tightly behind their backs—one for each arm so that they had no chance of breaking free.

He returned his gaze to Straif. "I think I might say the same to you." He was totally bluffing. He didn't really think he could defeat Straif, but now he was trapped by the bargain he'd made. His parents had always taught him to stand by his word, so there was nothing left to do but pretend he was tougher than he really was and hopefully fight his way out of this nightmare.

With an evil smile, Straif swung his spiky arm at Gabe's head. The movement was slow, almost leisurely, as though a mere demonstration. Gabe jumped back and the arm missed him by only half an inch. The entire circle of spectators stepped back in unison, widening the ring. No one wanted to be Straif's victim, accidental or intended.

Gabe remembered the mallet in his hand. Dorn's buddy had knocked away his stick, but hadn't seen the smaller weapon. Straif swung again and Gabe blocked the blow with the wooden hammer. A satisfying crack snapped the tense air. Straif bellowed, yanking back the broken branch. Sap the color of blood oozed from the shattered limb. The dark one's soulless eyes flared madly. Snarling like a mad dog, he advanced on Gabe, swinging his arms like a windmill in a storm.

At the very last second, Gabe dove forward, tucking into a somersault. Just before he reached Straif's legs, he came out of the roll and swung his leg around low and hard. Straif tripped, falling heavily to the ground. Gabe scrambled to his feet and spun around to face his opponent. Almost as quickly, Straif was standing upright, his horrid face distorted with fury.

The gasps from the crowd told Gabe he'd managed to do something few had done before him, if any. But small victories such as this came at a price, because now the dark one was furious. Several arms shot out from his torso and stretched toward the sky, each one sprouting half-foot long spikes like a prickly rash.

Gabe's palms grew wet as Straif mutated into what could easily be the spawn of Medusa and an octopus. What was he going to do now? Over the years he'd put in a lot of time learning karate moves from books and videos to help him combat Kris. But fighting an evil Dryad was an entirely different kettle of rotten fish. There simply weren't any moves invented to fight an opponent with more than two arms, which also happened to be the length of Gabe's body, or longer.

He would have to keep moving, quickly and with perfect timing, to avoid getting hit. It was a strategy that could work, but one he couldn't keep up forever. Within minutes he'd be exhausted. No, his best hope was to seek Straif's soft spots and attack them ruthlessly.

"Go for his head, Gabe!" Kris yelled. "Aim for the eyes!"

Thank you, Kris. You've just revealed my only strategy. Not that he could implement it. Straif's arms were too long and too plentiful. He wouldn't be able to get close enough to his head.

Straif, sensing Gabe's increasing fear, advanced on him. Each step made the earth beneath Gabe's feet shake and his whole body began to tingle. He kept backing up, but finally there was nowhere to go. The crowd wasn't giving way to him.

"Meet yer Maker, *Gabriel*," Dorn hissed into his ear, then shoved him forward. Gabe stumbled and tripped over his own feet, crashing to the ground. But for once, his clumsiness was a blessing. A whoosh of air passed over his left ear as Straif struck out at him.

"Father!" Dorn bleated, leaping out of the way just in time. A few of the other dark ones weren't so lucky. Straif's arm hit them with such force that it lifted them off their feet and threw them twenty yards away. If they were lucky, the worst damage would be a sore tailbone.

But if those thorns had connected to flesh… Gabe shuddered as their howls of pain reached his ears. That could have been him.

Rising to his hands and knees, Gabe crawled around to the other side of Straif's trunk until he was crouching directly behind him. Holding his mallet tight, he smashed it into his attacker's torso before rolling out of the way, stopping right at his brother's feet.

"Go for the eyes!" Kris hissed at him.

"And how do you propose I do that?" Gabe hissed back. "He's got a bit of a reach on him."

"I don't know. Just do it. We're counting on you, you know."

Gabe groaned. That was the last thing he needed to hear. Maybe he should give himself up right now. Then Kris and Jer and the Rogues could get away safely. He'd managed to escape them twice now so he thought he could find a way to do it again. And maybe pigs could fly, too. But giving himself up was all he had. No way was he going to be able to defeat Straif by fighting him. His best bet now would be to use his mind.

He jumped to his feet and put his hands above his head. "I give up!"

"What?" Kris cried.

"You can't give up, Gabe!" Jer shouted. "He'll kill you!"

Hollie's eyes were large. "Gabriel, ye don't understand! There's something ye need to know!"

Gabe shook his head. "You're not changing my mind. If I go with Straif, he'll have to let you go. That was the agreement." He took a step toward the dark leader. "Let them go and you can have me without a fight."

Straif chuckled. "Ye're comin' to me freely, then?"

Gabe nodded. "Just let my friends and my brothers go."

The dark one squinted up at the sky. "All right. It's a deal. Come over here to me."

Feeling a little sick, Gabe walked toward the tree-man. Straif's arms began to pull back into his body until only two remained. When Gabe was about five feet away, he stopped. "Let them go," he insisted.

Straif nodded at the ones holding Jer, Kris, Hollie, and Oswald. They loosened their hold and the four stepped away, shaking their sore arms. "So be it. Now come here."

A choking lump formed in Gabe's throat as he plodded the last few steps to Straif. When he was within arm's reach, the dark one grabbed him, spun him around, and shot his arm around Gabe's neck. The move was so quick and unexpected that Gabe couldn't react in time to stop it. Straif's rigid arm pressed against his throat, threatening to crush his windpipe. He inhaled the rancid odor of rotting leaves and spoiled blood, and convulsed with nausea and fear.

"Grab them!" Straif growled.

"But you said you'd let them go!" Gabe protested, watching in shock as the dark ones grabbed hold of the others.

Straif laughed, a malicious, spiteful sound. "I did let them go. And now," he chuckled, "I've got them again."

Chapter Twenty-Three

The Tree Within

Gabe couldn't believe how stupid he'd been. "That's a dirty trick!"

Straif laughed and the sound reeked of everything wrong with the world. The noise wormed its way into Gabe's brain and he writhed in humiliation. "Did ye really expect me to let all of ye go? What do ye take me for? A seedling?"

"You've got what you want with me. You don't need the others."

"They know too much. Besides, they'll make good meat. We're sick of livin' on bits of bark and lichen when we can't find the blood beasts."

Gabe's body began to tremble all over. He'd failed his friends, he'd failed his brothers, and now they were all going to die. "I'm sorry! I didn't realize…"

Kris shrugged. "Rule number one when you're dealing with bad guys, Gabe, they're gonna screw you every chance they get."

Gabe stared at his brother, shocked by his nonchalance. "This is all my fault, Kris! They wanted me. Just me! It isn't fair that you guys should suffer!"

"It isn't fair that anyone should suffer," Jer said. "Except maybe him." He pointed at Straif, his face flushed with outrage.

"Enough of this idiocy!" Straif hissed. "Ye were stupid to trust words. Ye aren't much good to anyone. Useless as the stars and about as smart." His followers laughed uproariously.

Hearing their shouts of amusement, Gabe's fear began to ebb, and something else, something more powerful, took its place. He was angry. Absolutely furious! And when he got angry, all he wanted to do was strike out at the world. He wanted to do damage. He wanted to do anything he could to make this unbearably explosive feeling go away.

His mom had taught him ways to handle his anger so that he wouldn't keep putting holes in the drywall or wrecking his stuff. Control was a good thing; he liked his video games intact. But there were times, he was just now figuring out, when it was okay to be mad, when anger was a necessity. Anger helped you survive.

And Gabe wanted to live.

So he gave his fury free rein and it grew and grew, like a monster rising out of his own blood and guts. His breath came faster, and his
head felt like a volcano about to erupt. At that moment, the sun came
out, shining on him like a benediction. Straif's skin started to crackle
and he let go of Gabe. He snatched up his cloak and struggled to cover
himself.

Instead of running, Gabe turned to face his tormentor. The sun was
hot on his skin. The heat felt good, and his blood flowed like spring
water. Guided by instinct, his yearning fingers stretched upward toward the sky. His legs and body expanded like balloons filling with water. Before long he was twice his normal size. Thorns appeared next,
erupting from his hardening skin like giant pimples. He lifted an arm to
see that it was a branch now, a spiky branch the color of an elephant's
hide. He was a tree.

A *tree.*

He looked around and the world was strange to his new eyes. Everyone seemed smaller, appearing as either a warm glow or a dark, viscous
cloud. Glancing upward, Gabe felt an overwhelming desire to touch
the clearing sky, bright blue and wondrous. The sun was his mother,
warm and welcoming, and he longed to reach her.

"What's happening to you, Gabe?" a familiar voice cried out.

"He's one of them! He's a Dryad!" another shouted.

"Stop him!" The shout came from a distance, a faraway chirrup, but
loud enough to shake Gabe out of his lethargy. A tremendous bellow,
stemming from the earth beneath his feet, poured out of him. He
started thrashing his arms about as Straif had done, which turned out
to be quite an effective defense. None of the dark clouds could get
near him. Again and again they tried, but he was a creature of destruction. More than a few ended up on their backs, howling in pain.

The smell of burning wood brought him around. Feltry and Dorn
had transformed into black, spiky trees, smaller than Gabe, but powerful and deadly all the same. They charged at him, their black bark
smoking like chimneys. With two simple movements, he flicked them
away and the tree brothers flew backward, mere twigs against his
wrath.

"I can fight just as well as my brothers!" Jer shouted. "Come on, I
dare you to battle me!" Gabe looked about, trying to find his brother.
"Hey! Let me go, you jerk!"

He blinked several times and his vision sharpened to find that Straif
had Jer grasped tightly in his thorny grip. Unable to cover himself in

time, his skin sizzled and smoked in the bright light. Despite the pain, he bared his ragged teeth at Gabe in a challenging snarl. Jer fought to get away, legs kicking and fists pummeling, but the dark one had no intention of letting him go. Kris and Oswald, who'd broken free in the melee, were fighting off a wave of dark ones and could do nothing to help Jer. It was up to Gabe.

"Let him go!" he ordered, his voice rich and deep. "Or I'll finish you off right now!"

Straif ignored him and began dragging Jer toward the woods, one bony hand working desperately to pull his hood on. Gabe tried to follow after them, but his lower half felt as though it were encased in cement. He watched helplessly as Straif neared the forest edge with Jer clasped firmly to his chest.

He was almost to the border when Oswald's voice shouted from below Gabe, "Get these Ko-goks off me back, Gabriel, and I'll go save yer brother!"

Gabe began to knock dark one after dark one out of Oswald's way. A Ko-gok charged Kris from behind and Gabe batted him to the edge of the forest with one well-placed blow.

"Home run!" Kris raised his hands in the air. He reached up to wipe a trickle of blood from his cheek. "We've got them on the run!"

"Straif has Jer," he told his brother in his new, manly voice, which he hoped he'd keep. He really liked the sound of it. "Oswald went after him. I can't. I'm stuck."

"I'm on it, Tree Boy." Kris took off. Gabe wanted to go after the dark leader himself, but he was a full-fledged tree now. Dame Hazel had said that trees could move, and Gabe had seen them do it, but he couldn't do it himself. He was rooted to the spot—*literally*.

"Ye must believe that ye're still a human, Gabriel." Hollie stood by his side, peering up at him, her glow tinged with flecks of red and green. "Ye cannot forget that, or ye'll never be able to go back and forth like we can. Worse, ye might always stay just as ye are." She glanced ahead. "They need our help! There are too many Ko-goks. I'm goin' in!"

Gabe looked up and saw what she meant. The dark ones had trapped Kris and Oswald against the elms, keeping them at bay so that Straif could escape with Jer. The giant trees had closed the gap, forming an impenetrable wall to block entry back into the forest. The dark ones battered ruthlessly at the trees with their thorns, desperate to break through. One of the elms, gouged and pouring sap, was weakening.

I am human. I can walk and run, Gabe told himself, even as he felt his branches reaching upward to the sky once more. The sun felt so good and warm on his bark. His veins filled with sugary sap; it flowed through him like nectar. All he wanted to do was bask in the sun and grow. A sweet odor filled his senses and he glanced around to find its source. He soon realized that the rapturous smell was coming from himself. Thousands of white flowers sprouted from his branches, unfurling like a child's hand and releasing a rich, intoxicating scent into the air. He inhaled deeply, feeling powerful and alive. The world around him disappeared as he became this tree, as he accepted what he truly was.

All thought of his brothers and friends faded away as Gabe reveled in the sheer power of his limbs, in the intense light from above, in the intoxication of being alive. Nothing else mattered.

"Gabe!" The sound was distant, like the buzzing of a bee. He was tempted to swat the annoying noise away, but felt too lazy to try. "Gabriel Hawthorne, wake up right this minute, or I'm coming up there!"

Whatever it was, it was insistent. He sighed and opened his sight to see a figure standing below him radiating such luminous light that his insides melted like ice cream. He sighed in delight. The tiny light was even better than the sun. He leaned toward it, but it darted out of reach. He tried to follow, but he felt so heavy. He groaned and the sound vibrated all around him.

The glow darted back to him. Just as he reached for it, it slipped away from his grasp once again. He wanted that light. He must go after it; he would have to move. But how? The action seemed impossible. He was stuck fast.

A memory slid into his mind of long limbs stretching outward, carrying him forward with great speed. The image seemed to come from a time long ago, as insubstantial as clouds, but he clung to it with all his might. Bearing this impression in his mind, precious as rain, he lunged forward. The effort was horrendous, like wading through quicksand. One step and he already wanted to give up.

But he couldn't. He tried again and the next step was easier. Each stride after that grew less difficult, until soon he'd nearly caught up with the glow. He made one final lunge for the luminescent figure, but the stubborn creature darted off to the left at the last second. He felt angry and thwarted.

"Help them, Gabe!" the glow begged.

He looked around. Help who?

Ah, the other glows. Where had they come from? None were as tantalizing as this little one, but he liked their light. Still, he wasn't sure he wanted to waste time on them when he could be using it to catch the mother of all dawns.

He was about to continue his pursuit when a dark shade smashed into one of the glows and it fell to the ground. Gabe didn't like those dark smogs; they ruined his delight. With the patient deliberation of one who has lived for centuries, he began to knock the shadows away. When most were gone, he gently picked up three of the brighter figures and placed them in his boughs, careful to avoid setting them on thorns. He thought maybe they would not be pleased to end up on one of those.

Now where had the luminous glow gone? "Gabe!"

His vision searched out the voice and found it. A dark shadow clutched at two struggling lights, one brighter than the other, yet each dimming with every passing second. They were dying. He gazed at them, befuddled. He was too clumsy, too big to help. He couldn't free them without hurting them.

"Gabe..." the two figures gasped like twin ghosts, their struggles fading along with their glow.

He reached for them, but the dark shape squeezed tighter. "Stay back, Gabriel. I'll kill them before ye can spit."

"Stick it to him, Gabe!" one of the glows on his branch called out. "Poke his eyes out!"

"Careful, Gabriel!" another one warned. "Straif never bluffs."

Gabe pulled his limb back; his mind whirled out of control. What could he do? How could he save his lovely light? Panic rising, his sap raced through his limbs, bent on creating havoc, when he suddenly remembered that trees weren't entirely without grace and agility, possessed as they were of slender branches with finger-like twigs. His particular limbs had the added benefit of being armed with thorns.

Gabe reached out a long branch, stopping several yards from the dark shadow. Here he hesitated. He had to get this right—he had to destroy the darkness without touching the light. His sap, flowing fast and free before, slowed, weighing the branch, making it heavy. He couldn't do it! His limb felt like a wet noodle, gangly and out of his control.

"Gabe..." the dawn glow gurgled.

Before he knew it, Gabe whipped the branch at the dark shadow, making contact just above the good lights. A hideous screech echoed all around him. He whacked the evil shade again, and again, until finally it dropped the glows and retreated. Gabe advanced, bellowing like an elephant on the rampage, trapping the dark figures, along with the seething black hole, against the line of trees. He was very angry now.

Every fiber of his being, every cell, every seed, called for the death of the dark shades. He raised all his limbs high into the air, intent on wiping them out in one fell swoop.

Gabrielll…

The voice, endearingly familiar, stayed his hand. He searched the swarm of dark stains, but the source of the voice remained elusive. Still, it was nearby, close enough that he couldn't risk decimating what would so willingly destroy him and all that he cared for. He let his branches fall.

"Let them through!" he called out. The elms didn't respond, didn't even seem aware he had spoken. "I am Gabriel!" he roared, his tree voice full of the world. "I am Yggdrasil! Let them through!"

Silence, then some frantic whispering, followed by a shout, "It's him! In his true form, he is! Open up!"

A strained groan echoed through the forest. It sounded like an ancient horn calling up warriors of old, and one of the trees—the battered one—made way. The dark ones poured through, practically crawling over each other to get away from Gabe. One shadow, more putrescent than the rest, paused.

"I'll be back for ye, Gabriel!" the dark creature threatened, and then it was gone, as were all the rest. The elms closed ranks once more, just as the sun fled behind a cloud.

Gabe shuddered miserably and shook his trunk. Something was wrong. His body was shrinking, caving in on itself. The air rushed out of him and he hit the ground with a thud. The glows jumped from his limbs, rolling away from his changing form. After one last tremendous convulsion, he was human once more.

"Gabe!" Abazi jumped to her feet and rushed over to him. "You did it!"

He looked up, surprised to see her. He thought she'd been on top of the hedge. "Did what? What are you talking about?" His mind was fuzzy, caught between two worlds.

"It'll come back to ye," Hollie explained. She stood next to Oswald and the Rogues, all of whom stared at him in wonder—all, that is, except Oswald. "Ye'll remember soon enough," she assured him. "Just give it time."

Gabe slowly climbed to his feet, the memories already starting to nudge at his consciousness. Flashes of heat, blue sky, rapturous glows and disturbing black shades, they filled his mind like movie stills. Had it all been a dream?

"Now do ye understand, Gabriel?" Hollie asked. "Ye're one of us. Dame Hazel told me everything last night. When ye were born, sixteen years past, she took ye from yer mother. She put a spell on ye to keep ye safe from yer other side. But then yer mother found ye and took ye back and Dame Hazel had to return ye to yer other parents—the ones ye live with now. During that time, I was yer companion. We got along right enough, though I warn ye, twere only pity on me part." She grinned impishly.

"My other side?"

Oswald, listening to everything closely, groaned. "Ye're a Dryad. That's yer other side."

"I guess now I understand why ye didn't see me as a human baby," Hollie mused. "Me power isn't strong enough to fool ye. Another Dryad, perhaps, but not a King."

"I'm not a Dryad, or whatever it is you called me," Gabe protested, his voice weak. "And I'm certainly no King."

"A Dryad is a tree spirit, nothing more, nothing less. And ye are one, Gabriel," Hollie insisted.

"You're telling me that I'm some weird, mythical creature that lives in a tree. I live in a house. A house!" he cried hysterically. "I'm *not* a tree!"

"Then what was that ye just changed into, hm?" she challenged.

"I don't know," he floundered. "Maybe it was that drink Dame Hazel gave us."

"We must be gettin' back," Oswald announced brusquely. "Straif's angry now. No tellin' what he might try next, or when. He's injured, though, from the burning. That's a small blessing. We Dryads do not heal so easily as we once did, especially those who partake of the blood. Ye've got some time before he'll attack again."

"Will you guys be okay?" Gabe asked.

Oswald nodded, his eyes settling on a spot over Gabe's head. He didn't seem to want to look Gabe in the eye. "Our kind has survived for centuries. It'd take more than a band of Ko-goks to bring us down."

"Well, I'm glad you're on our side, Oswald."

The Dryad finally looked at Gabe, his dark eyes troubled, then he gave a brisk nod. "We'll meet again." He turned to his band. "Follow the elms now...to Shambolic Stream and back home to the mountain." He held out his hand to Hollie. "Come."

She reluctantly went to him, taking his proffered hand. As they walked away, she glanced back at Kris. "Take care of yerself, Kristofer Hawthorne."

"You, too, Hollie. Stop by any time." He grinned and gave her a salute.

She laughed and turned away, then spun back around. "Ye, too, Gabriel." Her mischievous eyes sparkled with humor, and could that be admiration, as well? She nodded at him, then let Oswald pull her along. Like dissipating smoke, the Dryads disappeared into the woods, with Hollie and Oswald the last to go. Moments later, they were gone.

In silence, the bedraggled group limped back to the hedge. Without a word from Gabe, the thorny vines parted to let them through. On the other side, a distraught Kimber limped hurriedly up to Jer. "You're okay!" she exclaimed, looking him over. "I was so worried!"

He grinned. "I did get this cut on my hand." He pointed it out to her, and she clucked sympathetically.

"Mine's worse than that!" Kris started to limp on a banged-up knee. "I feel like someone removed my kneecap with a hammer." He gave a wookie-like bellow. Gabe never ceased to wonder at how tough and wimpy Kris could be at the same time.

"I hope Mom and Dad aren't home yet," he said to no one in particular.

"Me, too," Abazi agreed, falling in beside him as they headed back to the house. "It's getting late, though. I'm sure they must be back by now."

Hearing the sound of her voice, Gabe experienced a flash of remembrance, brief and elusive. "That was you," he realized. He frowned, knowing there was more to it, but was unable to decipher what it was. "You were the one who led me to the forest."

She shrugged. "I had to do something. You were just standing there…like a big tree, or something."

Gabe blushed. "Was I *really* a tree?"

Her smiled dropped away. "Unless we were all experiencing a group hallucination, you were really a tree."

Gabe's skin grew hot. "So Hollie was telling the truth. I'm one of them. That means my whole life is a lie. The family I thought was mine really isn't mine at all." Out of all that he'd learned and all that had happened to him, this seemed the worst part.

Abazi scowled at him. "You can't just dump your family because they're not your blood."

Gabe's eyes widened. "I'm not *dumping* them. It's just that…" He paused, not wanting to say the words aloud. But he couldn't avoid them in his head. It's just that—he had another family out there, in the woods. He had a mother who was looking for him, calling for him. She, his family, his roots, weren't something he could ignore, much as he wanted to forget that all this had happened.

Abazi let his sentence hang, though she studied him speculatively. "We'd better hurry. I'm sure my dad is freaking out and Kimber's mom is so protective of her, because of her CP and all. I can understand the worry thing, but she gets all moronic about it. I wouldn't be surprised if she's called the cops. Good thing I don't have a mom," she tried to snort mirthfully here, but it came out bitter sounding. "Though even if she were alive, she wouldn't act like one."

Gabe wanted to ask her more about her mom, but didn't. "What are you going to tell your dad?" he asked instead, wondering what he would say himself.

"I'll tell him that we were cutting through the woods when the fog hit and we took a wrong turn. He'll still flip out on me, but since I'll be safely at home during his spaz attack, he should get over it pretty quick. There'll be lectures galore for months afterwards, but I can live with lectures. That's what ear buds are for."

Gabe nodded in sympathy. He'd gotten enough lectures himself. What was one more? "Maybe we'll try that, too. I'll say one of the cats got loose again and we were looking for it. It might work."

When they approached the farmhouse, however, the truck wasn't there. "Wait here," Gabe told the others. "I want to check to see if the coast is clear. I don't want them seeing us like this." Like this was torn shirts, deep scratches, vivid bruises, and wild, betwigged hair.

Once inside the house, Gabe called out several times, but no one answered. No note waited on the table or a message on the answering machine. Either his parents hadn't returned yet, or they'd gone out looking for their missing kids. Bad news either way.

He ran back outside. "We'll walk you home," he told the girls, even though the last place he wanted to go was back into the woods. Something seemed odd to him about all this and he wouldn't feel right leaving the girls on their own.

"Whatever," Abazi replied readily—too readily. Maybe she felt the weirdness, too.

As they walked along the path, Jer and Kris recounted their war stories to Kimber, already embellishing on what had happened. Gabe recognized the trees that bordered the well-worn trail—they were birches, like the white-barked trees forming the spiral circle that led to Dame Hazel and Isis. He knew at once that this path would be safe—that he and his brothers and their friends could come and go without harm. He relaxed a little, but still felt anxious.

When they arrived at the girls' houses, set in a spacious clearing about fifteen yards from each other, they found that neither of the girl's parents was home. Abazi ran inside the second house, then quickly back out to rejoin them. "No note, no dirty dishes. He hasn't been home yet."

"We were never gone, then," Kimber said softly. She smiled. "That works for me." Everyone laughed, somewhat surprised at seeing this devious side of her personality.

"Works for me, too," Jer grinned.

"Doesn't that seem strange to you?" Here at last was the source of Gabe's uneasiness. At the very least, Kimber's mom and Abazi's dad should be back by now. The fog had cleared and it was mid-morning at the latest. The worried parents would've flown home at the first chance they got to check on their kids.

"Remember what Dame Hazel told us?" Jer replied. "She said our parents are 'otherwise occupied.' That they wouldn't know we've gone, nor will they know that we haven't returned."

"But how did she know that?" Gabe wondered, feeling a chill.

"Maybe she did something to them," Kimber whispered.

"Like magic," Abazi suggested.

"You've got to be kidding me," Kris scoffed. "Magic?"

"Gabe turned into a tree," she countered dryly.

"Oh, yeah. Forgot about that." He grinned, running a hand over his Mohawk.

"Whatever she did, it might be wearing off," Gabe said, worried that Abazi might be right. He remembered how he'd forgotten Repulsive and the other strange events happening to him. It was very likely that Dame Hazel and her 'magic' had made him forget. But eventually he remembered everything again. "We should be getting home."

"Well, boys and girls, it's been real," Kris announced. "So what do we need to remember from all this?"

"Stay out of the woods?" Jer ventured.

"No! You need to remember that I'm a *wicked* good fighter! An awesome warrior!" He struck a karate pose.

Gabe frowned. "Seriously, guys. I'm surprised we weren't killed. We need to keep out of those woods and stay in groups. No venturing out alone from here on out. Especially at night."

"And carry a weapon made of wood," Jer added. "They don't like the touch of wood."

"They don't like sunlight, either," Kris put in. "It toasts them like wussy little marshmallows."

"Fine with me," Abazi agreed. She held out the tomahawk to Gabe. "Better take this. I'd hate to have risked my life for nothing." She rubbed at the back of her head where Feltry had struck her. No doubt there was a painful lump beneath her thick hair. "I've got to get cleaned up before my dad gets home." She looked over her torn clothes and messy hair, the bleeding scratches and bits of moss sticking out of her shorts pockets. "I look like I've been in a bar-k fight." She looked at each of them expectantly. "Get it? Bar-k fight?"

Gabe rolled his eyes. "Funny, Abazi."

"At least I didn't say my dad's probably pine-ing to see me."

Everyone groaned. "We're leaving," he said. "See you guys later."

"See you later," Kimber replied. Abazi was already walking away, refusing to commit to anything that might involve a future between them.

Kris and Jer chorused a cheerful goodbye and Kimber blushed, ducking her head with a smile. Kris added loudly, "And we'll see you later, She Who Throws a Mean Hawk."

Abazi whipped around, pointed her finger at him like a gun, and pulled the trigger. "*Bang.*" With a grin, she headed back toward her house, her ponytail swishing saucily back and forth, while Kimber let herself into hers with a shy wave.

Gabe wished irrationally that Abazi's gun had been aimed at him.

Jer hoped that Kimber's wave was meant for his eyes only.

Kris wanted a sandwich.

As they headed back home, the three boys were unusually quiet, each mulling over the seriousness of what had happened. Or so Gabe thought.

"I have seven wounds," Kris announced. "Pretty good ones, too. They'll make really nice scars. I'm going to tell the kids at school that I got them in a knife fight back in San Jose."

"Kimber's really brave, isn't she?" Jer sighed, his blue eyes wistful.

Gabe wanted to shout at them, "I turned into a tree! Don't you think that's weird?" but he kept his mouth shut. Why make an issue of it if they weren't going to? So he let them rattle on about their wounds and about the girls and about fighting the Ko-goks.

Back home, Jer showered first, then got to work making lunch. The boys hadn't eaten anything substantial since around six o'clock the previous day and they were starving. Kris went next, leaving his clothes in a pile on the bathroom floor. Gabe gathered up all their dirty laundry and started up a load while Kris finished up.

While showering, Gabe worried about why his parents weren't home yet. Their delay might have nothing to do with magic and everything to do with his father fighting for his life. If he died, Gabe could only blame himself for it. The Ko-gok attack had been meant for him, but they'd gotten Dad instead. With his virtually destroyed immune system, he'd been unable to fight off the resulting infection. Gabe's own thorn cuts burned under the hot water, as though on their way to infection, and he made sure to clean each one thoroughly with Mom's homemade peppermint soap.

Afterwards, he got dressed, covering up his scratches and bruises with pants and a long-sleeved shirt. To keep his thoughts off his dad, he wandered around the house, returning their weapons to their rightful places, and cleaning up wherever he could. Kris, who was similarly covered up, except for the vivid scratch on his cheek, which they decided he'd blame on Little Joe, pushed the wheelbarrow out to the barn.

When he returned, he said to Gabe, "You forgot to take the box."

"What box?"

They were standing in the kitchen. Jer was making hamburgers and the sharp smell of cooking beef filled the space. Gabe's mouth watered and he frowned. How could he be a tree and crave meat? It didn't seem right. In fact, if he were a tree, wouldn't eating meat make him like the Ko-goks? They'd eaten meat and look what had happened to them. They stank and their skin boiled in the sun. He shuddered at the memory, at the possibility of something like that happening to him.

"The wooden one," Kris clarified, "with the clothes in it. The one Oswald wanted to keep."

"That box wasn't mine," he said shortly.

Kris rapped his knuckles on the table. "I don't know what happened to you out there with the whole 'turning into a tree' thing, but I'm pretty sure that what you did makes you one of them. Now we need to figure out why you're here with us and not out there with the Dryads."

Gabe bit his lip. "I don't want to be out there with them."

"No one says you should be. We want you here, right, Jer?"

Jer nodded without turning around. He was humming a tune, but judging by how intensely he was tearing up the lettuce, he was also listening to every word of their conversation.

"But we're not related," Gabe persisted, spinning away from Kris, afraid his stupid emotions were going to betray him and he'd start tearing up like a baby.

"Remember what Mom always tells us?" Kris said heatedly, grabbing Gabe's arm and yanking him back around. "You can't just stop being brothers, even if you want to. We're brothers and we always will be. So get used to it, dork."

Gabe gazed into Kris's brown eyes, searching for the trick, the smart aleck remark. "So you're saying we're *still* brothers? No matter what?"

"Just try and get rid of us." Jer turned around and grinned his agreement, then went back to shredding lettuce. "Besides, you aren't nearly as big a wuss as I thought you were. So I can't let you leave now that I know you can fight so good. We're about due for a rematch, aren't we?"

Gabe felt a weight that he hadn't even known was there slide off his shoulders like heavy snow. "You're on," was all he could think of to say, then bit his lip to stave off any impending tears that might be the result of his overwhelming relief and joy. "But not today."

Kris laughed. "Deal."

Chapter Twenty-Four

We Are Family

The sound of squealing brakes sobered Gabe, and he and his brothers dashed to the kitchen door to see who'd arrived.

"It's the truck!" Kris pushed open the screen door. The brothers pounded down the steps to the car, frantically searching for signs of their dad.

As they neared the truck, Mom slid out of the driver's side. There was a smile on her face. It was a tired smile, but a smile all the same. Gabe felt pure relief quiver through him.

"He's okay," she said quickly. "I didn't call to let you know we were on our way home because I couldn't get through. Stupid cell phone. I thought they were supposed to be for emergencies."

They each gave her a quick hug, then pelted around to the other side of the car. Dad opened the door and they hurried to help him out. He looked pale, but otherwise okay, though his arm was heavily bandaged. He gave them a hug with his good arm.

"So you missed me? Were hardly able to exist without my charm and winning personality to keep you going?"

"You bet," Gabe laughed.

"Are you hungry?" Jer asked. "I'm making a big lunch." His eyes widened. "The hamburgers!" He dashed back to the house yelling, "I will not pull a Gabe!"

Gabe and Kris helped their dad out of the car and up the porch steps. He was still weak from the painkiller he'd gotten at the hospital and each step was an effort. Mom grabbed her purse and joined them, clucking at them like a mother hen.

"Watch his arm! Careful now, Kris! For the love of Pete, pick up your feet, you're going to trip him!"

They finally got Dad inside and sitting down at the table, relatively unscathed. "It's good to be home," he said heartily. "And yes, Jer, I *am* hungry! In fact, I'm so hungry, I think I could eat an entire tree, bark and all!"

The three brothers glanced at each other, then burst out laughing.

~~~~~~

Exhausted from their ordeal, Mom and Dad went to bed early that night. Following their lead, Jer and Kris headed to their own rooms to crash. After checking the house and locking all the doors, then tossing the wet laundry into the dryer, Gabe wearily climbed the steps to the turret with Gypsy galloping along behind him.

Stripped down to his boxer shorts, he lay in bed on top of his covers, with his hands tucked under his head and one foot crossed over the other. As he stared at the ceiling, memories of the last couple days filled his mind. He thought about the tree-shaped key to the turret, about the tree etched into the half-moon window. He remembered the bookshelf filled with hundreds of books on trees.

What did it all mean? Was there a connection between his family and those creatures in the forest—the Dryads? There had to be. Someone interested enough in trees to make a key that looked like a branch and a window that threw the shadow of a tree into the room was someone who knew something. But what did they know? More specifically, *who* knew it?

Grandma May had wanted *Gabe* to have this room, not Kris or Jer. She'd also acknowledged that there were parts of the woods she avoided, yet she claimed ignorance as to why. "I've lived here all my life," she'd told him. "We go way back in this town. There's something about those woods nobody understands and our folk have learned it's just best to leave it be."

She also had claimed that she hadn't entered this room in decades, nor had she let Mom in here. Or had Mom said it was the *turret* that hadn't let her in? "They never allowed me to pass, either," Grandma May had stated matter-of-factly. But the turret had allowed Gabe to pass into its sanctum, just as she knew it would.

Was Grandma lying to him? She could very well know exactly what was going on in those woods, in the Forest Immortal, even be a part of it all somehow. Was that why he never quite felt at ease with her? Because she was hiding something? Even worse, if Grandma May knew something, then maybe his mother knew something, as well.

He pondered this for a few minutes before deciding he couldn't quite buy that his mom was involved. She seemed to fear the forest only because something unknown had come from it and taken him. Gabe didn't think she knew about the Dryads. If she did, she would never have brought her family back here after nearly losing one of her kids. She was very protective. If she thought any of her children were in real danger, she'd pack up and get out of Dodge.

Of course, maybe she felt like she didn't have a choice, that she had to stay here so they could pay the bills. And maybe she wasn't too worried since he wasn't really her kid and she knew the dark ones would only go after him. But did she really know he wasn't hers?

He was a Dryad, and he had another mother who lived out in those woods. The mom who'd raised him from a tiny baby, who'd stayed up with him when he was sick and sang him lullabies when he couldn't sleep, wasn't his true mom. It didn't seem right; just the thought of it made him feel nauseous.

But as awful as finding out that his mother wasn't really his, he couldn't help wondering what his Dryad mother was like. The voice he'd heard calling to him had sounded haunted, as though his mother had long ago lost her grip on reality. He wondered if losing her son had driven her crazy, especially when she'd had him back and then lost him again. Dame Hazel must have returned him, taking his memory of what happened with her.

But why? Why take him away from the Forest Immortal in the first place? Why the lies and secrets?

He wanted to believe that Grandma May and his mother didn't know about what was going on. He wanted to believe that his mother and father thought he was theirs, that he wasn't expendable. He wanted to believe everything was going to be all right.

But it wasn't all right. If what had happened with Straif and the Kogoks was real, then those two women, Mrs. Deacon and Mrs. Morrigan, would have to be stopped in their quest to clear the woods. They couldn't go into the forest. They'd die.

Or, if they managed to get permission to clear cut, the trees would die. Hollie and Oswald and Dame Hazel. His real mother and father. The mighty oaks and the wondrous beech trees, who'd saved his life when he fell from the treetops.

Then again, Mrs. Morrigan had said Mom would get paid for showing the guides around. And more tourists visiting Ranger would increase the money they could earn. Dad's latest hospital bill wasn't going to pay itself. And if the Forest Immortal was destroyed, the Kogoks would be destroyed...

It was a dilemma—one he wasn't sure he had the right, or the fortitude, to resolve.

He yawned and stretched, then groaned. His muscles were sore and he felt sluggish. Starting tomorrow, he vowed to run every day, even if a blizzard was raging—anything to avoid feeling like a hunted animal. Maybe he and his brothers would pick up archery again. They'd gone through a Robin Hood phase several years ago and had gotten quite good.

His eyes had begun to flutter when he heard a noise coming from behind the bookshelf. He turned on his lamp. Someone was at the door down below. Wide awake now, Gabe jumped out of bed and hurried over to the bookshelf. Grabbing the mallet he'd brought up earlier, he opened the shelf and slid down the pole.

Someone was jiggling the knob. "Blighters! He's gone and locked the door! Why's me life so cursed?" No one answered him, so Gabe figured his visitor was alone. He pulled open the door. Peering back at him was Oswald.

"It's about time," he growled. "Let me in."

Gabe backed up and Oswald barged past him. He was dragging something awkward and heavy behind him. "What do you want?" he finally managed to get out.

"Ye left this behind. It's yers. Best keep it." He didn't sound too thrilled at the prospect.

"What is it? I can't see anything down here."

"Climb to the top and I'll hand it to ye."

"How are you going to do that? It's twenty feet up."

"Have ye learned nothing this day?" Oswald sighed. "Just climb."

After tucking the mallet into his waistband, Gabe did as he was told. Once he was at the top, he called down to Oswald, "Hand it up."

A moment later, he spotted the box rising upward like an elevator. He reached out to grab hold of it and noticed the twig fingers holding the trunk tightly. Ah...of course. That explained the reach. Oswald was a tree spirit, after all.

Once Gabe had the box in hand, he carried it over to his bed and carefully set it down. He slipped his mallet under his pillow just as Oswald warily entered the room. "Never been this far," he said, looking around. "Hollie said it's a grand place, this room. Fit for a King, she said." His tone sounded belligerent.

Gabe's stomach clenched up. Oswald hadn't come here just to deliver the box; he'd come to deliver a message.

"I like it," he replied, choosing the most neutral route.

Oswald wandered around, touching things, peering into the dark, bubbling fish tank. Gabe went over and turned on the light. Oswald's irate expression changed to wonder. "What fish! I've never seen such colors." He continued to gaze at them for several minutes. Gabe felt himself growing more nervous with each passing second.

"So everyone is okay, then?"

"They're fine."

"That's good."

"Do ye know who I am, Gabriel?" Oswald asked, standing up to look Gabe straight in the eye.

Here we go, Gabe thought, feeling trapped. "You're Oswald, King of the Forest Immortal, if I remember correctly."

He shook his head. "Oh, no, Gabriel. When Dame Hazel said ye were King, I thought she was playin' some sort of ruse on ye. But I was wrong. Just now she told me the truth, that ye are me, and I am ye."

"Huh?"

Oswald drew in a long breath. "I'm supposed to be Gabriel Hawthorne, and ye're supposed to be Oswald Eik...King of the Forest Immortal. Now ye know why Dame Hazel switched us around. To protect *ye.*" His tone was bitter.

Gabe took a step back. "That can't be right! I can hardly believe I'm a Dryad, and now you're telling me I really am some kind of Dryad King?"

Oswald's smile was wry. "I wish ye luck with it, Gabriel." He spun on his heel and headed for the bookshelf. Gabe watched him go, his mouth hanging open in shock. The Dryad turned back. "And this family here," his hand swept outward, "is *me* family, not yers. When the time comes, I might think on collectin' on my heritage since I have no real family of me own." His threat delivered in a dark voice, Oswald spun about and disappeared into the darkness. Moments later the small door below banged shut.

Gabe numbly pushed the bookshelf back to its normal position and latched it shut. *King of the Forest Immortal?* It was ludicrous! He was Gabriel Hawthorne, ordinary kid. He liked to pick on his brothers; he liked to think about girls; he liked to play stupid video games. He couldn't be a King.

But in his heart, Gabe knew. He knew that's why he'd been scared of the forest. To him, the woods were more than just a bunch of trees—the woods were his home, his dominion. And he was their ruler.

Him. Gabriel Hawthorne.

He was the Changeling child.

And his tale had only just begun.

About the Author

When author, Kristina Schram, was growing up she wanted to be a star. When that didn't turn out quite like she expected, she turned her mind to achieving other goals: Earning her Ph.D. in Counseling Psychology, working as an Artist-in-Residence at local schools, being a free-lance editor and reader, coaching parks & rec basketball, protecting the earth through recycling and using green products, and publishing her first novel, a YA fantasy called The Chronicles of Anaedor: The Prophecies.

Knowing what it's like to struggle with self-doubt and lack of confidence, her biggest dream (in addition to owning a castle) is to stamp out low self-esteem for everyone, especially young people. She lives in beautiful, wooded New Hampshire with her husband, three boys, and various pets, and can also throw a tomahawk, if need be. One of her favorite things to do is walk with her dog in the woods, where she searches for the impossible around every corner. Sometimes she finds it.

For more information on Kristina Schram, feel free to make a trip to her website: www.kristinaschram.com. She's also on Facebook, Twitter, and Pinterest.

Other Books by Kristina Schram

The Chronicles of Anaedor: The Prophecies (Book One)

Strange things happen to fifteen-year-old Lavida Mors. Maybe that's why her father sends her to Portal Manor, a mysterious family estate she never knew existed. Lavida quickly discovers that not everything at Portal Manor is as it seems when she stumbles across a secret passage to a hidden world—Anaedor. Long ago, humans drove the Anaedorians, a civilization of magical and strange beings, into the dark world of huge caverns, frigid rivers, and bottomless pits deep within the earth. Malevolent forces, led by the evil Malvado, seek to control all of Anaedor, but an ancient prophecy tells of a hero who will save them from destruction. While trying to escape the dark realm, Lavida must battle overgrown leeches, survive a poisoned arrow, and outwit a giant, all while trying to convince the hopeful populace of Anaedor that she is not the savior they believe her to be.

The Chronicles of Anaedor: The Return to Anaedor (Book Two)

After escaping from Anaedor, fifteen-year-old Lavida Mors starts a training course with her guardian, Mrs. Keeper, in hopes of improving her magic skills before the dreaded Malvado returns. But while trying out a new spell, something awful happens, and she vows never to do magic again. When an unexpected discovery forces her to return to Anaedor, she is faced with her most terrifying challenges yet. Strife reigns in the hidden underground world as lootings and burnings break out, and numerous enemies conspire to capture Lavida, fight her, even kill her. Without magic, how can she possibly flee from dragons, escape the Goblins, outwit the ruthless Frio, and fight a duel with a young rebel intent on proving she's not the One? Time is running out. If Lavida doesn't learn to trust herself and her skills, a series of catastrophic events will ensure that she and her friends never make it out of Anaedor again.

The Chronicles of Anaedor: The Lost Ones (Book Three)

Sixteen-year-old Lavida Mors is in for a long, hot summer. With no way into Anaedor, the Lost Ones seeking refuge at Portal Manor are taking over the house, creating havoc and misery. Lavida is overwhelmed trying to keep up with her chores, learning magic, and fighting off the Pixies—tiny creatures who have made it their mission to harass Lavida at every turn. Meanwhile, unbeknownst to the residents of Portal Manor, the AAK is hard at work opening a Portal to the Upland. They are successful at last, and the twins, Loria and Darian, on the run from Malvado, and the AAK leader, Trey, manage to make it through the opening only to have it collapse behind them. With no way back into Anaedor, they are forced to take refuge at Portal Manor. As they try to settle into this strange new life, tensions between the humans and the Anaedorians grow, creating rifts between Lavida and her friends. To make matters worse, Frio, Amoral Hunter Leader, is hiding out in the Upland, and when he goes after Lavida, he starts in motion a series of events that could end up costing Lavida her life.

The Chronicles of Anaedor: The Uprising (Book Four)

In this final book of the Anaedor series, sixteen-year-old Lavida Mors is placed in grave danger when a group of young Anaedorians infiltrates the Upland. Their orders are to eliminate the evil one, whom they believe is Lavida, and then launch an Uprising to take over the Upland. Disguising themselves as humans, they befriend the unwitting Lavida and her friends, allowing them easy access to Portal Manor. Darian and Loria, Blendar twins and Lavida's friends, and Trey, ex-AAK rebel leader, have come to the Upland to warn Lavida about the intruders. But before they can, Darian learns something about Lavida's past that turns him against her. Surrounded by betrayal and danger, and faced with an astonishing revelation that makes her question everything about her existence, Lavida feels increasingly alone and afraid. If she cannot convince Darian and the others that she is not the evil being they think she is, she will lose everything to the Uprising.

Mayhem at Nepenthe Manor: A Pandora Belfry Adventure
(Book One)

Precocious and morbidly obsessed with death, Pandora Belfry has spent her entire life at Nepenthe Manor, a dark, Gothic mansion also known as the local loony bin. Recently turned fourteen and growing exasperated with her stifling life, Pandora wants two things more than anything else in the world—to make her escape from the asylum, and to get her mom to finally act like a real mom. Until these wishes are granted, she acts as self-imposed ringleader to a wayward posse of inmates. Known amongst themselves as the Secret Six, Pandora and her friends spend their time at Nepenthe Manor stirring up trouble—holding weekly Midnight Meetings to concoct schemes, sneaking into places like the Nepenthe family cemetery and the forbidden attic, and generally doing everything they can to avoid the curse of living a mundane life. But when a mysterious new inmate arrives at the manor, things change for Pandora, and not for the better. In retaliation for a trick she plays on him, the charming and handsome Xavier connives to take over the posse, threatens to divulge one of Pandora's biggest secrets, and refuses to tell her what he did to get himself locked up. This boy is obviously hiding something, and it's up to Pandora to use whatever nefarious means necessary to find out what it is, before he destroys the only world she's ever known.

The Labyrinth of Lunacy: A Pandora Belfry Adventure
(Book Two)

Pandora Belfry, along with the eccentric members of her posse, is back, and looking for trouble. The posse's first order of business is to break into the off-limits labyrinth, even though they can't find its door. Against her mother's wishes, Pandora also works to solve the mystery of her father's identity. Perhaps he's a staff member, or maybe he's the stranger haunting the beach late at night. Topping the list of possible dad candidates is the new therapist, Dr. Steele, who keeps popping up in Pandora's life like an annoying, but handsome, nanny. To add to her problems, Pandora's date with the slimy, but oddly fascinating, Dougie Daft, is fast approaching. She isn't sure how to get out of it, or even if she dares to. Her new acquaintance, Giganticus, certainly doesn't want her to go, but if she doesn't, she'll be obligated to Dougie Daft, and that's the last thing any sane person would want... Come join the posse on their latest, a-maze-ing adventure. Just one warning: Watch out for snakes!

I Shall Return: A Paranormal Gothic Romance

Journalist, Lily MacKenzie, is off to the Highlands of Scotland on a newspaper assignment. But in reality, she has another mission in mind, one she desperately needs to keep secret. Her arrival starts off unexpectedly when she encounters Greg Huntington, a stranger who seems to know her even though they've never met. Things grow more peculiar as she gets to know the Derings of Dundeid Castle, the lodging where she's staying. Andrew Dering, the god-like laird, is welcoming enough, but appears to be hiding something. His cousin, Vivian, seems intent on sabotaging Lily's efforts, while another relation, Ophelia, sees Lily as her savior from a mysterious illness. As Lily works to unravel the mystery that set her on her journey, events grow increasingly complicated and dangerous, and she finds herself caught between two very different men. The reason behind her mission makes it difficult to trust either one, but when she finally ends up choosing, things go very wrong, and Lily ends up fighting for her sanity and her very life.

The Wrath: A Paranormal Gothic Romance

When a cryptic letter arrives from Evalina Filmore's two aunts, she travels to England to find out what they want, figuring this will be the chance to experience the romantic adventure she has so often read about in her beloved gothic novels. When she arrives, she finds the eerie mansion, the strange atmosphere, and the adventure, as hoped. But there are troubles. On the train, she meets a man who, upon learning her name, walks away without a word of explanation Not long after, she passes unharmed through a wood called the Wrath, even though, as she later learns, no one ever has. While in the Wrath, she meets a tantalizing and seductive stranger, one who just might be her gothic hero. But he has a secret. It seems everyone in the village does, including her aunts, and it's up to Evie to figure out what is going on before the Wrath lures her in and never lets her go.

The Battle to Become an Author:
When Great Expectations Go Awry

 Are you looking to find an agent and/or get published? Are you a published author frustrated with the whole process? Or have you simply heard the horror stories and are looking for a ray of light before plunging into the fray? In this short booklet, author Kristina Schram discusses how one's unrealistic expectations about becoming an author can contribute to feelings of negativity and isolation. Dr. Schram offers a real-world discussion of this growing issue, humorously incorporating her own experiences throughout. She also offers insights and ways to cope with the increasingly difficult battle to become a published author. Come prepared to challenge your own expectations, to laugh and to cry, and to battle against the forces conspiring to keep you from reaching your writing potential!